a Gift of Wings

the light-bringer series, vol. 1

Stephanie Stamm

ZEKE & ME BOOKS
KALAMAZOO, MICHIGAN

This book is a work of fiction. Any references to historical events, real people, or real places are used fictitiously. All other names, characters, places, and incidents are the product of the author's imagination, and any resemblance to actual events, places, or persons, living or dead, is purely coincidental.

Published by Zeke & Me Books, November 2012

Cover design by Cindy Koshar, Designs & Otherwise
Author photograph by Laurie Phelps

ISBN 978-0-9883042-0-8

For Carol

PROLOGUE

Two Years Earlier

Aidan willed himself to stand still, eyes directed straight ahead and features impassive, as the silence that followed his statement of Renunciation lengthened. He refused to make eye contact with any of the Council members. He knew that most of them did not approve of his decision. But as far as he was concerned, he had no other option. After everything that had happened—everything he'd done—he couldn't imagine using his Gift ever again. And Renunciation was the best way he knew to make sure he'd never have a reason to.

It was Zeke who finally broke the silence, his resonant voice echoing in the expanse of the Council chamber. "I move that the Renunciation be considered temporary, with reinstatement in no more than two years."

Aidan's jaw clenched, and his hands curled into fists, but he said nothing as the motion was seconded and carried without hesitation, even his father giving a nod of assent.

You are sure this is what you want, Naphil? The Archangel Uriel's words seared through Aidan's senses.

"Quite sure," he responded. The only thing he wasn't sure about was the designation of temporary, but he'd deal with that when the time came.

Then so be it.

As soon as Uriel spoke, Aidan felt a brief, slicing pain on either side of his back, and the familiar weight was gone. He shrugged his shoulders, accustoming himself to the lack and clearing away the final energetic remnants of his wings.

Then, without saying another word, he walked out the door. He didn't look back.

CHAPTER 1

Lucky bit her lip and squeezed her eyes shut. She was not going to cry, *not* going to cry. But when Josh put his arm around her shoulders, she could hold back the tears no longer. His other arm went around her, and she stopped trying altogether. She just buried her face in the curve of his neck and shoulder and sobbed.

"I know, kiddo," he said, his own voice breaking, "I know."

They were standing by the car in the parking lot of the assisted living facility in Lincoln Park into which they had just moved their grandmother. Josh's parents, Lucky's uncle and aunt, were still inside talking with one of the staff members. After saying goodbye to G-Ma, Lucky had nearly run to the car, with Josh close on her heels. She hadn't wanted to break down at all, and she had been determined not to do it inside. It was hard enough leaving G-Ma behind in there; she couldn't make it worse by sobbing like a baby in front of everyone.

G-Ma was the only mother Lucky had ever known, her mother having died giving birth to her—and G-Ma had early-onset Alzheimer's. She had been diagnosed after almost a year of visits to various medical specialists, and in the months since the diagnosis, it had become increasingly difficult for her to function independently. Lucky, Uncle Matthew, Aunt Beth, and Josh had done their best to make sure she was taken care of and was left alone as little as possible. Just last month, though, she had wandered several blocks away from her Hyde Park apartment and hadn't been able to find her way back or tell anyone where she lived. By the time they'd located her, the rest of the family was frantic with worry, and G-Ma was close to panic. The incident had prompted Uncle Matthew to make the difficult decision to place his mother in an assisted living facility. He had visited several before settling on the one they had moved her into today.

Lucky raised her head from Josh's shoulder and took a deep breath. "I just miss her so much," she whispered.

"I know. I do, too."

Lucky stepped away from her cousin and leaned back against the silver Pontiac sedan, crossing her arms over her chest. The mid-September sun touched the light hairs on her arms with gold. How ironic that the day could be so beautiful, when she was feeling so bereft. After a moment she sniffed and rubbed the back of her hand across her nose. "I probably got snot all over your shirt."

Josh glanced down at the soggy cloth on his shoulder and raised his eyebrows. "Yeah, well.... What are best fams for?"

Lucky gave him a watery smile.

She and Josh had always been close, despite their five-year age difference. Even as a small boy, Josh had seldom objected to her trailing around after him wanting to play, and as they got older, their closeness had somehow remained.

Maybe it was because neither of them had any siblings. For Lucky, Josh was the brother she'd never had, and she knew he regarded her as his little sister.

Lucky looked up to see Uncle Matthew and Aunt Beth crossing the parking lot toward them. Uncle Matthew's lips were pressed together, and his hands were shoved into the pockets of his khaki pants. The sunlight reflected off his glasses and highlighted the gray in his brown hair. The brightness of Aunt Beth's blonde bob and sky blue sweater contrasted with the sadness reflected in her features. As they drew nearer, she tucked her hand in the curve of her husband's left arm.

No one said a word as Uncle Matthew unlocked the doors and they climbed into the sedan. They had driven a few blocks before Aunt Beth turned around in her seat and broke the silence. "I'm so glad you packed a bag so you can spend the night with us, Lucky. You don't need to stay there alone tonight."

"Yeah," was all Lucky could manage over the lump in her throat. She swallowed the new swell of tears and turned to look out the window.

"Tomorrow," Aunt Beth continued with forced cheerfulness, "we'll move the rest of G-Ma's things out of her room and get Josh's things moved in. Then you'll have someone to keep you company."

In a few weeks, Josh would be starting a graduate program at the University of Chicago, and the Hyde Park apartment would be a convenient location for him. It was an ideal solution really. Lucky wouldn't have to move, and Josh had a ready-made place to stay. Josh would have a part-time job in addition to his financial aid, and Lucky was about to start looking for a job. She had just graduated from high school a few months before. She had intended to start college the fall after she graduated, but she had been so preoccupied with G-Ma that she had let the application deadlines slip by. She had since decided it was probably best to work for a year or so before starting college anyway—to give her time to save some money and to get her bearings back. It had been a long time since she'd felt like herself, and she wasn't ready to focus on school just yet.

"It will be good to have Josh there," she said, directing a brief smile at both her cousin and her aunt.

She couldn't imagine not missing G-Ma, but the thought of sharing the apartment with Josh made her feel like an adult—independent. His brown eyes held a mixture of affection and sadness as he reached over to give her hand a quick squeeze. Aunt Beth smiled at them both and then turned back around.

Lucky sighed with relief and looked out the window, wanting to avoid further conversation. Her hand closed around the locket she always wore—a gift from her grandmother—seeking comfort in the feel of its familiar shape under her fingers. When they reached Lake Shore Drive, she stared out at the ruffled surface of Lake Michigan. The sun was bright, and the lake glistened in various shades of blue, darker with a hint of green as it deepened farther from the shore. Some part of her registered the natural beauty, but she was unable to appreciate it. At least, she wasn't the only one who seemed uninterested in talking; the rest of the trip back to Josh's parents' house in Evanston was completed in silence.

After a subdued dinner and an hour or so spent half-watching forgettable television shows, Lucky said goodnight and retreated to the bathroom to brush her teeth before she made her way to bed. As she pulled her favorite monkey print pajama pants out of her backpack, she remembered wearing them while curled up on the couch beside G-Ma doing homework, talking, or reading.

She was glad she was here—she didn't know if she could have borne spending the night in her and G-Ma's apartment alone—but she hadn't been able to stay in the family room with everyone else either. She still didn't feel like talking to anyone. What was there to say after all? The situation sucked, and there wasn't anything anyone could do about that. Lucky knew they had done the right thing. The assisted living facility was neat and clean, bright and airy, and the staff members all seemed to be both competent and compassionate. It was just…, well, none of it should have happened. She couldn't understand how someone as smart and funny and active and good as G-Ma could have lost herself the way she had. It wasn't fair.

Lucky took a deep breath and sighed. Then she pulled on the monkey pants and a soft, faded cami and climbed into bed. Unclasping the chain of her locket, she removed it from around her neck. The chain had a weak spot, and she was afraid she would break it in her sleep. She opened the locket and studied the small picture of her mother that was tucked inside. Her mother had been a little younger than Lucky was now when the picture had been taken. Short dark curls framed her laughing face. For the millionth time, Lucky wished she could have known her. After closing the locket, she placed it on the bedside table.

She thought she'd lay awake for most of the night, but after a few minutes of tossing and turning, she fell into a dream-filled sleep.

She was standing in the choir loft of an old church—with dark wood panels and arched beams in the high ceiling. The choir behind her was singing a wordless hymn. She stood looking down at the chancel below, knowing she needed to jump, but terrified of the fall. Lifting her gaze, she found one of the choir members standing next to her. The woman looked at Lucky with wise brown eyes and said softly, "Go on, honey. You'll be alright."

Looking into her eyes, Lucky felt a little of the fear slip away. The woman smiled, and Lucky stepped up to the railing. Her heart pounding, she swung her legs over and let go. To her amazement, she didn't fall but floated to the floor. She took a few steps forward and then turned and looked back up at the choir loft. The woman who had spoken to her was still standing in front of the rest of the choir. She raised her arms, and the wide sleeves of her royal blue choir robe transformed into a pair of shimmering wings.

Lucky awoke with a start, her mind going back over the events in the dream, which were unusually clear. She often had a hard time remembering her dreams, and they seldom felt so real. She had no idea what the dream might mean, but for all its strangeness, it left her with a sense of well-being.

She felt warm inside and even hopeful. Snuggling deeper into the covers, she wrapped her arms around her pillow and sank back into slumber—this time without any dreams.

CHAPTER 2

Lucky awoke to the smell of coffee. It took her a few seconds to orient herself, to realize she was in her aunt and uncle's house. Then she remembered: Moving Day. Hurrying into jeans, a t-shirt, and sneakers, she padded down the hall to the bathroom.

As she reached for a towel to soak up the cold water she had splashed on her face, Lucky caught a glimpse of herself in the mirror. Her jade green eyes looked bigger than normal in her pale, oval face. There were slight, bluish shadows under her eyes, and the freckles scattered across her nose were accentuated by the paleness of her skin. Her cheekbones seemed sharper than they had not so very long ago. She had lost weight in the last few months; between forgetting meals and a lack of appetite, she hadn't been eating enough. She ran a brush through her long dark corkscrew curls and, picking up the elastic band she'd left on the edge of the sink the night before, pulled her hair up into a ponytail. Then, with a last glance in the mirror, she headed toward the kitchen, arriving just as Uncle Matthew returned from the bakery down the street.

After a quick breakfast of coffee and donuts—accented with some good natured squabbling between Lucky and Josh over dibs on the custard-filled—the family split up for the drive to Hyde Park. Uncle Matthew and Aunt Beth took their Explorer, which was filled with Josh's things, while Lucky rode with Josh in his beat-up Mazda compact. It was another clear, sunny day, and several sailboats dotted the lake, flashing bright-colored spinnakers.

Josh cranked up the volume on the car's CD player as soon they left his parents' driveway, eliminating the need for conversation, and he and Lucky alternated between listening to the music and singing along. As they passed by the Field Museum, he turned the volume down a few notches.

"So, I was thinking," he said, "after the work is all done today, and Mom and Dad head back home, maybe we could go see Icarus. They're playing in Wicker Park tonight. What do you think?"

Icarus was a relatively new Chicago band that had already amassed quite a local fan base. Lucky liked their music and even owned their first CD—Josh had given it to her the year before as a seventeenth birthday present—but she'd never seen them play. Josh was friends with the bass player, so he'd been to several shows, but the few times he had invited Lucky, her schedule—with homework, her extra-curricular school activities, and the need to stay with G-Ma as much as possible—had not worked out so that she could go.

She realized with surprise and no small rush of excitement that she would have much more free time now. Of course, she had to find a job, and that would take up a lot of time, but not much more than school. And her evenings, for the most part, would be hers to do with as she chose now that she was no longer responsible for making sure G-Ma wasn't left alone.

Lucky's excitement was dampened by the guilt that followed close behind. It didn't seem right to revel in her own newfound freedom when her grandmother had lost so much. Still, she knew G-Ma would not want her to close herself off from life in some misguided attempt at solidarity. G-Ma had been almost childlike in the joy she took in nearly everything she did. Going to see Icarus with Josh was exactly the kind of thing she would have encouraged Lucky to do.

"That's a great idea," Lucky said. "I'd love to go see them tonight!"

Josh grinned. "Excellent! Maybe we can stay and hang out with the band for a while after the show."

Lucky smiled back at him. "Sounds like a plan."

Her smile faded as Josh took the 51st Street exit off Lake Shore Drive. In just a few blocks, they would arrive at the building where she had lived almost her entire life—with G-Ma, who wouldn't live there ever again. At that moment, her grandmother's absence felt almost palpable to Lucky, as if it were a kind of presence, a G-Ma shaped void that Josh, no matter how well-loved, would never be able to fill.

They found a parking space on the street less than a block away from the red-brick, three-story walk-up. Josh retrieved a stack of shirts on hangers from the back seat and placed them in Lucky's outstretched arms, before grabbing an armful for himself.

"Geez, you're such a clothes horse," Lucky teased, to take her mind off her grief. "How does a poor graduate student manage to have so many designer shirts?"

Josh unlocked the building door and held it open for Lucky. "Thank God for Costco is all I can say. It's the only way I can keep myself in the style to which I'd like to become accustomed."

Their apartment was at the top, the third floor. G-Ma used to joke that having all those stairs to climb would keep her healthy. Perhaps they had; physically, she was in great shape—except for the plaques that were presumably forming on her brain. Lucky shook her head to clear away the thoughts. Dwelling on them was useless and would get her nowhere but depressed.

Once inside the apartment, she tossed Josh's shirts across the back of one of the living room chairs. Turning toward the hall, she almost stumbled over the two gray tabby cats that were curling around her ankles.

"Hi, Shu, Tef," she said, reaching down to pet them both, as they meowed and purred greetings up at her. "How are my babies? Did you miss me?"

"Either that, or they want food," Uncle Matthew said, on his way back out the door.

Lucky wandered down the hall to the kitchen, passing by her own room and her bathroom. As she walked past G-Ma's—no, Josh's—room, she caught a glimpse of Aunt Beth setting up boxes. The raspy sound of the tape gun followed her into the kitchen.

Retrieving a couple of cans of Fancy Feast from the wire shelf in the kitchen corner, Lucky turned their contents onto two small pottery bowls, which she placed on the floor. She stood watching the cats attack their treats for a moment, steeling herself before heading back down the hall.

The morning was spent boxing clothes and shoes, purses and bags, jewelry and knickknacks, and all the other things G-Ma had accumulated over the years. The packing was difficult and emotional for Lucky. When she pulled a ragged denim shirt from the back of the closet, she felt tears spring to her eyes.

"She used to wear this to her pottery classes," she sniffed. "She'd come home all spattered with clay from the wheel."

Aunt Beth sighed and sat down on the edge of the bed, a sweater clutched in her hands. "She loved those classes—after she finally got the hang of centering."

Lucky smiled through her tears. "Yeah, that took a while. She was frustrated for weeks."

She sat down on the bed beside her aunt. "I keep thinking that maybe she'll get better, you know, that maybe she'll come back, and things can be the way they were. But I know that's not true. She'll never get better. Nothing's ever going to be the same again, is it?"

Aunt Beth reached over and folded her fingers around Lucky's hand where it rested in her lap. "Honey, nothing ever stays the same. No matter how much we might want it to. But your grandmother has had a rich, full life. And, whatever happens, however this disease changes her, you have to remember that she loves you very much."

"I know," Lucky's voice broke, and a tear fell on the hand that was clasped in her aunt's. "I love her too, and I miss her—more than I can even say."

Aunt Beth pulled Lucky into her arms, and Lucky wound her own arms around her aunt. When the older woman tightened her embrace, Lucky felt a sense of relief. It was as if the pressure could keep her from coming apart, from losing herself in the void of her grandmother's absence.

"Dad and I are thinking pizza for lunch. What kind do you want?" Josh entered the room carrying a box of books. He dropped the box by the bookshelf he'd emptied earlier, and turning, saw Lucky's face. "Hey… Lucky, you okay?"

Lucky wiped the tears from her eyes and gave a rueful smile. "Yeah, same old same old. How about stuffed spinach with mushrooms and fresh garlic? Oh, and whole wheat crust? That's my favorite."

"Sounds good to me." Aunt Beth gave Lucky's shoulders a last squeeze and rose to her feet. "I'll call in the order for pick up and go get some soda. Want to come with me, Lucky?"

"Thanks, Aunt Beth, but I'm okay. I'll finish boxing up the last of the stuff from the closet."

While Josh unpacked his books and organized them on the bookshelf, Lucky packed up the remaining items of clothing and carried the taped boxes into the hall for her uncle to load into the Explorer. Then she retrieved the step stool from the kitchen and returned to the bedroom to tackle the top closet shelf.

"There's a lot of stuff up here," she said, climbing onto the top step. "Josh, can I hand this down to you?"

Josh opened the first box and glanced in before turning to take the next one from Lucky. "That one looked like art supplies. We may want to keep some of this."

"Great—more things to sort through...."

"We don't have to sort everything out right now. We can stow some stuff in the computer room or the storage space in the basement and look through it later." He gestured toward the box he'd just taken from her. "This one's full of papers and pictures. We don't need to look at all those today."

"Good." Lucky handed him a stack of photo albums and sat down on the top step of the stool. "I'm not sure how much sorting I could stand right now."

Just then she heard the rattle of keys and the sound of the apartment door being opened.

"Pizza's here!" Uncle Matthew called from the living room.

Mouth watering and stomach growling, she launched off the stool to race Josh to the door.

After their much-needed break for lunch, it was back to work. Lucky and Josh looked through a few of the boxes from the closet, keeping some items and discarding others. The boxes of papers and photo albums they stashed in the computer room to be dealt with at a later date.

The rest of the afternoon they focused on the happier task of putting Josh's belongings in place. By the time they were finished, the bedroom was transformed. While some of the items of furniture remained, everything else was so different that being in the room didn't make Lucky miss her grandmother. The family pictures that had hung on the walls were replaced with masks from Africa and reproductions of East Indian art. The bed was covered with a black comforter, a few beat-up, multi-colored pillows scattered near the head, and a striped Mexican throw draped across the foot. From the walls to the bed to the shelf full of books beside the rummage sale floor lamp and the battered but comfortable-looking lime green reading chair, the space now reflected Josh's personality, not G-Ma's.

"This looks great, Josh," Aunt Beth said, as she scanned the room, her hands on her hips. "Comfortable and very you. I think you're going to be really happy here."

"Yeah, I think so too. If I can just keep this one in line," Josh grinned, giving Lucky a good-natured shove.

"We'll see who keeps who in line," Lucky replied, with a smack to his upper arm.

Uncle Matthew chuckled and draped his arm across his wife's shoulders. "What do you say we leave these two to fight it out? I, for one, could use a shower and a beer."

After hugs and a quick check to make sure everyone had all the keys they needed, Josh's parents were gone, leaving him and Lucky to collapse on the couch.

"Wow, even the living room looks different," Lucky said, glancing around.

"Without G-Ma's recliner and the rocking chair, there was a lot of empty space. We found those two armchairs in the storage room. They're not new, but they look pretty good, I think," Josh said.

Lucky agreed. The armchairs—one a faded paisley that managed to coordinate with the muted green sofa and the other a worn leather club chair—did lend a certain shabby chic to the room. And it all looked so new and different that Lucky again felt a nascent sense of excitement.

"We've got some time before we have to leave, right?" she said, pulling the elastic band out of her hair. "I'm going to take a shower—and then maybe a nap."

"Get your energy on, kid. It could be a long night." Josh's voice trailed after her as she headed down the hall to her room.

CHAPTER 3

"Mo just texted me," Lucky said as they were getting into the car. "I'm so lame. I haven't even thought about calling or texting her. I mean, she knew I was going to be busy these last few days, what with G-Ma, and you moving in and everything, but…. She's my best friend. I should have called her. About tonight, at least."

"Ask her to come along if you want."

"Really?"

"Sure. She's into Icarus, too, right?"

"Yeah. She'd be majorly bummed if I went without even asking her."

Seconds after Lucky texted her reply, the cell phone rang. As soon as Lucky accepted the call, before she could even speak, her friend was squealing into her ear. "Oh, my God! I'm changing right now. Can you and Josh swing by and pick me up? I can meet you there, if you can't, but it would be fun to ride together, right? I can't believe we're going to see them tonight! Oh, my God!"

"Can we—?" Lucky began.

"Pick her up?" Josh interrupted. "Yeah, no problem. Given how she's screaming into the phone, she's probably too excited to be trusted behind a wheel right now anyway."

"We're on our way, Mo. See you in a few. Yeah, I'm excited too. I'm really glad you can come." Lucky ended the call and turned to look at Josh. "Thank you. I know she bugs you sometimes…."

Josh glanced at her, one corner of his mouth lifted in a wry smile. "Just when she's all super-excited. It's like you can't find the off switch. She makes me tired."

"Mm-hmm…. And she's *so* not excited now," Lucky responded. "Like I said, thank you."

They pulled up in front of Mo's building, and before Josh could tap the horn, the blonde girl was running out the door and down the steps toward them. She burst into the back seat like a sudden storm, tossing bag and jacket aside before launching herself at the back of the seat in front of her. She gave Lucky a sideways hug and brushed a quick kiss across Josh's cheek, repeating "Thank you, thank you, thank you," throughout the entire process.

Lucky laughed. She'd forgotten how invigorating her friend's effervescence could be. Like Josh, she sometimes found Mo's overwhelming energy and excitability tiring, but most of the time, she found it comforting and a little bit contagious. It was very difficult to be sad around Mo. Even when Lucky was feeling her worst—in the depths of her initial grief about G-Ma, for example—Mo could tell her a story about her day and have her laughing so hard her stomach hurt. She had a unique and creative way of looking at the world, and she didn't take herself or anything else too seriously.

"I can't believe this," she gushed, pushing back the messy blonde locks that had fallen over her face. "Fifteen minutes ago I didn't have anything to do tonight besides paint my toenails in contrasting colors that would give my mother heartburn. And now I'm on my way to see Icarus. You guys are the best." Turning toward Josh, she added, "You know the band, right?"

Josh cleared his throat. "Some. My friend Ben is the bass player. You'll get to meet him tonight. Probably the rest of the band too."

Mo gave Lucky a backhanded smack to the shoulder. "As long as we get to meet Aidan, right? He's just"— she stopped speaking long enough for a rapturous sigh—"too gorgeous for words. And that voice…." She sighed again.

"Get a grip, girl," Lucky laughed. "It's not as if he'll even notice us. We're just barely out of high school."

Mo dropped the pose and replied in all seriousness. "He's not that much older. I think I read somewhere that he's only 20."

"I know he's good-looking, and he's got that voice and all, but he's just a guy, okay?" Josh interjected. "Could you two please try to restrain yourselves at least a little? I don't want to regret bringing you along."

"Oh, not to worry, Josh, you won't even know we're there. Right, Lucky?" Mo said, giving Lucky a wink.

"Okay, I have to ask," Lucky said, as Josh gave a resigned sigh. "*Did* you paint your toenails? What color this time?"

"*Colors*, plural. And not yet. But I'm going to do the left foot alternating purple and green and the right alternating yellow and turquoise. You just can't show up at the country club with toes like that. It's not done. Which is precisely the point."

"Is she seriously asking you to show up at the country club?" Lucky asked. After Mo's parents had divorced a few years ago, her mother had remarried and moved to the suburbs. Mo had chosen to remain in the city with her father, and she stubbornly resisted her mother's attempts to shape her into the daughter her stepfather thought she should be.

"Oh, there's some stupid fall dance, and I'm supposed to go and 'comport myself as a young lady should.'" Mo's voice went all snobby on the last bit. Then she snorted. "Young lady? You'd think she'd know me better by now. I mean, *really*. I'm not wearing any frilly, floofy dress. I'm thinking some short black frock with a wild beaded belt, a lime green feather boa, and strappy sandals with outlandish toes. That'll go over big, don't you think?"

Lucky giggled at the image. Before she could respond further, Josh spoke up. "Mo, do you really think it's a good idea to bait your mother like that all the time?"

"Oh, why not?" The girl let out a breath and flung herself back against the seat. "If she persists in thinking I can be turned into country club material, she deserves to be baited. I can't stand the thought of spending that much time listening to my evil stepfather and his snooty friends trying to out-snoot each other. Life's too short."

"I suppose you do have a point," Josh said. "Now, both of you, start looking for open parking spaces. The bar's just a couple blocks away."

After they parked and made their way to the bar, they had to wait in line for about fifteen minutes to get in. Once inside, Josh led the way toward a table near the stage that was marked "Reserved." Lucky and Mo gave each other wide-eyed looks at the special treatment.

The band was on stage finishing their equipment setup and performing a sound check. As the trio approached their reserved table, one of the band members, an attractive young man with shoulder-length straight black hair pulled back and tied at the nape of his neck, looked up. Catching Josh's eye, he smiled. After securing his bass into place, he stepped down off the stage and came toward them, pushing back a lock of hair that had escaped the leather tie. Lucky's already wide eyes widened even more in surprise as the young man embraced her cousin, and the two exchanged a brief kiss. *This must be Ben,* she thought, *and he and Josh must be more than just friends.* She knew her best fam was gay, but she didn't know there was anyone of interest in the picture right now.

Turning to her with a slight flush coloring his cheeks, Josh made the introductions. "Lucky, this is Ben Takada. Ben, my cousin Lucky and our friend Mo."

Ben's brown eyes sparkled with laughter as he held out his right hand to Lucky, his left arm still around Josh's waist. "Hi, Lucky. It's so good to finally meet you. I understand my boy here got all settled into his new space today. I can't wait to see it."

"It's good to meet you too," Lucky said, taking his hand. She felt an instant liking for the attractive young man with the mischievous eyes who looked at her cousin with such obvious intimacy. "We did a lot of work today. The place looks great."

As Ben turned toward Mo, Lucky gave Josh a pointed look which made his flush deepen. But before he could say anything, one of the other band members called Ben's name.

Untwining his arm from around Josh, Ben started back toward the stage. "Catch you all later. Enjoy the show!" he called, looking over his shoulder and giving Josh a wink.

After they'd seated themselves at the table, Lucky looked at Josh with raised eyebrows. "So?" she asked.

"Yeah, Lucy," interjected Mo, "you got some 'splainin' to do."

Josh gave Lucky an apologetic smile. "We've been friends for a while. We just started dating a month ago. I've wanted to tell you, but I wanted you to meet him first. Sorry to spring it on you like this."

"It's okay. I like him—I mean, I don't know him at all really, but I think I like him. If he makes you happy, that's what matters."

"He does. And you will like him. He's a good guy."

"Not to mention easy on the eyes," Mo chimed in.

"Do Uncle Matthew and Aunt Beth know?"

He shook his head. "I'll tell them soon. I kind of wanted to make sure it was going somewhere, you know, before telling everyone. But," he cleared his throat, flushing again, "it's feeling kind of serious."

"That's great!" Lucky replied, reaching across the table to cover his clasped hands with one of her own. "Good for you."

Josh smiled his thanks. Then they all turned toward the stage as the first chords filled the room.

Lucky and Mo both gasped a little as Aidan Townsend, the lead singer, stepped up to the microphone. The young man really was stunningly handsome. His golden hair curled just below his ears, and even from this distance Lucky could see that his eyes were the intense blue of a glacial lake. Everything about him shone as if he were lit from within.

When he started to sing, Lucky gasped again. She felt as if the husky baritone struck a chord in her chest and left it humming inside her. Listening to Aidan sing was unlike listening to anyone else she'd ever heard. She didn't just hear the music; it was as if she became the music, or the music became her. She couldn't take her eyes off him as his voice rolled over and through her. The lyrics were about love and loss, pain and joy. Lucky couldn't quite capture the words, but she felt every nuance of emotion conveyed in them. Aidan's voice was the echo of her own heartbeat, her heart the speaker through which his voice was conducted.

As the song ended, Lucky felt as if she were waking from a dream or coming out from under a spell. She shook her head to clear it, a frown wrinkling her brow as she continued to stare at the singer. Only then did she notice that he was looking at her with an equal intensity, his eyes narrowed, his gaze curious and probing. Lucky held his eyes for a few moments before turning away.

She hadn't realized she'd been holding her breath until she broke the connection with his eyes. As she exhaled, she saw that Mo was looking at her curiously. Then her friend grinned at her and repeated her earlier words back to her in a teasing tone, "'It's not as if he'll even notice us,' she says. I think *someone* just got noticed."

Lucky gave her a small smile. "Not like that. I mean…. That was…. Well, that was a pretty amazing song, huh?"

"Mm-hmm," Mo's brows drew together with concern. "Are you alright?"

"I'm fine. I think I just got a little swept away for a minute."

When she turned back toward the stage, Aidan was finishing the introductions of the band members. As the band played the intro to the next song, he scanned the audience, his eyes catching hers and lingering a moment before moving on.

The rest of the set did not affect Lucky so intensely. The music was great—from the driving anthems to the subdued ballads—but she didn't get caught up in it, swept away, as she had when the first notes from Aidan's lips had struck her ears. This was at least in part because now that she knew he could evoke such a strong reaction in her, she was somewhat on guard. The few times she felt the touch of his haunting voice inside her head and her chest, as if it were attempting to wrap around her and weave its way through her, she made a conscious effort to shield herself from its thrall. It was not that the experience had been unpleasant—quite the opposite—but it had been unnerving, a little frightening, to have lost herself like that, to have somehow merged with his voice so completely that she couldn't tell where her edges were, where she began or ended. Especially when she came back to herself and realized that no one else seemed to have been affected in the same way.

But that wasn't all. She had the curious sense that Aidan was singing differently too, that he had also been shaken by what had happened and was holding back, reining in his own voice so it didn't overcome her. She gave a little shake of her head at the thought. What was wrong with her? She was letting her imagination carry her into crazy territory. As if a human voice could have that kind of power. No, Aidan's voice was just one of the most beautiful she'd ever heard, and she'd been seriously moved by the song—there was nothing more to it than that. And thinking she'd felt it trying to enfold her? Well, she was just over-emotional right now, vulnerable to the suggestions of her own imagination.

The set ended, and Aidan announced that they'd be back after a brief break. Ben came over to their table with the drummer and the guitarist following behind. Aidan and the keyboard player headed toward the bar. After a few moments they returned armed with drinks for the whole band. Ben introduced Lucky and Mo to the rest of the band members. Lucky smiled but remained silent while Mo, to whom shyness was a completely foreign emotion, without hesitation told them all how much she'd loved the set and how excited she was to meet them. Lucky sat back in her chair and listened as the conversation unfolded around her.

"So, what kind of name is 'Lucky,' anyway?" The soft, deep voice came from close to her ear.

She turned in surprise to find Aidan seated next to her, one booted foot propped on the rung of her chair. "What do you mean?"

One side of his mouth crooked upward in a smile. His eyes were like blue flames. "I've never met anyone named Lucky before, that's all. How do you get a name like that?"

"Well, it's Josh's fault really. He was five when I was born. When his family first came to visit us, I guess I was wrapped in a blanket that had 'Lucy' embroidered on it. My real name is Lucinda, after my grandmother. Anyway, Josh was just starting to read, and he thought the blanket said 'Lucky.' So, that's what he started calling me, and I guess it stuck."

"It suits you somehow."Aidan tilted his head to one side, looking at her through narrowed eyes. "You liked the first song a lot, did you?"

Lucky's cheeks grew hot. "I… It…." She cleared her throat. "Yes, it was very… moving."

Aidan's eyes narrowed further. When he spoke, his voice was very soft. "You got lost in it, didn't you? You couldn't tell what was you and what was the song."

She opened her mouth to protest, but at his murmured "Don't bother denying it," she pressed her lips together without saying anything.

"How old are you, Lucky?"

"W-what?" Lucky was embarrassed at how inarticulate she was being, but Aidan's words kept knocking her off balance. Everything he said was so unexpected. She felt like she was trying to tread water while waves kept crashing over her head.

In a patient voice, he repeated, "How old are you?"

"Seventeen. I'll be eighteen later this month."

"Hmmm…." Suddenly, all the intensity went out of his expression, and nodding toward her glass, he gave her a carefree, flirtatious smile. "Hence, the club soda?"

"Hence, the club soda." She gestured toward the beer in his hand. "And you, I take it, are over 21?"

He nodded and took a long drink from the glass before responding. "Barely, but yes."

He swallowed the rest of the beer and rose to his feet as he set the empty glass on the table. "I better get back up there. See you after the second set." His eyes catching hers for a moment, he added, "I wonder if you'll find it equally… moving."

Before she could respond, he had left her side to make his way back up onto the stage.

"Tell me again that he's not interested," Mo hissed in her ear.

Lucky rolled her eyes.

"Well, I don't care if Mr. Gorgeous is all about the shy, quiet type. *I've* got a date with Eric." Mo waved at the long-haired young man who'd just seated himself behind the drum set. He grinned at her and saluted with one of his drum sticks.

Lucky laughed. "Mo, you're unbelievable. How did you manage to get a date with someone you've known less than twenty minutes?"

Mo's hazel eyes sparkled with mischief. "I told him about the whole country club dance thing. He said he'd like to see my mother's face when she sees me, so I told him he could—if he would come as my date."

"And he agreed?"

"Yep," Mo snapped her fingers, "just like that. He gave me his number, and I've already got him on speed-dial."

Lucky shook her head. "You never cease to amaze me."

"Yeah, well, you must have been taking lessons, 'cause the beautiful Aidan is looking all kinds of intense at you."

"Shut up," Lucky poked Mo with her elbow. "He is not."

But when she glanced toward Aidan, she found that Mo had spoken the truth. When her gaze touched his, he looked away, and then the music started up again.

Lucky couldn't just relax and enjoy the music, no matter how much she wanted to. Every time she started to get caught up in a song, she'd begin to feel that voice trying to weave its way into her, so that she had to shore up her defenses. Each time it happened, she found that Aidan's eyes were focused on her with a look of concentration. Again, she sensed that he was trying to hold something back, trying to lessen the effect his voice was having on her. Crazy as it sounded, there really did seem to be some kind of weird connection between the two of them.

Despite the mental effort it took, she managed to enjoy the show. She knew some of the songs and liked all of them. Listening wasn't a problem, as long as she kept a part of her mind focused on resisting the mysterious pull of Aidan's voice.

But during the last song, her shield crumpled. The song was the band's signature piece, called "Icarus Falling," and it was one of her favorites. As she recognized the first notes from the guitar, she unconsciously dropped her guard, and she was defenseless when Aidan began to sing. His voice enveloped her, and all her mental and emotional edges blurred. Some small part of her was still Lucky, but she was also Aidan's voice, and perhaps a little of Aidan himself, and she was Icarus too. She felt the weight of the wings, the freedom of flight, the blazing heat of the sun. She even felt the touch of burning wax on her back—though the part of her that was still her argued that the wax wasn't even mentioned in the lyrics.

She grabbed on to that protesting thought and concentrated, trying to pull herself free. Focusing her gaze on the stage, she stared in shock. Rising from Aidan's back and stretching across the stage was a pair of wings, made not of feathers, but of many tongues of flame, flickering red-gold. She gasped for breath as he sang of flying and falling, of the sweet freedom in flight that was worth the price of death.

The last notes faded away, and she pushed her hair back off her face with a trembling hand, her breathing ragged. She could still see the wings in a sort of transparent shadow. It must have been some kind of lighting effect, something to bring the show to a spectacular close. Somehow, her merging with the song must have magnified that too.

Everyone around her was applauding and whistling. Chairs were scraped back as the crowd began to stand. She felt a little unsteady as she rose to stand beside Mo, who turned to her with a wide smile.

"That was amazing, wasn't it? Just amazing," Mo shouted over the applause.

Lucky nodded, smiling back as brightly as she could. "Incredible."

As people milled around chatting, Lucky bolted down the remainder of her club soda as well as the last of Mo's, trying to calm herself, to still her spinning thoughts. At least, no one seemed to notice her odd behavior. Some more of Josh's friends had shown up, and he was preoccupied with talking to them. And Mo was focused on Eric, who had come back to their table as soon as the song had ended. Lucky captured Josh's attention long enough to motion that she was going outside for some air. When he nodded his acknowledgement, she headed for the door with a feeling of relief.

Outside, the chill of the evening sharpened her senses. She slid her arms into the sleeves of her jacket, and leaning back against the outside wall of the bar, she drew in a few deep breaths. When a masculine hand holding a bottle of water appeared in front of her, she followed the curve of the arm up to see Aidan looking down at her with concern.

"Hey," he said softly.

Her response was a grumpy, "Hey, yourself," but she took the offered water and lifted it to take a drink, looking out at the street and the passing cars.

After a few moments of silence, she turned back to Aidan. "That wing thing is quite something."

"What?"

It seemed as though she had knocked him off balance this time.

"That special lighting effect thing—you know, where you grow flaming wings during 'Icarus Falling.' Pretty amazing stuff."

"Oh, that." He ran a hand through his hair. "Yeah, our lighting and special effects guy is top-notch. That one's copyrighted—or whatever you call it with those things. I could tell you how he does it, but then I'd have to kill you."

She managed a weak smile. "Seriously, it was incredible. The whole show was great. You probably hear this all the time, but your voice… well…." She shrugged.

He acknowledged her half-spoken compliment with a tilt of the head. "Thanks. I'm glad you… enjoyed it." Another moment of silence passed, and then he took a deep breath. "So, when exactly is this upcoming birthday of yours?"

She frowned. "Next Sunday, if you must know. Why are you so concerned about my age and my birthday?"

He raised an eyebrow. "Maybe I just want to make sure you're legal before I ask you out."

"You're going to ask me out?" she asked, with no small share of skepticism.

He shrugged. "Maybe." Then he gave her a rakish grin. "When you're old enough."

Lucky rolled her eyes. "Right."

"It could happen."

She regarded him in silence for a few moments. Then, shaking her head, she muttered, "This is going to make me sound like I'm nuts." She paused before continuing. "Your voice—it does something strange to me." She searched his eyes, a crease between her brows. "But somehow I think you know that."

He opened his mouth to speak, but before he could say anything, they were surrounded by laughter and conversation as Josh, Ben, Mo, Eric, and the rest of the band joined them. Everyone said their good-byes, and then Lucky, Josh, and Mo started down the block to find their car. When Lucky glanced back over her shoulder, Aidan was still standing there watching her.

Aidan watched Lucky and her friends walk away from him with the uncomfortable sense that his life was about to change—and not for the better. From the first song of the evening, when he'd felt the power go out of him and realized that it focused solely on the solemn-looking, dark-haired girl, that no one else in the room was affected, he'd known she heralded nothing but trouble. Anyone who could evoke the Gift he kept hidden in his human life could mean nothing else. Watching her, though, he'd seen the shock in her unusual green eyes, and he had realized she wasn't drawing his power intentionally. She didn't understand what was happening. He'd tried to rein it in then, to lessen the impact, but with limited success.

She was a Sensitive—she had to be—and she had no idea what she was. And that wasn't even the worst of it. She had seen his wings, or at least the shadows of them. In the last few days he had begun to feel them again, had realized they were being returned to him—whether he wanted them or not. So far, he had been deluding himself into believing that if he ignored them, they would go away. Now he was forced to admit that such a response was out of the question. Even if he could just ignore the reinstatement of his wings or reply with some kind of cosmic "Return to Sender," there was the problem of the girl. He couldn't ignore her. She was going to be eighteen soon, and if she reached her birthday without knowing what she was, without realizing what was happening to her, if she came into the full force of her power without someone there to help her, she could well lose her mind, or even her life. To survive the process intact on her own, she would have to be very "lucky" indeed.

By all that was holy and unholy, he did not want to be drawn back into that world, but he couldn't live with himself if he didn't do whatever he could for her. He really had no choice; he had to contact Zeke.

Cursing under his breath, he turned and went back into the bar.

Lucky was flying. She could feel the wind on her face, the sun on her hair, the muscles of her back flexing with every beat of her wings. She was surrounded by nothing but blue sky and wispy, white clouds. She felt as light as air. She threw her head back and laughed at the delightful sense of freedom. Someone touched her hand, and she saw that Aidan was flying with her, great white wings beating against the air. She laughed again as they flew higher and faster, as if the pull of gravity was near non-existent. She called out to him in her excitement, and as he turned to look at her, his wings burst into flames. The force of the fire drew his bare shoulders up and back, his body arcing backward into a perfect bow. Lucky was awestruck by the beauty of it—the arc of his body, the flames, and the music. Each tongue of flame on his wings had begun to sing, and the air was filled with a resonating, haunting chorus. Then the arc of Aidan's body broke, crumpled, and the music stopped as he began to fall. She screamed in terror as she reached for him.

"No! NO!" Lucky jerked awake as she cried out, her heart pounding with fear. She sat up, pushing trembling hands through her hair.

After her breathing had slowed, she threw back the covers, got out of bed, and padded down the hall to the kitchen, where she retrieved a glass from the cupboard and filled it with water from the tap. Still feeling too shaken to return to bed, she wandered into the living room and curled up on the couch, wrapping a fleece throw around her shoulders to take away the chill.

The dream had felt so real—the freedom, the exhilaration, the fear. She listened to the noise from the street below—raucous laughter and loud conversation from a group of people walking by, the shrill sound of a city bus releasing its brakes, the bass beat from a passing car growing louder and then fading away. She let the familiar sounds comfort her, restore a sense of normalcy.

She didn't feel like going back to bed for quite a while, and when she did, her sleep was troubled and restless.

CHAPTER 1

It was almost 3:00 AM when Aidan parked his motorcycle outside Zeke's brownstone. He didn't hesitate to ring the bell despite the hour. He knew the angel never slept. Waking and working 24/7, that was Zeke. There was, he supposed, something to be said for that. Still, he was thankful that he was human enough to need a little shut-eye. He hadn't felt that way a year ago, but the nightmares weren't as frequent now, and he'd made friends with the oblivion found in dreamless sleep.

When no one answered, Aidan rang the bell again. The street was so quiet he could hear the sound echoing in the dark house. He tapped his foot impatiently while he waited for a response. He was about to ring a third time when the door opened. Zeke just looked at him, his face revealing nothing of his thoughts. Aidan couldn't tell if the angel was surprised to see him, or if he'd known who was at the door all along. He also had no idea if Zeke was pleased or annoyed by his presence at his door in the wee hours of the morning.

"Aren't you going to invite me in?"

Zeke moved aside and gestured for Aidan to enter. Aidan hesitated a fraction of a second before stepping into the house. He was anxious about this first conversation with Zeke after so long with no contact.

As Zeke closed the door behind him, Aidan walked into the formal living room. It still looked the same: filled with slightly faded but valuable antique furniture, the windows hung with dark drapes. The room had a cold, abandoned air, as if no one lived there. That was because, as Aidan knew, no one did. Zeke seldom used the formal living room. When he was home, he was most often in the library on the lower level.

Zeke raised his hand and pointed toward the door to the hall. "You know the way." His voice was deep and resonant, the sound so substantial it was almost like another presence in the room.

Aidan tilted his head in acknowledgement, and preceding Zeke into the hallway, he made his way to the stairs that led to the library. He was hit with a strong wave of nostalgia as he walked into Zeke's sanctuary. The room was filled with floor to ceiling bookshelves, every inch of them covered with books, stacks of folios, and ancient objects of power—statues of gods, religious symbols, and icons from various traditions. An imposing black walnut desk sat at one end of the room, its surface covered with curling parchment scrolls and opened leather-bound volumes. The sleek silver laptop pushed to one side looked incongruous sitting next to a statuette of an ancient Sumerian goddess.

Aidan couldn't help himself; he started singing, "One of these things is not like the others. One of these things just doesn't belong."

Zeke raised an eyebrow at him, but said nothing. Aidan stopped singing. "It's good to see you, Zeke," he said.

For the first time, Zeke smiled, and Aidan could see the affection in his light gray eyes. "It's good to see you too, my boy." Even though his voice was quiet, the sound rolled into the room like a wave.

"Have a seat." He nodded toward the four scuffed leather chairs that circled the heavy, low oak table in the middle of the room. Aidan took off his black leather jacket and tossed it over one of the chairs before seating himself in another.

"Would you like a drink?"

When Aidan answered in the affirmative, Zeke opened a small cabinet to the right of the desk and took out a bottle of cognac and two snifters. After pouring a generous amount of the liquor into each glass, he handed one to Aidan and then seated himself across from the young man.

Aidan slipped the stem of the snifter between his index and middle finger, cupping the glass in his palm and swirling the liquid to allow it to absorb the warmth from his skin. "How very civilized," he remarked.

A corner of Zeke's mouth quirked upward and he replied, "We must take our small pleasures where we can find them."

There was a moment of silence while the two men sampled the cognac. Then Zeke directed a rapier sharp look at Aidan. "What brings you here, young Aidan? The last time I saw you, I believe you swore something to the effect of never darkening my door again."

"That I did." Aidan grimaced. "And, believe me, I wouldn't be here now if it weren't important."

Zeke leaned forward. "Your wings have been returned." It was a statement, not a question.

"Yes, they have, but that's not why I'm here." Aidan settled more comfortably into the soft leather of the chair and took another sip of his cognac before continuing. "I had planned on ignoring them. If you don't use them, you lose them, right?"

"Still as cocky as ever, I see. If it's not the return of your wings that brings you here, what is it that's so important?"

"There's this girl," Aidan began.

Before he could continue, Zeke interrupted. "Isn't there always?" His light eyes shone with mischief, a look as incongruous on his serious face as the laptop was on his ancient desk.

"It's not like that," Aidan's tone was impatient. "This girl—her name is Lucky—she's a Sensitive, I'm pretty sure. But she doesn't know. She doesn't know anything. And she's going to be eighteen in less than two weeks. I wanted you to know, so you can do your thing—help her."

Zeke's eyes narrowed, and he leaned further forward in his chair. "A Sensitive? One of whom I was unaware? Who is this girl, and how do you know she's a Sensitive?"

"She came to the Icarus show tonight—well, last night, I guess. She's the cousin of the guy who's dating our bass player. From the first notes of the first song, she drew my Gift out of me. I thought she was doing it on purpose at first, that she was one of the Dark Ones trying to expose me or something. But then I could tell she was shocked by what my voice was doing to her. She had no idea, and she tried to put up defenses, tried to block it." When he continued, his voice was tinged with admiration. "She did a pretty good job, too. I could feel her pulling herself back together, marking her mental boundaries."

He paused to take another sip of his drink.

"Did you talk to her?" Zeke asked.

"Yes, when we took a break. That's when I found out she's just shy of eighteen. By that point, I was pretty sure she was a Sensitive, but what made me certain was the conversation we had after the show. During the final number, I sensed my wings. They've shown up in small ways over the past couple of weeks—the occasional muscle twinge or feeling of weight. But this was the first time they were really *there* on my back, a part of me again. I had the glamour up anyway, like always, just in case, and when I felt the wings, I turned it up a few notches."

He stopped for a moment, and his eyes locked on the angel's. "She saw them. She made some remark after the show about 'that special effect thing' where the lighting made it look like I grew flaming wings. I played along, pretended that's what it was. I mean, I couldn't just tell her that I'm half angel, and what she saw was real, could I? She would never have believed me." He hesitated and then continued, "I almost told her anyway a little later. But then her friends showed up, and everyone started saying good-bye. Then she was gone. So I decided to come to you."

Zeke leaned back in his chair and sighed. "Who knows what she might have believed? She probably had some inkling that what she saw wasn't an effect of the lighting—especially if she experienced even a part of your Gift. Did you find out exactly when her birthday is?"

"A week from Sunday."

"I'll see what I can do about contacting her before then. If she truly knows nothing of what she is or the world she's about to join, that makes matters a little more difficult. I can hardly walk up to her and introduce myself as the angel who's about to take on her training. I'll have to engineer some kind of event."

Aidan gave him a sardonic look. "I have no doubt that you'll come up with something. I've never seen you at a loss."

Zeke's face took on a somber expression, his eyes filling with sadness. "Yes, you have, my boy." His voice sounded like the waves at ebb tide. "Yes, you have."

Aidan knew exactly what the angel was referring to. Regretting his hasty comment and unable to shape any words in response, he just nodded in agreement.

"Well, then," Zeke said, as he stood up, "I will contact Malachi, see what I can find out, and arrange something suitable. I will be in touch."

Knowing he was being dismissed, Aidan swallowed the last of his cognac, appreciating the way it burned his throat, and rose to his feet. He grabbed his jacket and shrugged it on as he followed Zeke up the stairs and through the formal living room to the front door.

When he stepped outside, Zeke closed the door behind him without another word.

Lucky's first thought when she awakened late Sunday morning, after passing a less than restful night, was that she needed to visit G-Ma. It had been only a couple of days since they'd moved her into the assisted living facility, but Lucky didn't want her to think her granddaughter had abandoned her. Checking the time, she found that she could make it to Lincoln Park by lunchtime if she hurried. She rushed through her shower and towel-dried her hair as best she could before twisting it into a thick braid that hung between her shoulder blades. Pulling on jeans, a long-sleeved black t-shirt with a white Icarus logo on the front, and a pair of lime green Chuck Taylors, she swung her tattered backpack over her shoulder, grabbed her keys, and headed for the door.

She didn't see or hear Josh, and his bedroom door was closed, so she assumed he was still sleeping. She hesitated then turned toward the kitchen, where she scribbled a quick note on the small whiteboard stuck to the refrigerator door. That way he wouldn't wonder where she was when he found her gone. Since she was in the kitchen, she decided to pour herself a glass of milk as fortification for the trip. She downed the milk and walked back down the hall and out the door, her keys jangling as she locked the door behind her. Out on the sidewalk, she turned east toward Lake Park, where she could catch the #6 bus downtown.

Standing at the bus stop, she found herself thinking of reasons to go back home, to change her mind about going to visit G-Ma. She wanted to see her, but she didn't want to go to the assisted living facility. And, in all honesty, she wanted to see G-Ma as she used to be. She wanted to be able to talk to her about art and literature and politics, to curl up in her arms and know that she was protected and loved. Instead, she had to be the one doing the protecting, and conversations sometimes took a turn toward the surreal. Not only was G-Ma not always sure what year it was anymore, her grasp on reality was getting more tenuous all the time. Well, at least her grasp on reality as she used to know it and as the rest of her family knew it. Maybe there was some other reality that she was able to tap into now, some other level of awareness that those who thought they knew "the real world" couldn't begin to comprehend. Lucky liked to think so. Rather than seeing G-Ma as an aging woman who had lost too much of herself too soon, she preferred to think of her as moving beyond this realm and into another. It was just that her mind went there before her body.

Seeking distraction from her thoughts, Lucky rummaged through her backpack and located her iPod. Popping in the earbuds, she searched for one of her favorite playlists. When the music hit her ears, she smiled. This song always made her happy. Even though the words were sad in places, the music was upbeat, and it somehow made her trust in possibilities.

She tapped her foot with the rhythm and resisted the urge to dance. If she had been alone in her room, she would have. Here on a public street, waiting for the bus, on the other hand.... If Josh or Mo had been with her, she would have danced here too. She wondered why it seemed more acceptable to do silly or outrageous things in groups, even just a group of two, than it did alone. If strangers saw her dancing with a friend on the street, they would probably call them spontaneous or whimsical, but if they saw her dancing alone, they would be likely to question her mental stability.

Lucky's thoughts were interrupted by the arrival of her bus. Climbing aboard, she swiped her pass through the reader and made her way to one of the few empty seats. She sat down next to a young African-American man who gave her a slight smile before turning to look out the window.

Lucky glanced around her at the variety of people on the bus. Four white kids about her age sat in the seats across from her, the two in the front turning around in the seats so they could talk to their companions in the seats behind them. All were dressed in black, and three of the four had multiple earrings and facial piercings. One had a tattoo on the back of his hand. She guessed the others were tattooed as well, the marks hidden beneath their clothing. A few rows up, an elderly Asian woman in an orange coat sat next to a large African-American man in leather with gold rings in his ears. An old man in an overcoat and hat sat in one of the seats that faced in toward the aisle of the bus, his hands in his pockets and his eyes closed as if he were trying to sleep. He was sandwiched between two young women, one black and one white, who looked to be in their early twenties and were leaning forward to talk around him.

When the bus stopped, a few more passengers got on. One of them, a tall, sallow-skinned man with longish, jagged dark hair and wearing a charcoal gray duster, stopped in the aisle next to Lucky and stood holding onto the support bar. He glared at Lucky when she glanced up at him. An elderly woman got on at the next stop, and seeing there were no empty seats, Lucky stood to offer hers. The action brought her uncomfortably close to the man in the gray duster.

At Lucky's murmured "Excuse me," he looked at her through narrowed yellow-gold eyes and scowled, but he stepped aside to give her room to get around him so she could find a place in the aisle to stand. The bus took off before she could grab hold of the support bar and the movement knocked her against the man. The noise he made sounded to Lucky more like a growl than anything else, and the eyes he turned toward her when she apologized were filled with malice. Lucky jerked away from him and put as much space between herself and him as she could.

She was conscious of his proximity for the remainder of the ride to the Loop. He had turned so his back was towards her, but she kept remembering those venomous yellow-gold eyes. Her clumsy stumble hadn't been enough to warrant such hatred. Lucky had ridden city buses all her life and had encountered many angry, frustrated people over the years. She usually took such things in stride. But this man was different; something about him seriously scared her.

When the bus reached her stop at Michigan and Randolph, Lucky was a little unsettled to find that he was getting off the bus there as well. At the same time, she was glad, because that meant she didn't have to squeeze past him in the aisle and risk another malicious look.

He preceded her off the bus and was already several yards away by the time Lucky stepped down to the sidewalk. She stared after him, a frown furrowing her brow. As she watched, the breeze caught his duster and blew it upward.

For a moment she could have sworn he had a short, dark, pointed tail and leathery, bat-like wings folded against his sides. Then the duster fell back in place, and he was just a man in a long coat walking away from her with impatient strides.

"Miss?"

The bus driver's impatient query made Lucky realize he was waiting for her to move so he could close the door. She stepped away from the bus. Before she could get the word "Sorry" out of her mouth, the door was already closing, and the bus was pulling away from the curb.

She turned to look back down the block after the man in the duster, but he was nowhere to be seen. She sighed. Bat wings and a tail. Right. "Get a grip, Lucky," she murmured under her breath.

Adjusting her backpack on her shoulder, she held onto her iPod, taking comfort in the smooth, familiar shape of it in her hand, and settled in to wait for her next bus. The playlist switched to the next song, and she frowned as the opening to "Icarus Falling" filled her ears. It had been a weekend for weirdness. Momentarily hallucinating a tail and bat wings on an angry stranger paled in comparison to her experience at the Icarus show the night before. What had that all been about anyway? In the midst of the mundane activity of waiting at a bus stop, the almost mystical quality of her experience of the music seemed even more surreal and dreamlike. She must have imagined it all. And yet, she knew she hadn't imagined her conversations with Aidan, nor had she imagined the intensity with which he had stared after her as she and Mo and Josh were leaving. Whatever was going on, he had felt some part of it too, had *been* a part of it.

As she listened to the words of the song, she remembered the feeling of being inside the music, the song, the story. She recalled the sensation of the leather harness of the wings against her skin and the strangeness of the moment when she felt the heat of the melting wax on her back. She also recalled the sense of oneness with Aidan's beautiful voice. She could feel herself rising and falling with the melody, feel the rhythm of his voice stroking against the edges of her mind, wrapping her in warm, dark silk. She caught her breath as she remembered the flaming wings she had seen rising and spreading from his shoulders, wings she had seen again in her dream, when, like Icarus', they caught fire, and he fell from the sky. She had assumed the flaming wings were a part of the show, special effects, but now she was beginning to wonder. Aidan had seemed startled when she had first asked him about them, and now she had seen wings of another sort on someone else. Was it just her? Was she seeing things?

Her worries were interrupted by the arrival of the 151. Lucky swiped her card and took an empty seat next to the window. She stared out at the people on the sidewalk, wondering what they were thinking. She guessed they all had plenty of things to worry about. She wondered if any of them, like her, were starting to have doubts about the sureness of their grip on reality.

She had spent months worrying about G-Ma. What if her own mind was failing? It wasn't exactly normal to go around seeing angel or demon wings on people. She wasn't even sure she believed in angels and demons. She had attended Catholic school, but she had not been raised to be especially religious, so angels and demons for her were figures from fantasy or horror movies, not beings one encountered in one's daily life. But since she hadn't ever been particularly fascinated with them, why would she start imagining them now? It didn't make sense. Then again, it seemed that life often didn't make sense. Look at what had happened to G-Ma. Was it really so much more nonsensical for her to be imagining that people had wings than it was for a highly intelligent, independent woman to have suddenly lost the ability to remember where she lived, or how to operate a stove or a television? If such a thing could happen to G-Ma, then pretty much anything could happen to anybody at any time.

Lucky's jaw tightened as she realized they had reached her stop at Sheridan and Diversey. She got off the bus, quickly stepping away from the door this time, since there was no yellow-eyed, bat-winged stranger to distract her. She walked the remaining blocks to the assisted living facility and hesitated for a few moments outside the door. Then she took a deep breath, squared her shoulders, and went in.

After Lucky had signed in at the front desk, she started down the first of several somewhat maze-like corridors toward G-Ma's room. She hoped she'd find her grandmother there so she wouldn't have to wander around the building looking for her. When she turned down the last hallway, she was relieved to see G-Ma walking toward her down the hall. At the sight of her granddaughter, G-Ma's face lit up in a smile, and she spread her arms wide. Lucky was almost running as she closed the remaining distance and wrapped her arms around her grandmother. Tears filled her eyes as she was enveloped in G-Ma's embrace. It felt so normal, so right, and yet she knew that her relationship with her grandmother would never return to what it had been before.

"It's so good to see you," G-Ma said, pressing her cheek against Lucky's. "I've missed you, my dear."

"I've missed you too," Lucky replied, a slight break in her voice.

She tightened her arms around her grandmother's slight form. G-Ma had never been a large woman, and in the last several months, she had gotten smaller. She wasn't frail, but she no longer had the wiry muscular strength she had once possessed. After a final squeeze, Lucky stepped back from her grandmother.

Slipping her hand around Lucky's elbow, G-Ma turned back down the hallway to her room. "Let's go sit down and visit for a while."

Once in G-Ma's room, Lucky refused the offered recliner, which she knew was G-Ma's favorite chair, and settled into the rocking chair across from her. Looking around the room, she was pleased to see that it was bright and cheery. The curtains were pulled back and the blinds were open, allowing sunlight to stream through the window. The walls and shelves were covered with family photographs and artwork, the latter a combination of pieces by some of G-Ma's favorite artists and those she had made herself. G-Ma had been an art teacher, and she had explored various media over the years. Most recently, she had been working with oil paints. Lucky was pleased to see a partially finished painting and tubes of paint laid out on the artist's table in the far corner of the room. With all that G-Ma had lost, it was a relief to know that she still had her art.

"What are you working on?" Lucky asked, getting up from the chair and moving toward the art table.

"Well, I'm not sure," G-Ma responded.

Hearing the uncertainty in her voice, Lucky stopped and turned to look at her grandmother. The older woman's face wore a puzzled frown. "I had intended to paint a still life."

She gestured toward the dresser, atop which sat a small, lapis-colored ceramic bowl filled with vibrant yellow lemons and bright green limes. Next to the bowl was a narrow, clear blue vase which contained three cheerful daisies. G-Ma walked over to the dresser and picked up a lemon, cradling it in her hand.

"One of the girls brought me the flowers, and when I mentioned I'd like to paint them next to that bowl, and that it would be even better if there were some lemons and limes in it, she brought me those. Wasn't that nice of her?" G-Ma looked at Lucky and smiled, then lifted the lemon to her nose and sniffed. "It smells so fresh."

Turning back to the dresser, she replaced the lemon in the bowl and gazed at the little display with satisfaction. "It will make quite a nice painting, don't you think?" she asked.

"Yes, G-Ma," Lucky said. "It will make a very nice painting." She took another step toward the art table in the corner. "And what is it you're working on right now?" She glanced back at her grandmother.

G-Ma lost her smile and frowned again. Slowly, she walked over to join Lucky, and together they took the final steps to the table, moving around to the far side of it, so they could see the painting right side up. G-Ma put out her hand toward the painting, but paused before her fingers touched it.

"I don't know what this is," she said. "When I sat down to paint, the image came into my head, and I had to paint it. It's not finished, but I can't see the rest of it yet."

As Lucky examined the piece, she felt her own forehead crease with a frown. It was unlike anything G-Ma had ever painted before. Usually, her paintings were realistic—still lifes, leaves, trees, and flowers. She'd once said that she liked to paint natural images because, living in the city, she didn't get to see enough nature; if she filled her house with paintings, she could give herself the illusion of being surrounded by it.

This painting was definitely not a nature scene, although, like G-Ma, Lucky wasn't sure what it depicted. Approximately the right third of the sheet was filled with a dark, cloud-like image. Swooping diagonally across the canvas were swirls of gray and black with occasional streaks of red. Although the cloudy shape was abstract, it somehow gave the impression of animation, of personality—and of distinct malevolence. The longer Lucky looked at the image, the more convinced she was that the subject was some sort of being. She noticed two yellow-tinged red spots amidst the darkness that could even be representative of eyes.

The remaining two-thirds of the painting was little more than a sketch. The colors were lighter—blues, golds, some paler grays—and it looked as if several figures were beginning to take shape. Ultimately, though, the image was as yet indeterminate. Lucky found the painting both fascinating and deeply disturbing. Something in her clamored to see the finished version, while another part of her never wanted to look on the image again.

"I was going to paint a still life," G-Ma said in a small, uncertain voice, her fingers still reaching toward but not touching the half-finished canvas. Now that she had seen the painting, Lucky found that the words filled her with a strange sort of dread.

Shaking her head and looking up at Lucky as if awakening from a dream, G-Ma asked, "Would you like a cup of tea, dear? I'll heat some water." Then she looked around the room with a puzzled frown. "Oh, it looks like someone took my stove." She turned to Lucky and spoke in a lowered voice, as if sharing a secret. "They do that, you know. Things just disappear. My dishes and my silverware have almost all gone missing. Someone just comes in here when I'm gone and walks right out with my things."

Lucky wasn't sure how to respond. They hadn't brought any dishes or silverware when they had moved G-Ma into the assisted living facility. All her meals here would be in the facility's dining room, so she didn't need her own personal items. "I'm—sure they'll bring them back," she said.

"Yes, and if they don't, I'll let someone know about it," G-Ma stated.

Just then, there was a knock at the open door, and a pretty young black woman stepped inside.

"Lucinda, are you ready for lunch?" she asked.

Seeing Lucky, she smiled and held out her hand. "I'm DeShawn," she said. "You must be Lucky. Lucinda talks about you all the time."

Lucky shook her hand. "It's nice to meet you. Are you the one who brought G-Ma the flowers?"

DeShawn's smile widened. "Yes. They caught my eye when I walked past the flower display at the market yesterday, and I thought of Lucinda, because when I first met her on Friday, she said she liked daisies."

"Thank you," said Lucky with a smile. "That was very kind."

DeShawn waved away the thanks. "Oh, it was no big deal. She's a neat lady, your grandmother."

She held her hand out toward G-Ma, who took it without hesitation. "Are you hungry, Lucinda?"

G-Ma nodded. "I hope they have chicken," she said. "Chicken and mashed potatoes would be nice."

DeShawn laughed. "You know, I think we are having chicken today." She turned toward Lucky. "Would you like to have lunch with your grandmother? We can fix you a plate too."

Lucky looked at G-Ma. "Why not?" she said. "If you're sure it's no bother."

"No bother at all," DeShawn replied, leading G-Ma from the room.

Lucky stepped through the door after them, casting one last troubled glance toward the unfinished painting, before pulling the door closed.

The rest of Lucky's visit was uneventful. During lunch, she met some of the other residents. Although most of the people who shared her grandmother's table were several years older than G-Ma, they all seemed to be at much the same stage of dementia as she was. They were all still capable of carrying on conversations, even though those conversations were sometimes bizarre. Some of the residents at other tables were in later stages of the disease, several of them in wheelchairs, and many of them needing assistance eating their meals. It made Lucky sad to see all these people whose lives had been disrupted. She was sure they had never imagined that this would be how they would spend their final years.

After lunch was over, she and G-Ma wandered through the halls until they found the lounge, where G-Ma was going to sit with some of the other residents and watch television. Lucky kissed G-Ma good-bye and blinked away tears at her grandmother's prolonged embrace. When G-Ma released her, she reached up to pat her granddaughter's cheek.

"I love you so much, Lucky," G-Ma said, her hazel eyes filled with warmth.

"I love you too, G-Ma," Lucky responded. "I'll come back and see you soon."

G-Ma nodded. "That's good," she said.

Lucky had taken only a few steps toward the door, when her grandmother called her name.

"What is it, G-Ma?" Lucky asked, turning around.

G-Ma's face was serious. "Watch out for the dark, Lucky," she said, her voice filled with warning. "Watch out for the dark."

CHAPTER 5

G-Ma's warning echoed in Lucky's head all the way back to Hyde Park. Fortunately, she didn't have any more encounters with tall, menacing men who might or might not have wings and tails. Unfortunately, that didn't mean she saw nothing out of the ordinary. While waiting at the stop between buses, she glanced at a beautiful blonde woman with striking lavender eyes. When the woman returned her glance, Lucky could have sworn her eyes lost all their color, becoming blind white balls. Lucky gasped. Then the woman's lips curled in a small smile, and her eyes were lavender once again. Lucky looked away.

After she boarded the #6, Lucky sat by the window and made it a point to direct her eyes out toward the passing city; she didn't want to watch her fellow passengers anymore. While the bus was stopped at a light, she found her eyes drawn to a homeless man who was walking down the sidewalk toward the bus, pushing a shopping cart. As the bus began to pull away, he looked up at her, and Lucky suddenly saw two silvery wings unfolding from his shoulders, as if they'd grown from his back right through his tattered coat. The bus passed him by, and Lucky turned around to catch another glimpse of him, but the angle was all wrong, and she could no longer see him.

Disembarking the bus at Lake Park, Lucky covered the blocks to her building in record time. She was breathing fast when she reached the top of the stairs and put her key into the lock. Stepping inside, she found Josh and Ben slouched on the couch watching a movie. Josh paused the video as she threw her keys on the table by the door, dropped her backpack beside it, and flung herself into the faded paisley chair.

"How was G-Ma?" he asked.

"Okay. It was good to see her." Lucky hesitated. She wanted to tell him about the painting, but she wasn't sure what there was to tell. She didn't know how to convey the real sense of menace the dark cloud had given her, or how she couldn't help but connect the painting to G-Ma's warning about the dark, and she didn't want to sound crazy. Of course, given the things that were happening in her life lately, maybe *sounding* crazy was the least of her worries.

"Have you eaten?" Ben asked. "There's leftover pizza." He nodded at the box on the coffee table.

"Thanks, but I had lunch with G-Ma." Lucky grimaced. "Fried chicken, mashed potatoes, and Brussels sprouts. Old people food."

Both young men chuckled. "Sorry," Josh said.

"No, it was okay, and I got to meet some of the other residents. G-Ma seemed to get along with everyone, and they all talked to each other. The conversation was a little weird sometimes." Lucky's voice trailed off. As if she had any right to talk about weird.

After several moments of silence, Ben directed a pointed look at Josh, who shifted uncomfortably, cleared his throat, and said, "So, um, Ben is planning on staying over tonight." He paused and continued in a halting manner. "We just wanted to let you know. You know, in case it… bothers you,… or you want to talk about it… or anything."

"That was smooth," Ben muttered, with a smirk.

"Relax, Josh, it's fine," Lucky said. Then she raised her eyebrows and gave a toss of her head. "Just as long as you're okay if *I* have a guy stay over sometimes."

Josh frowned. "Not until you're eighteen," he said. "After that, fine. Until then, no way. And I mean it. I'm older than you, so that makes me the master of the house."

Lucky snorted. "Master of the house? You're not even master of your own domain."

Ben burst out with a laugh. "You must admit she's got a point."

"You don't even know what that means," Josh said to Lucky, blushing.

"Of course, I do." Lucky chuckled. "We have cable. I've seen almost all the episodes of *Seinfeld.* Besides, I'm well versed in YouTube."

"Nevertheless," Josh said over the laughter of the other two. "Not until you're eighteen. Your birthday is only a week away. No big deal, right?"

"Fine," Lucky said, grinning. "It's not like anybody's in the running anyway. Although, Aidan did hint that he might ask me out." She paused for effect and then continued, "For some reason, though, he insisted that he was going to wait until after my birthday."

"Aidan?" Josh said with a frown. "He's too old for you. What's he even thinking? I'm going to have to talk to him about this."

"Josh, no," Lucky interjected, embarrassed. "I was just teasing you. I don't think he meant it anyway."

Ben put his hand on Josh's knee. "Calm down, sweetie. You can't do that to her. Can you imagine how embarrassed she'd be if you had this little heart-to-heart with Aidan? Besides, you know him. He's a good guy. Sure, he's a little older than Lucky, but he's trustworthy. You should know that."

"He's a *guy*," Josh grumbled.

Ben chuckled. "Even so. Plus, as you just pointed out, Lucky *is* going to be eighteen soon, so it's really not your call."

"Fine," Josh muttered, stretching his legs out in front of him and crossing them at the ankles at the same time as he crossed his arms over his chest.

Lucky gave him an arch look. "I think this is going to be far harder for you than it is for me." Turning to his long-haired companion, she added, "Ben, I don't mind you staying over in the least—and thanks for being on my side."

Ben winked at her, as he pushed a stray lock of hair behind his ear. "Anytime, sister. We gotta stick together so we can help Josh deal with his control issues."

Josh looked at Ben through narrowed eyes, but when his softly uttered "Traitor" caused both Lucky and Ben to burst into laughter, his face relaxed and his lips curled into a smile.

"Alright, alright! So I overreacted." He uncrossed his arms and sat up straighter. "I can't help it if I'm protective of you, Lucky. You're like my little sister. I just don't want you getting hurt."

"I know, Josh," Lucky said, smiling at him affectionately. Pushing herself up out of the chair, she walked by the couch and reached out to ruffle his hair. She paused with her hand still resting on his dark curls as she added, her voice suddenly serious, "But I'm not at all sure you can do anything about that."

Before either of the young men could reply, she had left the room.

Aidan was in a bad mood. He'd awakened not much before noon with the strong conviction that he had to go see Zeke again, and he couldn't help but think that the conviction was not his own. That conniving bastard was messing with his mind again. Now that he had his wings back and had taken the first step by getting in touch with the angel, he was being pulled back into his world, like it or not. Aidan knew better than to ignore his compulsion. If he didn't follow through, the need to head toward that familiar brownstone would start giving him an itch that would make him want to scratch his own eyes out.

So to Zeke's he'd gone, and sure enough, the angel had been expecting him. That had been no surprise to Aidan at all. What had been a surprise—and not a pleasant one—was finding his half-brother Kevin lounging in one of the comfortable leather chairs in Zeke's sanctum sanctorum. After ushering him into the room, Zeke had left, closing the door behind him.

Only out of bed for an hour, and the day just keeps getting better, Aidan thought now, as Kev's eyes raked him from head to toe.

"The prodigal returns," his older brother drawled.

"Not by choice," Aidan responded, unsmiling, "as you probably well know."

Kev tilted his head in assent. "Not this time, it's true. But no one was compelling you last night—or rather, in the wee hours of the morning. Once I found out you'd come to see the old one, I asked him to do me the favor of bringing you back."

Aidan's jaw tightened. "So this is your doing?"

Kev responded with a wordless shrug.

"I should have guessed," Aidan muttered. Dropping into the chair across from his brother, he leaned back, shoving his clenched fists into the pockets of his leather jacket. "Okay, so I'm here. What do you want with me?"

"We want you to come back, Aidan."

Aidan pushed his hands deeper into his pockets and regarded his brother in silence. He'd figured that much, but that didn't mean he was ready to comply—and certainly not without more information.

Kev leaned forward in his chair, his features assuming the focused gravity Aidan knew only too well. His brother's eyes looked back at him from the face of a Captain rallying his troops.

"Let me rephrase. We *need* you to come back. Our situation is more precarious than usual—and getting more so by the day. The Metatron is on the verge of nullifying the Alliance."

"Right. The Metatron has been making noises about the Alliance for as long as I can remember—usually they're idle threats intended to make Lucifer toe some kind of line."

"Not this time," Kev said, his jaw tightening. "Jahoel has been killed. And the perpetrator did a very good job of making it look like Lucifer was responsible."

Aidan could feel the blood draining from his cheeks. "Holy hell," he breathed.

"Yep, that pretty much sums it up," Kev said.

"Who's Jahoel's replacement?"

"Adrigon has been promoted to first of the Metatron. A Principality named Margash has joined as fourth."

"Jahoel was the only one of the four who was sympathetic to the Fallen."

Kev nodded. "He was the only one as ancient as Zeke, the only one who was there from the beginning."

"What's Adrigon like?"

"He's young—in angelic terms—arrogant and, from what I can tell, unwilling even to acknowledge the existence of shades of gray. As far as he's concerned, Light is good, Dark is evil, and the Alliance is a huge waste of energy. If he had his way, there would be no Dark and no Fallen."

"And Margash?"

"He's something of an unknown quantity, but indications are he'll follow Adrigon's lead."

"So, where does that leave us?" Aidan was unaware of the pronoun he'd chosen until he caught Kev's raised eyebrow.

Kev uncharacteristically refrained from comment and just answered the question. "Lucifer has called for an investigation of Jahoel's murder, and despite their apparent willingness to accept the surface evidence, the Metatron has consented. A team is being assembled with members from both sides. In an effort to strengthen our position, I've agreed to serve as *Ha-Satan*."

"*What?*" cried Aidan, leaping to his feet. "Are you out of your mind?"

"Probably."

Aidan paced back and forth in front of his chair. "Gods, Kev. Caught between Lucifer and the Metatron, you won't stand a chance. You'll be dead before next Tuesday."

The corner of Kev's mouth lifted in a sardonic smile as he pushed a hand through his shoulder-length brown hair. "Believe me, I'm well aware that that's a distinct possibility. But it's the only way I can have access to both Lucifer and the Metatron, and I need to have some idea of what's going on in both domains. If we don't get a handle on this situation soon, we could all find ourselves caught in the middle of something much like Armageddon."

Zeke had entered the room while Kev was speaking. He carried a tray containing a Sèvres tea service, along with an assortment of breads, butter, hard-boiled eggs, and a plate mounded with bacon and sausage links. He placed the tray on the heavy oak table around which the leather chairs were clustered.

"I thought we could all use some sustenance," he said, as he poured strong, dark tea into the three cups. "Help yourselves to milk or sugar, if you like."

Aidan shook his head as he lifted one of the cups and studied its pattern. "Zeke, your civility never ceases to amaze."

"Nor does your enthusiasm for breakfast meat," said Kev, as Zeke lovingly placed several slices of bacon on a piece of buttered toast.

Zeke's light eyes sparkled with amusement as he lifted the open-faced sandwich toward his mouth. "Ah, Kevin, one should never underestimate the power of food. Even apocalypse looks less dire when viewed over a plate of bacon."

Chuckling, Aidan and Kev helped themselves to breakfast, and for a while, the three ate without speaking.

Aidan found his anger at being compelled to return to a world he had purposely left behind abating somewhat as he dropped back into the easy camaraderie he had once shared with his brother and Zeke. The angel could be a controlling bastard at times—Aidan knew that better than anyone—but even in the depths of his grief and anger, Aidan had never lost the respect and affection he felt for Zeke. A huge responsibility rested on the angel's broad shoulders—and had done so for millennia. Aidan guessed he could cut him some slack for assuming that gave him the right to put compulsive thoughts in other people's heads. Besides, he had to admit that he probably would not have agreed to see Kev otherwise. He just hadn't felt ready to face him yet. Now that he was here, though, he admitted to himself how much he had missed his half-brother.

His new fear for Kev reasserting itself, he broke the silence. "Are you sure you have to do this, Kev? Isn't there any other option?"

Kev placed his empty plate on the tray and settled back in his chair, his long legs stretched out in front of him. "I wish there were. Zeke, Malachi, and I have talked this over at length, and none of us could come up with a better solution. Really, I am the best candidate. It's a dangerous role for anyone, but as Lucifer's son and with my experience as Captain of the Forces, I'm in a better position than most. I'm good at protecting myself, and if it comes down to it, Lucifer will do what he can to protect me. While his familial feelings may be lacking in certain respects, he does have some sense of affection and obligation to us."

Aidan's mouth tightened. He questioned the use of the word "us." Lucifer might well have fatherly feelings for Kev, but any he had ever had for Aidan had been destroyed two years ago. Keeping those thoughts to himself, he asked, "Where do I come in?"

Zeke studied him for a moment before he spoke, and when he did, his voice rolled through the room like distant thunder. "Kevin becoming *Ha-Satan* leaves us with a void in the Forces of the Fallen. Malachi has taken Kevin's place as Captain, but he needs a second. Your Gift and your experience would be an asset to us, Aidan. We'd like you to step into that role."

"Zeke, I've been out of the ranks for two years. No one is going to accept me in a position of authority."

"Of course, they will," Zeke said. "Some few might be a little disgruntled at being overlooked themselves, but they all recognize and respect your power. They also understand why you did what you did. They may not have agreed with your decision at the time, but even then they understood your motivation. Just because you renounced this life and kept yourself apart from us for the past two years does not mean you have been forgotten. There was a reason we insisted the Renunciation be of limited duration. Not one of us thought permanent Renunciation was in anyone's best interest."

"Oh, one of us did," Aidan disagreed.

Zeke looked a question at him. "And do you still feel that way?"

Aidan sighed, "If you had asked me that yesterday morning, I'd have said yes, most definitely. Now, though,…." He paused, looking from his brother to Zeke and back to Kev. "If there's going to be a battle, then I need to be a part of it. If Kev can take on *Ha-Satan*, then this is the least I can do. I'm in."

"I was hoping you'd feel that way," Kev said. "Actually, I was pretty sure you would."

"Really? I thought you were one of those who viewed my decision to undertake Renunciation as nothing short of betrayal."

The corner of Kev's mouth lifted in a smile. "It pissed me off. I didn't want to see you throw it all away." His face sobering, he continued, "But I understood, Aidan. You'd lost too much. And I know I had a part in that." An unvoiced apology was in his eyes.

When he stood and held out his right hand, Aidan took it, closing his fingers firmly around his brother's.

"I'm glad you're back," Kev said.

Aidan nodded. "Me too."

"Well, now that that's out of the way," Zeke said, "we should get down to business. Would either of you like more tea?"

CHAPTER 6

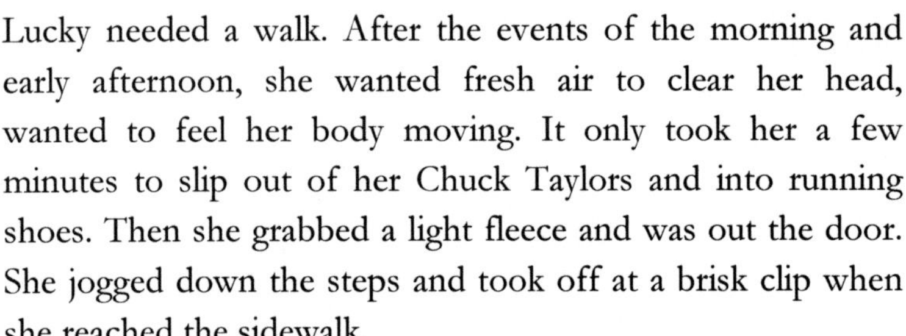

Lucky needed a walk. After the events of the morning and early afternoon, she wanted fresh air to clear her head, wanted to feel her body moving. It only took her a few minutes to slip out of her Chuck Taylors and into running shoes. Then she grabbed a light fleece and was out the door. She jogged down the steps and took off at a brisk clip when she reached the sidewalk.

Without a conscious decision, she found her steps taking her east, toward the lake. There was something about looking over the water, watching the movement of the waves and the changing reflections of light, that had always soothed her. Lake Michigan was a huge piece of nature on the edge of the city, and being in its presence helped her to think, to relax. And she did think of it as a presence. The lake was a kind of being, always there, always watchful, always changing, yet ever the same, a constant along the city's eastern boundary. Lucky had come to realize that the lakeshore provided not just a natural haven for her but a kind of spiritual solace as well. It reminded her that there was something larger than herself, larger than the city in which she lived, something that wasn't made by human hands. As she had walked beside it, swam in it, communed with it over the years, she had also come to realize that it weathered whatever came at it, greeting blue and gray skies, hot summer sun and icy winter winds, with the same acceptance. The lake simply *was*, and because it simply was, it gave her permission simply to be.

That was something she desperately needed right now. Someplace where she didn't have to worry about G-Ma's failing memory or her own crazy visions. Whatever was going on with her, being at the lakeshore would help her find a way to deal with it.

At 51st Street, Lucky walked up the ramp to the overpass bridge above Lake Shore Drive. Sometimes she went through the underpass at 55th Street, but today she wanted to be above ground, to have nothing over her but sky, and she wanted to be able to see the lake as soon as possible. She reached the top of the ramp and paused. There it was in all its liquid, blue beauty. Her shoulders instantly relaxed a bit. She stood there long enough for another couple of breaths.

Her steps a little slower now, she headed down the other side of the ramp and turned south toward Promontory Point. There were several other people on the path—walkers, joggers, bikers. Lucky navigated around them while keeping her gaze toward the lake as much as possible. When she reached the Point, a part of Burnham Park that jutted out from the rest of the shoreline, she took the track that looped south. A couple of people—college students, probably—were flying kites in the fall breeze. She watched the primary-colored shapes swirl and loop in the blue sky for a few moments, before her eyes moved on to the leaves that were beginning to show their own more muted yellows and reds. Then she turned back toward the walking path.

After rounding the edge of the Point, she stepped off the path and made her way over to the stone boundary at the edge of the shoreline. She climbed down a couple of levels, and locating a rock that offered the perfect combination of view, sunlight, and breeze, she sat down and wrapped her arms around her bent knees. She gazed out at the water and let her mind relax, drift with the lapping waves. No need to worry, to think, to plan. This was exactly what she had needed. Releasing her knees, she leaned back on her arms. The breeze tugged at the long curls she had pulled back into a braid, blowing a loose strand of hair against her cheek. She brushed it away and turned her face toward the sun.

She wasn't sure how long she sat there. After a while, the warmth of the sunlight and the lapping of the waves lulled her into a peaceful state somewhere between waking and sleeping. As she cast her sleepy gaze out over the water, her eyes caught and held on something her mind couldn't quite grasp.

There in the air, hovering a few hundred yards above the lake and at a distance of a mile or so, were two winged figures. Not birds or planes, but winged *human* figures: one with great white wings that glistened in the sunlight, the other with larger wings of deep velvet black. They appeared to be talking—or rather, arguing. They were too far away for her to hear what they were saying, but from the gestures she could make out she gathered their discussion was somewhat heated. She wondered what they were arguing about.

As the thought penetrated her consciousness, she came fully awake and shook her head, blinking to clear her vision. What an odd dream!

But as she looked back at the sky over the water, she saw that the two winged figures had not disappeared. She bit her lip and pinched her arm and then shifted her position on the rock to make sure she was awake. She glanced around her. A young woman was stretched out on a blanket reading a book. A group of teenagers laughed and joked as they climbed over the rocks. An older couple sat on a rock a few paces to her left holding hands and looking out over the water. A few other groups were scattered about, talking and laughing. No one else seemed to have noticed anything amiss in the sky above the lake.

Slowly, she turned back toward the spot where she had seen the winged beings, expecting—hoping for—an empty stretch of sky. No such luck. They were still there, wings and all, and the argument seemed to have escalated. They looked as if they were about to come to blows. Just as she thought the smaller one with white wings was going to throw a punch at the larger, black-winged figure, he drew back and, wings flexing, swooped upward and northward and then disappeared. The black-winged man hovered there for a moment more, and then he moved his wings in what looked like a shrug before winging upward and turning inland toward the city. He didn't disappear as quickly as his companion, but after a few beats of his powerful wings, he was no longer in sight.

Lucky sat looking after him with a pounding heart. So much for peaceful relaxation and escape from her worries. That was the most startling vision, illusion, mirage, or whatever it was, that she had had yet. She didn't think her imagination was good enough to have created those two out of thin air, and yet no one around her seemed to have seen anything out of the ordinary. Either she had some magical, mystical powers they didn't, or she was losing her freaking mind. While she wasn't exactly comfortable with the latter thought, it seemed more realistic than the former. Sure, she had always wanted to be special, but somehow she didn't think having angelic visions was the kind of special she might be in line for. Such an ability seemed far too important to be given to some random seventeen-year-old who wasn't ready to start college and hadn't yet managed to find a part-time job. Yeah, the happy alternative made much more sense—she was delusional, seeing things; her mind was starting to break apart at the seams.

Lucky felt her breathing accelerate as her heart kicked in her chest, and she forced her thoughts away from that path before she had a full-blown panic attack. She had only recently started seeing the visions, delusions, whatever. She'd just wait and see, give it some time. She'd been under a lot of stress lately. Maybe this was just her mind's temporary way of coping. If the visions didn't go away on their own, then she'd have to talk to a doctor, that was all. If the problem turned out to be chemical, then they could probably treat it with medication. There were all kinds of drugs for things like this, she was sure of it.

She rose to her feet, and with a last wistful look across the lake, she turned to climb up over the rocks. She might as well go back home; her peaceful state of mind had been completely disrupted, and there was no hope of corralling her circling thoughts enough to get it back.

Instead of walking back to the bridge over the Drive, this time she took the underpass at 55th Street. Exiting the tunnel, she wound her way north to Harold Washington Park, where she looked for the large nests that belonged to the green monk parakeets that, for some reason, had taken up residence there years ago. She wondered how it had felt for the birds, which were native to somewhere in South America, to settle in this Midwestern city with its long, cold winters. Hyde Park was the only home she had ever known; she had never had to experience being removed from her home and relocated. Instead, she had felt the disruption of losing the people closest to her—first G-Pa and then G-Ma. And now it looked like she might be losing herself as well. All in all, if faced with the choice, she'd much prefer the physical disruption.

Lost in thought, she wandered back toward home. A couple of blocks from her building, she started when she almost stumbled over a dead bird lying on the sidewalk. It was a robin, one wing twisted at an awkward angle and its red breast darkened with a spot of blood. She gently toed it to the edge of the sidewalk, where it would not be a target for careless pedestrians. The image of the bird lay heavy in her heart as she covered the remaining distance to her building door. Before going inside she took a last glance upward. The sun was beginning to go down, and a pale pink tinted the wispy cirrus clouds that feathered the sky.

After parking his motorcycle in the private garage of the Gold Coast high rise where he lived, Aidan made his way toward the elevator that would take him several stories up to his condo.

"Mr. Townsend," the guard nodded a greeting as Aidan passed.

Aidan nodded in return. Normally, he would have joked with the man, but right now he was not in the mood for humor. No, right now, he was worried—and somewhat pissed off. Even though he had accepted Kev's decision and had decided to rejoin the ranks himself, he was still a little angry at his brother—because he was terrified for him. What did Kev think he was doing anyway, becoming *Ha-Satan?* He'd heard Kev's arguments for taking on the position, but Aidan still wasn't sure if he should chalk his brother's choice up to bravery or insanity. And now he felt the same way about his own decision. He was just as crazy as Kev.

Stepping into the empty elevator, he pushed the button for his floor, grateful he didn't have to share the compartment with anyone with whom he would feel compelled to make small talk or whose eyes he would have to avoid. After the nearly silent ride upward, the doors swished open at the 12th floor, and Aidan walked down the elegantly appointed hallway to the door to his condominium. He kicked the door shut behind him and shrugged out of his jacket.

When he heard the chattering near his feet, his lips curved upward in a reluctant smile. He looked down at the ferret that was hopping sideways in a play-with-me war dance and chuckled. "Hey, little buddy. Yeah, I missed you, too."

The ferret skittered across the room to the toy box where he rummaged inside and dug out one of Aidan's socks. Carrying it back toward Aidan, he shook it as if to say, "Ha, look what I've got!" and danced a few hops to the right and then to the left. Aidan laughed. "Harley, you know those are my favorite socks. I don't know why I put up with you."

As the ferret danced backward away from him, Aidan followed him through the foyer and into the main room of the condo. Large glass windows overlooked Lake Michigan. The sun was lowering, and the sky was beginning to dim. Soon he would be able to see the lights of the cars far below on Lake Shore Drive, if he stood close enough to the windows. The sound of his booted footsteps echoed in the almost empty room as he walked across the polished marble floor to the liquor cabinet in the corner. After pouring himself a scotch, he moved to the black leather sofa, a small, dark island in a sea of marble tile. Besides the liquor cabinet, the sofa and the glass topped coffee table in front of it, the only furniture the large room boasted was a black baby grand piano that took up much of the opposite end of the room.

Aidan dropped onto the sofa and stared out the window at the lake as he sipped his scotch. "Damn it, Kev," he breathed.

It wasn't like his brother was going into this blindly; he knew what he was getting into. Still.... Working for their father was bad enough; having the sort of dual reporting that Kev was going to have made it all so much worse. Caught between Lucifer and the Metatron, there was no way he wasn't going to be royally screwed. And what about himself? He'd agreed to become second in command to the Forces of the Fallen. What did he know about being in command of anything?

Clenching his teeth, Aidan went to pour himself another drink. One wasn't going to cut it tonight. Calling on Zeke after all this time had been tough. It had been two years since he'd seen the angel, and that last conversation hadn't been pleasant for either of them. Aidan had been sure he had lowered himself in Zeke's estimation by renouncing his wings and leaving their world. But Aidan hadn't been able to stay. Not after what had happened to his mother, what he'd done to her. And it seemed that Zeke had understood all this time.

Then there was Kev. Encountering his older brother so unexpectedly had knocked Aidan for a bit of a loop. And finding out what Kev was taking on was almost more than he could bear. He didn't want to lose his brother too. Gods, now that he had been pulled back into that world, he was back in with a vengeance. He shook his head, his hand clenching around his glass, and bit out another curse.

Harley hopped up onto the sofa beside Aidan and climbed into his lap. Putting his front paws on Aidan's shoulder, he pushed his nose against his cheek before licking him and then settling down. He curled up in a semicircle with his belly and chin facing upward. Aidan sighed and rubbed his free hand against the ferret's belly. The warmth of the little creature and the softness of his fur helped to soothe some of his worries.

With a last pat, he moved the sleepy ferret off his lap and walked over to the liquor cabinet to pour himself a third. Then, remembering his new role, he thought better of it. He had to start serious training tonight; best not to drink himself into a stupor now. Instead, he carried the glass into the kitchen and placed it in the sink before making his way down the hall to his bedroom. Maybe he could manage to catch a little sleep before he had to get ready for tonight.

His footsteps echoed hollowly in the hall, a staccato accompaniment to the anxiety that was settling deep into his bones.

CHAPTER 7

When Lucky woke up the following morning, she felt amazingly rested, and she realized with surprise that she didn't remember having any dreams during the night. Given the events of the day before and the fact that her last two nights of sleep had been broken by odd dreams, she had gone to bed convinced she would get very little rest because her dreams would be filled with threatening dark clouds and menacing yellow eyes. Relieved that those fears had not been realized, she turned on her back, stretched, and relaxed. Shu and Tef had curled up on either side of her in the night, and she took both hands out from under the covers, so she could pet the two cats simultaneously. Her efforts were rewarded by a chorus of purrs: one quiet and somewhat motor like, the other a deep bass rumble that she felt in her chest as Shu pushed himself against her, turning to expose his belly. Lucky chuckled and rubbed his tummy, causing the cat to go boneless against her.

"You are spoiled rotten, aren't you?" she asked.

Tef, not to be ignored, butted her head against Lucky's other hand. "Sorry, sweetheart," Lucky apologized, scratching the tabby under her chin. "I didn't mean to neglect you."

For several more moments, Lucky luxuriated in the peacefulness of lying in a warm bed and doing nothing more strenuous than petting the cats. Then she glanced at the clock and decided she'd better get up and begin her day. She had a job to find. She couldn't work full-time until she turned eighteen, but since her birthday was so soon, there was no reason she shouldn't start a serious search as soon as possible.

Pulling a sweatshirt on over her pajamas, she wandered into the kitchen in search of something quick for breakfast. Shu and Tef followed meowing, hoping for some breakfast of their own. After popping a slice of bread into the toaster, she shook some kibble into their bowls, made sure they had fresh water, and then poured herself a glass of milk and got the jar of peanut butter out of the cupboard.

Carrying her peanut butter toast and milk, she padded back down the hall to her room. She stacked up pillows to lean against, powered up her laptop, and curled up against the pillows, her legs crossed under her, the computer on her lap, and peanut butter toast and milk within easy reach.

First, she had to work on her résumé. She hadn't had that many part-time jobs as a student, but she had had a few, and she'd made good grades and had been involved in several extra-curricular activities. She hoped that would count for something. She also knew she had to figure out what kind of job she hoped to find. She was unsure about waitressing; although, she'd heard from her friends who'd done it that they made decent money in tips. It was all dependent, of course, on the restaurant and the clientele. Maybe she could find a job at a library—she loved books. She checked through a few job ads online, but didn't see anything that interested her.

Flipping back to her skeletal résumé file, she filled in all the details she could think of. She left her objective statement pretty general for now, since she hadn't yet settled on a particular type of job. She saved the draft, then went into the computer room to turn on the printer. Her eyes caught and held for a moment on the boxes of papers and pictures they had moved from G-Ma's closet, but she looked away, focusing on the printer instead. She couldn't face those boxes just yet.

Back in her room, she thanked the powers that be for wireless networking as she hit "Print" and heard the soft clicks from down the hall as the printer began spitting out her file. She'd ask Josh to look it over and give her advice before she handed it to anyone.

While she had been working, she had heard Josh and Ben leaving his room and heading to the kitchen. From the slamming of drawers and the clanging of pots and pans, it sounded like they were making real food for brunch. She wondered if they would mind if she joined them. Not that she was all that hungry—it hadn't been that long since she had finished her peanut butter toast—she just hadn't had real breakfast food in a while, and the idea of sitting down at the table and sharing a meal like a family seemed suddenly appealing.

Retrieving her résumé from the printer, she tossed it on her bed and then followed the sounds of cooking to the kitchen, where she found Ben beating a bowl full of eggs and

Josh chopping vegetables. Lucky grabbed a mushroom from the stack next to the cutting board and popped it in her mouth. Speaking around the mushroom, she asked, "Are you making enough for me too?"

"We were planning on it, squirt, but we won't be able to if you keep eating the veggies." Josh added the last remark as a piece of red pepper followed the path of the mushroom. Lucky wrinkled her nose at him as she chewed the crunchy vegetable.

"Is there anything I can do to help?" she asked.

"Toast," Ben answered, gesturing toward the loaf of bread sitting on the breadboard. After pushing Josh out of the way so she could retrieve the bread knife from the drawer, Lucky began cutting the sourdough round into medium-thick slices for toast. She slid a couple slices into the toaster as Josh dumped the chopped vegetables in the skillet to sauté.

"Smells good," Ben said, adding some cream to the eggs before handing Josh the bowl.

"I'm a master at the art of scrambled eggs," Josh asserted.

"Master?" Ben remarked, giving Lucky a wink. "You probably shouldn't start that again. Last time, it didn't go so well for you."

"Very funny," Josh responded, but the smile he directed toward Ben was warm and affectionate.

Josh spooned the egg-vegetable scramble onto three plates to which Lucky added toast, while Ben rummaged through the refrigerator to find butter and some cherry preserves. With an extra trip for coffee, they carried the food into the dining room where someone had already placed napkins and silverware.

"What are you up to today, Lucky?" Ben asked as they sat down.

This really is like a family meal, Lucky thought. What she said aloud was something about getting a start on her job search. "I'd like you to take a look at my résumé, if you don't mind," she said, looking at her cousin.

"Sure, no problem," he replied. After taking a sip of coffee, he continued, "Have you thought about checking at that little gift shop in the Oriental Institute—what is it called? The Suq or something? I know you're into archeology and all. Maybe they would be willing to hire you, at least part-time."

Lucky's eyes lit up. "That's a great idea. I'll walk down there this afternoon. You can give me comments on my résumé before then, right?"

"Yeah, I can take a look at it as soon as we're finished with breakfast. School doesn't start for another couple weeks. Until then, I'm a free man, and my time is my own. After that, I'm a slave to the books." Despite the dire sound of his words, Lucky could sense his anticipation. She knew how excited he was about beginning his graduate studies.

"Just make sure you find time in your busy academic schedule for us," Ben teased. "You can't be taking your loved ones for granted."

"No worries there. If I don't take some time to play, I'll go nuts. Too much studying and no play make Josh a very cranky boy."

The light-hearted conversation continued while they finished breakfast, cleared the table, and cleaned up the dishes. Lucky found herself liking Ben even more the more time she spent with him. He and Josh were good together, and she was comfortable around him. She had known him for just over two days, and already he felt almost like family.

After the kitchen was all tidied, Lucky went to take a shower while Josh reviewed her résumé. When she was ready, he went over the marked-up copy with her, explaining what he meant by his comments. Lucky thanked him for his help, and after making the suggested changes to the electronic file, she printed a handful of copies and placed them in a manila folder which she tucked into her backpack.

"See you guys later," she called, heading out the door.

As she walked toward the university, Lucky noticed that she was casting furtive glances at almost everyone she passed, looking for anything out of the ordinary. She didn't know whether to be relieved or disappointed when she found nothing the least bit odd.

She was walking down Woodlawn toward 58th Street when it finally happened—in a way she hadn't been expecting. A trio of crows flew over, cawing loudly, and then fluttered down to the sidewalk about half a block in front of her. She was a little startled, but also pleased. They were attractive birds, their dark feathers shining in the sunlight. But when they all turned in her direction and, to a bird, began eyeing her up and down, she was more than a little spooked. And when they began marching toward her, their black eyes glittering with intelligence and a strange sense of purpose, she had an almost irresistible desire to turn and run in the opposite direction. Refusing to give in to what seemed a completely irrational fear, she continued her course, but she did slow her steps. With little more than a yard of distance between them, the birds suddenly took to the air, flying past her head and shoulders. They were so close she could feel the breeze generated by the beating of their wings against her cheeks and hair. They circled her once, twice, three times, and then, with a final chorus of caws, they flew up and away.

Lucky stared after them, stunned, her hand pressed to her rapidly beating heart. What in the world had that been about? She'd always had a fondness for crows: the lonesome sound of their rough calls heralded fall for her, and she had heard that they were extremely intelligent. Now she wondered if maybe she needed to rethink her attitude toward them. The birds hadn't exactly been threatening, but they hadn't been friendly either.

After her heartbeat had returned to normal, Lucky jaywalked and turned onto 58th Street. The entrance to the Oriental Institute was on the far end of the block, adjacent to the main quad of the University of Chicago. Climbing the stone steps, she walked through the open outer door and into the lobby of the museum.

The Suq gift shop was to her immediate left, and tables and shelves with books and items for purchase spilled out into much of the lobby. An information desk was on the opposite wall, the space between it and the Suq offering a direct path to the glass doors leading into the museum proper. Only a few people were looking at items in the shop, and the girl at the check-out desk was reading a book, glancing up periodically at the few shoppers.

Lucky walked up to the girl and asked if there was someone she could talk to about the possibility of working there. When the girl informed her that the manager was currently unavailable, but that she'd be happy to take her résumé and pass it on, Lucky handed her one of the printouts she had tucked into the folder in her backpack. She started to leave, then turning back to the girl, asked if she could have one of the manager's business cards, or at least a name and number. After looking through the desk drawer for a moment, the girl handed her a card. Lucky smiled and thanked her.

Stepping aside for a shopper who was waiting to pay for the articles she'd selected, Lucky glanced at the glass doors to the museum. While she was here, she decided, she might as well go visit the winged bull. After dropping a couple of bills into the slot of the clear plastic bin on the side of the information desk, she headed through the glass doors. Once inside the museum, she stood still for a moment, staring at the majestic sculpture at the far end of the room. Displays were set up to either side of an open corridor, giving an unobstructed view of the massive creature that was both the room's centerpiece and guardian spirit.

Walking slowly toward the statue, Lucky felt her lips curve into a smile. She'd loved coming here ever since the first time G-Ma had brought her when she was five or six. Her eyes had grown wide when she had first seen the huge, winged bull, then she had laughed with delight. She had felt much the same every time she'd come back to the museum. Sometimes, over the past eighteen months, she had popped in for a quick visit when she was having an especially rough day. Seeing the great bull with his wings arching over his back and his smiling human face had always lifted her spirits. Maybe it was because he was supposed to have been a protector.

"He's quite something, isn't he?"

Lucky turned toward the speaker in surprise. She had thought she was alone in the room. Giving him a brief glance before directing her gaze back to the object of their conversation, she smiled and nodded. "Yes, he is."

"He's a *lamassu*," the man continued, moving closer to her, "a protector deity or guardian spirit of ancient Assyria." His voice was oddly resonant, almost as if the sound had a kind of spatial dimensionality. "They used pairs of them, one on either side of the entryways into courtyards, to protect those who were inside and to keep a watchful eye on those who entered."

Lucky really looked at the man for the first time. He was tall, nearly a foot taller than her average five and half feet, and dressed like a clichéd academic in brown leather oxfords, khakis, a white shirt, and a tweed sports jacket with suede patches on the elbows. His hair did not match his attire. It was quite long, falling in wheat and honey streaked waves to the bottom of his shoulder blades. The locks at each temple had been pulled back and were secured with a tie at the back of his head. His eyes were a pale gray and seemed to hold a wisdom beyond his apparent forty-odd years.

"I know," Lucky said, looking from the man back to the huge stone sculpture. "I've been coming to see him for a long time."

"Ah, I should have sensed a devotee." Lucky could hear the smile in his rolling voice.

She shrugged. "I like him. He comforts me when I'm having a bad day. He somehow manages to be awe-inspiring and friendly all at the same time, you know?" Lucky looked at the man to try to gauge his response to her remark and found that he was studying the statue, a curious smile curving his lips.

"Oh, yes, I know very well," he said softly.

He gazed at the winged man-bull for a few moments in silence and then, somewhat abruptly, turned toward Lucky and held out his right hand. "I'm Zeke, by the way," he said. "Might I find out the name of my fellow admirer?"

"Lucky," she responded. "My name is Lucky." She took his proffered hand and was surprised when, instead of shaking it, he turned it in his palm and raised it to his lips to brush a chaste kiss across her knuckles.

"Are you interested in ancient religions, in general, Lucky, or just our large friend here?" he asked, releasing her hand. His pale eyes twinkled as he met her gaze.

"I'm interested in general," she said with a smile. "I just have a special fondness for this guy. When I go to college, I think I'd like to study archeology and ancient traditions."

Zeke raised an eyebrow. "Is that so? Well, then, you might be interested in a lecture I'm giving here on Friday afternoon. I know—terrible time. Why would anyone want to attend a lecture on a Friday afternoon? But so it goes. In any case, I'll be speaking about this big fellow and others of his ilk." Lowering his voice to a stage whisper, he added, "I may even provide some information that's new to you."

"What do you say?" he asked, his voice at normal volume.

Why not? Lucky thought. It wasn't as if she had any special plans for Friday anyway, and it sounded interesting. "What time? And you said it would be here?"

"It's at 2:00, in the small lecture hall upstairs," said Zeke, pulling a card out of his pocket and scribbling on the back. "I'll write the date, time, and room number on the back of my business card. There we go." This last was added as he pocketed the pen and offered Lucky the card.

She barely glanced at it before sliding it into her pocket. "Thanks. I'll be looking forward to it."

"Indeed," Zeke said, "I believe you will find it most enlightening."

Lucky gave a slight chuckle, wondering for a moment if he were joking, despite the seriousness of his tone. But when he just looked at her, she decided he definitely wasn't joking. Well, he was a professor, after all; he probably did have a vast store of interesting and esoteric information to impart. She supposed she could forgive him a little arrogance. "I'm sure I will," she said. "Thanks for telling me about it."

"See you Friday, then?"

Lucky opened her mouth to give a noncommittal reply, but at that very moment she was struck with a strange certainty that the lecture hall upstairs was exactly the place she should spend her Friday afternoon. With the first part of her intended answer already on its way from her brain to her tongue, the message short-circuited, and she found herself responding in the affirmative. "Yes, see you Friday."

As if her confirmation were a form of dismissal, Zeke nodded a farewell and, turning on his heel, walked back down the center of the room toward the double glass doors. As she looked after him, Lucky thought she glimpsed a much larger, shadowy form trying to take shape around his figure, but she blinked, and the illusion was gone. Then Zeke was gone too, as he passed through the doors, and they closed behind him. She stared after him for a moment, her forehead knotting in a frown.

Looking back at the *lamassu*, she said, "Bye, my friend. Since it seems I'm going to be here anyway, I'll stop by and see *you* Friday as well." Then she turned her back on him to walk toward the glass doors. Her frown settled into a smile as she did so, for she could feel his protective gaze following her all the way to the exit.

Standing in the cold, bright ante-room waiting for the angelic guard to return and grant him entry to the Metatron's council chamber, Kev wondered, not for the first time, if agreeing to become *Ha-Satan* was really such a good idea after all. He had known the Metatron would not exactly be rolling out the welcome mat like he was a long-lost family member finally coming home. But he hadn't fully grasped the reality of the suspicion under which he would be held until he had stepped through the Gates into the ante-chamber to find himself in the presence of two very large angels—either

Powers or Dominions, he wasn't sure which—who were armed with glowing swords and bedecked in the silvery white angelic armor that resembled nothing so much as chain mail but was more effective than Kevlar.

Since this was his introductory visit, Kev had deferred to ceremony and replaced his usual blue jeans, boots, buttoned shirt, and leather jacket with the traditional garb of *Ha-Satan*. The loose-fitting black silk trousers and the blood-red, knee-length, open-fronted robe offered next to no hiding places for weapons, but that hadn't kept one of the large angels—Dominions, he'd decided—from patting him down, while the other eyed him coldly, sword at the ready.

Satisfied that he was unarmed, the Dominion who had felt him up had indicated that his companion could announce Kev's presence to the Metatron. The second Dominion had left to do so, and Kev was currently awaiting his return, while the first stood guard over the door into the council chambers.

Kev suppressed a shiver. The room was as cold as his welcome, and he felt as if all his body heat was leaking out through his bare feet and chest. The medallion that indicated his station, a large obsidian pendant with the seal of *Ha-Satan* inlaid in jasper, lay heavy against his sternum. He waited in silence, eyes trained on the door, for what felt like an eternity before it finally opened and the guards gestured that he could enter. When his legs responded easily to his brain's command to walk, he guessed that his feet hadn't frozen to the floor after all.

After ushering him into the council chamber, the guards accompanied him every step of the way across the large room. Like that of the waiting room, the council chamber's floor was of white marble. The walls too were white, with narrow, window-like openings through which shone a bright, silver-white light. The ceiling, which arched high overhead, seemed to be made of some clear crystal, but instead of blue sky beyond, all Kev could see was more of that silver-white light. At the far end of the room was a large council table, also made of crystal, which looked to Kev like a massive, ornate ice sculpture. The legs of the table were carved in the form of angels, kneeling and bowed over; the angel's spread wings formed the table's surface.

Behind the table stood four figures, all tall, slender, and at first glance, as silvery white as the room. As he drew closer though, Kev saw that their skin was not quite as silvery as he'd thought. Its transparent paleness revealed the tracery of veins beneath, and the angelic ichor in those veins gave their skin the faintest golden glow.

Centered in front of the table and a few feet away from it was a single crystal chair of the same design as the large table. Evidently, that uncomfortable-looking piece of furniture was to be his seat for the meeting. Kev took his place in front of the chair, inclining his head to each of the members of the Metatron in turn in the formal gesture of respect. He was somewhat disappointed, but not at all surprised, when each accepted his gesture without offering one in return. As one, the four angels indicated that he should take his seat, and they seated themselves as he did so. The Dominion guards flanked him, one on either side of the crystal chair.

The chair was every bit as uncomfortable as it looked—and just as cold. Now, every part of his anatomy was freezing. No matter its actual duration, this was going to be a long meeting.

The tallest of the angels, who was seated almost directly in front of Kev, just slightly to his left, and whose long silver-white hair flowed over his shoulders, introduced himself as Adrigon. The angel to his left, who was just to Kev's right, was Tatriel. He was a little shorter than Adrigon and wore his long hair pulled back from his temples. The angel to Kev's far right was Galiel. Margash was to Kev's far left. Both had shorter hair, which just brushed the tops of their shoulders; Galiel's was straight and Margash's curly. Except for slight differences in height and the distinctions of hairstyle, the four angels were virtually identical. All had the same long, narrow features and the same pale eyes, an odd color, part blue, part green, and part gray, that somehow seemed to Kev to be the exact shade of ice.

Introductions over, Adrigon continued, "So, Kevin Drake, you are the latest to come to us as *Ha-Satan*. This time Lucifer has seen fit to send his own son."

The angel paused as if awaiting a response. Kev wasn't sure he'd heard a question in there anywhere, but he inclined his head in silent assent.

"Your mother, Katrin, was not fully human, but was herself Naphil, half-Seraph, the child of the Fallen, Semyaza."

Again, the pause. Again, Kev inclined his head.

"And what messages do Lucifer and the Fallen send through you, *Ha-Satan*?"

Kev felt a sense of relief when he heard the question. That one he recognized as the standard formal opening of the diplomatic meeting. Now, he was on more familiar discursive turf. He delivered the response he had been practicing in preparation for today's meeting. "Rumors have reached the ears of Lucifer and the Fallen. They have heard that some believe the time of Alliance between Light and Dark is at an end. They respectfully ask if the Metatron is of such an opinion. Does the Metatron seek an end to the Alliance?"

"And does not the act of war perpetrated on the Light by the Dark constitute a revocation of the Alliance? Has the Alliance not already been violated by the Dark?"

Kev had expected Adrigon to respond, but the questions came from Tatriel. His words were not angry or accusatory, but were calm and rational, as if affirmative answers to his questions were a given. Kev found the very reasonableness of the angel's voice chilling. Nevertheless, he forced his own words into the same coolly rational tones.

"Certainly, if the crime was indeed committed by the Dark, then the *terms* of the Alliance have been violated. It does not necessarily follow that the Alliance itself has been destroyed. We could work together, Light and Dark—and Fallen—to seek out the perpetrators and see that they are punished. That would be in keeping with the terms of the Alliance."

This time it was Galiel who responded. "And what would be the advantage to the Light in attempting to maintain this Alliance that has already been broken? Why should we not consider it ended?"

Kev answered with a question of his own. "Do you truly wish for war? If the Alliance is ended, such will be the outcome."

"Are we to consider that a threat?" asked Margash.

In the midst of castigating himself for not choosing his words more wisely, Kev paused a moment to wonder if the members of the Metatron always took turns responding in the formal meeting. Then, weighing his words with care, he responded, "My apologies, Most High. No threat was intended. Please allow me to rephrase. As you are no doubt aware, there are certain among the Dark who merely tolerate Lucifer's position among them. Their continued tolerance is, in large part, due to the Alliance. If the Alliance is ended, then their tolerance will decrease, putting Lucifer's leadership at risk."

"And why should we be concerned if Lucifer loses power?" Adrigon interrupted. "Lucifer is no longer a great favorite of ours."

Once again, Kev inclined his head in assent. "We do not, of course, expect the Metatron to be concerned with the leadership struggles of the Dark or the Fallen in general. But, in this instance, the Light could be affected by these struggles. If Lucifer loses his power over this—recalcitrant—element among the Dark, then they will see no need to even attempt to maintain peace with the Light. You have stated that the violation of the Alliance is a declaration of war, but I would respectfully disagree. I humbly submit that it is a mere salvo, a calculated attempt to get the Most High to call for an end to the Alliance. It is the end of the Alliance itself that would be the declaration of war."

"But if the Dark has fired this first salvo, as you call it," said Tatriel, "then has not war already been declared?"

Kev considered his response, taking a grim satisfaction—albeit minuscule—in the apparent accuracy of his guess about the Metatron's speaking patterns. "While we would agree that whoever committed this act intended it to start a war, we neither consider it, in and of itself, a declaration, nor do we believe war is inevitable. First, we would respectfully submit that we do not know for certain that this act was committed by a member or members of the Dark. Second, even if it were, that act was in no way condoned by the Dark at large, nor was it in any way sanctioned by the Dark's leadership. I speak the truth when I say that Lucifer does not desire warfare with the Light, nor do the Fallen."

When Kev finished speaking, the members of the Metatron silently rose to their feet. He followed suit, uncomfortably aware of his Dominion guards stepping nearer to him, their swords at the ready.

"We will take your words under advisement," said Galiel coolly.

Margash then closed the meeting. "We thank you for your visit, *Ha-Satan*. You are dismissed."

Kev directed the small ceremonial bow to each of them in turn and then, flanked by the Dominions, made his way back to the ante-chamber. Before he was allowed to leave, he had to submit to the indignity of another pat-down. He wondered where or when the guards thought he could possibly have acquired any weapons—at least one of them had kept an eye on him the entire time. When he was given permission to step back through the Gates, he breathed a silent sigh of relief. As far as he was concerned, he couldn't get out of there soon enough.

CHAPTER 8

For her first foray into the world of job hunting, Lucky decided it only made sense to target places where she thought it might be fun to work, like the Suq—or one of the neighborhood book stores. After leaving the OI, she walked across the street to the closest book store on her list, the Seminary Co-op. She knew that one was a long shot, since most of the employees were university students, but she thought it was worth a try. Besides, she liked wandering around in the cramped little store with its narrow aisles and shelves and tables full of books. It didn't take her long to find out that her assumption had been correct, but the manager gave her the bad news kindly. Lucky thanked him for his time and readied herself for her next attempt.

Back on the sidewalk, she headed north on University toward 57th Street—and 57th Street Books. Filled with *New York Times* best sellers, shelves of classic and contemporary fiction, poetry, cookbooks, art books, and children's books, the store was one of Lucky's favorite places. She had been known to spend an entire afternoon there, browsing the shelves and collecting volumes, before curling up in a chair with a stack of books to peruse more closely in order to decide which one or two she would purchase. A couple of blocks beyond 57th Street Books was Powell's, a used book store with a huge stock of popular fiction and non-fiction as well as scholarly volumes in various disciplines. Lucky nearly salivated at the possibility of being able to spend several hours each week working in either of the stores. She hoped that one or both of them would be hiring and would be willing to take her on.

She was pleased to find that the managers at both stores were, in fact, looking for help and were happy to take a copy of her résumé and consider her as a possibility. She filled out applications at both places. She couldn't resist a brief stroll through the fiction, poetry, and history sections of both stores, but she resisted the urge to buy anything. She decided she should be judicious about the money she spent before she found a job.

As she turned her steps toward home, she felt positive enough about her afternoon's adventure to want to celebrate in some small way. She wondered if Mo was around and would be interested in getting a coffee or something. She was disappointed when, after several rings, she was dumped into voicemail, and her friend's recorded voice spoke into her ear, "Unfortunately for you, this is not Mo. It's just her voicemail. Leave a message though and she might call you back."

"Hey, Mo, it's Lucky. I've been passing out one-page summaries of my education and brief work life in the sunny hopes that maybe someone will offer a poor girl just out of high school a job. I was hoping maybe you were available and could meet me somewhere for a little while."

She flipped her phone closed with a sigh. Apparently, home was in her immediate future after all.

She hadn't even made it to the end of the block, when her phone rang. It was Mo, her voice slightly desperate. "Lucky! I'm so glad you called. I've been dying for an excuse to get out of the house. Where do you want to go? Wherever it is, I'll be there in five minutes."

Lucky laughed. "What about the Med?" The restaurant was back in the direction from which she had come, but it was one of her and Mo's favorite meeting places.

"Okay, maybe ten minutes, but no longer than that. See you in a few." Mo hung up without waiting for Lucky's response.

Smiling, Lucky shook her head, as she pocketed her phone and turned back toward 57th Street. She had no doubt Mo would make it to the Medici in ten minutes. She would have made it in five if will alone could overcome the laws of physics. Mo was one of the most strong-willed people Lucky had ever met. Whatever obstacles stood between Mo and something she wanted had better watch out, because Mo wasn't going around—she was coming through. Sometimes, Lucky wished she had half Mo's drive and confidence.

She strolled to the Med, since she was so close, knowing she'd arrive before her friend. She had just gotten seated in one of the carved and graffitied booths, when Mo rushed in and propelled herself onto the opposite bench.

"Good timing." Lucky grinned at her friend as the blonde girl caught her breath.

"Thanks. I strive to ever exceed the expectations of myself and others. You said something like that on your résumé, right? Or wait, I guess that's better suited to a cover letter. Whatever." She waved her hand in the air. "I'm sure you put it wherever it's supposed to go."

She paused and looked up at the waiter, who put glasses of water in front of them and asked if they were ready to order. "I need coffee and chocolate, and lots of both."

"Are you sure you need any more energy?" he asked with a grin.

At her nod, he responded, "I think we need a second opinion on that." Looking at Lucky with one eyebrow raised, he added. "What do you think? Is it safe to give her coffee and chocolate?"

"Only if the coffee is decaf," Lucky laughed. "But don't skimp on the chocolate. Hell hath no fury like Mo when she's cocoa-deprived."

"Got it," the waiter turned back to Mo. "So, is that a decaf coffee and a Vaguely Reminiscent or a mocha?"

Mo pursed her lips and considered for a moment. "Let's make it a mocha *and* a Vaguely Reminiscent."

"Excellent choice. And for you?"

Lucky barely heard the waiter's question. All her attention had been irresistibly drawn to a man who had just entered the small room and was now taking a seat at a table for two just across from their booth. Nothing about his appearance seemed at all out of the ordinary. Well, perhaps the long, black trench coat he wore was a bit of overkill, given that it was a reasonably warm September afternoon; otherwise, he looked completely normal. He was middle-aged, had short dark hair shot with gray, and he sported a small, tasteful moustache. Wire-rimmed glasses perched low on his nose as he tried to find the right focal point to read the menu through his bifocals. Yes, he seemed quite ordinary. But something about him was wrong. Every internal alarm bell Lucky possessed was ringing at full volume. She had no idea why. The man hadn't even looked their way. Although he was going to soon if she didn't stop staring.

"Lucky?"

Mo's voice finally penetrated her preoccupied thoughts, and she turned to look at her friend, feeling slightly dazed. "Hmmm?"

"Uh," Mo jerked her head toward the young man who was taking their order, "he's waiting for you to tell him what you want."

"Oh, um, sorry. A mocha for me too. And could you bring two forks for the Vague Rem?"

The waiter looked at her a little oddly, but said only, "Sure, no problem."

Before heading toward the front of the restaurant to place their order, he stopped to take that of the man in the long black coat. Lucky again found her gaze drawn to him. This time as her warning bells clanged, her head started to throb. She turned quickly back toward Mo as pain lanced behind her right eye.

Mo leaned across the table toward her and looked into her eyes. Tilting her head ever so slightly to the left toward the man in the coat, she asked, "What gives? Do you know him?"

Lucky gave a tiny shake of her head, which caused a series of pains to spiral out from the invisible knife sticking into her skull. "I've never seen him before," she said weakly.

Mo frowned, and her face took on a look of concern. "Are you alright?"

"I have a headache," Lucky responded, lifting her glass to take a long drink of water. "It'll probably go away soon."

"Do you want to go? We can cancel our order."

"No, we can't. He's bringing our stuff out right now." Lucky paused until the waiter had placed their drinks and the mocha mousse pie on the table. "I'll be fine. The caffeine and sugar should help."

Mo grimaced. "Yeah, since you didn't specify decaf for yourself."

Lucky chuckled. And it didn't cause the right side of her head to feel like it was going to explode. Good, she was feeling better. Unable to help herself, she looked out of the corner of her eye toward the man at the small table, who was now drinking a cup of coffee and scribbling on a notepad. As her gaze passed over him, another pain shot through her skull. Okay, so that was completely weird. Not only did this guy totally freak her out, but just glancing at him hurt. Well, the solution to the latter was not to look at him anymore. She wasn't sure what to do about the former. He obviously posed no threat, yet every fiber of her being screamed out that he was beyond dangerous. It made no sense whatsoever. Lucky fought down the panic that threatened to well up inside her.

Maybe she really was losing her mind. Was this how paranoid schizophrenia started?

Pushing that thought aside, she took another sip of her mocha followed by a bite of the pie. She savored the chocolate dessert, concentrating on its flavor and texture in her mouth. By the time she had swallowed that bite and another, she was much calmer.

"Are you sure you're okay?" Mo asked.

Lucky thought a moment before she replied. She wanted to confide in her best friend, but she wasn't sure how to begin. Too many weird things had been happening to her lately, and she didn't want Mo to start having doubts about her sanity. She had plenty of her own, thank you very much.

She had just opened her mouth to speak when the man in the black coat rose to his feet. Taking a few bills from his wallet, he tossed them on the table, before turning to leave. On his way toward the door, he stepped around a waitress who was carrying coffee and dessert to another table, and as he did so, he glanced toward Lucky. Their eyes met only momentarily, but it was long enough for her to see that his were a sulfurous yellow that glowed with an eerie light. Lucky was blinded by the pain that exploded behind her eyes. She cried out and pressed both palms to her head.

"Okay, that's it," Mo said, standing up and coming over to kneel beside Lucky. "As soon as you can move, we're out of here. We've got to get you home."

"No, really, it's alright," Lucky breathed, lowering her hands. "I'll be just fine in a minute. He's gone now."

"Who's gone?" Mo asked in surprise. Then, "Oh, you mean the man in black that you've never seen before? What is going on, Lucky? Talk to me. I'm your best friend, and I'm worried about you."

"Okay, I'll tell you," Lucky sighed. Then, with a grin, she added, "But I want to finish my mocha first."

"I guess you are feeling better." Shaking her head in mock disgust, Mo abandoned her kneeling position and resumed her seat across the table from Lucky.

After several moments, she broke the silence with a frustrated sigh. "Well, since you're apparently refusing to tell me anything while we're here, I guess I'll fill you in on the latest about the country club dance." She paused, then continued with a pointed look, "Mom said that in addition to a date, I can bring a friend."

Lucky started to protest, but she was silenced by the sincerity in Mo's voice when she added, "And I really want you to come. Please. I need you there, for moral support."

"What about Eric?" Lucky asked. "Won't he provide moral support?"

Mo shrugged. "Sure, some maybe. But he's not you. You've been there for me through every really difficult thing I've had to survive since first grade. And I want you there for this one."

Lucky laughed. "A country club dance is a 'really difficult thing'? Oh, come on, Mo, it can't be that bad."

Mo looked down at the table in silence for a minute or two. When she looked back up, her face was serious. "Lucky, please? This is really hard for me. I feel like I'm going to be walking out in front of a firing squad. Please say you'll come."

Seeing the nervousness in her friend's hazel eyes, Lucky couldn't refuse. "Okay," she sighed. "When is it anyway?"

Mo's expression lightened immediately. "Oh, thank you, thank you, thank you!" she gushed. "It's Friday night. I think the dance starts at 7:00."

"Friday!" Lucky exclaimed. "Mo! How am I supposed to find a suitable dress by Friday?"

"What? It's not like you have a job yet. You have four days to shop."

"Yeah, but since I don't have a job, I also don't have a lot of spare money to be spending on fancy dresses I'll never wear again."

"We can go vintaging." Mo's eyes sparkled with excitement. "It'll be so much fun! We'll find you something really cool and retro chic."

"And cheap," Lucky added.

"You mean 'inexpensive,' dear," Mo said in a snooty drawl. "A girl never wants to look cheap."

"Whatever," Lucky laughed. "As long as it's cool, retro, and affordable."

Mo reached across the table to squeeze her friend's hand. "I'm so glad you said yes. You can bring someone too if you want." Her eyes took on a speculative gleam. "Maybe Aidan would be willing to go with you? Wouldn't that be a coup? The lead singer and the drummer from Icarus at my mother's country club dance."

Lucky was horrified. "Oh, Mo, please don't start plotting anything that involves Aidan."

The other girl continued as if Lucky hadn't spoken. "You wouldn't even have to ask him yourself. I could ask Eric to ask him, as a favor to me."

"Mo," Lucky said loudly, making sure she had her friend's attention. "No. I mean it. I won't go."

"Alright, alright," Mo said, with a frown. "I won't say anything. I just thought it might be fun."

"Mo." Lucky's tone brooked no opposition.

With her thumb and index finger, Mo mimed a zipping motion across her lips.

"Okay, then." Seeing that the waiter had left their bill without their even noticing, the girls dropped their payment on the table and rose to go. Feeling somewhat embarrassed by her odd behavior, Lucky left a generous tip.

"Okay, spill," Mo ordered, after they had walked about half a block in silence.

"I don't know where to start," Lucky muttered.

"How about with the black-coated man whose very presence made you scream in agony?" Mo asked, as if she were stating the obvious.

Lucky shrugged. That was probably as good a place as any. "I don't know what it was about him. He just gave me the creeps. I felt like every nerve was on alert, like I was waiting for him to leap to his feet and try to kill us all or something. And when I looked at him, my head started to hurt."

"And when he left? What happened then?"

"I don't know. He looked at me for a second or two, and I saw his eyes. They were this weird, creepy yellow, and they kind of glowed. And then my head hurt so much I couldn't see anything."

Mo frowned. "His eyes weren't yellow and glowing. I mean, I didn't get a good enough look to see exactly what color they were, but I'd say brown or gray or something. They were just ordinary eyes."

"Oh," Lucky said in a small voice.

"Not that I don't believe you," her friend reassured her. "I just think you were in so much pain you didn't know what you saw."

"You mean, I imagined it or hallucinated or something."

When Mo didn't respond, Lucky continued with a sigh, "It wouldn't be the first time."

She told Mo about the strange experiences she had had over the last few days, leaving out only the ones that involved Aidan. She loved Mo dearly, but she didn't want to risk the possibility of her sharing it with Eric. It wasn't like it really mattered if he passed it on to Aidan—Aidan was already well aware that something out of the ordinary had happened between them. It was just that the experience felt too intimate, too raw, to share with anyone. It had been both terrifying and exhilaratingly freeing.

By the time Lucky finished recounting her tale, the girls had reached Mo's building. They paused outside, leaning against the brick half-walls on either side of the steps. Mo didn't say anything for a while. Lucky had rarely seen her friend speechless, but she supposed if anything merited such a reaction, this did.

"Well," Mo finally said, "I can understand why you didn't want to talk about it. It's all really freaky."

"I'm afraid of losing my mind, Mo," Lucky said. "There's G-Ma and.... I know I'm not old enough to get dementia or Alzheimer's, but she wasn't old enough either. What if 'crazy' just runs in the family?"

Mo stepped close to Lucky. "You are not crazy," she said. "I don't know what's going on, but I do know you, and you are one of the sanest people I know. And 'crazy' doesn't run in your family. Look at Josh and his parents. They're all, like, supernaturally normal."

"Good point." Lucky's smile was half-hearted.

"Besides," Mo continued, "do you really feel crazy?"

Lucky looked at her friend as if she had suddenly sprouted a second head, which she supposed, given the things she had been seeing lately, wasn't outside the realm of possibility. "What kind of question is that? How many crazy people actually feel like they're crazy? If you're crazy, doesn't crazy seem normal to you? And, come to that, how many normal people are really normal? I mean, none of us can really know how anybody else perceives the world, can we? What I experience as the color blue, you might experience as what I think of as green or purple, right? No, I don't feel crazy, but that doesn't mean that I'm not, does it?"

Mo started laughing before Lucky finished speaking. After she caught her breath, she responded, "I don't know whether to tell you you're talking like a crazy person or to reassure you that no one who's really crazy would ever use such a philosophical argument."

Then, sobering, she repeated, "You are not crazy. You're just stressed. You've had a lot of major things happen to you lately, and they're bound to take a toll. You just need to get some sleep." She grinned as she continued, "And spend more time playing with me. Let's take the next few days to hang out and shop for your dress. I know you have to find a job, but no one's going to hire you before your birthday anyway. Come on, what do you say?"

"Alright," Lucky agreed with a smile. "Why not?"

What could it hurt to take a few days and just be a girl with no worries?

"Excellent." Mo gave her a hug and started up the stairs. "I'll call you tomorrow, and we can decide on a game plan."

"Sounds good." Lucky called over her shoulder as she started down the block. She had to admit she was looking forward to a few days of playing. She steadfastly refused to listen to the little voice that kept insisting that her carefree days were numbered.

CHAPTER 9

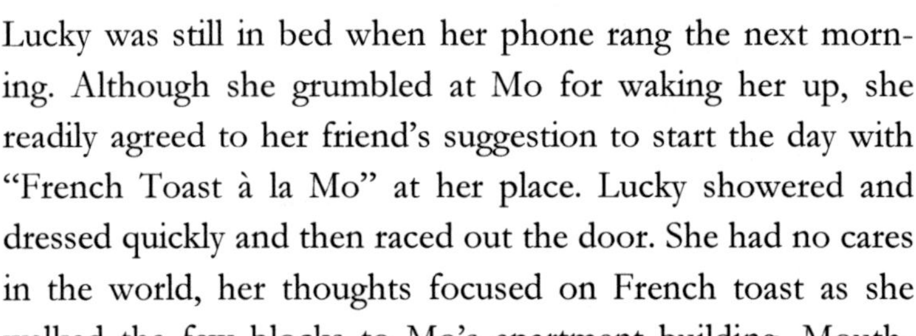

Lucky was still in bed when her phone rang the next morning. Although she grumbled at Mo for waking her up, she readily agreed to her friend's suggestion to start the day with "French Toast à la Mo" at her place. Lucky showered and dressed quickly and then raced out the door. She had no cares in the world, her thoughts focused on French toast as she walked the few blocks to Mo's apartment building. Mouth-watering smells were already wafting from the kitchen when Mo let her into the apartment.

Tossing her jacket on the arm of the sofa, Lucky made herself at home in the kitchen, helping Mo put the finishing touches on breakfast. She was almost as comfortable at Mo's place as she was at her own. The two girls had been best friends since first grade and had been in and out of each other's homes ever since.

The French Toast à la Mo was as good as Lucky remembered. Made of thick slices of ciabatta bread dipped in egg batter, fried in ghee, and finished with a liberal sprinkling of powdered sugar and generous drizzles of maple syrup, it was delectable, and she never refused it when it was offered. Mo's repertoire of recipes was not extensive, but the few dishes it included were delicious.

While they ate breakfast, the girls sketched out their plan for the day, deciding to hit the vintage and resale shops along North Halsted in Boys Town, where they had both previously had good luck finding things. Meal over, cleanup was a matter of minutes. Then they were out the door and headed to the bus stop. A short ride on the #6, and they were downtown, where they transferred to the red line which would take them north to Belmont, shopping, and—Lucky hoped—the perfect dress.

The trip was largely uneventful. Lucky was disconcerted to find that she did catch occasional glimpses of wings where they didn't belong—like growing out of people's backs—but she was relieved that there were no more encounters like yesterday's. No one she saw gave her the heebie-jeebies or caused her skull to feel like it was going to implode. She didn't mention the wings to Mo. She didn't want to freak her out any further. Besides, today was about fun. If she caught the occasional glimpse of a pair of wings, well, it was starting to feel almost like a normal part of the way she saw the world. She wasn't going to let it bother her. Not today.

They spent the remainder of the morning and early afternoon drifting through resale and vintage shops. They were unsuccessful in their attempt to find a dress for Lucky, but they did find lots of other things to try on. Mo ended up buying a man's tuxedo jacket, which must have been made for a fairly small man, since it was just fashionably baggy on her, and a dark gray felt fedora.

"I've always wanted one of these," she said, popping the hat on her head at a rakish angle.

Lucky didn't find anything she needed to own; she was saving her money for the as-yet-undiscovered dress. She didn't know exactly what she was looking for, but she would recognize it when she found it.

Around mid-afternoon, they took a break to grab a sandwich and soda at a neighborhood deli. As they made their way from the deli toward the next shop on their list, they passed a small antique store, its windows crowded with an odd assortment of expensive-looking antiques and kitschy novelty items. After casting a disinterested glance at the windows, Mo started to pass the store by, but Lucky caught her arm.

"This place looks fun," she said. "Let's go in."

Although Mo protested that they would find no dresses in the dusty little shop, Lucky insisted on going inside. Something about the window displays whetted her curiosity. Inside, the shop was stuffed with shelves and tables. Items seemed to be arranged at random. A set of leather-bound volumes was neatly stacked next to a somewhat haphazard display of Pez dispensers, and a lovely Tiffany lamp shared a small table top with a garishly painted bust of Elvis. For some reason, Lucky found the crowdedness and lack of order enchanting. She felt as if she could happily spend the rest of the day exploring the little store's contents.

She had made it about a quarter of the way through the shop, when she saw the sculpture. As soon as she laid eyes on it, she knew it was why she had been drawn to the shop. After carefully winding between the tables and shelves that stood between her and the item that drew her like a beacon,

Lucky reached out her hand to pick up the statuette. Roughly a foot in height, it depicted a beautiful warrior angel in gilded armor, his sword raised in triumph and one foot planted on the body of the dragon he had defeated. The piece had been lovingly crafted: each feather on the conquering angel's great wings and each scale on the conquered dragon's hide had been painstakingly carved and then painted. Some of the paint had worn away over the years, but the touch of wear only increased the statue's appeal.

"That's a very lovely piece, isn't it?" said a scratchy voice to Lucky's right.

She turned toward the sound in surprise. She hadn't heard anyone approaching.

The speaker was a small, elderly woman, with masses of white hair pinned up on her head. She was wearing a vintage black dress, and a large jeweled spider was pinned to one shoulder. Seeing Lucky's startled glance at the brooch, she chuckled hoarsely. "She may look alarming, my dear, but I assure you she's completely harmless."

She lifted the black cane in her right hand and pointed toward the statue Lucky was holding. "He has a beautiful face, doesn't he?"

When Lucky nodded, she added, "That's the Archangel Michael, the Dragonslayer, the Prince of Light. Do you need a protector, dear?"

Lucky still didn't say anything, but she looked a question at the old woman, to which she responded in a voice like the scratching of a fountain pen on paper. "I've been watching you since you came in. As soon as you saw him, you were drawn like a moth to candlelight."

Lucky replaced the statue back on the shelf where it had been, her fingers lingering a moment before she drew back her hand. The little woman made Lucky uncomfortable, and she didn't want her thinking she was going to buy the piece. She hadn't seen a price on it, but she was sure it was beyond her means.

As if guessing her thoughts, the old woman said, "It's not as expensive as it might appear—at least not to the right buyer."

She tilted her head and studied Lucky with piercing eyes that were as pale as moonlight. After several moments, she nodded as if satisfied. She moved nearer to Lucky, leaning heavily on the cane with each step, and then reached up and lifted the angel statue off its shelf with her free hand. She gazed at it fondly for a moment and then held it out to Lucky.

"Take him, dear," she said. "He is meant to be yours."

Lucky took the object from the old woman's hand, her fingers closing around it with a sense of inevitability. As she clasped the statuette close to her, she felt something settle into place inside her. Yes, it was right that she have this, no matter what the cost.

"What do I owe you?" she asked.

The old woman patted her arm. "Don't you worry about that." She turned toward the back of the store and gestured for Lucky to follow her. "Let's wrap him up well, so you can get him safely home."

Lucky followed her into a little office as cluttered as the rest of the store. Somewhere amid all the items that seemed to fill every available inch of space, the woman located some thick paper and twine, which she used to wrap the statue, her fingers moving more nimbly than Lucky would have thought possible. After she cut the loose ends off the twine, she handed the wrapped statue to Lucky as if presenting her with a gift. Instead of taking the package, Lucky reached into her backpack for her wallet.

"How much does it cost? I don't have much cash, but I do have a credit card."

The woman shook her head as she pressed the parcel into Lucky's hands. "There is no charge. He is yours."

"Are you sure?" Lucky asked, slipping her wallet back into her backpack and closing her hands around the package.

The old woman nodded as she covered Lucky's hands with her own. "I am sure. He has not spoken in such a way to anyone else. No one else has the same need of him." Her hands tightening for a moment, she added, "He is the leader of the Forces of Light. He will protect you from the Dark that is coming."

"Lucky, there you are," Mo said, sounding relieved, as she appeared in the door of the crowded office. "I thought I'd lost you. This place is a maze." Seeing the package in Lucky's hands, she raised her eyebrows in surprise. "You bought something?"

"Well, not exactly," Lucky said.

Turning to the old woman, who had moved away from her to sit down in the single chair beside the cluttered desk, she offered a thank you that she couldn't help feeling was inadequate, no matter how heartfelt. "Thank you for this. I'll take good care of him."

The woman nodded. "As he will of you," she said, as softly as her scratchy voice would allow.

Then she waved her hand at them, dismissing them from her little room and her store.

"What was all that about?" Mo asked, when they had closed the door of the little shop behind them.

Lucky motioned to the parcel. "She gave this to me. She saw that I wanted it, and she wouldn't let me pay for it. She said it was meant for me."

She paused to shrug her backpack from her shoulder so she could tuck the package inside it.

"What is it, anyway?"

"A statue, a carving, of an angel." Lucky answered. "She said he's the Archangel Michael, and that he'll protect me from the Dark."

"Okay, so that's a little strange. But given what's been going on with you, maybe you need him, right?"

Lucky nodded as she repositioned her backpack on her shoulders. "Maybe so."

It was late afternoon, and the girls were about to give up any hope of success in finding Lucky a dress for the dance. With only fifteen minutes before closing time, they stopped in one last shop, not really expecting to find anything, but feeling they should make one final attempt before calling it a day. They split up so they could scan the merchandise more quickly. Lucky was half-heartedly flipping through a rack of prom dresses when she felt a tap on her shoulder. She turned around to find Mo holding something behind her back and looking very excited.

"What did you find?" she asked.

Mo kept uncharacteristically silent, but her expression became smug as well as excited as she showed Lucky the dress she had found. Lucky's eyes grew wide. It was beautiful. "So, do you want to try it on?" Mo asked.

"You know I do," Lucky answered, taking the dress and hurrying toward the small dressing room in the back of the store, with Mo following behind.

Lucky pulled the curtain to the dressing room and slipped out of her sneakers, jeans, and t-shirt. She dropped the dress over her head, pulled up the side zip, and was stunned by the reflection she saw in the mirror. The dress was sleeveless with a scoop neck and made of satin with an overlay of filmy lace shot through with a scattering of small, glistening beads. The variegated color darkened from a pale jade at the bodice to a deep sea green at the base of the skirt. The lines of the dress clung close to Lucky's body, the skirt flaring slightly at the hips and falling to just above her ankles.

"Oh, Mo, it's perfect," she breathed.

As soon as the words left her mouth, her friend had pulled back the dressing room curtain. "You look amazing in that," she agreed, her smile widening as she gazed over Lucky's shoulder at her reflection in the mirror. "I know just what we should do with your hair, and you can borrow my strappy silver sandals. They'll be perfect with that dress."

"Thanks," Lucky said. "That would be great. Now, get out. I have to get changed—the store is going to be closing any second now—and there's not enough room to move with both of us in here."

Mo ducked through the door and pulled the curtain as Lucky shimmied out of the dress. After she put it back on the hanger, she peeked at the price tag, which she hadn't even thought about looking at before. The cost was a little more than she had planned on spending, but she loved the dress. She knew she'd regret it if she didn't buy it, and she rationalized the expense by telling herself she'd never find anything else that looked as good on her for less. She yanked on her jeans and t-shirt, shoved her feet into her sneakers, and before she could have second thoughts, hurried to the cashier at the front of the store to make her purchase.

Carrying their shopping bags, the girls made their way to the closest 'L' stop. While they were standing on the platform waiting for their train, Lucky scanned the other travelers, looking for anything strange. On the opposite platform, she noticed a woman with a girl who looked to be her daughter, both of whom seemed to have shadowy, transparent wings if she gazed at them at just the right angle. Her eyes lingered on a group of four young people about her own age, two boys and two girls, who were standing only a few yards away from her and Mo. Something about them seemed different, but she wasn't sure what it was. As she stared at them, one of the boys looked up and smiled at her. His gleaming, white teeth were all unnaturally long and pointy. Lucky looked away. She waited a few moments, and making sure none of them seemed aware of her attention, she studied his companions. One of the girls appeared to have the same predatory teeth as the first boy. The other boy and girl did not, but if she allowed her eyes to lose focus, she found that they looked to be much larger than they at first appeared, and their skin no longer looked smooth and tanned but gray and rough.

Lucky was surprised at the clinical nature of her observations as she studied the crowd. She found that she wasn't in the least shocked upon catching glimpses of wings or pointy teeth or rough, gray skin. She also discovered that, for the first time since she had begun seeing such things, she wasn't questioning her own sanity or doubting the truth of what she was seeing. She stopped her little experiment when the train arrived, and she and Mo hurried aboard, finding places to stand amid the crowd as the doors closed behind them. But as she and Mo chatted about the events of the day, their purchases and the upcoming dance, in the back of her mind, she was wondering what had changed to make her suddenly accept her strange, new way of seeing the world as somehow real?

Aidan was exhausted. No, exhausted didn't even begin to describe the depth of tiredness he felt or the pain he experienced every time he moved. He was tired and achy all the way down to the bone. He was aware of every single muscle and sinew in his body, and they all groaned in agony. Even his hair hurt. He was undergoing serious training alright, and it felt like a serious butt-kicking. He had known that after two years off the field he wasn't going to be at the top of his game, but this was ridiculous. The muscles in his right hand trembled as he held his heavy sword at shoulder height, the point just touching Kev's throat.

"Good," his half-brother said, lifting his hand to press down on the flat side of the sword, indicating to Aidan that he could drop his arm. "You're getting better. A few more days of this and you'll be almost as good as you were."

"A few more days of this," Aidan groaned, "and I'll be dead."

Kev chuckled. "Being the lead singer of a popular band made you soft?"

Aidan lifted his middle finger, and the muscles of his hand protested at the gesture. He sighed. "Being human has made me soft," he conceded.

Backing up a few feet so he could lean against the wall behind him, he slid to the floor, placing the sword beside him, point angled away so he wouldn't do himself any damage if he suddenly toppled over onto it in exhaustion.

"What's it like?" Kev asked, lowering himself to a seated position a few feet away.

Aidan's eyes had drifted closed, and he opened them to look a question at his brother. "What's what like?"

"Being human. Living a normal, human life."

Aidan blew a small breath out in a "hmmph," closing his eyes again as he considered the question. It wasn't like his life had been exactly normal—or even completely human—for the last two years. But it had been a lot more humanly normal than it had been before or, it seemed, than it was going to be, at least in the foreseeable future.

"It's peaceful," he finally answered, his eyes still closed. "In comparison. Don't get me wrong—everyone has their worries and fears, their losses and sorrows. But they aren't cosmic. You aren't carrying the weight of the world on your shoulders every second of every day."

"I doubt that it's the same for them," Kev commented.

Aidan opened an eye in inquiry.

Kev shrugged his shoulders. "Well, they aren't used to, as you put it, 'carrying the weight of the world.' So, their worries and fears and losses probably feel pretty cosmic to them."

"Yeah, I guess so," Aidan agreed, closing his eye again.

After a few minutes, he opened both eyes and looked at his brother with a serious expression. "I think I always knew it was just a kind of vacation for me. Even though I swore I'd never come back, that as soon as my wings were returned, I'd undertake permanent Renunciation, some part of me always knew this was where I'd end up."

"You mean, on the floor, after getting your butt kicked by your big brother?" Kev asked with a grin.

Aidan lifted his middle finger again. It hurt a little less this time; his body was already starting to recover. Being half Seraph had its advantages.

Chuckling, Kev rose to his feet. He stepped over to Aidan and held out his hand. Aidan took it, allowing Kev to help pull him up to standing. Aidan groaned as all the aches and pains reasserted themselves. They were less intense than they had been before his rest, but he still felt like hell. He winced as Kev clapped an arm around his shoulders, his hand closing in a squeeze on Aidan's bicep.

"Let's call it a day," Kev said. "You get some sleep. I'll see you back here tomorrow, bright and early."

Aidan slid out from under his brother's arm, and turning, reached out a hand to clasp Kev's. "Bright and early. I'll be here."

Kev's eyes glinted. "Be prepared for company."

Aidan groaned. That couldn't bode well.

Lifting his hand in a half-hearted farewell, he walked across the training room floor to the outside exit.

Once outside, he took a deep breath, mentally preparing for the pains that would assault his body when he summoned his wings. He felt the heavy weight of them as they took shape on his back. He paused a moment, allowing himself to readjust to the feel of them, his muscles tightening and recalibrating their effort as his center of gravity shifted. Flexing the extra muscles in his shoulders and back, he spread his wings and launched himself into the sky. He stifled the groan that threatened to escape his lips as he executed a couple of practice loops above the training center. This was his first flight since he had renounced his wings two years ago. He probably needed flight training too, and despite his aching body, he might as well get that started.

He flew a few more loops, practicing climbs and dives, sudden stops and hovers, before he felt prepared to activate his secret weapon. He finished a multi-level figure eight, with a few full body rolls thrown in just for giggles, and then came to a hover. Closing his eyes, he drew on the depth of energy within and around him, and then he opened the door behind which he hadn't even looked since the day he'd kissed his feathered appendages good-bye. As soon as the door cracked open, he felt the force throughout his whole body, a kind of electricity humming through his veins. With a sort of mental muscle flex, he flipped the switch, and those heavy wings of his burst into flame.

He shot upward into the fastest climb he had executed this evening, feeling a surge of exhilaration inside him. Gods, this felt good. Sure, he was still aching all over, and every flame-feather twitch sent a twinge through some muscle or other, but he was flying again, shooting through the sky on wings of flame that carried him faster and farther than mere feathers ever could.

He went through the same series of exercises that he had executed before, with greater speed and increased agility, as his abused body recalled from the depths of muscle memory the precise and sometimes minute shifts and movements necessary to maneuver through the twists and rolls. When he finally brought himself to a horizontal dead-stop from a high-speed dive that ended barely a foot above the top of the training center, he was breathing hard and had added several new muscle aches to his already considerable quota, but he was grinning from ear to ear and filled with a greater sense of accomplishment than he had felt in a long time.

With a single beat of his wings, he swooped upward and then lowered himself to the sidewalk in front of the building. He flipped the mental flame switch to the off position and retracted his wings, pleased to find that he was able to perform both actions smoothly and without hesitation.

"It's nice to see that you are in such good form so soon," Zeke said, taking shape beside him. "You fly almost as if you've never been without your wings."

"Thanks," Aidan said, the self-satisfied grin still on his face.

Zeke smiled back at him. "And it's more than nice to see you looking pleased with yourself. That I haven't seen in a long time."

Aidan lost the grin and eyed Zeke with suspicion. "You haven't seen *me* in a long time. Have you?"

"The fact that you renounced our world didn't mean we renounced you. I've been keeping an eye on you in my own way. I have resources of my own, you know."

"Oh, trust me, I know," the young man said, adding after a slight pause, "which means I should have realized that you would be aware of my every move over the past two years. Once you're on Zeke's radar, you're never off, are you?"

For a moment Aidan thought he caught a glimpse of something resembling hurt in the ancient angel's eyes, but if he did, it was gone in an instant. "Not your *every* move, Aidan. I wasn't spying on you—well, technically, I suppose I was—but it was not my intention to violate your privacy." He captured Aidan's gaze with his own and held it as he continued, "I just wanted to be sure you were safe. There are some over whom I will always keep a watchful eye—as long as it's in my power to do so."

"Sorry," Aidan muttered, looking down and away from Zeke's penetrating gaze.

Aidan didn't really believe Zeke had spied on him for any nefarious purpose, but he was finding it difficult to let go of the bitterness and sense of betrayal that had led to his perhaps precipitous action two years ago, and which had been his ever-present companion since. Now, though, he was beginning to realize that he needed to put it all behind him if he wanted to get on with his life. And that entailed not only forgiving Zeke and Kev, but forgiving himself. He was getting closer to coming to grips with the former, but the latter was going to be a lot more difficult.

"I am available to talk," Zeke said, as if reading his thoughts, "whenever you are ready."

In his current mood, the angel's tone set Aidan's teeth on edge. "Patronizing much?" he asked, all attitude again.

Zeke sighed. "Go home, Aidan. Get some rest. I'll see you tomorrow." Zeke inclined his head in a slight bow and then dematerialized.

Aidan cursed under his breath before focusing his own energy so he could disappear himself. He rematerialized high above Lake Michigan a few miles out from the city, wings extended but not in flames, and glamoured so that humans couldn't see him. He executed a few easy loops, trying to reclaim the sense of satisfaction he had felt earlier, but it seemed to have abandoned him. Feeling his fatigue reassert itself, he abandoned the effort and pointed his wings toward home.

He dropped to the ground in an empty alleyway about a block from his building and, after dismissing his wings, released the glamour that kept him hidden from human eyes.

Emerging from the alley, he made his way to his building on foot, as if he were the ordinary human being he had pretended to be for the past two years. When the doorman greeted him, observing, "You look like you've had a hard day," he felt the corners of his mouth lift in exhausted amusement.

"Yeah, you could say that," he responded.

CHAPTER 10

When his alarm buzzed the next morning, Aidan hit snooze and turned over, hoping to catch a few more minutes of shut-eye. His hopes were short-circuited by the wide-awake Harley, who pushed his nose into Aidan's face before catching the blankets between his teeth and pulling them down. As the cool air hit his bare skin, Aidan sighed, "Seriously, ferret, there are days when I wonder what I was thinking when I took you in."

He'd really had little choice in the matter; Kev had presented him with the ferret after his mother's death, hoping the little animal would help coax Aidan back to life. And Aidan had to admit that, as annoying as the little guy could be, the gift had been a pretty good call.

Sitting up, he switched off the alarm, raked his hands through his hair, and then rose and padded into the adjoining bathroom. In the shower, he turned the cold on full blast, hoping the shock would not only wake him up but help prepare him for the many physical discomforts he would undoubtedly face before the day was over.

Showered, dressed, and breakfasted, he pulled on his leather jacket and started to hit the door. Then he stopped in a moment of stunned surprise as he realized he didn't have to use the door. He could dematerialize from anywhere; he didn't have to be outside to do it. He shook his head at himself, thinking about how very human he had become in the past couple of years. It hadn't even occurred to him the day before to dematerialize from the apartment. And, once he had left the building by the door, he needed to return the same way. He didn't want the security cameras to record him exiting the building but not record him returning. Not that anyone would probably ever notice, but you never knew. He didn't want to raise any questions.

But today he would neither exit nor enter the building. As far as anyone knew, he would have stayed inside all day. Still shaking his head in wry amusement, he dematerialized and reformed in front of the training center. Here, he had no choice but to materialize outside. The building was protected by wards that made it impossible to dematerialize or materialize inside it. Since it was where the members of the Forces underwent numerous kinds of training, it had a security system of cosmic proportions.

The training center existed at a dimensional remove from earth, the Heavens, and the Dark Realms, and its location was known to and accessible by only those in the Forces. Still, since it was always possible that their enemies could learn of its existence, it was equipped with an elaborate physical and magical security system. In addition to the building security, the area for several miles around in all directions was warded to prevent anyone unknown or unauthorized from crossing the boundary line. The troops underwent extensive training outdoors as well as in, and Zeke and the others in charge made sure they were as protected as angelically possible.

Stepping up to the door, Aidan pressed his right hand against the security panel and braced for the surge of heat and pain as the sigil on his palm flared to life. Recognizing his sigil, the door slid open, allowing him entry. The room in which he had trained with Kev the day before was empty, but he heard voices coming through the open door on the far side. Heading toward the voices, he crossed the expanse of floor, his footsteps loud and echoing in the near empty room.

As he entered the smaller room, he was greeted by three pairs of eyes that turned in his direction. Zeke and Kev were seated at one end of a large conference table. The room's other occupant leaned against the window sill a few feet away, his legs crossed at the ankle and his arms crossed over his chest. Looking into the familiar amber eyes that stared back at him, unsmiling, from the man's dark face, Aidan inclined his head in greeting.

"Malachi," he said, stepping up to the man and extending his hand.

"Aidan. I understand that you have not only returned to us, but have also agreed to command our Forces," Malachi responded, his deep voice cold. "I must say, I am somewhat surprised."

"And what is it that surprises you, Malachi, my return or my agreeing to serve as your second?" Aidan asked, allowing his hand to drop to his side, since the other man had made no move to uncross his arms.

"Both."

"Aidan, have a seat," Zeke's resonating voice interrupted the frosty exchange.

Aidan dropped into the chair closest to him, which happened to be next to Zeke, and leaning back, crossed his own arms over his chest. He was beginning to realize just what a hard road lay ahead of him, winning back the favor of those he had abandoned. For so long, he had felt as if they had all abandoned him. Now, he understood that they were going to see the situation in just the opposite light. He had been the golden boy, the Gifted one, the one they had all viewed with such promise—and he had walked away from it all, walked away from *them*, with no intention of ever returning. Malachi's attitude would be shared by many. They would be surprised by his return, and they wouldn't readily trust him as second. Zeke and Kev had put him in a difficult and awkward position. No, he admitted grudgingly, in this case he had no one to blame but himself. He was the one who had walked away, and he was the one who would have to re-earn their trust.

"Zeke tells me you were practicing flying exercises after we parted yesterday," Kev said, giving Aidan an evil grin. "Good. Today, we fight in the air. And today, you have two opponents."

At those words, Malachi stepped up beside Kev's chair, arms still crossed, teeth bared in a predatory smile. "My battle skills have improved in the time that you have been gone," he said.

Improved? Aidan thought. Hard road didn't even begin to describe the day ahead of him then. Malachi had always been one of the best fighters in the Forces. Two years ago, Aidan had been better, but just barely. Now, he probably didn't have a prayer against the other man, let alone against both him and Kev, who was equally as good.

He rose to his feet, determined to face the music with good grace. He inclined his head toward Malachi. "Then I will have my work cut out for me indeed. I couldn't ask for a better opponent."

He was gratified by the gleam of respect that lightened the man's amber eyes as Malachi inclined his head toward Aidan in turn, a few of his long braids sliding forward over his shoulder as he did so.

"Okay, fellas," Kev said, rising to his feet and clapping his palms together, "let's get geared up. We've got training to do."

Zeke's satisfied chuckle followed them as they headed for the weapons room.

Two hours later, Aidan felt as battered as he had by day's end the day before. *Double the pleasure, double the fun,* he thought, as he parried a thrust from Kev's sword while simultaneously dodging a well-aimed arrow shot from Malachi's bow. All three men had multiple weapons strapped to their chests, backs, waists, and thighs, and the demands of the battle were as much mental—keeping focused and in the moment, so he could anticipate which weapon was going to be used against him and which to use in return—as they were physical. As he had anticipated, Malachi was a formidable opponent, as was Kev. So far, he had been pretty much holding his own, but it was early in the day, and his own was beginning to take a down turn.

Giving a strong beat of his wings, he shot straight upward out of range of both swords as each of his opponents came at him from opposite directions. Seeing Malachi abandon the sword to notch another arrow into his bow, Aidan changed course—and barreled straight into Kev, who wrapped him in a wrestler's hold, pinning one wing against his back, and dived toward the ground. Aidan thrust upward with the other wing with all his might, but it had little effect against both his and Kev's weight combined with the strength of Kev's dive. As it occurred to him that he could pull a "flame on," Kev brought them to a sudden stop, and he felt the point of Malachi's sword at the back of his neck.

A well-executed move, he thought. Another few millimeters and he'd have been facing paralysis—at least until his half-angelic body managed to heal itself.

"Uncle," he groaned.

The other two men chuckled in satisfaction as they released him, and all three of them dropped to the ground, disappearing their wings as they landed.

"Break time," Kev called.

He jogged over to the cooler they'd left at the edge of the practice field, where he grabbed three bottles of Gatorade before jogging back to join Aidan and Malachi.

From his half-reclined position, legs stretched out in front of him, upper body supported on his elbows, Aidan regarded his new opponent for the day. Malachi was seated in a cross-legged pose and taking slow, deep breaths as if he were meditating.

"By all that's holy and unholy, Malachi," he groaned, "did the last two hours have any effect on you?"

Malachi looked at his left hand and slowly rotated his wrist. "I think I might have strained my left wrist a little," he answered, a smug smile in his voice.

Aidan resisted the urge to flip him the bird and took a long swallow from the bottle Kev had handed him.

When Aidan made no response to his comment, Malachi lifted his gaze to Aidan's. "You did well in that last exercise. Extremely well, considering that you have been out of practice for so long. Do not worry. You will be back in form before you know it."

"What exactly do you think we are up against?" Aidan asked after a moment. "I know I have a lot of training to do just to get into good enough shape to be a fit second. But I don't know what kind of battle—or war—I need to be prepared to lead the Forces into. Are we talking Dark Forces, Angelic Powers, what?"

"Yes," both men responded.

Kev continued, "We're caught in the middle on this one, bro. We have enemies on both sides, and it's difficult to know if, when, or from where the threat might come."

"Fortunately, we have allies on both sides, too," Malachi added. "Not all of the beings of influence in the Heavens support the new Metratron. And many of the Dark Ones continue to recognize the need for alliance. Those on either side who support the Alliance will fight with us should the extremists on either side precipitate a war. Of course, the problem is, if that should happen, we're also caught in the crossfire between the two."

"How's that for a morale booster?" Aidan quipped. "Welcome to the Forces of the Fallen, friend to none and enemy to all."

Kev's voice was dead serious as he shot back a brief "Welcome to my world."

Aidan showed steady improvement as they moved through the day's remaining drills and battle exercises. He could feel his senses sharpening and his instincts refining to the point where he felt as if every cell in his body was capable of experiencing all five bodily senses and a few extras. As his senses and skills improved, he was amazed to find that his powers were stronger than they were two years ago. He had expected them to grow weak from lack of use. Sure, he was out of practice—a fact to which his tired, aching body could attest—but he was remembering old moves and techniques with ease and learning new ones more rapidly than he could have imagined. As the day wore on, the mock battles stretched longer as it became increasingly difficult for the combined forces of Kev and Malachi to defeat him, and he even brought the final exercise to an end by besting both his opponents with an economical series of elegantly lethal maneuvers.

Aidan left the training facility battle-scarred and weary, but filled with a growing sense of certainty that his life was back on track. That certainty was stronger than any resistance he had had to returning. He now realized that the very strength of his resistance had sprung from his innate knowledge that the outcome was inevitable. He had been fighting against the life he had been born to live. Now that he had accepted that, well, it didn't mean that the path would be filled with roses, but it did mean that he no longer felt as if his day-to-day existence was ripping him apart from the inside out. That had to count for something.

Lucky left her apartment for the Oriental Institute about 1:30 on Friday afternoon. Mo had tried to convince her to skip the lecture and hang out with her until it was time for them to get ready for the dance, but Lucky had adamantly refused. She didn't know why she felt so compelled to go to Zeke's lecture. She had liked Zeke, and she was interested in finding out more about her friend the *lamassu*, but her desire to attend the lecture went way beyond that. Almost more than a need to go, it was an utter inability *not* to go. For some reason she didn't understand, she felt with great urgency that she had to be at that lecture.

As she walked the mile or so from her apartment to the OI, she had the sense that she was being followed. She zigzagged through a few of the blocks to see if she could shake the feeling, but to no avail. A couple of times, the sensation that some unknown someone right behind her was reaching for her was so strong that she swung around to confront whoever it was. No one was there. By the time she reached the OI, her pulse was racing.

After a quick stop in the museum to say hi to the *lamassu*, she hurried up the stairs to the lecture hall and made her way to a seat that was roughly in the middle of the room. The crawling sensation on the back of her neck during the walk there had made her paranoid, and she wanted to be sure she was in a very visible position.

"Mind if I sit here?"

She jumped at the question, pulling hard enough on the locket she had been holding like a talisman, to cause the weakened chain to give way. Now a little annoyed as well as anxious, she enclosed the broken necklace in her hand and looked up at the speaker who had startled her, realizing she recognized the voice at the same moment as her eyes fastened on Aidan's familiar features. A blush stained her cheeks as she met his intense blue gaze, and she pressed her empty hand against her thigh to hide the fact that it was trembling.

"No, please do," she answered, giving a small shake of her head.

As Aidan seated himself next to her, Lucky was struck by his size. His jean-clad legs were so long that his knees knocked into the seat in front of him, so he parted them, placing one to either side of the seat's curved back. When he was settled, his right thigh was brushing Lucky's left knee, and his right arm was resting on her side of the armrest. She bumped against him as she retrieved her backpack from under her seat and tucked the locket with its broken chain into the inner zippered pocket. His nearness did nothing to alleviate her racing pulse.

As the silence between them lengthened, it occurred to her to wonder what he was doing there. Why would he even have known about the lecture, let alone cared to come to it?

She turned toward him to ask the question at the same time as he turned toward her.

"What are you—"

"So, what brings—"

When their words collided, they both stopped speaking. At Lucky's small, self-conscious laugh, Aidan smiled, the corners of his eyes crinkling. Gazing into those warm blue eyes through the fringe of his lashes, Lucky was struck dumb for a moment. Then taking a deep breath, she began again, "I was just going to ask how you came to be here."

"Yeah, me too." Aidan's smile widened. "Zeke is… an old friend of mine. I heard he was giving a talk and thought I'd see what he has to say. What about you?"

"I ran into him in the museum downstairs on Monday, and he asked me to come. It seemed important to him. And then, for some reason, it became important to me too. It was like I couldn't *not* come, if that makes any sense."

Aidan responded with a humorless chuckle. "Yeah, Zeke sometimes has that effect on people." He didn't look at her as he spoke, his face turned toward the stage at the front of the room. As if just becoming aware of the first part of her comment, he turned to her with a question, "What were you doing here on Monday?"

"I was hoping maybe I could get a job at the Suq—the gift shop downstairs. The girl took my résumé, but I think the chances are pretty slim. Anyway, while I was here I stopped in to see the *lamassu.* Zeke came in while I was visiting him."

"*Visiting* him?" Aidan's lips quirked in amusement. "You visit the huge, winged man-bull on a regular basis?"

Lucky frowned at him, her nervous awareness of him dissipating somewhat in a brief surge of annoyance. "Yes, I *visit* him on a somewhat regular basis. What's so funny about that?"

Aidan shook his head, making not even the slightest effort to wipe the amused smirk off his face. "It's just that when you say it like that, it sounds like you're just stopping by to see a friend, like he's—what's her name? your buddy? Mo, isn't it?—like he's her or something."

Lucky shrugged. "I do sort of feel like he's my friend. I mean, it's not like we have long, heartfelt conversations or anything—I am aware that he's a statue. I've just always liked him." Blushing a little, she admitted, "I went in to say 'hi' to him before I came up here."

At her words, Aidan laughed out loud. The sound was soft and warm and rich, wrapping around Lucky like a blanket and banishing her annoyance in another crashing wave of awareness. Couldn't Zeke just start, already? What was he waiting for anyway?

Scanning the room, she saw that the lecture hall was about half-filled. Her senses still largely occupied by the young man sitting next to her, she didn't pay much attention to the other attendees, but she had the impression that there was no one else there that she recognized, besides the long-haired man who, she saw with relief, was just stepping up to the podium. Zeke looked much as he had when she'd met him, only this time his shirt was a pale olive green, and his sports jacket was a deep chocolate brown.

She had forgotten how substantial his voice seemed until he spoke, and the sound flowed into the room like the waves of the ocean, rolling and resonant and ancient. After thanking his audience for generously choosing to spend part of their Friday afternoon listening to him, he began the lecture. Dimming the lights, he switched on a slide presentation, flashing a picture of Lucky's large, winged friend on the screen behind him.

"You are all no doubt familiar with this fellow," he began, and Lucky was distracted by the elbow Aidan poked into her side as he chuckled in response. She pushed him away, casting a glare at him that he, unfortunately, probably couldn't see since the lights were down. Zeke was mid-sentence when she tuned back in.

"...*lamassu* or *aladlammu*, a guardian or protector figure from ancient Assyria, also referred to by the Babylonian term *karabu.* Statues of these winged bulls or lions with human heads were placed at the entrances to gateways and palaces. The Babylonian *karabu* is linguistically related to the Hebrew *cherubim.*" He pronounced the Hebrew term with a hard "ch" so that it sounded like a "k". "And it is thought that the descriptions of the *cherubim* may derive from these hybrid figures. See how the prophet Ezekiel describes the *cherubim*, in one of the few biblical passages in which angels appear—I read from the New Revised Standard Version:

"This was their appearance: they were of human form. Each had four faces, and each of them had four wings. Their legs were straight, and the soles of their feet were like the sole of a calf's foot; and they sparkled like burnished bronze. Under their wings on their four sides they had human hands.... As for the appearance of their faces: the four had the face of a human being, the face of a lion on the right side, the face of an ox on the left side, and the face of an eagle; such were their faces. Their wings were spread out above; each creature had two wings, each of which touched the wing of another, while two covered their bodies."

As Zeke continued speaking, Lucky's head began to feel strange, as if it were expanding. It didn't exactly hurt; it just felt sort of detached from her body, floaty, like a balloon. Looking around her, she saw flashes of vari-colored light around the other people in the audience, and she wasn't all that surprised when, as she watched, some of the flashes resolved themselves into transparent, flickering light-shadows of wings that stretched up and out from the shoulders of their owners.

But she was shocked when she turned her attention back to Zeke. In the dim light, it appeared as if his form were shifting. Right in front of her eyes, he changed in an instant from a man to an eagle, to a lion, to a bull, and then, once again, his form was that of the man she knew. Before she could even try to rationalize what she had seen, he was shifting again, growing larger. His face was somehow simultaneously those of man, eagle, lion, and bull, and his form, while still that of a man, was also encompassed by that of a bull with huge wings arching up and away from his back. As she stared, he grew larger and larger until his presence, like his voice, filled the room, and it hurt to look at him, but she couldn't look away, and she couldn't comprehend, and she couldn't breathe. She was awed and terrified. Something was wrong, so terribly wrong with her. Gasping for breath, she lurched to her feet. She had to get out of this room.

Turning toward Aidan, to ask him to move his long legs so she could get by, she was surprised to find him already standing. Looking up toward his face, she clapped a shaking hand over her mouth to stifle the cry that struggled to escape. Extending upward and outward from his shoulders and back were the great flaming wings she had seen at the Icarus show. Drawing deep gasping breaths, she looked from Aidan's wings to Zeke's incomprehensibly morphing form. Back to Aidan, back to Zeke, back to Aidan. It was too much, and none of it could be real. Her heart was beating so hard she could feel it pounding against her chest, and her pulse was drumming in her ears, drowning out Zeke's rolling voice as he continued to speak. If she could just get to the exit. With a choking cry, she tried to push past Aidan, then she felt herself stumbling and falling as everything went black.

Aidan caught the girl as she fell, scooping her up in his arms and heading toward the doorway with long strides. He hadn't expected her to lose it so soon; then again, considering the terrified expression on her face, he was surprised she'd lasted that long. He wondered what she'd seen. Given her own developing powers plus the twist he was sure Zeke had provided, it was hard to say. He figured he'd find out soon enough.

Pushing the door open with his hip, he slipped through, careful of the girl in his arms, and strode down the hallway to the room that served as Zeke's office when he was acting in his semi-regular capacity of visiting professor at the OI. Clutching Lucky to him with one arm, he turned the knob with his free hand, pleased to find the door unlocked. Not that a lock would have stopped him at this point, but things were easier this way. Once inside the office, he located the familiar, battered leather sofa against one wall. Taking two steps forward, he kicked aside a stack of papers that covered one end and lay Lucky gently on the sofa. When his scanning glance revealed nothing that would serve as a blanket, he stripped off his jacket and tucked it around her shoulders. Then he pulled Zeke's office chair over to the sofa and sat down to wait. Once the lecture was over, Zeke and the others would be coming in this direction.

The girl made a noise as she shifted positions, but she didn't open her eyes. He wondered if it was safe to leave her alone long enough to find her some water. He guessed she might need some—or something stronger—when she came to, but he didn't want her to wake up alone. At least she seemed to be breathing just fine, and she wasn't shaking as if she were going into shock or anything. As he studied her unconscious form, he noted the darkness of her hair and lashes against her pale skin, the soft curve of her lips. In the silence of the room, he could hear the soft inhalations and exhalations of her breath. He felt strangely protective of her, and he had an urge to reach out his hand and stroke her cheek, to soothe her if he could. Just as he gave in to the desire and was at the point of brushing her cheek with his thumb, her eyelids fluttered open. He quickly pulled his hand away so as not to startle her.

Lucky came awake as if she were swimming upward into consciousness. The first thing she saw when she opened her eyes was Aidan bending over her, a concerned expression on his handsome face. At the sight of him, the memory of what had happened before she had blacked out came rushing back to her, and she gasped in alarm and tried to push herself up to sitting.

He put out an arm to restrain her. "Don't try to get up just yet," he said. "Rest for a little while longer."

Lucky complied, relaxing back against the cushions of the sofa on which she lay and pulling the covering that was draped over her shoulders closer around her. She heard Aidan asking her if she was cold at the same moment that she realized that her blanket was his leather jacket. She shook her head.

Glancing around the room, she discovered that she was in what appeared to be an office. The light in the room was switched off, but the door was open, letting enough light spill in from the hallway that she could get a general idea of the room's contents. Bookshelves and filing cabinets stood against the walls, and a desk sat perpendicular to the far end of the sofa, its surface cluttered with books and papers.

Papers littered the floor near the sofa as well. Aidan was sitting in the desk chair, which he had drawn up to her side.

"Is this—is this Zeke's office?" she managed to ask. The words almost stuck in her throat, her mouth was so dry.

Aidan nodded. Leaning toward her, he stared into her eyes. "I'm going to go find you some water. Promise me you won't try to leave while I'm gone."

When she shook her head, he asked, "Does that mean you won't leave, or you won't promise not to?"

"I won't leave," Lucky whispered.

"Good girl," he said, squeezing her shoulder through his jacket. "I'll be right back."

Lucky watched him go in silence and then closed her eyes and relaxed into the sofa cushions. She was so tired and thirsty, not to mention confused and scared. What was happening to her? Too tired to do more than ask herself the question, she lay there letting her thoughts drift as she waited for Aidan to return. He had been afraid she would leave, but right now she didn't have the energy to go anywhere. She lifted her heavy eyelids when she heard him step into the room from the hallway.

As soon as her eyes fell on the figure in the doorway, pain sliced through her head. Along with the pain came fear, as she realized not only that the person who had entered the room was not Aidan but that she had a pretty good idea who he was. Blinded by her pain and terrified of what the man in the door might do to her, Lucky screamed as loudly as she could.

CHAPTER 11

Almost as soon as the sound of her scream had faded, Lucky heard pounding footsteps, and then the pain in her head faded as Aidan ran into the office, calling her name.

Crouching down beside her, he grasped her shoulders. "What happened? Lucky, are you okay?"

She shook her head and started to sob. His arms slid around her, and he pulled her close, pressing her head against his shoulder. Lucky let him hold her as the tears came. Strangely enough, given the experiences of the last few days—including those of the last hour or so—she felt safe with him. The concern in his eyes and voice had been real, and his arms wrapped around her were strong and warm. Even though she was as confused and scared as ever about what was happening in her life, here in his embrace she somehow felt as if everything would be alright.

She let out a final sob and then drew back from Aidan, raising a hand to brush at the wetness on her cheeks. He found a box of tissues on top of the filing cabinet and handed them to her. Worry still showed in his eyes as he scanned her face. After she had wiped away the remnants of her crying fest, he handed her a bottle of water. *Well, at least his search was successful,* she thought, as she opened it and drank until she had drained the bottle.

Taking the empty from her and handing her another, Aidan asked, "Do you feel up to telling me why you screamed? Which scared the hell out of me, by the way."

Lucky gave him a wry smile. "Well, I was pretty terrified myself, although I'm not sure if the explanation will make any sense to you."

"Try me," he urged.

"Someone came in here, a man. When I heard him, I thought it was you, but when I looked at him, it hurt—a lot—and I knew who he was—well, sort of—because only one person has ever made my head hurt like that. I was scared. I didn't know what else to do."

"You knew who he was because he made your head hurt?" Aidan asked the question as if it made perfect sense.

"The other day, I was with Mo at a restaurant a few blocks from here, and this man came in. He looked so ordinary—middle-aged, average size, graying hair, moustache, glasses—but he gave me the creeps. And every time I looked at him, it made my head hurt. Then, when he was on his way out, he looked me straight in the eye for just a few seconds, and his eyes were all strange and yellow and glowing. And then my head hurt so badly I couldn't even see. He left, and almost as soon as he was gone, the pain went away. The same thing happened just now. After I screamed, I heard you running down the hall, and I could tell he was gone, because my head didn't hurt anymore."

A frown had creased Aidan's brow as he listened to her story. "This man is the only person who's ever affected you like this?"

She nodded again, and then, gathering every ounce of courage she possessed, she asked a question of her own. "So, tell me, do you really have wings, or am I losing my mind?"

Aidan looked at her for a moment, his expression showing no surprise at her question. Then he stood and turned his back to her. In about a second, two large white wings appeared on his back as if they had sprouted right out of his t-shirt. Where the appendages connected to his body, they formed a sort of inverted V, nearly meeting at the top of his spine and growing farther apart as they moved down his back to end just below his rib cage. The tips of the wings, folded in as they were now, almost brushed the floor, and the curves at their tops stretched above his head by at least a foot. In the light from the hallway, the white feathers glistened as if they were sprinkled with gold dust.

Turning to face her, Aidan asked, "Does that answer your question?"

"Sort of." Lucky frowned a little. "Do they burn? When I've seen them before—or thought I've seen them—they've looked like they're on fire."

Aidan nodded. Then, disappearing the wings, he sat back down in the chair facing her. "Yeah, they flame. Have you ever heard of Seraphim?"

Lucky vaguely remembered the term from her Catholic school theology classes. "They're a kind of angel, right?"

Aidan nodded. "Yes, and they have the ability to appear as fire. I'm half Seraph—on my father's side. I got the flaming wings from him."

Lucky swallowed. "What about your mother?"

Aidan smiled. "She was human, a concert pianist."

"Was?" Lucky asked.

He pressed his lips together. "It's a long story."

Understanding that he didn't want to talk about his mother, Lucky asked another question. "How do the wings come and go without ripping holes in your clothes?"

Aidan chuckled. "You know $e=mc^2$? Matter and energy are the same and all? It's sort of like that. The wings are energy that we can summon as matter. And matter is mostly empty space. The wings take form around the molecules in the fabric of whatever we might be wearing."

"Okay," Lucky said, and then giggled, struck by the strangeness of the situation. How many people sat around discussing scientific equations with a self-professed half-angel? And if Aidan was half angel, what did that make Zeke?

Before she could ask the question, the being himself appeared in the doorway, flanked by a couple of people Lucky didn't recognize.

"Ah, good," Zeke said, "you're awake. Shall we adjourn to the lounge down the hall? I think my office may be a bit cramped for all of us."

The little group formed a procession and followed Zeke down the hall to the lounge to which he had referred. Lucky and Aidan were at the rear of the group, she with his jacket still wrapped around her shoulders. Entering the lounge,

Lucky moved to sit on one end of an empty sofa, and Aidan positioned himself beside her. Zeke sat in an armchair across from them. A tall, broad-shouldered man with mocha skin and many long dark braids pulled back into a ponytail at the nape of his neck leaned hip-shot against the arm of the chair to Zeke's right. He was dressed in unrelieved black, the sleeves and shoulders of his long jacket adorned with large patches of leather. The final member of the group, a small woman with long white hair, clothed in a pale gray smock-like dress, perched on the edge of the chair to Zeke's left. Given the whiteness of her hair, Lucky was surprised that her skin looked unlined.

Zeke broke the silence, his many-timbred voice surrounding and enveloping them. "I suppose some introductions are in order before we get started. Lucky, the lady to my left is Sambethe, and the gentleman to my right is Malachi. Sambethe and Malachi, as you have no doubt surmised, the young lady sitting next to our Aidan is Lucky Monroe, the guest of honor at this afternoon's event."

The woman said nothing, merely nodded once in greeting as her piercing grey eyes, even paler than Zeke's, raked Lucky from head to foot.

"It is nice to meet you in person, Lucky," said Malachi, in a voice both deep and dark. "I have had some small knowledge of you from friends."

At his words, three crows descended from the shadows near the ceiling and, circling the room once, came to rest, one on each of Malachi's shoulders, and one on his extended right forearm. They looked at Lucky with their bright, intelligent eyes, each in turn bobbing its head as if in greeting.

"I apologize if they frightened you," Malachi continued. "They were merely confirming that you were the girl we sought. Aidan had given us some information about you and your powers; the birds were sent to find the one who matched the description given. They had to pass quite close to you to be certain you were the one."

Lucky stared at the man and his avian companions in wonder. She felt as if she were in the middle of a dream or, like Alice, had fallen down the rabbit hole.

"It was quite a happy coincidence that you were on your way here at the time," Zeke picked up the tale. "It made my job of contacting you much simpler. Once I discovered your interest in the *lamassu*, making sure you came to my lecture seemed the easiest course. It was then a matter of a few moments to engineer the presence of some specially chosen friends in the audience. *Et voilà!* Here we are."

Lucky opened her mouth to speak, but finding no words at the ready, she closed it again. It took her another minute or two to form her incoherent thoughts into speech. "I may be missing something here, but I don't understand why you were looking for me, why you wanted to contact me, or why you thought I needed to be here today. Who are you? And what do you want with me?" Her words were directed primarily at Zeke, but she cast a glance in Aidan's direction as she spoke. His hand briefly covered hers where it rested on her thigh.

"We're here to help you, Lucky," Zeke answered. He looked at her in silence for a moment; then, leaning forward, he brought his face a little nearer her own. When he spoke, his voice was quiet, and his attention focused solely on her, as if they were alone in the room. "Lately, you've been experiencing the world a little differently, haven't you? Seeing things that weren't there before? Sensing things that make no sense in the world as you know it?"

Swallowing the lump that formed in her throat, Lucky nodded.

"And you're going to turn eighteen in a few days, right?"

Casting a frowning glance in Aidan's direction, Lucky responded impatiently, "Yes, in just a few days. Why is my birthday so important to everyone?"

"It is no accident that eighteen is the number associated with the Hebrew word *Chai*, which means 'living,'" Zeke said, his gray eyes warm and reassuring. "Your powers will come fully alive on your eighteenth birthday, Lucky. It was important that we find you and talk to you before then. I would guess you've recently had some fears for your sanity. Am I correct?"

Again, she nodded.

"Well, imagine your experiences of the last few days magnified tenfold." As Lucky's eyes widened, he continued, answering her unspoken question. "Yes, even your experience this afternoon. Imagine that times ten, and you have some idea of what your birthday could be like. Then imagine that with no one there to take care of you or to help you understand what's happening."

"Okay, I get the birthday thing now. Can we move on to the explaining part? What is going on anyway?"

Zeke sat back in his chair. "You are what we call a Sensitive, Lucky. You're one of a group of humans who have the ability to recognize us as we are, to see beyond the glamours we sometimes cast."

As he spoke, his face became translucent, like the image from a film projected onto a screen, while behind it alternated the faces of a bull, a lion, and an eagle. Around his human body appeared the shadowy form of a great winged creature, equal parts eagle, lion, and bull.

"Am I seeing you as you are?" Lucky asked in a shaky voice.

The shoulders of the winged creature and the human-looking shoulders of the man she knew as Zeke both shrugged. "Only in part. It is very difficult for human Sensitives, or even Nephilim—half-angel hybrids like Aidan here—to comprehend me as I truly am. What you are seeing is the closest approximation your mind is capable of making at this moment. It may change over time, as your powers develop."

Lucky studied him in silence, watching his form shift and morph. Then the images coalesced into a human form once more, and she saw just Zeke: light gray eyes above high cheekbones, long honey-wheat hair, conservative attire.

"What are you?" she asked.

He smiled. "Didn't you pay attention to my lecture at all, my dear?" he teased gently.

When she shot him a look, he relented. "Yes, I know, you were somewhat distracted at the time. To answer your question, I am what you would call a Cherub, one of the order of Cherubim. Not exactly what you would expect, eh? Definitely not a chubby baby with wings. The best description that has been recorded of my kind is the one I quoted from the book of Ezekiel, from which, incidentally, I adopted my name."

"Zeke isn't your real name?"

He shook his head. "No. My real name would be unpronounceable for you. When I chose to live among humans, I needed to adopt a human name. As I wanted one that would seem normal to your kind and yet have some connection to the truth of my being, 'Ezekiel' seemed the best choice. It has evolved into 'Zeke' over the years."

Lucky shifted her gaze to Malachi, who was now seated on the arm of his chair. The crows no longer perched on his shoulders and arm, but had flown to various windowsills, where they walked back and forth and looked out onto the street below. "And what about you, Malachi? You're not a Cherub or a Seraph. I can see the shadows of wings around your shoulders, but they don't burn like Aidan's, and the feathers are black."

Instead of answering her question, he first offered her additional information. "Not all half-Seraphs have flaming wings like Aidan's; they can take other forms. But you are correct in your assertion—I am neither Seraph nor Cherub. I am something altogether different." As his eyes met hers, she noticed for the first time that they were a startling shade of amber, warm against his dark skin.

Zeke cleared his throat. "Malachi was once a Sensitive, just like you, Lucky. Now, he is—something more. But we will get to that later. Our present task is to determine how to help you through the next few days and, after that, how to attend to your education and training."

"Education and training?" she asked.

"Oh, yes. You will need much of both in order to make use of these new powers of yours. Fortunately, we have the resources available to help you. I, for example," he continued with a smile, "can offer you a wealth of information—relevant and irrelevant—as well as help you focus your mental powers, so you can both use them to better effect and shield yourself from those who would turn them against you. Sambethe can teach you about spells, potions, divination, and healing. And Aidan and Malachi can teach you how to protect yourself and train you for battle."

"Battle?" Lucky's voice was alarmed.

"Zeke," Aidan inserted, "maybe we could save some of this for another day. She's been through a lot already."

"Yes, of course," the angel responded. As he rose to his feet, the others stood as well. "Suffice it to say that you are very important to us, Lucky, and we will do all we can to help you fulfill the promise of your—"

A voice both young and old cut across Zeke's words in an eerie sing-song, as Sambethe's body stiffened, and her eyes rolled back in her head: "The Destroyer awakes. Ancient and undying, it takes its form. Both Naphil and not Naphil, she will unwind the threads. Light and Dark, she will unwind the threads. Only then will the Destroyer sleep once more. Both Naphil and not Naphil, she will unwind the threads. Light and Dark, she will unwind the threads. She will unwind the threads. She will unwind the threads. She will unwind the threads…."

The sing-song voice trailed to a whisper as Sambethe repeated the words over and over. When she finally stopped speaking, she collapsed against the arm of her chair. As Malachi moved to assist the woman, Lucky swung her eyes back to Zeke to find him studying her with a face grown stony in its gravity.

"She was talking about me, wasn't she?" she asked. "What did she mean 'both Naphil and not Naphil'?"

It was Sambethe, not Zeke, who answered her. Her words were halting and breathless, and she leaned against the arm the kneeling Malachi had placed around her. "It means… that you must… be Made Nephilim."

"No!" Aidan rose to his feet. "Zeke—"

The angel cut him off with a wave of his hand. "As you so correctly pointed out earlier, Aidan, Lucky has had a long day. Let's save this discussion for another time. I would like to talk to Sambethe about it more myself in private. Lucky, your birthday is Sunday, I believe?" When Lucky nodded, he continued. "Can you meet me here, outside the OI, Sunday morning, early, say 7:00?" He paused, reaching into his jacket pocket. Coming up empty-handed, he continued, "I was going to give you my card, but I seem to be out of them."

"I already have one. You gave it to me when you told me about your lecture."

"Right. Good. In the meantime, then, please don't hesitate to call me if you need anything—if you see or sense anything that frightens or unnerves you, or if you just need reassurance that what you are experiencing is normal." He reached out to take her hand in his. "No matter how strange this all may seem, I am here to help you, Lucky, and I take my responsibilities quite seriously."

"Okay," Lucky responded. "I'll call if I need to, and I'll see you here on Sunday." After a pause, she added a "Thank you" that sounded suspiciously like a question.

Zeke released her hand and turned to leave the room. Still leaning on Malachi, Sambethe paused in front of Lucky and grasped her arm with bony fingers, studying her without saying a word. Then she released Lucky's arm and gestured to Malachi that she was ready to follow Zeke. Whistling to the crows, Malachi inclined his head toward Lucky. As he and Sambethe fell into position behind Zeke, the birds settled onto his shoulders and arm. Lucky stared at the empty doorway for several moments after the strange assembly had departed.

Then she looked to Aidan with wide, anxious eyes. He settled an arm around her shoulders, giving her a brief hug. "It's overwhelming, I know. But you'll get used to it—well, some of it. Now, I should probably take you home."

"Oh, no," she said, her hand flying to her mouth as she looked at her watch. "I was supposed to be at Mo's an hour ago to get ready for the dance. I have to call her." Looking around her, she realized something was missing. "My backpack. I must have left it in the lecture hall."

Lucky raced back to the lecture hall with Aidan by her side. She went straight to the seat where she had been sitting, remembering that she had placed the bag under it when she had first sat down. Finding nothing under the seat, she glanced around the neighboring seats, a worried frown creasing her forehead.

"Over here," Aidan called from the side aisle closest to the hallway exit.

Lucky was filled with relief when she saw her green backpack, in all its buttoned and graffitied splendor, dangling from his fingers. She weaved her way through the rows of seats toward him and, taking the proffered bag, looked through the pockets to see if anything was missing. Wallet, cell phone, keys, everything was there, except for the locket and broken chain she had tucked into the inner pocket.

"That's weird," she said.

"What's weird?" Aidan asked. "Is something missing?"

"Just my locket. The chain broke earlier—"

"When I startled you," Aidan interrupted.

Lucky glanced up at him. So he had noticed. "Yes. I put it in the zipper pocket inside. And now it's gone. But my phone is here and my wallet." She opened the wallet and extracted a few bills. "Even the money. Why would anyone leave all that and take a broken necklace? It doesn't make any sense."

Aidan's brows drew together. "The locket—I'm guessing that was something you wore all the time?"

She nodded. "It was my mother's. My grandmother gave it to me when I turned sixteen. She had given it to my mother on her sixteenth birthday. When she found it in my mother's things after she died, she saved it for me."

Aidan's frown deepened, and a muscle worked in the side of his jaw. "Lucky, can you tell me anything more about the man you saw in the office earlier, the one who made you scream?"

She shook her head. "I think I told you everything. He's average-looking. The first time I saw him he was wearing a long, dark trench coat."

"And you've only seen him the two times?"

"Yes. Why? Do you think he took my locket? Why would he want it?"

"Objects that are worn close to a person's skin, especially those that are worn regularly, carry with them a connection to the wearer. Such objects are very powerful and can be used to track the wearer or to perform other acts of magic focused on the wearer."

Lucky's eyes widened. "You think he took the locket so he'd be able to find me again? Why would he be looking for me? What does he want with me?"

Aidan shook his head. "I don't know what he wants with you, but, yes, I am afraid he took the locket as a way to locate you. The fact that he's even aware of you may be our fault. We have some powerful enemies, and if they think you're important to us…." He cursed under his breath, then added, "In trying to help you, we may have just made your life a lot more complicated."

CHAPTER 12

Lucky put a hand on Aidan's arm. "This isn't your fault. From what Zeke said, it sounds like if you hadn't contacted me, I might have been in pretty bad shape in a couple of days. Not that that's completely out of the question now, I guess, but I have a better shot of getting through it."

Her hand slid from his arm as her cell phone started ringing. "Mo!" she exclaimed. "She's probably worried about me."

Retrieving the phone from her backpack, she flipped it open and said hello to her friend.

"Lucky, thank God!" Mo's voice said in her ear. "Where are you? I've been calling and texting for almost an hour now."

"It's a long story, Mo. I'll fill you in later."

"Well, you better get over here soon, because you don't have much time left to get ready. We have to leave in less than an hour."

"I'll be there as soon as I can. 'Bye." Cutting off a flood of words, she flipped the phone shut.

"Come on," Aidan said, tilting his head toward the door. "I'll give you a ride."

Lucky followed Aidan out of the building in silence, jogging to keep up with his long strides. Her eyes widened in surprise and alarm when he stopped at a motorcycle parked against the curb a block or so from the OI.

Straddling the bike, he tossed her the helmet. "Get on behind me."

After struggling with the helmet strap, she swung her leg over the motorcycle and settled onto the seat behind Aidan. He turned on the engine and called over his shoulder, "Put your arms around my waist, and hold on."

She complied, her breath hitching in her throat as the action brought her into very close contact with his body.

At his loud "Where to?" she leaned even closer, if that was possible, and shouted Mo's address in his ear. He nodded and, releasing the brake, pulled the bike away from the curb. Lucky tightened her hands on his waist, and then she wanted to jerk them away as she felt the hard muscles of his abdomen flex beneath her palms. Feeling the heat in her cheeks, she hid behind his back, glad he couldn't see her face. Staring at the cotton of his t-shirt and the muscles outlined beneath it, she realized she was still wearing his jacket. The knowledge caused her flush to deepen.

During the short ride to Mo's building, she was able to get her treacherous cheeks under control—at least enough so that any remaining pinkness could be attributed to the motorcycle ride itself. She disengaged her arms from Aidan and hopped off the bike almost before he had cut the engine.

He interrupted her hurried thanks. "Where are you going tonight?"

"There's this dance at Mo's mom's country club. She wanted Mo to go, and Mo wanted me to go with her."

Aidan said nothing for a moment as emotions warred on his face. When he spoke, both his voice and features indicated his reluctance. "I don't suppose you would be willing to take me with you?"

Lucky shot him a look of surprise. "You're welcome to come. Mo said I could bring a guest. You don't sound like you really want to though." The last sentence came out sounding like a question.

"Well, I'm not exactly a dance kind of guy," Aidan said, looking uncomfortable. "But I don't like leaving you alone knowing that a Dark One might be after you."

"Dark One?" she asked.

He raised his hand, saying only, "It'll keep 'til later."

"Fine," she said, watching as he dismounted the bike. "Does this mean you're coming with me?"

He nodded as he took her arm and pulled her toward the stairs. "You better hurry up and get in there, or your friend is not going to be happy with you."

Mo buzzed them in almost as soon as Lucky rang the bell, and Lucky raced up the stairs to the second floor with Aidan on her heels. Before Lucky could knock, Mo opened the door with an impatient "It's about time!"

Any further comment died in her throat as she registered Aidan's presence. A look of surprised speculation crossed her face, but to Lucky's relief she said nothing more than "Aidan! This is a surprise!" as she held the door open for them to enter.

Mo ushered Aidan into the living room, asking if he'd like something to drink while he waited. Lucky slipped out of the leather jacket and handed it to its owner, before hurrying down the hall to Mo's room.

She was sliding the multi-toned green dress over her head when Mo burst through the door. Slamming it behind her, she hurried to Lucky's assistance, tugging the dress into place and pushing Lucky's arm aside so she could pull up the side seam zip. Then, dragging Lucky over to her dressing table, she pushed her into the chair and started pulling a brush none too gently through her long curls.

"Ouch!" Lucky exclaimed, grabbing the brush from her. "Let me do this part. You clearly don't have curls."

"Well, not like those," Mo acknowledged.

Her blonde hair was wavy, and she usually wore it in a messy, shoulder-length bob. Tonight, Lucky saw, looking at Mo's reflection in the mirror, she had twisted it up into a loose knot, with tendrils escaping at the sides of her face. From what Lucky could see, two bejeweled chopsticks seemed to be all that held the knot in place. The style somehow managed to be both casual and sophisticated, and it looked perfect on Mo. The bright colors of the gemstones on the hair chopsticks were duplicated in the earrings that dangled halfway to her shoulders. The jewelry offset the soft champagne color of the off-the-shoulder gown she wore.

"Mo!" Lucky said. "What are you wearing? I thought you were going for short and black."

Mo's reflected cheeks flushed. "My mother gave me the dress, especially for tonight. She was so excited, and I couldn't disappoint her." She caught Lucky's eye in the mirror and grinned. "Besides, it is pretty stunning," she said, executing a spin to show off the back of the dress.

"It's beautiful," Lucky agreed.

"I didn't completely sell out though," Mo said. Lifting the hem of her dress, she alternately stuck out each of her sandaled feet for Lucky's inspection. True to her word, her toenails were painted in various shades: turquoise, yellow, lime green, and hot purple. In addition, a jeweled ring decorated each of her second toes. "A girl's gotta do what a girl's gotta do."

When Lucky laughed, Mo reclaimed the brush from her and began to tug her hair into some kind of up do. "Now," Mo said, "enough about me. What's going on with Aidan? Can I assume the fact that he's here means he's going to the dance with you?"

"Yes," Lucky sighed. "He's going to the dance. It's a long story, Mo, and I don't have the time or the energy to go into it all right now. I will tell you later, though." As the last words left her lips, Lucky wondered if they were true. Would she be able to tell her friend the whole story? How much could she reveal of what had happened this afternoon without endangering Mo too?

Mo's eyes sparkled at her in the mirror as she brandished the hairbrush in a threatening manner. "You better, girlfriend. I want *all* the juicy details."

The doorbell rang as she finished speaking. "That'll be Eric," she said, tossing the brush aside. "Your hair's done. Use whatever makeup you want. The sandals I promised you are by the bed." Before she closed the door behind her, she added, "Hurry up! We have to leave in about five minutes."

Lucky barely glanced at her hair as she hurriedly brushed on mascara, blush, and lip gloss and inserted a pair of dangly rhinestone earrings into her ears. Wrestling her feet into the silver sandals, she took a deep breath and then opened the door.

Three pairs of eyes turned toward her as she stepped into the living room, the heels of her sandals clicking against the hardwood floor.

"You look amazing," Mo said. A mischievous note in her voice, she added, "Doesn't she, Aidan?"

Cheeks flushing, Lucky shot her friend a warning look before turning her gaze toward the young man in question. Intensely blue eyes scanned her from head to toe and slowly made their way back up her body. Lucky was sure her cheeks were flaming by the time Aidan's eyes locked on hers. One corner of his mouth lifting lazily, he drawled, "I don't think my leather jacket will work with that dress, so looks like we're going to have to figure out another way to keep you warm."

Though she hadn't thought it possible, Lucky's blush deepened. She said nothing as Aidan chuckled. Then Mo was thrusting a wrap into her arms and motioning them toward the door. "Let's go, let's go!"

Lucky was surprised when Aidan took the wrap from her and settled it around her shoulders. His hands were warm through the soft cloth as he slid them down her upper arms, smoothing the wrap into place.

"Thanks," she said, the word barely audible.

"My pleasure." His voice was a breath against her ear.

Lucky's breath caught in her throat.

Aidan moved to her side and offered her his arm for support as they descended the stairs. "I've never understood how women walk in those things," he said, looking at her strappy high-heels.

"Honestly, I'm not always very good at it." Lucky lifted laughing eyes to his, her hand closing around his arm. "You may be sorry. One wrong step and I could take us both down."

He chuckled. "That might not be an altogether negative experience," he said in a low, soft voice that Lucky felt like a feather-stroke down her spine.

Her thoughts completely scattered, she said nothing as they located Eric's car and piled in.

The country club was in the northwest suburbs, and the drive took almost an hour. Mo and Eric bantered throughout the trip, with Lucky and Aidan interjecting an occasional comment. For the most part, the latter pair was silent. It wasn't that Lucky had nothing to say to Aidan, it was just that everything she wanted to talk about was something that couldn't be mentioned in front of the other two. She wanted to know more about Zeke and Malachi—and the seemingly ageless woman who, except for her single outburst, had said almost nothing throughout the entirety of their odd afternoon gathering. And what had her strange words meant anyway?

Casting about for something to say, Lucky remembered the statue of the Archangel Michael the old woman at the antique store had given her. She had intended to do some internet research to see what she could find out about Michael, but she hadn't gotten around to it yet. Thinking that might be a safe enough topic to broach in company, she turned toward Aidan.

"What do you know about the Archangel Michael?" she asked quietly.

From the expression on his face, she could tell the question had taken him by surprise. He considered for a few moments before he responded, his voice equally quiet. "Michael is the fiercest of the Archangels. He's a warrior, the leader of the Forces of Light. In your traditions, it's said he defeated Lucifer in the battle in Heaven, causing the Light-Bearer to be cast out." Lowering his voice to make sure that only Lucky could hear him, he added, "While that statement is accurate as far as it goes, the actual battle was—somewhat different. Why do you ask?"

"The other day when Mo and I were shopping, we went into an antique store, and I found this statue of an angel standing on a dragon and holding a sword. Something about it—I don't know—*called* to me. The old woman who ran the store ended up giving it to me. She wouldn't accept any payment. She kept telling me he was mine and that he would protect me from 'the Dark that is coming.'" Lucky dropped her voice even lower. "Why would some complete stranger give me a statue of Michael? And what do you think she meant by 'the Dark that is coming'?"

Aidan leaned closer to her, so that when he spoke she could feel his lips moving against her ear. "I don't know, unless she means something like what Sambethe calls the Destroyer. I'd guess the woman may be a Naphil or a Sensitive. Maybe she sensed something similar in you. Then again, she could just be an eccentric old lady who gets her kicks making strange comments to impressionable young girls."

Before Lucky could begin to argue that she wasn't as impressionable as all that, Mo twisted around in her seat. "Okay, you two. We're here. Time to stop being such lovebirds and start interacting with others."

Lucky was glad for the dark when she felt her cheeks stain with heat once again. Keeping her face turned away from Aidan as the car doors were opened triggering the inside light, she silently cursed fate for giving her fair skin that blushed so easily.

Her embarrassment was forgotten as they approached the doors to the country club. Tiny white lights wrapped the pillars on either side of the entrance, and more lights were strung on the elegant potted topiaries that created a pathway leading to the ballroom. It was like something out of a fairy tale—or at least a Disney movie version. So far, this day had turned out nothing like she'd expected; she wondered what other surprises it might hold.

Aidan stayed at Lucky's side as they fell in line with the other guests to file into the ballroom. White-draped tables topped with candles and fall floral centerpieces lined the edges of the room. A band playing soft jazz occupied the raised dais at the room's far end. Otherwise, the floor was open, providing ample space for dancing. Aidan clenched his jaw as he looked around the room, wishing he were just about anywhere else. He had spoken nothing less than the truth when he had told Lucky he wasn't much of a dancing sort. Nor was he much into formal social gatherings. He had had to attend enough of them with his mother, and he hadn't liked them then. Now, affairs like this made him want to break out in hives.

His jaw relaxed a bit as his gaze came to rest on Lucky. Not that spending time with her was any hardship. In addition to feeling protective of her, he was also realizing that he liked her. She was tough and intelligent, and she had greeted the afternoon's revelations with a strength and acceptance he hadn't expected. Rather than being traumatized by the experience, she seemed curious and eager to learn more. Of course, she was frightened too. Not only had her whole life been upended, but she was also being tracked by something Dark and nasty. In her position, who wouldn't be scared? But she had seemed to take it all in stride, and even after the afternoon she'd had, it hadn't occurred to her to back out on her commitment to her friend. He had to admire that.

And that wasn't the only thing worth admiring about her. Lucky's wrap had slipped down her arms when she leaned over to greet Mo's mother, and Aidan's eyes lingered on the graceful line of her neck and the smooth planes of her upper back. Getting to look at her in that dress might just make the evening bearable. Resisting the urge to slide his palm along her bare skin, he thought maybe he could even manage a dance or two, if it gave him an excuse to touch her.

Hearing Lucky introduce him to Mo's mother, Helen, he held out his hand and made the appropriate polite responses, mentally shaking his head to change the direction of his thoughts. The point of his being here at all was to protect the girl, not to seduce her. Instead of wondering if he could get his hands on her, he needed to pay attention to their surroundings. If the Dark One used that locket to track her here, then there could be trouble, especially if he brought friends. He needed to be at the top of his game, not distracted by her pale skin and jade green eyes.

"So, young man," said Mo's stepfather, raking Aidan's jeans and leather jacket with a critical eye, "do you, like my stepdaughter, have a compelling need to disregard the niceties of appropriate attire?"

"Gerald," Mo's mother cautioned, casting a concerned look toward her daughter, who quickly masked the hurt in her eyes.

Unconcerned with his own appearance, Aidan replied, "My decision to attend this event was kind of last minute, so it was something of a 'come as you are' for me. Your step-daughter, on the other hand," he added, glancing at the blonde girl before directing his eyes back to her stepfather, "looks absolutely stunning. I wouldn't be surprised if my friend Eric has to fight off half the guys here in order to dance with her." He looked back at Mo as he finished speaking, acknowledging her expression of gratitude with a small smile. Her stepfather, he decided, was either an arrogant ass or completely clueless, and odds were in favor of the former.

Fortunately, the MC for the evening chose that moment to ask everyone to be seated, while she offered some opening remarks about the dance and the dinner that would be served. As she spoke about the charity which would be the recipient of the proceeds of the event, the wait staff moved discreetly about the tables, supplying the guests with freshly baked bread, butter, and small, beautifully plated salads. Aidan was seated between Lucky and Mo's mother, and he turned toward Lucky when she touched his arm.

"I'm sorry about that. You didn't even have the opportunity to think about 'appropriate attire,' since you were sort of roped into this."

He smiled into those striking eyes of hers. "My 'attire' doesn't bother me if it doesn't bother you, and you look 'appropriate' enough for both of us. In fact, you look so good no one's even going to notice me."

He was captivated by the light flush that stained her cheeks. When her low-voiced, "Every female here already has" only caused her color to heighten, he couldn't resist leaning closer to her and asking if that meant *she* had noticed him.

Instead of looking coy or flirting as most girls he knew would have, she narrowed her eyes and responded with a crisp "Don't push your luck."

When she picked up her salad fork and speared a piece of lettuce, he felt as if he'd been dismissed. His lips curling with amusement, he picked up his own fork and began to eat his salad.

Dinner was over, and the band was beginning the music for the third dance, when Lucky had the first inkling that something was not as it should be. She and Aidan had sat the first two dances out, which was okay with her, since she was afraid she'd trip over his feet or do something else equally embarrassing. At the same time, she couldn't help wondering what it would feel like to be in his arms, pressed against him as they moved in time to the music. She was jarred out of such thoughts by a flash of cold down her side, as if a window had been opened nearby. Looking over her shoulder, she saw neither window nor door through which a breeze could have come. The glass doors which opened onto the patio and the gardens were on the opposite side of the room. Giving a quick glance around, she felt the hairs on the back of her neck rise in warning.

Aidan must have felt it too, because as her hand moved toward him, he turned to grasp her arm. "Dance with me," he said, pulling her none too gently to her feet. "It'll give us an excuse to circle the room."

Sliding into his arms, Lucky felt as if she were at the center of a storm of sensations. The cold prickling at the nape of her neck warred with the warmth of Aidan's hand pressing into the small of her back. The soft glide of her skirts against her legs was in marked contrast to the hard muscles of his thighs moving against hers as he led her into a turn. Scanning the room for a glimpse of anything or anyone out of the ordinary, she couldn't begin to tell how much of the pounding of her heart was due to fear, and how much was a result of being this close to Aidan's body.

"There," he said in her ear, directing her attention to a figure that was standing in the shadows off to one side of the room.

Lucky gasped as two other dark shapes coalesced out of the shadows to join the first. As glowing yellow eyes began to turn in their direction, Aidan spun them between two other couples so they were hidden for a few moments in the center of the dance floor. With carefully guided steps, he took them to the opposite side of the circle of dancers. Sure enough, more of the fiery-eyed shapes had taken up residence on the other side of the room.

"So, what do we do now?" she whispered. "I don't know the first thing about fighting other humans, let alone—whatever those things are."

"They won't attack here, while you're surrounded by people. They'll try to get you alone. Your job is to make sure that doesn't happen. Let me worry about the fighting."

Lucky considered being offended by his you-stay-put-and-let-me-protect-you attitude, but she was smart enough to realize that she would be in way over her head in any kind of altercation with glowing-eyed shadows. "Can the others see them?"

"No. Well, at least not unless there are other Sensitives here that I don't know about."

As two other couples left the dance floor and began moving toward the large doors at the front of the ballroom opposite the dais, the shadowy figures fell in behind them. His eyes still tracking the shadow men, Aidan ushered Lucky back to the table where Mo and Eric were once again seated.

"Stay with them," he commanded, as he half-pushed her into the chair next to her best friend, before striding toward the exit.

"What's with him?" Mo asked in surprise.

"I—think he just needs some air," Lucky answered.

"Not buying it," her too perceptive friend responded. "That's usually an excuse to get the girl away from everyone else for some alone time, and our golden-haired boy seemed pretty clear that you should stay put."

"Whoever knows with Aidan?" said Eric. "He can be pretty moody sometimes. He'll probably be back in a few minutes."

Lucky said a silent thanks to her friend's date for saving her from replying. She was too worried to think of any explanation that didn't sound just as lame as her first one.

"Eric," she said, to change the subject, "tell me about Icarus. How did you all meet? Was it really hard getting started? Have things changed for you all now that the band is getting successful?"

Even though she was interested in his responses to her questions, Lucky couldn't focus on his words. Her mind was chasing off after Aidan in pursuit of the shadow creatures. She tightened her hands around the seat of her chair, holding herself in place. She knew there was nothing she could do to help Aidan—that her presence would no doubt interfere with whatever he was doing to combat those walking shadows—but she itched to get up off her chair and run outside after him. Fortunately, Mo had her own questions for Eric, so the two were able to keep the conversation going with nothing more than the occasional smile and nod from her.

Aidan followed the shadow creatures down the hallway, keeping several feet of distance and a handful of people between them. The shadowy things didn't seem to notice that they were being followed, perhaps because they were focused on the couples they were stalking like prey.

Once outside, the couples turned to the right to go around the corner of the building to a small patio that overlooked the golf course. The women, who were carrying on an animated conversation which, as best Aidan could tell, was about something inane like home decorating, seated themselves at one of the patio tables and continued talking, while the men stepped to the edge of the patio, where they practiced clubless golf swings and discussed technique. The shadow creatures clustered around the two men.

Aidan kept to the shadows just outside the soft glow of the in-ground lights that studded the edges of the patio. What were the creatures doing? Their positions in relation to the two men suggested an interest in improving their golf game, but Aidan seriously doubted that was their goal. Maybe it was because the proportions of their vaguely humanoid bodies were way off, with short, ape-like legs and long, brawny arms, but somehow they just didn't seem like the golfing type.

Aidan was wondering if he should make his presence known in the hopes of scaring the creatures away or at least distracting them, when two of the shadowy forms stepped closer to the taller man, who looked to Aidan like a former high school football star whose gut had been thickened with the onset of middle-age and a fondness for beer. As Aidan watched, the forms of the two creatures became thinner, less substantial, more like smoke than shadow. Then the two misty forms merged, combining into one, which stepped directly into the man, slipping him on like a suit of clothes. Almost at the same time, two more of the creatures performed the same operation on golfer number two, while the remaining shadows dissolved into a mist that drifted back toward the windows of the club. Golf swings forgotten, the two men hurried back inside the club, raising their voices as they went.

Trouble was definitely brewing, but Aidan wasn't sure of the location of the brewer. He had determined that the shadow creatures were just instruments, tools wielded by someone whose location and identity he had yet to discover.

Cloaking himself with a glamour that would not only make him invisible to human eyes, but would also hide his presence from the Dark One who was commanding the shadow creatures, he summoned his wings and, lifting himself into the air above the clubhouse, performed a quick survey of the grounds. He could see nothing amiss, but he knew better. He opened his senses, expanding them outward from his body, and—bingo. Some sort of dark energy seemed to be emanating from the stand of trees that separated the rear garden from the golf course. With a few beats of his wings, he reached the edge of the trees farthest from the emanation. Lowering himself to the ground and dismissing his wings, he crept toward the source.

As Mo and Eric suddenly fell silent, Lucky became aware of raised voices coming from across the room. She couldn't make out the words, but the tones were masculine—one sounding arrogant and condescending, the other angry and belligerent. Along with her friends, she rose to her feet, and they all turned toward the sound just as the crowd parted to reveal a tall, stout, red-faced man delivering a staggering punch to Mo's stepfather's jaw. The blow was strong and unexpected enough to knock the man off his feet. When he hit the floor, his assailant was on top of him, raining blows on the arms Gerald had raised to protect his face.

With a yelp of distress, Mo ran to her mother with Eric close behind. Lucky moved to follow, but her motion was halted as arms as cold and strong as steel wrapped around her. A hand covered her mouth to smother her cries, and she was dragged into the shadows near the wall. She tried to struggle, but her captor's icy hold was so tight she could hardly move, and her efforts had little effect. He didn't even react when she kicked back against his shin as hard as she could with the sharp heel of her shoe. Twisting her head to try to free her mouth to scream, she cast a desperate glance toward the center of the room, but everyone's attention was focused on the fight or its aftermath, and no one noticed her struggling in the arms of the shadowy creature, who swiftly circuited the room to the patio door and slipped outside into the night.

The creature crossed the well-lit patio in an instant, then entered the garden and made for the thick shadows cast by the trees on the garden's far side. Lucky's panic increased in direct proportion to the distance between herself and the people inside the country club. They were about halfway across the dimly lit expanse of lawn when Lucky saw someone emerge from the shadows and advance toward them. As she tried to discern features in the dimness, she felt as if a dagger were being driven through her forehead. Well, that answered that question, didn't it? Closing her eyes against the pain, she sagged in her captor's arms.

Suddenly, she was released, the pain in her head joined by lesser ones in her knees and forearms as she hit the ground. Rolling to her side, she fought back the pain enough to open her eyes.

A few yards away, the shadowy creature that had held her was grappling with something or someone that shone with the light of a small sun. Then great wings of flame unfurled from the back of the glowing one, breaking the hold of the shadow creature. The fiery wings spread and flexed, their myriad tongues of flame becoming more defined, and the glow receded from the shadow creature's opponent enough for Lucky to realize that it was Aidan. In the light cast by his wings, his hair took on the appearance of fire, and his face was set in hard, determined lines. As she watched wide-eyed, a sword appeared in his right hand and a spear in his left. Both looked as if they were made not of metal but of light; they glowed white-hot like steel heated to the point of being molten.

Aidan raised the sword to strike the shadow, but Lucky never saw the blow descend. Pain shot through her head as the gray-haired man she had seen at the Medici bent over her and lifted her in his arms.

In a voice rough as gravel under car tires, he said something that sounded like, "Yes, I can see the resemblance."

Mustering the will to fight through her pain, Lucky twisted in his arms and managed to jab a knee into his groin. Caught by surprise, he loosened his hold enough so that one strong push against his chest had freed her to tumble to the ground—which was farther away than she had expected. Landing with a thud that jarred her teeth, Lucky looked up to see that her would-be captor was hovering in the air a few feet above her. He had no wings that she could see, and yet he hung there as if suspended.

She heard him curse as he began to dive toward her. A flaming shape intersected his path, knocking him away from her and lifting him several feet higher into the air. Aidan had landed only a few blows before the man twisted away from him and shot backward several feet to put some distance between him and his opponent. Looking toward Lucky, he wiggled his fingers in a mocking wave and then—disappeared. One second he was there; the next, there was nothing to block her vision of the light-polluted night sky.

She was just scrambling to her feet, struggling with the tail of her dress and the heels of her shoes, which kept sinking into the soft ground, when Aidan landed beside her.

"Are you alright?" he asked, holding out his hand as he dismissed his wings.

"I'm fine," she answered, reluctantly accepting his offered assistance. "Unfortunately, I can't say the same for my dress."

Even in the dimness she could see patches of dark on the material that were probably either grass or mud stains. She didn't think she was bleeding anywhere, although now that the pain in her head was gone, and she could feel her other aches, she was pretty sure she had amassed quite a nice collection of bruises.

"Too bad," Aidan murmured, sliding a gentle arm around her shoulders. "I really like that dress."

Lucky directed a half-hearted punch at his side and felt an electric thrill shoot up her arm as her fingers connected with his hard muscles.

"What?" he chuckled. "I do like it. It makes you look kind of like a mermaid."

Lucky chose to ignore that comment, but when his arm tightened around her shoulders, she allowed herself to lean against him and slide her own arm around his waist. "Thank you," she said. "I couldn't fight the shadow thing. Nothing I did had any effect on it."

"That's because it couldn't feel anything. It wasn't real, wasn't a living thing. None of the shadows were. They were conjured, made of magic. The combination of the sword and spear took care of them."

"Will you teach me that—when you and Malachi train me to fight?"

He grinned down at her. "That and a whole lot more," he promised.

They found Mo and Eric standing in front of the country club with Mo's mother and stepfather. The latter was holding a towel-wrapped bag of ice to his face, while Mo's mother patted him and offered words of comfort.

"How is he?" Lucky asked as she stepped up close to Mo.

"He'll be alright," her friend answered, "but we think his nose is broken." Lowering her voice so that only Lucky could hear, she added, "I can't say I'm too concerned, since I've wanted to break it myself often enough."

She handed Lucky the wrap she had retrieved from her chair. "What happened to you anyway? I looked all over for you and couldn't find you anywhere. Did you go after Aidan to 'get some air,' after all?"

As Lucky folded the wrap about herself, her mud-stained, scraped hands caught Mo's attention. Eyes narrowing, she took in Lucky's messy hair and the stains on her dress. "Are you alright? Did he do this to you?" Her voice was filled with concern and the seeds of righteous anger.

"No!" Lucky gasped. "It was nothing like that. Aidan didn't do anything to me. We went for a walk, and I fell." Her lips twisted in a self-deprecating smile. "You know what I'm like in heels."

Mo said nothing, but Lucky could tell she wasn't satisfied with the story. "Really, Mo. You don't need to worry about Aidan." Then she added for good measure, her voice ringing with the truth of her words, "He was a perfect—angel."

CHAPTER 13

When they arrived back at Mo's apartment, Eric and Aidan waited outside while Lucky went inside with Mo. Moving as quietly as she could, so as not to wake Mo's father, Lucky washed her hands and face and changed out of her mud-stained dress. She sighed as she folded the garment and tucked it into her backpack, wondering if the cleaners would be able to get out the stains. Mo waved away her offers to clean the borrowed shoes, saying she'd take care of them the next day. In only a few minutes, Mo was standing in the open apartment door as Lucky stepped out onto the landing to make her departure.

"I actually had a good time tonight," Mo said. "Go figure. I guess my mom was right about this one." Grinning, she added, "Seeing Gerald get his nose punched was icing on the cake."

Lucky chuckled softly. "I'm glad he wasn't seriously hurt. What was the fight about anyway?"

Mo shrugged. "Nobody could figure that out. Gerald said he didn't even know the man. I guess the guy just started yelling at him for some reason, and then he started throwing punches. Weird, huh?"

"Yeah," Lucky sighed. "You can say that again." Blowing a laughing kiss at her friend, she headed down the stairs.

When she stepped outside, Eric was nowhere to be seen, and Aidan was lounging against the brick half-wall at the bottom of the stairs, his fingers tucked into the pockets of his jeans. His eyes caught and held hers as she came down the stairs toward him.

Neither of them said a word as they walked slowly to his motorcycle.

"I'll give you a ride home," Aidan said, handing Lucky the helmet she had worn earlier.

She strapped the helmet on and told him where she lived as she climbed on behind him. Sliding her arms around him, she locked her hands at his waist and leaned into the strength of his back on the all-too-short ride home.

Aidan cut the engine in front of her building, and Lucky slipped off the seat, unstrapping the helmet and holding it out to him. Still straddling the bike, he took the helmet from her and turned it over and over in his hands. His eyes on the rotating helmet, he said, "I don't like leaving you alone, but you should be safe. I don't think he'll try anything else tonight."

"Do you know who he was?" she asked.

Raising his eyes to meet hers, he shook his head. "No. And, before you ask, I don't know why he's after you." Those blue eyes held responsibilities beyond his years and a deep sadness she didn't understand. "I'll talk to Zeke and the others. See what we can find out."

She nodded.

"Let me see your phone."

Retrieving the requested item from her backpack, she placed it in his outstretched hand. After a few moments, he returned it to her. "I've added my number. Call me if you need me."

Again, she nodded. Giving him a smile made of equal parts worry and reluctance to leave him, she turned toward the stairs, only to be halted as he called her name.

Reversing her steps, Lucky watched as Aidan fumbled at the back of his neck. Then he held out his hand toward her. Dangling from his fingers was something that glinted in the glow cast by the streetlights. When she took it from him, she saw that it was a gold amulet—a dragon, raised in relief against a stylized sun. The metal was warm from having lain against his skin.

"Put it on," he said. He waited until she had slipped the chain around her neck before he continued. "It's an object of power that was given to me by my father. I've worn it so long it's almost a part of me. As long as you're wearing it, I'll have a sense of your location, and if you're in danger, I'll sense that too." One corner of his mouth lifted in a half-smile. "It's not exactly voicemail, but I'll get the message."

"Thank you," she said. "I know it must be important to you, and it means a lot that you're letting me use it." She grinned. "Don't worry. I'll give it back to you soon. Once you and Malachi teach me all your fighting strategies, I won't need it anymore."

"There's no hurry," he said, a smile crinkling the corners of his blue eyes. "By the way, the band has a gig tomorrow night. Want to come?"

"Sure, that would be great." She cast him an inquisitive look. "How do you manage this weird double life of singer-songwriter and avenging angel?"

He chuckled as he shrugged. "I'm not really sure. I've never been both at the same time before. I'll let you know how it works out." As he was speaking, he strapped on his helmet. "I'll call you tomorrow," he said, starting the engine.

With a wave, Lucky turned and walked up the stairs and into the building. He waited until she was inside before he pulled away.

When she slipped into her room, Lucky found Shu and Tef settled in the exact center of her bed. After brushing her teeth and changing into her pajamas, she was about to switch off the light and do battle with the cats to stake her own claim, when the statue of Michael, which she had placed on the bookshelf opposite the bed, caught her eye. She stared at the dragon under the angel's foot, her fingers rising to touch the outline of the dragon on the amulet Aidan had given her. Looking around the room, she considered for a moment. Then she walked to the bookshelf, picked up the statue, and carried it over to the room's lone window. Only after placing the statue on the windowsill did she turn out the light and climb into bed.

The cats meowed in protest as she squirmed under the covers and positioned herself between them. Snuggling her tired and bruised body into the bed's softness, she sighed with relief. Her hand moved again to the amulet around her neck, and she realized that she did feel safe. Michael guarded the window, and Aidan was right beside her. That sense of his closeness stayed with her as she drifted into sleep.

When Aidan reached Lake Shore Drive and headed north toward the Gold Coast, he cranked the accelerator well beyond the regulation 45 mph speed limit. He laughed out loud as the wind of his passage whipped around him. There was definitely something to be said for speeding down the highway straddling a machine boasting 162 horsepower. Not that he wasn't grateful he could motivate under his own wing power again, but he loved his Ducati. It had satisfied his need for speed for the two years he had been wingless, and he had no intention of giving it up now that the wings were back. Those flaming flight providers were a part of his being; his Ducati, well, that was a toy. Besides, sometimes it came in handy, like today, when he was able to give Lucky a lift.

As his thoughts turned to the girl, his brows drew together in a frown. He really did believe she'd be safe tonight. Whoever the Dark One was, creating and controlling those shadow boys would have cost him quite a bit of power, and he'd need some time to recharge his metaphysical batteries. Plus, Aidan had given her the Light-Bringer's Medallion, which would provide him with the necessary bare bones information—*I need your help; here's where I am*—should she be in trouble. What he hadn't told her was that it would also offer her some strength and protection in and of itself. The amulet emitted a kind of energetic net that merged with the wearer's own energy field, enhancing his or her own natural powers. His not wearing it meant he'd be a bit more vulnerable now than he would have been with it around his neck, but there was no question that she needed the protection more than he did.

Aidan sped through the overpass around the museum campus and, weaving between a few cars, shot up past Navy Pier and reluctantly decelerated to slip onto the Oak Street exit. Traversing the few blocks to his building, he entered the parking garage and eased the bike into its spot. A short elevator ride later and he was inside his own space, trying not to trip over the vibrating ferret that was weaving figure eights around his ankles.

After filling Harley's bowls with food and water, he hung up his jacket, removed his boots and socks, and poured himself a scotch. He raised the glass to his lips as he walked across the cool marble tiles toward the floor-to-ceiling windows overlooking the night city. Catching the reflection of the baby grand in the window glass, he hesitated for a second and then changed course.

He stood beside the piano for a few moments, a muscle working in his jaw, before he set the glass down on its sleek surface and seated himself on the bench, where he sat for several moments more, head down, hands clenched around the bench's edge. Finally, heaving a sigh, he lifted his fingers to the keys and lightly stroked a few. A perfect minor D broke the silence. He played through the first chords of the "Lacrimosa" from Mozart's *Requiem*, and then let his hands fall back to rest on his thighs. He picked up the scotch and threw back the remaining contents, before placing the empty glass on the piano. The hand that returned to rest against the keys trembled.

Gods, he missed his mother. The piece had been a favorite of hers. She had taught him to play it on the piano when he was only ten. Tears filled his eyes as his right hand repeatedly fingered a few notes. Sometimes the weight of her loss—and his own guilt—was still almost more than he could bear. This world in which he lived, the one he'd just returned to, was not meant for humans. Involvement in it had cost his mother dearly.

Visions of her broken and bleeding body still haunted his nightmares. And always they carried with them the knowledge that he was responsible—that his recklessness and arrogance had caused her death. He remembered kneeling over her, staring in silent horror, beyond speech, beyond tears, beyond grief. Everything in him had screamed in agony, but no sounds had passed his lips other than those made by his ragged breathing.

It was Zeke who had finally drawn him away from her, as it was Zeke who had stood by his side at the funeral ceremony and, later, at the formal hearing, where his brother, as his Captain, stripped him of his rank, demoting him to the Fallen equivalent of foot soldier. A few days later, in front of Zeke, Lucifer, and the other members of the Allied Council, Aidan had taken his punishment further, resigning his commission in the Forces and formally renouncing his wings. Against his wishes, Zeke had intervened and petitioned the

Council to make the Renunciation temporary, a request they had readily granted.

When he had walked out of the council chamber that day, Aidan had had no intention of ever returning, and he had been bitterly angry with Zeke for refusing to grant him permanent Renunciation. He had taken up residence in the condo his mother had owned, and which she had left to him, and proceeded to empty it of almost all her possessions, except for some photographs and keepsakes and the baby grand that had been her pride and joy. This living space had been selected and designed to be both his refuge and his personal emotional torture chamber.

His left hand joining his right on the piano keys, Aidan played another few bars of the "Lacrimosa." He originally intended to stop there, but, almost of their own volition, his fingers continued to stroke the keys until he had played the piece through to the end. As the last notes faded from the nearly empty room, he bowed his head. He remained in that position for several moments. Then, taking a deep breath, he rose to his bare feet and retrieved his empty glass, which he half-filled again, before walking slowly down the hall to his bedroom.

Discarding his battle-stained clothes, he moved into the bath and turned on the shower. After giving the water a moment or two to warm, he stepped under the hot spray, allowing it to wash away not only the niggling aches and pains from the evening's battle, but also some of the anguish of the memories he had carried for the past few years. Tonight was the first time he had been able to play the "Lacrimosa" in its entirety since his mother's death. And while the pain of her loss and the role he had played in it still felt like a constricting band around his heart, he felt as if that band had loosened a notch or two, as if he had somehow turned an emotional corner. He had no illusions that his past was entirely behind him, but he realized that the last two years—even the last few days—had changed him. He was being given a second chance, and he was determined to do his best to meet the challenges ahead of him—including keeping Lucky safe.

As a fully human Sensitive, the girl had none of the extra strength and healing abilities his angelic half provided; she was as physically vulnerable as his mother had been. Even worse, since she hadn't yet come into her full Sensitive powers or learned how to use them, her very abilities could sometimes be a handicap to her. He had begun to suspect—and hope—that the pain she experienced in the presence of the Dark One whose attention she had for some unknown reason already attracted was a result not of intentional affliction on his part but of the erratic nature of her own new powers. If that was the case, she would be considerably less vulnerable to him in the next few days, once her powers were complete and she began her work with Zeke.

Shower finished, Aidan pulled on a pair of loose flannel pajama pants and stretched out on his bed, leaning back against the pillows he'd stacked against the headboard. His thoughts were still spinning around Lucky and the encounter with the Dark One at the country club. He wished he had some idea of what the being wanted with her. Did it have anything to do with her personally? Were her powers such that the Dark would have some special interest in her? Or was it the result of the attention that the Fallen had focused on her since he had told Zeke of her existence? Or—his jaw clenched at the thought—was it because of him? Had the Dark One somehow known of Aidan's reinstatement among the Forces of the Fallen as well as his connection to the girl? Was he hoping to hurt him by hurting her?

As his thoughts darkened, Aidan reached for the half-full glass of scotch on his bedside table. Swallowing the last of the alcohol, he focused on its smoky taste and the warmth sliding down his throat. Well, he resolved, he would be ready this time. He was going to keep the girl safe if it was the last thing he did.

Turning out the light, Aidan slid under the covers, dislodging the ferret that had draped itself around his shoulders. Harley chittered at him, before resettling at the foot of the bed.

Aidan's sleep was troubled by dreams in which, bound and powerless, he was forced to watch as fiery-eyed shadow creatures twirled his mother's bloody body through the movements of a macabre and torturous dance. When she was directly in front of him, the tormented, pleading eyes she turned toward his were not the soft blue he remembered but an unusual shade of jade green.

Aidan woke himself with his scream. His chest rocked by the beating of his heart, he took several deep breaths to steady himself and raised his hand to stroke the ferret who was standing on his chest making noises of concern.

It took him a long time to fall back to sleep.

CHAPTER 14

Lucky was awakened by Josh pounding on her door and calling, "Get up, sleepyhead."

"Go away, Josh," she groaned, turning over and pulling a pillow over her head.

Undeterred, her cousin replied, "Not happening. I've got plans for you today."

Then Lucky heard the door open and two light thuds followed by the patter of feline feet on hardwood as Shu and Tef jumped off the bed and headed for the open door. The next thing she knew Josh's weight came crashing down on the foot of the bed.

"Come on, get up," he said, grabbing her foot through the covers and giving it a shake. "The day awaits."

Muttering under her breath, Lucky withdrew her head from under the pillow and pushed herself into a seated position. "Just come on in, why don't you," she grumbled, brushing her long curls back out of her face.

"How late were you out last night anyway?" Josh asked. "It's almost noon."

"Noon?" Lucky looked up in surprise. "Wow. I think it wasn't much after midnight when I got in. I was just really tired, I guess. So, what's the deal? What are your plans for me?"

Her cousin grinned, looking so much like the naughty little boy he used to be that she wanted to reach out and ruffle his unruly brown curls. "Well, since tomorrow's your birthday, I thought we could spend this afternoon just playing. You know, go to Navy Pier, wander around downtown, play tourist."

"I haven't been to Navy Pier in a long time," Lucky said, catching Josh's enthusiasm. "Can we ride the Ferris wheel?"

"If we must. But you have to get up first, so we can get going." As he finished speaking, Josh gave her leg a smack through the covers and then hopped off the bed. "Hurry up! I'm hungry."

"Then eat something," Lucky grumped at him, throwing back the covers and climbing out of bed.

"Huh-uh," Josh shook his head. "I'm saving myself for a Chicago dog."

Lucky reached down to draw the covers up over the pillows, and as she did so, the dragon medallion around her neck swung forward, catching the light. Reaching a hand toward it, Josh asked, "What's that you're wearing?"

Lucky instinctively closed her fingers around the amulet. Feeling a slight flush rise to her cheeks, she let her hand fall to her side, so Josh could see the necklace. "Aidan gave it to me. It—it's supposed to be for protection or something."

"Protection?" Josh frowned. "Protection from what?"

Lucky shrugged.

Josh's frown deepened. "You were with Aidan last night? I thought you were going somewhere with Mo."

"I did go somewhere with Mo. It just so happens that Aidan and Eric were with us. What difference does it make?"

Josh sighed, rubbing a hand back through his hair. "I just didn't want to think you'd lied to me about where you were or who you were with. I know you're not a child anymore, Lucky, but I can't help worrying about you."

"I didn't lie to you, Josh," Lucky said, her fingers rising to touch the amulet again. "I didn't know Aidan was going to be there. I ran into him at the—lecture—I went to at the OI, and he ended up going to the dance with me."

"Just be careful, will you? He's older than you, and he's—well, best I can tell, never had a shortage of potential girlfriends. I just don't want to see you get hurt."

"It's sweet of you to be concerned, Josh. Annoying, but sweet," Lucky said. "You really don't need to worry though. Aidan is the least of my problems."

Josh frowned again, "That's supposed to make me feel better?"

Lucky laughed and gave him a push toward the door. "Come on, it's not like my other problems are life-threatening," she lied. "I'm about to turn eighteen, I need to find a job, and my live-in cousin is over-protective. Oooh, scary! Now, get out so I can get dressed."

After pulling on clothes and catching her hair up into a ponytail, Lucky grabbed her backpack and started for the door, hesitating for a moment as the statue of Michael and the dragon once again caught her eye. Going back to the closet, she retrieved an old sweatshirt, which she wrapped around the statue, before tucking the bundle into the backpack. She shrugged her arms through the straps of the backpack, taking comfort as the weight of it settled between her shoulders. With the statue at her back and Aidan's amulet nestled against her skin under her sweater, she felt as protected as it was possible for her to be, and she had every intention of enjoying her day playing tourist with Josh.

When they arrived at Navy Pier, the first thing they did was make their way to the food court. By this time Lucky was hungry too, so when Josh ordered his Chicago dog, she added a New York dog to the order.

"I don't know how you can eat those things," she said to her cousin as he pulled the Chicago-style hot dog, laden with pickles, relish, tomatoes, and peppers out of its box. "It's more like a salad than a hot dog."

Opening her own hot dog box, she eyed the kraut dog within with satisfaction. "Now, that's what a hot dog should be."

Josh chewed and swallowed a large bite, then looked at Lucky's hot dog with disgust. "Well, I can't believe you're so misguided as to actually like sauerkraut. Give me tomatoes, pickles, and celery salt any day."

They walked as they ate, taking in the sights and sounds of the pier, stopping at vendor stands to look at everything from t-shirts to funky, imported jewelry. Surrounded by people and shops, her mouth filled with the salty and pungent taste of her food, Lucky felt more light-hearted than she had in days.

"I want to ride the Ferris wheel," she said, excitement beginning to catch her, "and then I want to go in the Fun House maze."

"Can we please go through the stained glass museum first?" Josh asked. "I'd like to give the hot dog a chance to settle before getting on the Ferris wheel."

"Still afraid of heights?" Lucky teased, as she popped the last of her hot dog into her mouth.

"A real man is not afraid to admit his fears," her cousin replied. "So, yes, I confess that the thought of being in that thing that far off the ground makes me want to lose my lunch."

"Alright, then, stained glass it is," Lucky said, looping her arm through his. "But prepare yourself. We're going up in the Ferris wheel before the afternoon is over."

They spent over an hour wandering through the stained glass museum. It stretched almost the entire width of the pier mall and contained over a hundred stained glass pieces of various periods and styles. Lucky liked many of them, but her favorites were the Tiffanies with their intense, layered colors—and their angels. She was especially drawn to the Tiffany Annunciation, a two-paneled piece, the right half depicting Mary and the left the angel Gabriel, who had come to tell her she would bear the son of God. Mary's features were so delicate; the purples and blues of her robes, so rich. The angel of the Annunciation shone with a golden light that extended from its own panel into the upper left of Mary's. Lucky gazed at the piece in silent admiration.

Suddenly, all the color faded from the glass, leaving behind white panels, against which Mary's face and hair and hands showed dark in stark contrast. The leading around Mary's robes and the cushions on which she knelt was still visible, but the angel had almost disappeared.

It took a moment for Lucky to realize what had happened and what she was seeing. The light source behind the windows had been turned off, hiding the rich colors. Tiffany had layered milky white glass panels over the colored pieces—except for Mary's face, hair, and hands—and the leading of the angel's form was on the far side of the glass. With the light behind the panels extinguished, the angel could no longer be seen. As Lucky watched, a soft light began to glow behind the windows, increasing in intensity until Mary and the angel showed clearly once more.

Lucky was enraptured: all that color and depth, all that richness, hidden away just waiting to be revealed by the coming of the light. She stood and watched the windows change as the light went off and on for several minutes. She was struck by the changes in Mary's face. As the light brightened behind the glass, her features appeared out of darkness, gradually moving from a soft glow to a delicate and exquisite radiance, as if she were awakened and illumined by the angel's shining presence.

Looking at the piece, Lucky couldn't help but think of Aidan's glowing form and flaming wings. She could feel the slight weight of his amulet against her breastbone, and her fingers rose to touch it through her sweater.

"Thinking of me?" said his voice in her ear, as if her thoughts had conjured him.

Gasping, Lucky spun around to face him. "What are you doing here?"

With the spot-lighting from above making a halo of his golden curls and his lapis eyes glowing as if lit from within, Aidan looked as if he could have stepped out of one of the windows, but for the clothes he wore. The faded jeans, black t-shirt, black leather jacket, and boots spoiled the effect somewhat; although, Lucky had to admit, as her pulse picked up a beat, the look was a good one for him.

"I sensed you were here, and I wanted to make sure you were okay," he said. "Besides," he added, when she remained silent, "I needed to talk to you to make plans for tonight."

"You could have called," she said.

He shrugged, his hands in his pockets.

"Aidan!" Josh said, as he joined them. "What are you doing here?"

"That's exactly what Lucky said. You're going to give a guy a complex."

"It's not that we don't want you here," Lucky said, directing a pointed look at her cousin. "We're just surprised to see you is all."

"I live not too far from here. Sometimes I come down to the Pier to be around other people, to get out of my own head."

Although she knew there was a different reason for his presence here today, Lucky somehow understood that what

Aidan said was true. Josh must have heard the same veracity in his tone, as he accepted the explanation without question.

Turning to Lucky, Aidan added, "The show's at 9:00, which means I have to be there about 8:30 to help get set up. Pick you up at 8:00?"

"Ben and I can give Lucky a ride, save you the trip," Josh inserted, before Lucky could reply.

"It's no trouble," Aidan said, his eyes never leaving Lucky's. "I'd like to pick her up, if it's okay with her."

"It's okay with me," she said.

"See you about 8:00 then." Aidan lifted his hand so the tips of his fingers rested against her cheek. "Be careful," he said, his voice dropping so that only she could hear.

She nodded, a shiver going through her as the movement caused her cheek to brush against his fingers like a caress. He dropped his hand, his fingers curling into his palm as he lowered his arm to his side.

Then, with a wave toward Josh, he turned and left the room.

Aidan wasn't sure why he had followed the impulse to seek Lucky out. After his dream-filled night, he had awakened feeling restless and worried. He had decided to take a walk to Navy Pier to clear his head, to stop the mental hamster from running round and round the wheel of his thoughts. Once he had reached the Pier, he had felt the pull of the amulet and had known the girl was nearby. Although he hadn't sensed that she was in any danger, he had been helpless to resist the desire to go to her.

She had seemed so fragile standing in front of the Tiffany Annunciation, the colors of the stained glass reflecting on her delicate skin. And, although he knew from experience that she was a lot stronger than she appeared, when she had looked at him with the jade green eyes that had haunted his dreams, it was all he could do not to pull her into his arms and fly away with her to somewhere he could keep her safe. *And just where would that be?* he thought.

Enough of this. He had to get out of here. Fly, train, something. He needed physical exertion to burn off the excess adrenaline pumping through his veins. Stepping to the edge of a crowd of people near the Ferris wheel, he made sure no one was paying any attention to him before he dematerialized.

He reformed outside the training center. Pressing his palm against the security panel, he felt the familiar burn as his sigil was activated. Once inside, he headed toward the weapons room, his long strides making short work of the distance. He was gratified to find Malachi and several other members of the Forces donning guards and gathering weapons.

"Are you joining this morning's session, Commander?" asked one of the men, a huge Naphil named Gareth.

Aidan was taken aback by the unaccustomed title, but he recovered quickly, responding in the affirmative. While he had no doubt that Malachi had noted his momentary surprise—the man was preternaturally aware of almost everything that went on around him—he didn't think any of the others had noticed.

"Tell me where you want me, Captain," he said to Malachi as the geared-up group headed out to the training field. "Make me earn my place."

Malachi clapped a hand to Aidan's shoulder with enough force to knock him slightly off balance. "As you wish, Commander," he said. "As you wish."

"Tell me again I have nothing to worry about." Josh scowled after Aidan's retreating figure.

"Oh, for goodness' sake," Lucky sighed in exasperation. She took her cousin's arm and pulled him toward the exit. "What is wrong with you?"

"I saw the way you looked at him—as if he were an angel sent from heaven specially gift-wrapped for you. And he looked at you like—I don't know—like you were the last chocolate in the box. He's going to break your heart."

"No, he's not," Lucky said with more force than she felt. She realized that her cousin was probably correct. She was falling for the handsome, young angel-man, and while his actions toward her led her to think he was developing feelings for her as well, she knew better than to think anything could ever come of them. She was connected to his world by her newfound abilities, but she would never be of that world in the same way he was. She was human, and he most definitely was not.

Before it was out of sight, she turned her head for one final look at the Annunciation. She wanted to hold on to the image of Mary turning toward the angel's golden light for a little while longer.

After exiting the museum, Lucky and Josh headed toward the Fun House, where they laughed their way through the strobe-lit maze. Lucky felt somewhat disoriented by the time they reached the end and came back out into the mall—but not so much that she was willing to give up on the Ferris wheel. When she asked Josh if he was ready to face the ride, and he responded with a reluctant "I suppose," she dragged him outside to the huge, circular contraption.

"This one isn't so bad," she said, giving his arm a reassuring pat. "The seats are big, and they're all enclosed. It's not like the little ones, where there's nothing to save you from a sudden plummet toward death."

He pushed her hand away. "Lucky, that's not helping."

"Sorry?" she said, the word less an apology than an amused question.

"I really don't think you are."

"You don't have to go up with me," she offered. "I can do it by myself. I just want to see what everything looks like from up there."

Josh's face brightened. "Are you sure? You don't mind?"

"Well, I'd rather you went up with me, but I know you don't want to, so I'm okay going alone." Eyes twinkling with mischief, she added, "Scaredy cat."

When her cousin responded equally maturely by sticking his tongue out at her, she laughed.

"You know, the original Ferris wheel was introduced here in Chicago in 1893 at the Columbian Exposition," Josh said, as they waited in line. "It was meant to compete with the

Eiffel Tower, which had been built for the Paris Exposition a few years before."

"You're such a geek," Lucky told him.

"I know; it's part of my charm," he replied, continuing undaunted. "The Museum of Science and Industry is the only building still left from the Exposition. The other buildings were just made out of plaster, but that one was built with a brick substructure."

"It would have been pretty amazing, wouldn't it, to have seen everything set up on the Midway like that?"

"Mm-mm. The White City, they called it. Have you read that book about the serial killer, *The Devil in the White City*?"

Lucky shook her head.

"It's really interesting—and creepy. All the time the architects and planners were setting up this amazing display for the Exposition, there was this guy taking advantage of the presence of a lot of strangers in town to find and prey on these poor women. It's like the story of good and evil living and developing side by side."

"Okay, stop now," Lucky said. "You're creeping me out."

As if the story about the serial killer wasn't enough, Josh's words made her think of the shadow creatures at the country club the night before. She shivered as she recalled the feeling of the cold, hard arms holding her so tightly she could barely move. And Aidan had said the things hadn't even been real, that they had been created by that levitating man who made her head hurt. She could hardly wait to begin her studies with Zeke and her training with Aidan and Malachi. She didn't like feeling this helpless against whatever was after her.

They had reached the front of the line, and Josh stepped to the side to wait for her as Lucky handed the attendant her ticket and stepped into the empty car alone. She waved to Josh as the Ferris wheel moved her forward to load the next car. Looking out over the crowd as she was raised higher in the air, Lucky realized that she hadn't been troubled by visions of angels or demons all day. Funny, she would have thought her experiences would have been even more pronounced today, given that her birthday was tomorrow—and from everything Zeke and Aidan had said, it was likely to be intense.

She scanned the people below her, trying to open her mind to her new abilities. She caught the transparent shadows of a few glimmering wings and the deeper, more opaque shadows of some that seemed more leathery and bat-like. As best she could tell, none of the people she saw resembled the man from the night before. At least, none of them seemed familiar from this distance or caused her pain when she looked at them.

Then the Ferris wheel started to turn in earnest, and she was caught up in the views of the city and the lake as she was raised high in the air. How beautiful it all was! Aidan had said he lived not far from here. She wondered which of the many buildings was his. She wondered if she'd ever get the chance to visit him in his own place.

As the wheel descended, she looked for Josh, trying to pick him out of the crowd. She thought she caught a glimpse of him talking to someone, but she wasn't sure. Up, up, she ascended again. She looked down at everything spread out before her, from the huge white canopy over the Skyline Stage all the way to the end of the pier and Lake Michigan beyond. Too bad Josh wasn't up here with her to see the views. She didn't understand why it scared him; the wheel turned slowly, and each car was completely enclosed.

She looked for him every time the wheel descended, and she was almost sure she was looking in the right place, but she couldn't find him. She told herself he had probably just decided to get a Coke or something while he waited, but she couldn't suppress the niggling fear that something was wrong.

By the time the Ferris wheel stopped and Lucky exited the car, she was feeling almost panicky. She raced around to the place where she had left Josh, but he was nowhere to be seen. Shrugging her backpack from her shoulders, she rummaged through it with shaking hands, searching for her cell. She found Josh in her contacts list and punched the button to dial the number. After several rings, the phone went to voicemail.

"Josh, it's Lucky. I just got off the Ferris wheel, and I can't find you. Where are you? Call me." Her voice was as shaky as her hands.

This was all her fault. If she hadn't left him alone.... If she hadn't been so insistent about going up in the stupid Ferris wheel.... It was little comfort to tell herself she couldn't have known that *he* would be in any danger. She studied the people all around her trying to catch a glimpse of him. Nothing. Keeping her phone in her hand, she slid her backpack over one arm and jogged through the crowd, focusing her mind, searching for something that might help her find her cousin. Still nothing. She swore.

After several minutes, she made her way back to the spot where she had last seen Josh, in the futile hope that he had returned. Her hands shaking so badly she could barely punch the buttons, she dialed him again. Again, she was dumped into voicemail. She left a second message, hung up, and then, pressing the button for contacts, she located the number Aidan had programmed into the phone. When he didn't answer either, she almost threw the phone against the pavement in frustration.

Tears filling her eyes, she tugged on the chain around her neck to lift the dragon medallion out from under her sweater. Clenching her trembling fingers around the amulet, she pictured Aidan in her mind and concentrated as hard as she could, focusing all her fear and frustration into a silent scream, praying he'd get the message.

CHAPTER 15

Aidan was thoroughly enjoying demonstrating combat techniques. His adrenaline was running high, and he was more than holding his own against Malachi. He was about to bring the other Naphil to the ground, wings pinned, when he felt Lucky's scream. The non-sound went through his body like an electric shock, causing him to loosen his hold on Malachi for just an instant, which was all the other man needed to break his hold, execute the same move Aidan had just used against him, and drop Aidan to the ground, his wings pinned and useless. He must have realized something had happened to cause Aidan to fumble the maneuver, because he shot his second a questioning look as Aidan got to his feet.

"I have to go," Aidan called over his shoulder as he ran into the training facility, stripping off his guards and weapons as he ran.

He flung them all aside except for the short sword that was strapped to his left thigh. Then he was out the front door, where he could dematerialize. Lucky was still at Navy Pier, and he was back there in an instant, cloaking himself as he materialized, so as not to frighten any innocent bystanders. He let the glamour fade in such a way as to make it seem as if he had just stepped outside from one of the many shops. He kept the blade at his thigh masked. No need to scare the natives.

There she was. Aidan located Lucky where she sat slumped against a short concrete wall across from the Ferris wheel. He was relieved to see that, though she looked upset, she appeared to be unharmed. Closing the distance between them, he crouched down by her side.

"Hey," he said softly. "What happened?"

Lifting her tear-stained face, she launched herself into his arms.

"Josh is gone," she said through her tears. "I went on the Ferris wheel, and he didn't want to go, so he waited for me. And when the ride stopped, I couldn't find him. I've called and called, and he doesn't answer. I tried your phone too at first. When you didn't pick up, I didn't know what else to do."

Lucky felt some measure of relief as Aidan's arms closed around her. At least, she wasn't alone anymore—and he'd be able to help her find Josh. She knew he would.

Drawing away from him, she sniffed. "It's my fault. I shouldn't have left him alone. I had the amulet and the statue." She paused as she indicated her backpack. Then, her eyes again filling with tears, she added, "I just never thought anything could happen to him. It didn't even occur to me that they'd take him."

"Did you see anything? Anything at all?"

"That's just it. Mostly I haven't seen anything out of the ordinary today. When I was up on the Ferris wheel, though, I concentrated, and I could see that some of the people here had wings, and a few—a handful maybe—had leathery ones. But even then I didn't think Josh was in any danger—not until he wasn't there, and I couldn't find him, and he didn't answer my calls."

"Okay, come with me," Aidan said, as he stood and drew Lucky to her feet. "You and I are going to my place. I'll contact Zeke and Malachi—and we'll find Josh. I promise."

Lucky was stunned to discover that Aidan lived in one of the ritzy high rises you could see from Lake Shore Drive. She had never dreamed she'd ever get to see inside one of them. As the elevator carried them higher and higher, she wished she were there under better circumstances.

They exited at his floor, and after unlocking the door to his condo, he held it open for her. She gasped as she stepped through the door. The entire wall across from her was made of windows, reaching from floor to ceiling and looking out over Lake Shore Drive, Navy Pier, and the expanse of Lake Michigan. Drawn like a moth to flame, she crossed the light marble floor on her sneakered feet.

"Make yourself comfortable," Aidan called, his voice and the sounds of his boots on the tiles receding as he walked away from her down the hallway. "I'm going to get in touch with Malachi and Zeke."

When Lucky was able to tear her eyes away from the spectacular view—which was *way* better than the one from the Ferris wheel—she looked curiously around the room. She was surprised to find that the large luxurious space was very nearly empty. Behind her, facing the window, was a black leather sofa fronted by a glass-topped coffee table. A small ebony wood bar topped with a half-filled bottle of some kind of liquor and an empty glass sat against the small side wall between the windows and the hall down which Aidan had disappeared. The only other item of furniture in a room that stretched well back from the single sofa was a black baby grand piano.

No, there was something else. Against the other side wall was a medium-sized wooden chest, with its lid open and a blanket and various items that looked like cat or dog toys spilling out of it. As she gazed at the chest, wondering who—or what—the toys belonged to, a pointy, whiskered nose poked from under the edge of the blanket. The nose was attached to a masked face, which along with two small sable paws, preceded the rest of the long, narrow body of the creature as it squirmed out of the toy box. Seeing Lucky, the animal faced off against her and began hopping from side to side, making sharp chattering noises.

"She's a friend, Harley," said Aidan, who had emerged from the hallway.

Shrugging off his jacket, he crossed back over the expanse of floor to hang the garment in a cleverly disguised closet near the entry door, before turning his steps toward the liquor cabinet. He splashed some of the liquid from the half-filled bottle into the empty glass and lifted it to his mouth, half-emptying it with one drink. As he caught Lucky's wide-eyed stare, his expression took on a touch of defiance.

"Do you want something to drink?" he asked in a voice that was a little rough around the edges. "I think I have some club soda—and there's water."

Her voice subdued, Lucky requested club soda.

Her eyes followed him into the spacious kitchen that was separated from the huge living room by a granite-topped bar. Suddenly, she felt ill at ease with him. Here in his own space, which, except for the presence of the ferret, seemed to Lucky quite cold and barren, Aidan was like a stranger to her.

After a few seconds, she heard him pouring the club soda, and then she heard the soft sound of a cabinet door opening and the spill of something dry into a metal bowl. Apparently, that was ferret kibble, since at the sound, the little animal who had chattered at her trotted into the kitchen, emitting eager squeaks.

Returning from the kitchen, Aidan handed her a tall glass of club soda.

"I talked to Zeke," he said, in that unfamiliar rough-edged voice. "He'll contact Malachi, and they'll let us know when they find out anything." He gestured toward the sofa, adding, "Might as well have a seat. It could be a while."

Aidan seated himself on one end of the sofa, propping one booted foot against the opposite knee, and Lucky perched uneasily on the sofa's other end. Turning toward him, she saw that he was jogging his lifted foot up and down, and she wondered if he was as uncomfortable as she was.

"Isn't there anything we can do?" she asked.

He shook his head. "Malachi will find him. Provided he has the right information, there's very little Malachi can't find."

"Will he use the birds?" Lucky asked, mostly because she couldn't think of anything else to say.

"Perhaps. Or he may use magic. Malachi is a man of many talents."

When he finished speaking, Aidan raised his glass to his lips and drained the remaining liquor. Uncrossing his legs, he leaned forward to place the empty glass on the table, then, resting his elbows on his knees, he turned toward Lucky.

"I wish," he began, and then stopped as he looked down at his hands. After a moment or two, he began again, "I wish I could promise you that he'll be okay." The eyes he turned toward Lucky were haunted. "I want to tell you that, that he'll be fine, that there's no need to worry. But I can't. I've seen…" His voice broke, and he paused a moment before continuing, "things I pray you never have occasion to see."

Lucky's hand rose to her throat, and she choked back a sob. Then, standing abruptly, she set her glass down on the coffee table, starting at the sharp clink of glass on glass. She wrapped her arms around herself and walked over to stare unseeing out the window. She didn't realize she was crying until she felt the chill on her face as the tears began to evaporate.

Glued to his seat, Aidan watched Lucky as she stood at his window. She was so quiet and still, not making a sound. What had possessed him to say such a thing to her? Sure, it was the truth, but did she really need the truth right now? No, what she needed was the comforting words he hadn't been able to provide. He raked a hand back through his hair. He didn't know how to comfort her. Not this time. He just kept remembering his mother and what had been done to her. He wanted to go to the girl, to put his arms around her, but given what he'd just said, he feared she would push him away.

After a few moments, he found he could no longer bear her stillness. Moving as quietly as he could on the tiles, he stepped up beside her and rested his hand between her shoulder blades. When she didn't pull away, he applied enough pressure to turn her toward him and then slid his other arm around her. She came into the embrace without resistance, but it was several moments before she unwrapped her arms from around herself to slide them around his waist. Feeling her relax against him, Aidan hugged her a little closer, his hand stroking over her soft, dark curls as he pressed her head against his chest. Her hands flexed on his back, and he tucked her head beneath his chin, tightening his arms around her to pull her as close as possible.

They stayed that way for a long time, with him holding her as she had earlier held herself. When she pulled back just enough to look up at him, he drew his thumb across her cheekbones to wipe away the dampness of her tears.

Then it seemed the most natural thing in the world to lower his head toward her. He paused with his mouth just millimeters above hers. If she wanted to pull away, she could. He felt a surge of satisfaction when she moved a tiny bit closer. Closing the remaining distance, he pressed his mouth to hers. Her lips were soft and warm, and he could taste the salt of her tears. When he felt the flow of new tears against his lips, he released her mouth to press little kisses on each of her cheeks, catching the salty drops with his lips and the tip of his tongue.

Lucky held on to Aidan as her knees went weak. She had wanted him to kiss her, but she had never imagined it would feel like this, his mouth somehow firm and soft at the same time, and tasting slightly smoky from the liquor he had been drinking. Her emotions were overwrought as it was, and the sweet slide of his lips on hers caused a fresh batch of tears to flow down her cheeks. When he began kissing them away, she was sure she would have fallen but for the support of his arms. She could hardly breathe. She slid her hands up his back, feeling the hard muscles flex beneath her palms as he tightened his arms around her, lifting her until only her toes touched the floor. She sighed into his mouth as his lips settled on hers once more.

"Pardon the interruption."

The dry voice rolled into the room like a desert tumbleweed, causing Lucky and Aidan to shoot apart. Reflexively, Lucky wrapped her arms around herself again, trying to hold on to the heat of Aidan's body as long as possible.

"Hello, Zeke," Aidan said, pushing a hand through his golden curls as his breathing steadied. "Any luck?"

"I see that I don't need to ask the same of you," the long-haired Cherub responded with dry amusement, causing hot color to flood Lucky's cheeks. Then he nodded and added in a serious tone, "Yes, Malachi is ever resourceful."

Turning to Lucky, he continued, "Your cousin was in the Crystal Garden, unconscious, stretched out on one of the benches. He's suffered a blow to the head and likely has a concussion. He'll need to be monitored for the next several hours."

Zeke looked toward Aidan once again as he asked, "Shall we bring him here?"

"Yes," Aidan nodded. "As you well know, this place is warded against everything but you—and a select few others. He'll be safe here."

"Excellent. I'll pass that on to Malachi, and he will be here shortly with Josh. In the meantime," he fluttered his hand at them as his form began to fade, "please continue as you were."

Lucky blushed, and Aidan scowled at the empty spot where Zeke had stood. Then turning to her, he said, "I hope you're okay with Josh coming here. It's safer for both of you here than at your apartment."

"That's fine," she replied. "How long will we have to stay?"

"I don't know. At least overnight, long enough to make sure Josh is okay."

She nodded, saying nothing.

"I'll go make up the guest bed," Aidan said, and turning, disappeared down the hall.

This time Lucky followed him. The hallway, she found, was even barer than the living room. No rug, no occasional tables, no pictures on the walls. A small frown had knitted between her brows by the time she followed Aidan through the farthest door. The guest room seemed a bit more lived-in, if only because of the thick Oriental rug that covered much of the floor. Mostly a deep red, with touches of ivory, gold, blue, and green, the rug brightened the room, adding a warmth that seemed lacking in the rest of the condo.

Turning from the closet with a stack of sheets in his hands, Aidan looked surprised to see her standing in the doorway.

"I thought I could help," she offered.

"Thanks," he replied, tossing the sheets onto a chair near the bed.

He delved into the closet again to come out with a blanket and comforter. Neither of them spoke as together they spread the fitted sheet over the bed. Then Lucky slipped the pillows into cases, while Aidan tucked in the top sheet and blanket. As they both worked the comforter into place, Lucky wondered if offering to help had been a good idea after all. She already had a stomach full of butterflies because of what had happened between them such a short time ago, and looking at him across the bed made the little winged creatures fly around even more furiously, knocking themselves against her stomach walls. She cast about for something to say, but all she could think about was how it had felt to be in his arms, pressed against his body.

She was literally saved by the bell. As they finished tucking the comforter around the pillows, the doorbell rang, alerting them that Malachi had arrived with Josh. Aidan hurried from the room to buzz them in, with Lucky following behind him at a slower pace.

When the two men entered the room, Lucky restrained herself from rushing to Josh. Her cousin was leaning on Malachi, and his face was pale and drawn with pain. As Aidan led them down the hall to the guest room, she contented herself with following behind. She could talk to Josh after he was off his feet and more comfortable. When he was stretched out on the bed, she perched gingerly beside him holding one of his hands in both of hers.

"How are you feeling?" she asked softly.

"My head hurts." Josh's voice was thin. "My whole body aches."

"I'll get some ice," Aidan said, already on his way out the door. In a few minutes, he returned with a bag of frozen peas and a towel, both of which he handed to Lucky before dropping into a chair in the corner of the room.

After wrapping the frozen veggies in the towel, she placed the bundle on the goose egg that had risen on the side of Josh's head and positioned a couple of extra pillows to hold the ice pack in place. When she was sure it wasn't going anywhere, she settled back down on the bed beside Josh and took his hand again.

"Can you tell us what happened?" Aidan asked.

Josh started to shake his head and then grimaced in pain. "I don't know what happened." He paused for a moment, as if searching his memory, before he continued, his words quiet and uneven. "One minute I was watching Lucky go round in that god-forsaken Ferris wheel, then the next thing I knew, this guy"—he gestured weakly toward Malachi—"was half-carrying me out of the Crystal Garden."

Malachi was leaning against the window sill, one ankle resting on the other and arms crossed over his chest. As he had been the first time Lucky had seen him, he was dressed all in black. This time his garments appeared to be made of a soft matte leather, studded with myriad straps, buckles, and pockets that seemed meant for weapons of various shapes and sizes. He had yet to say a word since he had entered the apartment.

"Does Zeke have any tricks up his sleeve to jog his memory?" Aidan asked.

Malachi lifted his shoulders in a shrug. "There are things he can try." His voice was deeper than Lucky remembered. "But I would suggest waiting until tomorrow, to give the young man some time to recover." He uncrossed his ankles and stood, adding, "If you no longer need me, I have another battle practice to lead."

Aidan rose with him, and together they left the room. Lucky could hear the murmur of their voices, Aidan's mellow baritone alternating with Malachi's dark bass, but she couldn't make out what they were saying.

She lifted her hand and brushed the curls back from Josh's forehead. "I'm so sorry," she whispered.

His hand tightened on hers. "Lucky, what's going on?" Josh asked, a hint of puzzled anger giving strength to his voice. "Who is Malachi anyway? And why did he bring me to this place—which I gather belongs to Aidan? Why were you here?"

"When I couldn't find you, and you didn't answer your phone, I—called Aidan. Malachi's a—friend of his."

"Not good enough," Josh answered, looking at her through narrowed eyes.

She nodded. "I know," she said. "I'll tell you more later. Right now, you should probably rest."

"Fine, be that way." Josh's response was short, but the sigh he released as his eyelids fluttered closed sounded relieved.

Lucky remained on the bed beside him, holding his hand, until his slowed breathing indicated he'd fallen asleep. Then she carefully disengaged her hand from his and, kicking off her sneakers, curled up in the chair which she had moved closer to the bed.

Hearing Aidan's footsteps in the hall, she looked up to see him standing in the doorway. At his gesture, she rose and moved out into the hall to join him. Stepping off the deep pile of the red rug, she felt the chill of the marble floor tiles through her thin socks.

Gesturing for her to follow, Aidan moved down the hall toward the living room, past what appeared to be a large well-appointed bathroom, and stepped into what Lucky assumed was his bedroom. She hovered in the doorway, looking around, as he entered and pulled open a drawer.

Like the rest of the apartment, the room was decorated sparely, but Lucky was relieved to see two framed pictures on top of the dresser. The larger of the two was a black-and-white photograph of a woman sitting at a piano. She was turned slightly away from the instrument, looking toward the photographer, but one hand rested on the keys as if she had been interrupted in the middle of a piece. Long light-colored hair fell forward over her shoulders, framing a delicately beautiful face alight with love as she smiled into the camera. The smaller picture was in color and showed the same woman, her arms around a boy with messy golden curls, who looked to be about eleven years old.

"My mother," Aidan offered.

"She's very beautiful," Lucky said.

"Yes," he responded, "she was."

"Will you tell me what happened to her?"

He looked at her for a moment before responding. "Someday, maybe. Not tonight."

He handed her the clothing he had taken from the drawers, a couple of t-shirts and a pair of sweats. "For you and Josh. I thought they'd be comfortable for you to sleep in."

"Thanks." Lucky felt a hint of warmth in her cheeks at the thought of sleeping in his shirt.

"I have to leave soon, to meet the rest of the band and get set up for tonight's show. You'll be okay here while I'm gone. It's true, what I told Zeke. After my mother's death, we made sure to protect this place with every ward and spell imaginable. Only Zeke, Malachi, and Kev can pass freely through the wards without my permission."

"Kev?" Lucky asked.

"That's right," Aidan said, his lips quirking upward, "you haven't had the pleasure, have you? Kev—Kevin—is my brother, half-brother really. We share a father."

"The Seraph," Lucky's words were half statement and half question.

"Yes," Aidan replied, offering no additional information.

"Thanks again for these," Lucky said, indicating the clothes in her hands, as she moved toward the door.

Waving away her thanks, he began tugging his t-shirt over his head. "I should get changed," he said, his voice muffled by the cloth.

Lucky's jaw dropped as the shirt lifted, exposing the well-defined muscles of his abdomen and chest. With a little squeak, she turned and fled back down the hall to the guest room.

A few minutes later, she heard Aidan's booted footsteps leave his room and move down the hall away from her, and she followed him into the living room.

"Do you have something I could read while you're gone?" she asked.

"There's a bookshelf in my room," he said, shrugging his leather jacket on over his long-sleeved black t-shirt. "Help yourself to anything you want." After a pause, he added, "And if you get hungry, there's food in the fridge. Some spaghetti, sandwich stuff, leftover pizza. Help yourself to that too. It's nothing spectacular, but it'll keep you from starving."

"Thanks," Lucky said. Although the thought of food held no appeal at the moment, she appreciated the offer.

Walking over to her, Aidan lifted his hand to her cheek for a moment before letting it fall back to his side. "I'll be back as soon as I can," he said, and then he was out the door. She heard the click as it locked behind him.

Lucky went back to the guest room and, feeling guilty for doing so, shook Josh awake and showed him the t-shirt and sweats Aidan had found for him to wear. When she was sure he was okay to stand and move about on his own, she left him to change, taking the partially thawed peas with her. After replacing the bag of peas in the freezer, she went in search of reading material.

Inside Aidan's room, she paused for a few moments before the photographs on his dresser. His mother looked carefree and happy in both of them, her face filled with love. In the larger, black-and-white photo, that love was directed at the photographer; in the smaller one, it was directed at the boy in her arms, a young Aidan, his overlong, messy curls glinting in the sunlight. Lucky picked up the picture and held it in her hands for a moment as she studied the boy. He was attractive even then, his boyish features showing signs of the handsome young man he would become; otherwise, he looked much like any other well-loved eleven-year-old boy. His mischievous eyes were as yet innocent of the dark knowledge that haunted those of the Aidan she knew. With a sigh as much for her own loss of the carefree days of childhood as for his, she set the picture back in place.

The reason she had not noticed the bookshelf before was because it sat along the same wall as the door in which she'd been standing, not because it was small and inconspicuous. Quite the contrary, it covered almost the entire wall. Apart from a few scattered items—small art objects or icons—its shelves were filled almost exclusively with books. Modern paperbacks mingled with ancient-looking, leather-bound tomes, subject matters including popular and classic literature of various genres, science, history, politics, art, and mythology. Lucky was curious about the leather-bound ones with no titles indicated on the spines. Lifting a tall, thin volume from the shelf, she opened its cover to a frontispiece that displayed an engraving of a demonic-looking figure. Flipping to the title page, she found that the book was written in a language she couldn't even recognize, let alone read.

When her next few selections proved to be similar, she decided she was intrigued enough to look through them even if she couldn't read them. She chose a stack of volumes of various sizes and shapes, which she carried back to the guest room. Finding Josh asleep, she picked a book from the stack and curled up in the armchair next to the bed. She passed over the pages of text quickly, since she couldn't begin to decipher it, but she paused to study the drawings and engravings. Showing scenes peopled with figures both winged and unwinged, they depicted a world that had become increasingly familiar to her over the last few days. With a change of scenery and clothing, the people represented could have been among those she had seen on the bus, on the street, or in the lecture hall at the OI. She found the pictures somehow reassuring. Many other people had known about this world over the years. She wasn't alone.

Her thoughts were pulled from the book and its drawings when Josh spoke her name. Setting the book aside, she turned to find him tugging at the covers, trying to pull them more closely around himself.

"C-cold," he stammered. "S-so c-c-cold."

Lucky jumped up and ran to the closet where Aidan had gotten the linens and comforter. She grabbed a stack of blankets from one of the closet shelves and, hurrying back to Josh, covered him with all of them. A couple she left folded double in an effort to warm him up. Tucking the blankets in around him, she laid a hand on his forehead and found it to be oddly cold, the polar opposite of feverish. She tucked the blankets in a little more tightly, and promising to return with something warm for him to drink, she headed down the hall to the kitchen.

Filling the tea kettle with water, she set it on the stove to heat while she rummaged through the cupboards. Her search finally turned up a couple of boxes of tea and some hot chocolate mix. After locating mugs, she put a teabag in one and the contents of one of the hot chocolate packets in another. When the water started to boil, she switched off the burner, removed the kettle from the heat, and tipped some of the boiling water into each of the two mugs. Careful so as not to spill the hot liquid, she made her way back to the guest room and her cousin.

Josh was not shaking as badly as when she had left him. The blankets seemed to be helping, but his forehead still felt cold to the touch. Keeping the blankets tucked around him as much as possible, she helped him sit up.

"Tea or hot chocolate?" she asked.

When he chose the chocolate, she held the steaming mug to his lips, so he could sip the hot beverage. By the time he had consumed half the mugful, his shivering had subsided, and he was able to remove one hand from under the blankets to hold the cup for himself. After Lucky handed him the mug, she closed her fingers around his cool ones for a moment, pressing them against the mug for warmth. When she released his hand, he lifted the cup and drained the rest of its contents before handing it back to her.

"Thank you," he said, tucking his arm back under the blankets. "I don't f-feel like I'm turning into an ice cube anymore."

"Do you want the tea too? Or more hot chocolate?"

He shook his head as his eyes began to close. "I think I'm going to go back to sleep now."

Lucky helped him keep the blankets around him as he lay back down, and she remained beside him until he fell asleep. Then she went back to the chair, where she retrieved her book.

She had looked through the pictures in two of the books and was halfway through a third, when her attention was arrested by one of the pictures. Against a dark background stood a winged man, with lines radiating from him indicating rays of light. Arching from his shoulders were wings like those of a dragon, and around his neck was a familiar medallion. As she studied the picture, Lucky's hand rose to clasp the amulet resting against her chest. Turning the page, she found another drawing of the same man surrounded by figures of darkness, bat-winged and owl-eyed. They seemed to be looking to the shining man with the amulet as a kind of leader. A few pages later was a detailed drawing of the amulet itself, the dragon outlined against the background of a fiery sun. She wished she could read the language in which the book was written. She wanted to know what it had to say about the amulet and the man who was shown wearing it.

"Ah, the Light-Bringer's Medallion," said a familiar resonating voice, startling her so she nearly dropped the book.

Lucky turned to face the long-haired Cherub who had materialized beside her, asking irritably, "Don't you ever knock, or give some kind of warning before you just show up?"

Zeke's eyes held a mischievous glint as he replied, "I find the element of surprise frequently puts me in a position of advantage."

The angel wasn't wearing his usual conservative academic khakis and sports coat, but was dressed in loose flaxen pants and a long tunic that fell to just above his knees. His feet were bare.

"Don't you feel guilty about invading people's privacy?"

He cocked his head as if he were thinking for a moment, then he shook his head. "No, not really."

Giving the argument up as a lost cause, Lucky registered the words he had spoken when he materialized into the room. "The Light-Bringer's Medallion?"

"Yes." Zeke pointed at the drawing on the page in front of her. "That is what the drawing you are looking at depicts. And," he added more slowly, his eyes looking from her rising hand to the pendant it moved toward, "what you are wearing around your neck. Aidan gave that to you?"

She shook her head, "He *loaned* it to me. He said it would protect me and would help him find me if I was in danger."

She looked down at the amulet cradled in her hand. "It was how I called him today when Josh—"

As she said her cousin's name, she glanced at the bed, where he was moving restlessly beneath his blankets. By the time she had reached the bed, he was throwing off the covers. Her hand brushed his when she reached to help him, and she was stunned by how warm it felt. Placing her hand on his forehead, she discovered that his skin was now as hot as it been cold earlier.

"Something's wrong with him," she said. "Something more than a concussion. A while ago he was freezing, and now he's burning up. I don't know what to do for him."

Before she had finished speaking, Zeke had taken one of Josh's hands in one of his own and had placed his other hand on her cousin's forehead. As Lucky watched, pale blue light began to emanate from both of Zeke's hands, and then the two puddles of light began to grow and extend, reaching fingers toward each other, until a shaft of light stretched from Josh's hand up his arm to his forehead. When Zeke released that hand and reached across Josh's body to clasp his other hand, the light extended from one hand to the other. Soon, a third shaft of light covered Josh's remaining arm, so that the upper half of his body was encompassed by a glowing triangle of blue light. Zeke removed his hands from Josh's body, uttering a word that Lucky felt more than heard, that was less sound than the sense of the tumblers of a lock rolling into place. She gasped as light shot from each corner of the triangle to meet in its center, where it formed a fist-sized, glowing ball—located almost directly over the place where Josh's heart would be.

Zeke watched Josh for a moment in silence and then turned toward the door, gesturing for Lucky to follow. He paused at the doorway to direct a last glance toward her cousin as he said, "He'll rest easier now."

The angel moved silently down the hall on his bare feet, and Lucky tried to make as little sound as possible as she followed him into the kitchen. She watched as he filled the teakettle she had emptied earlier and, locating cups, dropped teabags into them. After he'd poured the hot water over the tea bags, he motioned for Lucky to lead the way into the living room. He waited while she took a seat at one end of the couch, and then he handed her one of the steaming cups before seating himself at the other end.

"I find tea a helpful aid to conversation," he said, breaking the silence.

Lucky took a small sip of the hot beverage and then asked, "What did you do to Josh?"

"It's a kind of healing spell. It will help him to rest and seek out what ails him. It cannot heal him, but it will alleviate his symptoms and keep the problem from progressing until we can find out what is wrong with him."

"Keep it from progressing?"

"The spell will hold your cousin in a kind of stasis until we can determine what is at the root of his symptoms. We do not know who took him or what they did to him. He could have been injured by magic or by some kind of poison or venom. Sambethe is looking into the matter."

Lucky frowned. "How did she know to do that?"

Zeke smiled. "I've been monitoring him. I knew before I arrived that something was amiss."

"Oh," Lucky said. "Thank you."

Zeke inclined his head.

Touching the amulet around her neck, Lucky directed another set of questions toward the angel. "Who is the Light-Bringer? And why did you seem so surprised that Aidan let me wear this?"

Zeke studied her in silence for a few moments before he answered. "It might be best if you asked Aidan those questions."

"But I'm asking you," Lucky responded.

Zeke sighed. "Very well. Does the name 'Lucifer' mean anything to you?"

"Lucifer? You mean like the devil?"

"Not exactly, no. But in your traditions, yes, the two terms have become synonymous."

"Our traditions.... Wait. Aidan said something about us getting the story of the battle in Heaven wrong. I think he called Lucifer the 'Light-Bearer.'"

"Yes. The name 'Lucifer' means 'Light-Bearer' or 'Light-Bringer.'"

"So, the Light-Bringer's Medallion is Lucifer's medallion?" Lucky frowned as she looked down at the pendant. "This belonged to Lucifer?"

Zeke nodded.

"Aidan said his father gave it to him...." Lucky's voice trailed off as her eyes widened. "Aidan is—Lucifer's son?"

Again, the angel nodded.

Lucky felt as if the ground had just dropped away beneath her feet. Given everything that had happened in the last few days, she supposed she shouldn't be surprised, but learning that Aidan, on whose couch she was currently sitting, who sang with the most beautiful voice she had ever heard, who had danced with her and rescued her from the dark shadow creatures and their creator, and whom she had held and kissed only a couple of hours before, was the son of the being many regarded as the father of all evil was a little more than even she was expecting.

"But Aidan isn't evil," she said in a small voice. Raising her eyes to meet Zeke's, she added, "Is he?"

"No." Zeke shook his head. The light glinted off the paler streaks in his honey-wheat hair, and for a moment Lucky saw his face flicker, as bull, eagle, and lion were superimposed over human. Simultaneously, she saw the transparent forms of multiple pairs of wings moving around him. As he continued to speak, the images faded away, and she could see only Zeke sitting before her. "No, Lucky, Aidan is not evil. Nor, for that matter, is Lucifer. He certainly has his faults, but he is not evil incarnate."

"That's good to know," Lucky said, her voice still subdued.

Zeke reached out a hand and patted her on the knee. His hand felt much heavier than it looked, and Lucky thought she could feel the slightest brush of feathers against her cheek. "Go get the book you were looking at when I barged in, and I will tell you a story."

CHAPTER 16

Lucky walked quickly down the hall to the guest room. Retrieving the book from where she had dropped it beside the chair, she stood looking at her cousin wrapped in lines of glowing, blue light. What had she gotten them into with this unexpected newfound ability of hers? What had been done to him because of her?

"I'm so sorry, Josh," she said quietly, before turning and heading down the hall to rejoin Zeke.

Handing the book to the angel, she sat down beside him, so she could see the pages as he turned them. He stopped at the page that showed Lucifer surrounded by dark figures.

"The myriad beings that have come to be called angels do not all hail from the same place—nor do those referred to as demons. That which you call Heaven could more accurately be called the Heavens, plural. The same is true of what you call Hell; there are a number of those as well—Hells, Dark Realms, or Underworlds. The beings who live in the Heavens and the Dark Realms have been in existence for millennia, and humans have considered many of them—many of *us*—to be deities, gods, at one time or another. As you might imagine, this has led to rivalries and power struggles. Rituals and acts of worship possess a kind of inherent magic that can both bestow and enhance power. Being worshipped can be a heady thing, and in the early days, some simply reveled in the power of it all rather than acknowledge any sense of responsibility they might have to those who chose to worship them. Needless to say, battles ensued—on earth as well as in the other realms. Humans frequently bore the brunt of the struggles, victims of 'natural disasters' visited upon them by their 'gods.'"

Zeke's last words were tinged with a weary bitterness. He was silent for a time, his expression distant and haunted. Then, with a sigh, he continued, "In an effort to create some order and end the needless sacrifices of human life, a group of angels banded together and chose a ruling council, a body of four that became known as the Metatron. The Metatron established a kind of military unit they called the Forces of Light, which was headed by the Archangel Michael. Together, the Metatron and the Forces of Light were able to unite many of the warring individuals and factions into a collective now known as the Angels of Light. Another group united under the leadership of a being called Ba'al-zebul. In the spirit of opposition as much as anything else, they chose to call themselves the Angels of Darkness."

Zeke paused again and, glancing at Lucky's empty teacup, said, "I think I'd like another cup. What about you?"

When he had refilled their cups and returned to his seat beside Lucky, Zeke resumed his story. "The major difference between the two groups was how they viewed their relationship with and responsibility to humans. To simplify matters, let's just say that the Light felt a greater sense of responsibility toward humans than did the Dark, who had far fewer qualms about using humans for their own pleasure and power." He directed a sad smile toward Lucky. "You can probably guess where this is headed."

"War?" she asked.

He nodded. "Inevitably. Suffice it to say that the Angels of Light eventually won, though many were lost on either side."

At Lucky's look of surprise, he interrupted his narrative again to answer her unspoken query. "Oh, yes, we can be killed. While we recover quickly from most injuries, some methods are quite effective. Beheading, for example, when performed with the right kind of weapon, usually does the trick."

Lucky refrained from comment, and Zeke continued, "After the Light defeated the Dark, the Metatron sent one of their own—Lucifer, the Light-Bringer—to govern the Dark and keep them under control. Knowing that he would be in danger from those unwilling to submit to the rule of the Light, the Archangels created for him an amulet of protection, one that would both heighten his powers and help to shield him from harm. That amulet came to be known as the Light-Bringer's Medallion."

"And this is that same medallion?" Lucky asked. "The one the Archangels created for Lucifer?" Her voice trembled, as did the hand with which she held the amulet. "I shouldn't be wearing this."

She reached up to unfasten the clasp at her neck, but Zeke stayed her hands. "Lucky, Aidan gave the amulet to you for the same reason the Archangels originally made it for Lucifer, for protection. He would not have done so if he did not think it necessary."

"Why did Lucifer give the medallion to Aidan?"

"That question you will have to ask Aidan. It is not my story to tell."

Lucky accepted his answer without argument and asked another question. "If Lucifer went to the Dark at the Metatron's orders, how did he end up in battle with Michael?"

"Though Lucifer was sent to rule the Dark, to teach them the ways of the Light, he was as changed by them as they were by him. As he began to better understand the Dark, he came to believe the restrictions the Light sought to impose were more stringent than necessary. Never one to meekly submit to orders, he then took it upon himself to act as a kind of Dark ambassador with the Metatron, who did not appreciate what they saw as his rebellion against their authority. It was not long before they began to consider him an adversary. The conflict escalated until, under the Metatron's orders, Michael ousted Lucifer from the Heavenly Council. He retained his position of authority over the Dark, but he was banished from ever returning to the Heavens. A new ambassador—known as *Ha-Satan*—was appointed to serve as intermediary between Lucifer and the Metatron. As you might imagine, it was—is—not an easy role to fill. Over the years, many have tried, some have succeeded, and none have held the position for long."

"Is that how *you* fit into all this?" Lucky asked.

"As *Ha-Satan*? No, that is a role I have never been called on to perform, though my position is somewhat similar," the angel replied. "While Lucifer and the Metatron—with the aid of *Ha-Satan*—have managed to maintain an alliance over the years, that alliance is uneasy at best. In addition, there are still those among the Dark who view Lucifer as something of a usurper, a kind of colonial ruler. As you can see, there are limitless potentials for conflict, and the resulting battles were—and are—often played out in the earthly human realm. There are those of us who felt bound to watch over and protect humanity from the fallout. We are most often referred to as the Fallen."

"Why 'Fallen'?" Lucky asked.

"Because in our choice to live among humanity, we have 'fallen' to earth from the Heavens. Those who originally coined the term viewed our choice as nothing short of folly. Some sense of responsibility to the humans who deified us was one thing, but a desire to understand and protect all humans—to live among them and become, in some ways, like them—was another altogether. Many could not understand the impulse. Others of us saw it as both an obligation and a privilege. So, living among humans and doing what we can to protect them puts us, like *Ha-Satan*, in the unenviable position of trying to keep the peace between Light and Dark."

"And if that fails?"

"Then we fight, which is why I mentioned the importance of battle training to you the other day. Your friend Aidan is the new second in command of the Forces of the Fallen. Malachi is his Captain."

"And who do you fight against, the Light or the Dark?"

"That can vary, depending on the specifics of the conflict. Since we are caught between the two, we often end up fighting against both sides. But we usually have supporters on both sides as well."

"Does that mean Aidan could be fighting against his father?"

"No. Lucifer has great loyalty to the Fallen and, in some ways, considers himself one of us. That has created some problems for him with the more extreme of those among the Dark. And it is the extremists on both sides that we have to worry about. Unfortunately for all of us, the new Metatron consists entirely of extremists, who, against all odds, seem to have a large number of followers among the Angels of Light. There are plenty who do not accept their views, who long for a peaceful alliance and do what they can to sway the powers that be. Sadly, they are not making much headway these days. And as the extremists among the Light grow stronger, so do those among the Dark, the intolerance of one feeding that of the other. Thus, the uneasy alliance between the Metatron and Lucifer is looking very shaky indeed. If it disintegrates, I fear all-out war between the two is inevitable."

As the angel finished speaking, Lucky heard the door to the hallway open. The sound of Aidan's footsteps preceded him into the room.

Removing his jacket and tossing it aside, Aidan looked from Lucky to Zeke and back to Lucky, before he turned, stepped over to the piano, and retrieved the bench. Placing it at an angle to the couch, he seated himself astride it, muttering as he did so, "I really have to get some more furniture."

Harley, who during his master's absence had made himself scarce somewhere, trotted in from the hallway and, placing his front paws on Aidan's knee, twitched a whiskery nose at him, requesting a pat.

Aidan complied, asking, "What brings you back, Zeke?"

Before the angel had a chance to respond, Aidan cast a sharp glance at Lucky. "How's your patient?"

Lucky shook her head. "Not so good."

"Which," Zeke picked up the sentence, "is why I'm here. His condition has worsened, but we are not sure of the cause. I have placed him in a healing stasis while Sambethe investigates."

"I see," Aidan replied. His face took on a guarded expression as, tilting his head toward the book in Zeke's lap, he added, "And in the meantime, you've been regaling Lucky with tales of my father?"

"Just an old one, Aidan," Zeke responded gently. Lucky was reminded of him saying the story of how Aidan had obtained the amulet from Lucifer was not his to tell.

"How was the show?" she asked, to change the subject.

"Good. We had a good crowd," Aidan answered, shifting his position so Harley could climb into his lap. "I wasn't able to keep my focus a hundred percent on the show, what with worrying about Josh—and you." Shooting Lucky a teasing glance, he added, "It's probably a good thing you weren't there. I would never have been able to keep you from drawing out my Gift with that untrained power of yours."

Now, he had Lucky's full attention. "What do you mean by that?" she asked. "You never have explained to me what happened that night."

"I'm going to check on our patient and see if Sambethe is making any progress," Zeke said, rising to his feet. "As if either of you will even notice I'm gone."

Aidan acknowledged the angel's departure by shifting from the piano bench to the spot Zeke had vacated on the couch, cuddling the ferret against him as he did so. Once he was reseated, Harley settled into an upside down circle on Aidan's lap, exposing his tummy for a rub.

"Well?" Lucky prompted, moving so she faced Aidan.

"You know what happened," he replied.

"No, I don't," Lucky said. "I know the wings I saw were real and not a lighting effect. But I don't know why your voice did what it did to me."

Aidan took a deep breath before he answered. "Every angel and every Naphil, like me, has a Gift. It sort of comes with the wings. Zeke, for example, has the Gift of Knowledge, which is what makes him an excellent teacher and mentor. It enables him to know all he needs to know to lead and coordinate the efforts of the Fallen—and to pass that knowledge on in ways other than the conventional. You remember how you felt as if you were unable *not* to attend his lecture? Part of his Gift is that he can compel people to do things when he deems it necessary for their knowledge or protection. Mine is the Gift of Song. When I sing, I can do things with my voice—make people feel things, believe things."

"No wonder Icarus is so popular!" Lucky exclaimed. "That's cheating!"

Aidan shook his head. "I don't use my Gift when I sing with the band; I just sing. But it was different with you. Something about you drew the Gift out of me, and I couldn't hold it back. I was able to lessen the effect, but I couldn't stop it. Just as you were able to block it, but only in part."

"I thought I could sense you trying to hold back once you saw the effect your voice was having on me. But it all seemed so crazy, I wasn't sure what was real and what I might have imagined." The relief Lucky felt at learning it had all been real was audible in her voice.

"I have to say," Aidan responded, "I've never experienced quite the same thing before. No one else has ever drawn my power like that. At first, I thought you might be one of the Dark, someone who knew who—what—I was and was trying to expose me. Then when I saw how shocked you looked"—he cast a teasing grin in her direction—"I realized you were probably a budding Sensitive, and a clueless one at that."

Lucky grimaced. "Yeah, well, I'm a little less clueless now. And I'm not altogether sure that's a good thing."

"Trust me," Aidan said, losing the grin. "If you have any place in this world, cluelessness is a definite disadvantage."

After a brief silence, he asked quietly, "Zeke told you who my father is?"

Lucky nodded.

"And are you okay? With me? Did he tell you enough to reassure you that Lucifer's not what you might think he is?"

Lucky hesitated only a moment before she nodded again. "It's strange—finding out the traditional story is wrong. But I don't know that I ever believed it all anyway. And in the last few days, pretty much everything I thought I knew has been turned upside down. But I trust Zeke—and you." As she spoke, she held her hand out toward him.

"Thank you," he whispered, catching her hand in his and rubbing his thumb across her knuckles.

"Malachi and Sambethe are on their way," Zeke announced as he reentered the room. "Sambethe believes she has isolated the source of your cousin's malady, Lucky, in a toxin of Dark origin. She's bringing an antidote. Aidan, you must give her permission to breach the wards."

Aidan released Lucky's hand and stood. Walking to the center of the room, he raised his arms above his head as if invoking the heavens. He spoke a few words in a lilting language Lucky did not recognize, and as he spoke, his great wings shimmered into being and spread wide in the emptiness of the room, white feathers dusted with gold glistening in the light. Lowering his hands to shoulder height but keeping his arms outspread, he opened his mouth and—sang, but what he sang was unlike any song Lucky had ever heard before. The voice that issued from between his lips was haunting and utterly inhuman, sounding of wind and leaves, feathers and stones, fire and water, and the rattling of bones and the flow of blood through the veins.

As he sang, a network of golden threads appeared all around the walls and ceilings and floors, an intricate and beautiful pattern, the nodes where one thread connected with one or more others shining more brightly, like tiny beacons. The notes Aidan sang altered somehow, but Lucky couldn't say just how, and the network of golden threads shifted ever so slightly, the change in pattern almost imperceptible, something she could only glimpse through the corners of her eyes.

Then the song disappeared into silence, and the golden pattern melted into the walls and ceilings and floors. Lucky turned wide eyes back to Aidan to see his wings fading as he lowered his arms.

"Good," Zeke said, turning on his heel and heading back down the hallway. "They'll be here at any moment."

"Do all wards work like that?" Lucky's soft-voiced query dropped into the moment of silence following the angel's departure.

Aidan shook his head. "All wards are different, shaped by the ward-maker's powers and Gift. Mine are coded to my voice and are activated and altered by song."

"Not just any song," Lucky muttered.

"No, not just any song," Aidan chuckled. "Only by a very special song, that only I can sing."

The sound of voices heralded the arrival of the expected guests, and they followed the sound down the hallway to the bedroom where Josh lay encased in Zeke's healing spell. When they entered the room, they found Zeke and Sambethe on either side of the bed, looking down at the patient. Malachi had taken a position off to the side, where he was out of the way but could still keep an eye on the proceedings. He gestured to Lucky and Aidan to stay back as well, and they took up positions similar to his own on the opposite side of the room.

At a softly spoken word from Zeke, the ball of light over Josh's heart faded away as the shafts of light that met to form it retracted back into the corners of the glowing blue triangle that surrounded his upper body. Placing a hand on each of Josh's hands, Zeke spoke again, and then he moved one hand to Josh's forehead. With his final utterance, he removed his hand from Josh's forehead, and the shafts of blue light retracted into the hand which was still placed over one of Josh's. When Zeke lifted that hand, Lucky could see the light flickering around his palm for a moment like tiny blue flames, before it was snuffed when he closed his fingers into a loose fist.

As soon as the spell was removed, Josh opened his eyes and began to move about restlessly, muttering under his breath.

"Bring me a glass of water, please, Aidan," Sambethe requested.

When Aidan returned with the water, she placed the glass he handed her on the bedside table, and removing a small brown bottle from the folds of her pale gray robes, she added several drops of its contents to the water. The liquid in the glass turned a deep crimson.

Zeke repositioned himself so he could hold Josh still while Sambethe held the glass to his lips. At the first taste, Josh turned his head away as if to refuse more, and some of the liquid dribbled from the corner of his mouth down his chin. It looked thick, and its crimson color made Lucky think uncomfortably of blood. Sambethe and Zeke overcame Josh's protests with a combination of coaxing and threats of dire consequences should he refuse the treatment, and within a few moments, he managed to drain the glass, despite his evident aversion to the medicine. Settling him back down in the bed, Zeke once again placed a hand on his forehead. Speaking a few words in a soothing tone, he passed the hand slowly over Josh's face and allowed it to hover for a moment over his heart. When Zeke stepped away, Josh appeared to be in a deep slumber.

"Good," said Sambethe. "We will need to administer the antidote twice more throughout the night. When he wakes in the morning, he should be fully recovered."

Acknowledging her words with a silent tilt of his head, Zeke turned to Malachi. "Thank you for your help, Malachi. You may leave now if you wish, as I am sure you have plenty of other matters to address. Sambethe and I will tend to the patient."

The tall, dark man responded to the angel's words with a slight bow. Then he gave a silent nod to Lucky, and directing a "See you tomorrow, Commander," at Aidan, he faded from sight.

Zeke turned to Aidan and Lucky. "You should both get some sleep. Don't worry," he added, catching and holding Lucky's gaze with his own. "We will take good care of Josh."

"Thank you," she said, directing the words to both Zeke and Sambethe.

The long-haired woman responded only with an almost imperceptible tilt of her head, but Zeke put a big hand on Lucky's shoulder, giving it a comforting squeeze.

Then Aidan took her arm and led her toward the door. He didn't speak until they'd reached the door to his room. Drawing her to a stop, he said, "You can have my bed. I'll sleep on the couch. Just let me grab a few things. There's an extra toothbrush on the bathroom counter. Make yourself at home."

"I can take the couch," Lucky protested, as he moved to the closet to retrieve sheets and a blanket.

"Really, I don't mind," Aidan responded, snagging a pillow from the bed and adding it to the stack of bedding in his arms. "I probably won't sleep that much tonight anyway, and there are things I need to discuss with Zeke. You've had a long and difficult day. You'll be more comfortable in here."

When she started to protest again, he silenced her by placing a finger on her lips. "Shh, I insist." Moving his hand to cup her cheek, he leaned down and placed a gentle kiss beside her mouth. "Sleep well. You know where to find me if you need me."

Before Lucky could think of anything to say, he had left the room.

She stepped through the door behind him—and then collided with him when he unexpectedly turned back toward her. The pillow and blankets fell to the floor as his hands came up to catch her shoulders. She made a breathless sound, half laugh and half gasp.

"Sorry," he said softly, on a chuckle. She felt his breath against her face. "I meant to tell you that you might want to lock the door, unless you don't mind a sleeping companion."

"What?" she said, as she felt the tell-tale color staining her cheeks.

"Harley likes to snuggle under the covers. He may sleep on the couch with me, but since he's used to the bed, he's likely to want to be in here. If you don't want him to climb in bed with you, you'd better lock the door. He can open it easily if it's not locked."

"Oh," she said, still a little breathless, since he hadn't stepped away from her. "I don't mind if he comes in."

"Alright. I just thought I'd warn you," he said, trailing a fingertip down the side of her face from her temple to her jaw line.

"Consider me warned," she breathed.

The amused light in his eyes heating to something warmer, he slid his finger across her cheek to trace the outline of her lips. "Maybe you should lock the door anyway," he whispered. Then, leaning closer, he pressed a quick, hard kiss on her mouth, which was already tingling from the touch of his finger. She barely heard his quiet "Good night" over the pounding of her heart.

CHAPTER 17

Lucky's sleep was troubled and dream-filled, one disturbing image fading into the next.

She saw Josh on a bed encased in a blue triangle of light, but instead of resting peacefully, he tossed and turned, his skin pale, with dark circles around his eyes. "I'm so sorry, Josh," she said, and the eyes he turned on her glowed crimson. She was in a shadowy cavern surrounded by dark-winged creatures with golden, owl-like eyes, the only light radiating from the dragon pendant around her neck. She was in Aidan's arms, kissing him, his great wings arching up and around them as he held her, but she was dragged from his embrace, screaming his name, as he was pulled away from her. She was flying, her own massive wings beating the air, Aidan and Malachi on either side of her and countless others behind them, a growing sense of urgency rising within her as they sped forward.

When she finally awoke, the sunlight filling the room assured her it was morning, which meant she had slept through the night, but she was as tired as if she hadn't slept at all, and a dull pain throbbed in her head. Harley was nowhere to be seen, and the unlocked door was still closed, so he must not have tried to enter the room during the night. Slipping out of the t-shirt Aidan had loaned her, she pulled on the clothes she had worn the day before. After dragging her fingers through her hair and securing it in a ponytail at the back of her head, she opened the bedroom door and stepped out into the hallway.

She walked slowly down the hall to the living room, where the bright light shining in the floor-to-ceiling windows had her blinking rapidly. It seemed to her as if the room was filled with tiny golden lights and miniature rainbows, and the effect was dizzying. She grasped the back of the sofa to support herself. Finding, to her relief, that the sofa was empty, the stack of bedding beside the coffee table the only indication that Aidan had slept there the night before, she slid onto the seat, leaning her head back and closing her eyes against the dazzling play of light and color.

"Happy birthday."

Zeke's resonant voice was as soft as Lucky had ever heard it, its usual evocation of ocean waves replaced by something less substantial and more cloud-like. She was grateful; she had a sense that his normal tones would have increased her dizziness and the slight roar in her head exponentially.

"Thanks," she whispered, opening her eyes to look at him.

She almost closed them again as the rush of images hit her. Zeke was standing before her, long hair falling over his shoulders, dressed in his usual khakis and button-down shirt, with royal blue Chuck Taylors on his feet. But he was also something huge that towered over her, simultaneously bull, lion, eagle, and man, faces shifting, bodies blurring from one to another, all surrounded by three pairs of wings, which were the dusky blue of a twilight sky.

"Is this what you really look like?" she asked.

Zeke, in all his forms, shrugged. "It is what I really look like to you at this moment."

He spoke more loudly this time, and the sound rolled over her, wave-like. But instead of feeling overcome by it, she felt herself lifted and borne upon it, supported and somehow taken out of the din in her head.

"How is Josh?" she asked.

"Your cousin is well. When he awoke this morning, he was completely recovered, just as Sambethe promised. I made a few attempts to retrieve his memories of the time between when you left him at the Ferris wheel and when Malachi found him in the Crystal Garden, but to no avail." The angel, in all his multiple forms, frowned as he continued. "The memories are not blocked, and there is no blank expanse to indicate that they have been erased. His memory simply stops at the point where you got on the ride and starts again when he woke to find Malachi with him. It is as if the time between the two events did not exist for him at all."

"I want to see him," Lucky said, beginning to rise from the couch.

Zeke stayed her with a gesture. "He is no longer here. Aidan has taken him back to your apartment. Aidan and I agreed it would be best if your cousin did not remember his time here either. When he leaves him, Aidan will trigger a suggestion I planted in Josh's mind, and he will remember nothing of yesterday's odd events. He will instead remember a pleasant day spent with you at Navy Pier, followed by a restful night at home."

"Is that safe?' Lucky asked. "What if whoever hurt him comes after him again? Shouldn't he be prepared instead of having no knowledge of it whatsoever?"

"We did not leave him unprotected, Lucky. He will be monitored for a time, to ensure his safety. Even so, I do not think he faces further danger. I believe yesterday's attack was meant as a message—and though Josh was the unfortunate victim, he was not, I think, the intended target."

"A message?"

"For the Fallen. Someone wants us to be aware that they know we have taken an interest in you—and that they are watching you as well."

Lucky scowled. "Sounds like I need to start battle training as soon as possible."

"Perhaps that would be wise," Zeke chuckled.

"Oh," Lucky gasped suddenly, remembering the messages she'd left when she'd called Josh the day before, "Josh's voicemail…."

"Taken care of," Zeke reassured her. "Aidan said you'd mentioned calling Josh. He found your cousin's cell phone in his pocket and deleted your messages."

The angel held out a hand to help her to her feet. "Now, shall we see about finding some birthday breakfast?"

As it turned out, Zeke spent the entire day with Lucky. After dropping Josh at home, the angel informed her, Aidan was going to work with Malachi and the rest of the troops. Included in the substitute memories Zeke had given Josh was one of Lucky telling him she had made plans with friends for the day, so he wouldn't be worried about her. At some point, she would have some explaining to do with Mo, but she would cross that bridge when she came to it. In the meantime, she was free to spend the day with Zeke, experiencing the full force of her powers and beginning to experiment with them, to learn to master them rather than letting them master her.

They started with breakfast at a downtown diner, because, Zeke said, the crowd of patrons would provide Lucky with ample opportunity to work with her expanding senses.

The trip to the restaurant alone made Lucky feel as if she were living in a very different world from the one in which she had grown up. She knew she was in Chicago; she recognized the buildings, the sounds of traffic, and the hustle and bustle of the city. Yet, at the same time, everything was different. There was a new depth to her vision as she looked around her.

She still saw myriad tiny rainbows and spotlights when the sun shone brightly. When it dipped behind a cloud, they disappeared, but only to be replaced by dancing shadows in various shades of gray. The lights and shadows played around the buildings, even the cars and buses, so that it looked as if over the brick and stone, the metal and glass and plastic, each was wrapped with an intricately patterned quilt of light and dark. And the people! Each person was enveloped in a field of colored light, each one unique, with threads of gold and black mapping their bodies. Lucky felt a little as if she were looking behind the scenes of a play she had been watching all her life, seeing how the parts came together to make the whole. She felt dizzy from it all and held on to Zeke's supportive arm to keep from losing her balance.

"In time, you will learn to turn it off and on at will," the angel assured her. "You will find it impossible to sustain such heightened perception for an extended period of time. The human mind—even for a Sensitive—is not designed to comprehend so much at once."

Inside the restaurant, Lucky was not as distracted by the play of light and shadow, which was much less pronounced indoors. But she was more than compensated for the loss by an increase in her awareness of the people—well, beings—around her. The restaurant was crowded, and she and Zeke had to wait for several minutes before they could be seated. Lucky gazed around the room, dazzled by the colors and patterns surrounding the patrons, a number of whom didn't seem to be human. She noticed that many of those non-humans seemed to know Zeke. Some offered him small nods in greeting, while others glanced at him with recognition, but looked away without acknowledgement.

Before Lucky could ask Zeke for an explanation, a waitress, menus in hand, arrived to show them to a table. As Lucky scanned the menu, her stomach growled, and she remembered that she hadn't eaten anything since lunch the day before. When the waitress returned with glasses of water, Lucky was ready to order. She asked for French toast and grinned when Zeke requested pancakes with *two* sides of bacon. While they waited for their food, he asked her to look around the room and describe to him what she saw.

She described the auras of the humans and the shadows of wings she saw on those she assumed to be angels, as well as the sharp-looking teeth and stony looking skin she saw on others. And she asked Zeke about the beings who had nodded to him and those who seemed to know him but refused to acknowledge him.

"There are very few among the Fallen or the Dark who do not know me—or at least know of me. Some I have taught or fought beside. Others I have had to—discourage—from certain behaviors. One consequence of being a leader is that one seldom pleases everyone."

When their waitress arrived with the food, Lucky smiled at the eager way Zeke reached for one of the many slices of bacon on his plate, as well as his evident enjoyment of it. Then she tucked into her own breakfast. She was surprised to find that her sense of taste also seemed to be heightened. The flavors of the food were more intense, more layered, than they had ever been before. While they ate, Zeke continued to ask her questions about what she perceived in the room. She responded, asking occasional questions of her own. By the end of the meal, she felt not only physically fed, but as if she also had a great deal to digest mentally.

As they left the restaurant, Zeke asked if there was anything special she would like to do for the rest of day. Lucky started to respond that she had no real preference, but then she realized that it had been several days since she had seen G-Ma. Her grandmother had been a part of all her birthdays, and despite the change in G-Ma's health and the corresponding change in their relationship, Lucky didn't want this year to be an exception. She explained the situation to Zeke, who agreed to accompany her on a visit.

Lucky was pleased to find that the play of light and shadow did not seem as dizzying to her now. She was able to adjust her visual focus so that the flickering colors and patterns no longer interfered with her vision, but appeared as a kind of screen overlaying what she had formerly thought to be the "real" world.

Not having to direct single-minded attention to her vision and her balance on the way to the 'L' stop, she told Zeke about her last visit with G-Ma. She remembered her grandmother's half-finished painting and her final warning. Now that she knew Zeke and had learned about the conflict between the Angels of Light and the Angels of Darkness, she found both even more ominous than before. But when Zeke asked her to describe the painting, she was able only to give a vague impression of massing gray clouds. She couldn't begin to capture the sense of menace the image had conveyed. She wondered if G-Ma had made any progress on the piece in the last several days.

After entering the 'L' station, Lucky swiped her card to go through the turnstile before turning to offer it to Zeke, who was behind her. With surprise, she saw that he was already sliding a card of his own through the reader.

"You take the 'L' often?" she asked, a smile tugging at the corners of her lips. "I wouldn't have thought that would be necessary for you."

The Cherub returned her smile with twinkling eyes. "I do indeed usually prefer—less conventional—methods of transportation," he assented, looking down at the card in his hand. "But as it is sometimes necessary to travel with others who do not share my abilities, I find it useful to keep one of these on hand."

While they waited for the train to arrive, Lucky found herself again grasping Zeke's arm, as this time the sounds threatened to overwhelm her. There were so many people, and the din of their conversations combined with the noise of the trains entering and leaving the station and the blaring trumpet of a street musician, all magnified and expanded, made her want to cover her ears. It was all too much. When she began to *see* the sounds in waves and zigzagging lines of color, she thought she might pass out. Closing her eyes didn't help; the colored lines and waves were still projected against the insides of her eyelids. Zeke's other arm went around her for support as she gasped and leaned against him.

"I completely understand now why you had to get to me before today," she muttered into his shirt. "I can't imagine how I'd have handled this on my own."

"The worst will pass in a moment," he told her.

His words proved to be true. In a short time, the clamoring din receded, and instead of cacophony, Lucky could now hear layers of sound, nuances, notes, and cadences that were previously outside her range. Everything she heard now had more texture, sounding like Zeke's voice had always sounded to her, as if it were substantial, multi-dimensional. The additional lines and waves she saw settled into another visual screen through which she viewed the world.

By the time their train arrived, she was steady enough to release Zeke's arm and step aboard. But that didn't mean she felt confident of her ability to balance on a moving train. Instead of standing inside the doorway, she moved farther into the car to find a couple of empty seats.

Settling into the seat next to her, Zeke said, "You are doing quite well, you know. You are a very strong young woman, Lucky. I have known many Sensitives who were nearly traumatized by the sudden onslaught of their abilities, even with adequate preparation and support. You, on the other hand, are integrating them very quickly. I believe Sambethe may have been right about you."

"Right about me how?"

Zeke held her gaze with his own for a moment before he spoke. "She said that you will somehow play a decisive role in the coming conflict between Light and Dark. She does not know how or why, only that it is so."

Lucky felt a chill running up her spine as he spoke. His resonant voice was so serious and his eyes, looking into hers, so grave.

"I'm not sure I'm ready for that kind of responsibility just now," she said.

Zeke's gray eyes softened as the corners of his mouth turned upward. "You don't have to be. Now, we are just going to visit your grandmother, and you are going to continue receiving and integrating your new powers. Whatever the future holds, we will face as it comes."

The rest of their ride was completed in silence, as was the walk to the assisted living facility. When Lucky lifted her hand to open the door, Zeke stopped her, offering to shield himself with a glamour that would hide him from everyone but Lucky, if she preferred. That way he wouldn't interfere with her visit with her grandmother, but would be there to provide support if her powers threatened to overcome her.

Lucky thanked him, but refused the offer. "I would like you to meet G-Ma," she said, "and I'd like her to meet you."

They found G-Ma in her room, working on the still life she had said she wanted to paint when Lucky last visited. At their entrance, she looked up from the painting to smile absently at Lucky.

"Hello, dear," she said, before directing her focus back to her artwork.

Pasting a bright smile on her face, Lucky returned her grandmother's greeting and leaned down to kiss her cheek. She was used to G-Ma getting caught up in her work—when she was in the middle of a project, she would often forget to eat—but before the onset of Alzheimer's, no matter how involved she had been, her eyes had always warmed when she looked at her granddaughter. Now, such moments of connection were hit or miss. Lucky wondered if she would ever get used to her grandmother looking at her with the same smile of general affection she directed toward relative strangers, if she could ever accept that the deep bond that had always existed between them was now tenuous at best. She knew that as the disease progressed, G-Ma would recognize her less and less often. Lucky could only hope that the pain she felt at the lack of recognition would also lessen over time.

"G-Ma," she said, placing a gentle hand on her grandmother's back. "There's someone I'd like you to meet."

At Lucky's words, her grandmother again looked up from her painting, and Lucky introduced her to Zeke. When he took one of G-Ma's hands between both his own, she greeted him with a smile several times brighter and warmer than the one she had directed at her granddaughter. Lucky felt the difference as a swift, sharp stab to her heart. The intensity lessened quickly, but she knew the dull ache that followed would be of much longer duration.

While Zeke asked her grandmother polite questions about her painting in gentle tones, Lucky looked around the room to see if she could locate the unfinished canvas from the week before. As her eyes scanned over the corner farthest from the direct light coming through the windows, she gasped in surprise and fear.

Crouched in the shadows was a creature she had never laid eyes on before in real life, but it was familiar to her from the engravings in the book she had examined with Zeke the evening before. In form, it looked very much like a gargoyle, with dark, bat-like wings of leathery skin stretched over a frame of sharp, curving bones. Its body appeared to be covered with short, fine fur of deep sable, and its eyes were large and golden, with huge pupils, like those of an owl. If it were to stand at full height, rather than crouching as it was now, its head would probably reach the base of her sternum. Somewhat to her surprise, Lucky could detect no malice in its expression, although the curiosity in its gaze seemed to be mingled with suspicion. Since she didn't know how G-Ma would react if her granddaughter suddenly started talking to the corner of her room, Lucky offered the creature a tentative smile and lifted her hand in a wave by way of greeting. Looking at her with deepened curiosity, it inclined its head in acknowledgement.

Lucky turned away from the creature to find that Zeke was watching her, observing her reaction to the being in the corner. She noticed that neither Zeke nor the creature greeted the other, but she sensed no animosity between them. Instead, they seemed to be so familiar with one another that no acknowledgement of recognition was required, as if each regarded the other as an expected and necessary part of the order of things. When Zeke moved toward the door, gesturing for her to follow, she complied. G-Ma had returned to her painting and was paying them no attention, and Lucky was grateful for the opportunity to satisfy her curiosity.

As soon as they had stepped into the hallway, Lucky whispered to Zeke, "It's like the creatures in the book, the ones with Lucifer in the cave. Is that a Dark angel?"

Zeke nodded. "One of them, yes." He spoke in an equally soft voice. "There are as many different kinds of Dark angels as there are Light."

A few steps farther down the hall, he added, "Look around you, Lucky. What do you see?"

Lucky's eyes widened as she gazed down the expanse of the hall. A creature like the one she had seen in her grandmother's room was standing in each doorway. A group of them had gathered at the hallway's end. Spinning around, she saw more of them in the doorways of the rooms behind her.

Every pair of round golden eyes was directed toward her. She stopped moving, heartbeat accelerating, as they came toward her from all directions.

She looked to Zeke, unsure if she wanted advice or protection, only to discover that the Cherub was nowhere to be seen. He had disappeared, and the mass of Dark angels was almost upon her.

CHAPTER 18

As the creatures closed around her, Lucky fought back a wave of panic. That internal battle intensified as the ones closest to her began pulling at her arms and legs and clothing. She struggled against them, trying to push them away, but her efforts were futile against so many. In a matter of seconds, she was on her knees. Kneeling put her at much the same height as the creatures surrounding her, and she could no longer see over their heads. Her panic now flavored with the added zing of claustrophobia, she gasped for breath as the creatures moved inward.

It took a few minutes for her to realize that they had stopped tugging at her limbs and clothing once her knees were touching the floor. Now, they were stroking her with clawed appendages that were somewhere between human hands and paws. When one of them placed gentle fingertips on her cheek, she responded in like manner. After an initial jerk of surprise, the creature accepted her touch. Their dark fur, Lucky discovered, was as soft as it looked.

Sliding its hand from Lucky's cheek to her neck, the creature slipped a claw under the gold chain she wore and tugged the amulet from beneath her shirt, so it lay exposed against her chest. The golden medallion caught the light, and the creatures drew back from her. None of them had made a sound, but Lucky sensed the wave of surprise that moved through the group. Those nearest her drew those behind her to positions where they too could see the amulet. They all gazed at her in silence, their eyes moving from her face to the Light-Bringer's Medallion and back.

Lucky knelt before them, unmoving, not knowing what to say or do. As she contemplated whether or not she should try to explain that she was just borrowing the amulet, she felt a circle of heat against her breastbone. She looked down and could not contain a cry of surprise. The medallion was glowing, the light and heat it radiated gathering intensity by the second. When it had increased to the point where she felt as if the pendant was burning her skin through the thin material of her shirt, the light exploded outward, enveloping her and all the Angels of Darkness around her.

For what was probably only seconds, but which seemed to Lucky like an eternity, she hung suspended in a sphere of heat and light, surrounded not only by the creatures from the hallway of the assisted living facility but by a myriad of other Dark angels, as varied in form as the nocturnal creatures of the earth, all looking to her for something she did not, could not, understand.

Then she crashed back into the reality of the tiled hallway, her chest tight from holding her breath. Releasing the air from her lungs, she sat back on her heels as her torso fell forward over her bent knees. Half-rising, she sucked in a lungful of fresh air and saw that the owl-eyed Dark angels were retreating from the hall, going back into the rooms from which they had come. She remained kneeling on the floor for a few breaths. Then she tucked the medallion back beneath her shirt with an unsteady hand and rose to her feet.

Retreading the short distance to her grandmother's room, she stepped through the door to be greeted by another curious sight. G-Ma was sitting in her rocking chair, head back and eyes closed. Perched on her left shoulder was the Dark angel, shrunken to the size of a small house cat. Its little hands moved over G-Ma's hair in soothing motions as it brushed its soft-furred cheek against her own. Zeke stood by G-Ma's art table, examining the still life as if nothing out of the ordinary had occurred.

"What happened to you?" Lucky hissed at him in a stage whisper. "Did you really think that was a good time to just up and disappear?"

Lifting a finger to his pursed lips to silence her, the Cherub strolled toward the door. It was all Lucky could do not to punch him in the arm. How dare he shush her after he'd abandoned her like that? She stalked along beside him in silence as they made their way down the hall and to the exit. Once they were back on the sidewalk, she turned on him accusingly, "Will you answer me now? Why did you leave me alone back there?"

"I did not leave you alone. I removed myself to a place where you could no longer see me, but I never lost sight of you."

"Why didn't you want me to see you?"

"Because you needed to face them alone. You weren't in any danger."

"I didn't know that!" Lucky huffed. Then, more calmly, she added, "Did you know what was going to happen?"

Zeke shook his head. "I know the Still Ones well enough to guess that they would want to touch you, to get a sense of you. They can perceive the truth of a being's motivations and impulses through a simple touch. I assumed that, realizing you could see them, they were curious about you. What happened with the Light-Bringer's Medallion was as much a surprise to me as it was to you. Now, I wonder if that was part of what drew them to you, if they sensed its presence on you."

"What did happen with the medallion? Why did it do that?"

"In all honesty, I am not quite sure. I may have the Gift of Knowledge, but there are plenty of things that I don't know. I've never heard of the Light-Bringer's Medallion doing anything of this sort. It clearly gathered a great deal of power to itself and then forced that power outward. To what end remains to be seen."

Lucky wondered if Zeke had seen what she had when the light exploded out from the medallion. Had he seen her surrounded by all the Angels of Darkness? Surely, if he had, he would have mentioned it, wouldn't he? Tired of asking questions that led nowhere, she kept those to herself, inquiring instead about the Dark angels.

"Tell me more about the—what did you call them?—Still Ones?"

"They are the gentlest of the Dark angels, and they are drawn to those who have suffered deep and irreversible personal losses. They feed on the feelings of pain and grief and loss."

"That doesn't sound gentle at all," Lucky interrupted. "It sounds horrible."

"It may sound so, but it is not," Zeke said. "It is a mutually beneficial relationship. The Still Ones feed through touch. Each caress, each stroke, takes away some of a sufferer's pain or grief. Even if a being is not consciously aware of a Still One's presence, its touch will provide comfort. Sometimes people like your grandmother, for whom the veil between this world and the others is less tangible, even recognize that a Still One is with them—though they would not be able to describe what it looks like or call it by name."

"But if they feed on suffering, doesn't that make them want to cause pain, to create more—food—for themselves?"

"There is enough suffering in the world already to provide for all the Still Ones many times over. They do not create suffering, although they can, in some way, be said to benefit from it. They are not gluttonous for suffering; they feed to provide a service. When a being no longer requires that service, their Still One will move on to someone else who does."

"Like part of a cosmic ecosystem," Lucky said.

Zeke nodded. "Exactly so."

"Speaking of food," Lucky remarked, as they entered the 'L' station, "will you be ready for lunch by the time we get downtown? That little encounter in the hallway took a lot of energy, and I think I need to refuel."

After lunch at a coffee shop, Lucky and Zeke spent the afternoon wandering around downtown Chicago. They strolled through Grant Park and passed an hour or so in the Art Institute. Lucky found that her new powers increased as the day progressed, each of her senses becoming heightened, so that the world she perceived was more layered in every way. The enhancements in her vision and hearing were followed by an increase in her senses of taste and smell and touch. By afternoon's end, her brain was so saturated with sensory information she couldn't begin to process it all.

At her suggestion, they walked to the lakeshore, since she thought being away from the people and noise of the city streets, looking out over the expanse of Lake Michigan would give her some much-needed mental space. Her assumption was at least partly correct: the presence of fewer people and the decreased street noise did provide a little relief. Still, the natural world itself offered an overabundance of sensory input. She could hear, as well as see, the dancing display of sunlight and cloud reflections on the water, a duet of alto and tenor, spiked with soprano notes and supported by the occasional rumble of baritone or bass; in addition to seeing and hearing the lapping of the water against the shore and the ruffling of the lake's surface in the light wind, she could also feel the flow of liquid over rock and concrete, the texture of the ripples on the surface of the water. Even the gentle touch of the breeze on her over-sensitive skin, especially when she could not only feel it, but hear it, taste it and smell it, was too much.

She closed her eyes and covered her ears with her hands to shut it all out, only to find to her dismay that she could now see the fine pattern of veins on the insides of her eyelids and hear the pounding of her own pulse and the rush of blood through her veins.

"I can't take this anymore, Zeke," she cried out. "Make it stop. Please make it stop."

"I am afraid I cannot."

"You're an angel! You must be able to do something."

"I cannot take this away from you, Lucky. Only *you* can control your powers. Concentrate as best you can—I know it is hard—on the deepest place inside yourself. Find the stillness, the calm, there. See yourself there; hear the quiet; feel the absence of touch."

"I can't!" she sobbed. "There's too much, too much noise, too much light, too much—everything!"

"Yes, you can." Zeke's firm, resonant tones cut through the cacophony in her head like a shaft of light in a dark room. "Because you must. Now concentrate. And breathe."

Lucky took a deep breath, and another, and another, trying to move inward, trying to concentrate on a place of stillness she wasn't sure she possessed. After several more breaths, she gradually relaxed the clasp of her hands over her ears and let her arms fall to her sides. She could still hear all the things she heard before, but she discovered that if she didn't try to shut the sounds out, didn't fight them, they didn't seem so intense. In breath, out breath, in breath, out breath. She could still see the pattern of the veins in her eyelids, but she was able to observe them instead of feeling as if she must somehow block them from her sight. In breath, out breath, in breath, out breath. The air brushed her skin, and though its touch was not as delicate as it had seemed only the day before, she no longer felt as if it were trying to wound her.

Going further inward as she continued to breathe deeply, she found herself in a dark cave, sitting cross-legged in a pool of soft light. Images, sounds, tastes, smells, and textures flickered, throbbed, burst, wafted, and slid over the cave's velvet black walls. Looking around, she paused on an image of water. Concentrating on it, she took it in—and the image brought with it the smell of rain, the clean taste of fresh water, and the chill of the lake against her skin, as well as the sound of lapping waves. Releasing that image, she chose the tactile sense of sunlight on skin, which brought not only warmth, but a flooding of yellow-gold light, the trill of birdsong, and the remembered sweetness of summer peaches.

One after another she chose, learning that she could turn the senses on and off at will, choosing to experience as much or as little as she wanted of any of them at any one time. After a while, she chose none at all and simply rested in the soft pool of light.

It was there that Zeke's voice found her several minutes later. "Good, very good."

The words circled around her, deep-voiced and warm, soft like the fur of her cats, and tasting of approval. "Now, come back."

Gathering herself, breath by breath, Lucky left the still, calm center and opened her senses to the world once again.

Sights, sounds, smells, flavors, and textures rushed over her. Taking another breath, she sank a mental taproot into that internal stillness and selected from among the myriad sensations clamoring for her attention only those she knew she could bear. Then, feeling more complete and capable than she had felt in her entire life, she opened her eyes and turned an exhausted but exhilarated face to her mentor. The smile he bestowed on her held all the warmth and radiance she could feel in her own.

"Bravo," he said, placing an arm around her shoulders and tucking her into his side. "Now, let's get you home."

"Home," Lucky discovered, really meant back to Aidan's, since Zeke did not want her to be alone until her birthday was officially over. Even though she had probably weathered the worst the day had to offer and come out on the other side triumphant, if exhausted, he deemed it best to remain with her until midnight. And since Zeke's presence in their apartment would, at best, cause Josh to ask uncomfortable questions about who he was and why Lucky was bringing him home with her and, at worst, could interfere with the memory switch Zeke and Aidan had pulled on him earlier, Aidan's seemed the more logical choice.

By the time they arrived at Aidan's high rise, Lucky was ready to call it a day and crawl into bed. When she greeted Aidan, a yawn escaped her, and making her excuses through another yawn, she headed down the hallway. She was hesitating outside Aidan's room, since that was where she had slept the night before, and she had left the t-shirt she'd slept in folded up on the bed, when she heard his boots on the tile.

"What's wrong?" he asked. "Do you need something?"

"I just...," she stopped, shaking her head. She couldn't tell him she wanted to sleep in his room and not the guest room. Now that Josh wasn't using the other bed, that's where she belonged.

"It's okay if you sleep in my room," he said, as if sensing her unspoken request. When she lowered her eyes, he added in a quieter drawl, "Trust me, I don't mind in the least."

Flushing, she lifted her eyes to meet his teasing, intensely blue ones. "It's just... Josh...."

"I know," he said, his tone and expression becoming more serious. "I wouldn't want to sleep in the guest room either if I were you." Then the flirtatious smile returned. "And I'm quite happy to have you sleep in my bed—again. I kind of like the idea of you tucked between my sheets."

She narrowed her eyes and tried to glare at him, but the effect was ruined by another yawn.

Aidan's flirtatious smile shifted to a grin. "I was going to ask you how today went, but you can tell me all about it later." Leaning forward, he dropped a light kiss on her forehead. "Get some sleep," he said.

As she stepped inside the bedroom and closed the door, Lucky listened to the sound of Aidan's footsteps retreating down the hallway and tried not to contrast that brotherly kiss he'd just given her with the embrace they had shared the evening before. Sure, he'd also flirted with her, but that didn't mean anything. It was best not even to think about him, she decided, discarding her clothes and pulling the borrowed t-shirt over her head. Unfortunately, it was difficult not to when she was wearing his clothes and sleeping in his bed.

But her last thought before sleep claimed her had nothing to do with Aidan. It was the remembrance of the sense of satisfaction and completeness that had filled her when she had stood at the lakeshore with Zeke, knowing she could master her own powers.

CHAPTER 19

Lucky was startled out of sleep by a moist nose poking into her ear. As she came fully awake, she also felt the pressure of two little paws, one on her head near her ear and the other planted on her cheek.

"Harley," she said, turning her head, "get off me."

She shifted over in the bed and turned on her side, so she could face the ferret. Harley was sitting back on his hind legs and looking at her. She could see his bright eyes glittering in the dimness that passed for dark in the city. She reached out a hand and stroked his soft fur. After a couple of minutes, he curled up in an upside down ball beside her.

Lucky lay there for a few more minutes trying to get back to sleep, but she was wide awake. A glance at the clock on Aidan's bedside table told her it was not quite midnight. She threw back the covers, careful not to disturb Harley, and slipping through the door which the ferret had left ajar, she padded down the hall toward the kitchen to get a glass of water.

About halfway down the hallway, she became aware of voices coming from the living room. Zeke and Aidan were still talking then. Feeling self-conscious, she glanced down at herself. Her legs and feet were bare, but Aidan's t-shirt was long enough on her to be a dress, so she decided it was foolish to turn around. She might as well get that glass of water after all. A few steps later, she stopped in her tracks, realizing that they were talking about her. She crept as near to the end of the hallway as she could without being seen and pressed close to the wall as she listened.

"Sambethe keeps insisting the girl should be Made Nephilim," Zeke's voice was a soft rumble.

"No!" Aidan responded. "Absolutely not. It's too dangerous. You know that as well as I do. I didn't ask you to help her survive the onset of her powers so she could be sacrificed to some misguided attempt at a Making. By all that's holy and unholy, Zeke, even Malachi…." Aidan's words trailed away, leaving the rest of the thought unspoken.

It was a moment or two before Zeke replied, and his voice was as quiet as Lucky had ever heard it. "And what happened during Malachi's Making was unprecedented, a direct result of his Gift. We could not expect anything similar to save Lucky."

"I was at the ceremony." Aidan's voice was subdued. "It was terrifying. He had to have been in so much pain…. And when he died…."

Lucky was puzzled by Aidan's words. Malachi *died?* But she had met him, spoken with him. What was Aidan talking about?

"I just wanted to get out of there," he continued, "but we had to stay for the full three hours—even though he was dead. They were getting ready to remove his body—and I was already scoping out the quickest path to the door—when the sigils on his back began to glow, and he started gasping for breath. Then those huge black wings of his appeared."

"The Making killed him, but his Gift brought him back," said Zeke.

There was a moment of silence, and then he continued, "I have asked him if he has a sense of whether or not Lucky would survive. He does not. He says his vision is clouded. Perhaps the girl's fate has already become too intertwined with his own, as it has with all of ours. Or, perhaps, since the subject of the question is a Making, it is too similar to his own past to allow clear vision. Whatever the cause, he sees nothing."

Lucky knew they were motivated by concern for her, but she still felt a sudden flash of anger at the fact that they were talking about her and whether or not she should go through this thing called a Making as if the decision were theirs, and she had no say in the matter. No one had even mentioned it to her. Wait, Sambethe had said something about it, hadn't she? In the lounge at the OI, after she had spoken about the Destroyer and unwinding threads in that strange sing-song voice. Lucky had asked what she meant, and Sambethe had said she, Lucky, must be Made Nephilim. The words had meant so little to Lucky at the time that she had forgotten about them until now. But Zeke obviously hadn't. Zeke had been talking to Sambethe about it all this time. Zeke. Her anger found its focal point. He had spent the entire day with her, and he hadn't said a word about this. Now, here he was talking it over with Aidan as if it had more to do with him than with her.

"I can't believe you!" she said, storming into the living room.

Two pairs of surprised eyes turned in her direction. Well, five pairs of eyes, since she could see all four of Zeke's faces. Staring into his gray human eyes, she continued, "Were you ever going to tell *me* about this? Ask *me* what *I* think? Give me enough information to make a decision about it myself?"

"How much did you hear?" Zeke asked.

"Enough to know you were talking about Making me Nephilim—as if you all have the right to decide what happens to me," she flashed back. Her eyes finding Aidan's, she added in a more subdued tone, "And I heard the story about Malachi."

"Then you heard enough to know how dangerous a Making can be," Zeke said. "You should not even be asked to consider it unless there is no alternative. The process could cost you your life."

Lucky shivered. Aidan picked up his blanket from the night before, which was still lying folded beside the couch, and held it out to her. Although she was unsure if her shiver was due to the chill in the air or the thought of losing her life at a Making, she accepted the blanket and draped it around her shoulders. When Aidan shifted positions to make room for her beside him on the couch, she shook her head and settled on the floor near his feet. Pulling her legs up under the blanket, she wrapped her arms around her knees.

"What exactly is a Making?" she asked, her anger forgotten. "How does it work?"

Zeke sighed, but he answered her question. "It is a ceremony in which a number of angels or Nephilim each bestow a portion of their powers on a human Sensitive. If the Sensitive survives—and many do not—then he or she will become a Naphil, no longer fully human, but part angel. Made Nephilim have the same powers as born Nephilim: superior strength, accelerated healing, wings—and a Gift. Each Gift is different, unique to the Naphil, and first manifests anywhere from three hours—as in Malachi's case—to several days after the actual Making."

"Why do people do it—if they know they may not survive?"

Again Zeke sighed. "Different reasons for different people. Some do it for the promise of power; some because they—or we—believe it is necessary to help our cause. Some do it to help someone they love."

"Why does Sambethe think I must be Made Nephilim?"

Zeke sighed yet again, this time heavily. "Lucky, please, could we not have this conversation at this time? I do not want to discuss this as long as there are other options."

"Zeke," Lucky's voice sharpened as she felt that flash of anger again. "I'm in this now, whether you like it or not, and you can't just exclude me from conversations or decisions, because you're afraid I'll be hurt. I need to know why Sambethe thinks I should go through the Making ceremony."

Aidan's hand closed on her shoulder. "I don't like this any more than Zeke, but I agree you have a right to know. Sambethe says she's seen a gathering Darkness—she calls it the Destoyer—that she says is unlike anything we've encountered before, and that could mean the destruction of—well, everything. And she says that you have to be Made Nephilim to help us defeat it."

"Then she must know that I'd survive the Making, right?" Lucky turned to look up at Aidan as she spoke.

The hand on her shoulder tightened. "You'd think. But it doesn't really work that way."

"The future is not fixed, Lucky," Zeke supplied. "Sambethe's visions show probabilities only. And she sometimes sees more than one. Yes, she has seen you as Naphil help defeat this Destroyer, but she has also seen you perish as a result of the Making."

"Oh." Lucky rested her head against her drawn up knees and leaned into Aidan's leg, which pressed against her side as he slid closer to her. "So, what do we do?"

"Look for another option," Zeke said.

Rising, he continued, "I have work to do—and I'm sure you both could do with some rest." He smiled at Lucky. "Or some *more* rest. It is now well past midnight, so it seems your birthday is over. You did very well today, Lucky. I could not have asked for more. Would you like me to take you home?"

"Don't worry about it, Zeke. I'll take her," Aidan offered, standing and helping Lucky to her feet. "I need to get out and clear my head anyway." Looking at Lucky, he added, "If that's okay with you?"

When she nodded, Zeke said, "That will make my trip a little easier, I suppose. I had thought we might start your training tomorrow, Lucky, but I think you deserve a day off. Let's postpone our meeting until Tuesday, shall we?"

As he finished speaking, his form shimmered, and he disappeared.

"Yeah, I guess he couldn't have done that with me, could he?" Lucky remarked.

Aidan chuckled. "Go get dressed, and we'll get you home another way."

After she'd pulled on her clothes and retrieved her backpack, Lucky met Aidan back in the living room.

"Do you want to take the motorcycle? Or," he raised his eyebrows as his wings appeared, arcing above his shoulders, "would you prefer to use a different method?"

Lucky's eyes widened, and a smile tugged at the corners of her mouth. "Really? You could fly me home?"

A grin stretched across Aidan's face as he nodded. Lucky laughed. A night flight through the city sounded like just what she needed. From the daylong sensory overload to the grimness of that conversation about Making, the day had been too intense by far. When Aidan held out his hand to her and gestured toward the door with a tilt of his head, she put her hand in his without hesitation.

They took the elevator to the very top floor of the building and then climbed a flight of stairs to the roof. The wind was strong, and Lucky clung to Aidan's hand. He had dismissed his wings for the walk through the building, but now they sprang from his back once more, opening and spreading wide.

"I don't usually do this with a passenger," he said, pulling her close. "Hold on tight."

Lucky wrapped her arms around his waist, below the point where his powerful wings ended at the base of his ribs, and did as he commanded.

His own arms pressing her close to his chest, Aidan flexed his wings and lifted into the air. Lucky cried out as her feet left the ground and then turned a laughing face to Aidan as she felt the wind blowing through her hair and the slight rise and fall of their bodies in rhythm with the beating of his wings. He grinned back at her, and she laughed again. Turning her head, she looked out over the city with all its lights bright against the night sky. It was magical.

"We can do this better," Aidan said in her ear. "Let go of me."

When Lucky looked down at the city far below them and gasped, he chuckled, but his words were reassuring, "Don't worry. I've got you."

Hovering in the air, he turned her in his arms, so that her back was to his chest. "This would be easier if you weren't wearing that stupid backpack," he muttered, "but we'll make it work."

Shoving the backpack as far to the side as possible, he wrapped his arms around her waist and then twined his legs with hers. "Now," he said, "you're not going anywhere. Just relax and enjoy the ride."

Then, with a powerful surge of his wings, he thrust them even higher into the air before leveling out, so that they were looking directly down at the city.

"It's so beautiful!" Lucky exclaimed. She had never imagined looking down on the skyline.

At her words, Aidan turned to circle back over the Loop, varying the elevation of their flight as they moved over and between buildings.

"What if someone sees us?" she asked, as he executed a turn mere feet from the windows of one of the skyrises.

"They can't," he answered. "We're glamoured. Someone might notice a slight smudge where we are, but no one will see us."

Angling them upward, he looped south.

"Show off," Lucky said, as he took a few dips and dives around the top of the tallest building.

He chuckled and then laughed out loud when a sharp dive caused her to scream. Still laughing, he urged his wings to a faster beat and headed out toward the lake.

"Oh!" Lucky sighed as they sailed out over the water.

The lake stretched black, ink blue, and gray beneath them, the moonlight painting flashes of silver on the water's undulating surface. She loosened her hands, which had been clutching Aidan's arms where they circled her waist, and spread her arms wide, as if to embrace the lake, the sky, the night, this experience. A smile spread across her face at the sheer joy of it all. When Aidan jokingly ordered, "Keep your arms and legs inside the vehicle at all times," her laughter bubbled over.

With small shifts of his wings, Aidan turned them in slow, swooping curves. Then he took them lower, so close to the water that the tips of his wings just skimmed its surface on the downbeat. He kept them just above the water for a long time, as his wings carried them south toward Lucky's home.

When they had almost reached the Point, Aidan lifted up from the water and flew into the city again, bringing them to ground in an alley a couple of blocks from where Lucky lived.

"Sorry about the touchdown location," he said, as he disappeared his wings, "but I don't want anyone to see us materialize out of thin air."

As his arms slid from around her, Lucky turned toward him. "Oh, Aidan, thank you," she said. "That was just—wonderful."

She shivered as the wind touched her back, surprised at how cool the night air felt now that his arms were no longer wrapped around her, and his body was no longer pressed against hers.

As if reading her thoughts, Aidan put an arm around her shoulders, tucking her against his side. "It was, wasn't it?" he said.

They walked the rest of the way to her building in silence. Lucky was aware of little except the warm weight of Aidan's arm across her shoulders and the brush of his hip and thigh against her with each step they took.

"Well, this is it," she said when they stood in front of the steps that would take her up and away from him.

Aidan remained silent as she stepped out from under his arm and pushed her hands into her pockets. Neither made a move to leave, the silence stretching between them. Then Aidan reached out a hand and lifted her chin with his fingertips. "I never did wish you happy birthday, did I?"

Lucky shook her head, her heartbeat accelerating.

Taking a step closer to her, Aidan lowered his head until his mouth hovered just over hers. "Well, then," he breathed against her lips, "happy birthday." Then he kissed her, soft and gentle and sweet.

When he moved away several moments later, Lucky felt somewhat dazed.

"So, sounds like you get tomorrow off?" Aidan asked, one corner of his mouth quirking upward.

"I guess so," she responded, hoping she didn't sound as breathless as she felt.

"The band has a gig tomorrow night. Since you couldn't make the last one, do you want to come?" When she nodded, he added, "I wonder if my voice will have the same effect on you now that you know what I am and what you're capable of."

Remembering what she'd told him the last time, Lucky grinned back at him. "I'm sure it will be very… moving."

He chuckled. "I'll pick you up about 8:00 then."

"I'll be ready," she replied, smiling up at him.

He leaned in for another brief kiss and then gently pushed her toward the steps. "I'll wait here until you're inside."

When she had opened the door, she turned around and looked back at him. "Good night," he called softly.

She waved at him, then stepped inside and closed the door behind her. When she looked back through the glass, he was gone.

CHAPTER 20

Josh was sitting at the table, alternately scribbling notes in the margin of the book he was reading and spooning cereal into his mouth, when Lucky stumbled through the dining room the next morning on her way to the kitchen for coffee.

"Hey," she said, unsure of what to say to him. The last time she had seen him he had been lying on the bed in Aidan's guest room, after drinking some blood-red potion that Sambethe had concocted. But he wouldn't remember any of that.

Josh looked up from his book. "Hey. Happy belated birthday. Did you have a good time with your friends?"

Even though Lucky knew his memories were altered, she still found his matter-of-fact manner disconcerting. She nodded, and as he waited for her to elaborate, she tried to think of something to say about the day before. "We—spent a lot of time—wandering around downtown. I—saw the city in a way I've never seen it before."

He raised his eyebrows in a question, and she sought for an explanation that would make sense of her odd statement. "Maybe it's because I turned eighteen, I don't know, it just all seemed—magical—somehow." Before he could question her further, she added something about her need for coffee and escaped to the kitchen.

Josh didn't seem at all concerned or surprised when, instead of joining him, Lucky took her coffee and headed back down the hallway to her room. She wondered how long it would take her to feel comfortable with him again, to stop being afraid that she'd say something to trigger the ghost of a memory from a series of events of which he was currently blissfully unaware.

She considered calling Mo, but the thought of her friend served only to increase her discomfort. She couldn't tell Mo what was going on either, so she'd have to make up some story about the day before.

Lucky had never been a good liar—had never had to be—and the knowledge that she was probably going to have to practice a certain level of deceit for the rest of her life made her insides squirm. Now that she walked in two worlds, she would be forever dissembling with her friends and family who knew just one. The new world of angels and demons of which she was now a part was not something she could share with them. They wouldn't believe her if she tried. And if, by some miracle, they did, their knowledge could put them in danger. She couldn't do that to them. With a sudden sense of loss, Lucky realized that she might never be completely comfortable in her old world again.

As she was contemplating that disquieting thought, Josh appeared in the open doorway, wearing a jacket and with a backpack slung over his shoulder. "I'm off to the library.

Then I'm going to meet Ben later so we can hang out for a while. They're playing tonight, by the way. Did you know?"

Lucky nodded. "Aidan's picking me up. Are you going?"

She was surprised when Josh didn't remark on her relationship with Aidan, but just nodded in return. They exchanged a few comments about seeing each other later, and then he left. The sense of relief that filled her when the door closed and locked behind him, and she heard him descending the building stairs, carried equal parts guilt and sadness in its wake. Lucky had never felt such a sense of distance from her best fam, and her discomfort was only amplified by his ignorance that anything was amiss.

Thoughts about the loss of friends and family and the very real drawbacks to leading a sort of double life preoccupied Lucky as she fixed and ate her breakfast. By the time she had finished eating and cleaned up the few dishes she had used, she had decided that despite the fact that she didn't know what to tell Mo about the day before, she was going to call her anyway. She missed her friend, and she really wanted to talk to her.

Guilt assailed her when she turned on her cell—she had turned it off the day before at Zeke's suggestion—and found that Mo had called her several times. She had left three messages, starting with a cheery "Happy Birthday" message and ending with a frustrated and hurt "Where are you? And why are you not returning my calls?"

Feeling like the worst best friend in the world, she dialed Mo's number. The feeling was not alleviated when Mo answered the phone with a reserved "Hello."

"Hey, Mo," Lucky said quietly. When she didn't receive a response, she continued, "I'm sorry I missed your calls yesterday. I was—out. And my phone, well, it got turned off—and I forgot about it."

"You forgot?" Lucky could hear the hurt in Mo's voice. "Yeah, well, I guess you forgot me too. When you didn't return any of my calls, I called Josh, because I was worried about you. He said you were spending the day, and I quote, 'with friends.' I thought *I* was your *best* friend. We've celebrated every one of both our birthdays together ever since we've known each other. I can't believe you didn't even have the courtesy to let me know you'd made plans that didn't include me."

Lucky felt about the size of the catnip mouse Tef was batting and chasing around the room. Shu was a warm weight on her lap, and she sank her free hand into his fur, seeking some kind of comfort from one of the few creatures she didn't have to lie to. "I'm sorry, Mo. I'm—really sorry. I—"

"I suppose you were with Aidan?" Mo interrupted.

Since Mo's assumption was at least in part correct, and her having spent the day with Aidan would make more sense than what had really happened, Lucky took the explanation and ran with it. "Yes. We went downtown, did some sightseeing. I met his friend Zeke." She threw the name in just in case she slipped and mentioned him later.

"So, you were okay hanging out with *his* friends, then?"

"Mo, it wasn't like that. I didn't deliberately exclude you…" Lucky stopped, realizing she had done exactly that, but for very good reasons. Unfortunately, she couldn't share those reasons with her friend.

Mo didn't give her a chance to continue. "I never thought you'd be *that* girl, Lucky. You know, the one who drops her girl friends as soon as she gets a boyfriend? I thought you'd still want to hang out with me and would still include me in things—like, oh, I don't know, your eighteenth birthday celebration. I guess I got that wrong, didn't I?"

"I don't know what else to say, Mo," Lucky said, feeling miserable. "I'm sorry. I really am. I don't want to—be that girl. I do still want to hang out with you. I guess I just got a little—carried away with it all yesterday." That last statement was vague enough it could mean anything. She would allow Mo to read into it whatever she would.

Her words were greeted with silence. After an uncomfortable pause, Lucky added, this time completely truthfully, "I was hoping maybe we could do something together today."

It took Mo a few moments to answer. When she did, her words were like a knife in Lucky's heart. "I don't think so. I'm not sure I want to see you right now. Besides, I'm having lunch with Eric, and if he has time, maybe we'll spend some of the afternoon together."

"Okay," Lucky responded in a small voice. "Um, are you going to see Icarus tonight?"

"Yeah. You?"

"Yeah. So, I guess I'll see you there then."

"I guess so." With those words, Mo disconnected the call.

"Oh, Shu," Lucky said, burying her face in the cat's fur, "I seem to have made a mess of everything."

She climbed back into bed and burrowed under the covers, hoping that surrounding herself with warmth would help alleviate the internal chill of loneliness. She was marginally comforted when both cats took up their standard positions on either side of her, bookending her between purring warm spots. She eventually fell into a fitful sleep, haunted by dreams of running through empty rooms in strange houses trying to find someone she'd lost.

When Lucky awoke, it was early afternoon. She had several hours to kill before Aidan picked her up, and she felt at loose ends. She guessed she could look for a job, but she wasn't sure how a job was supposed to fit into her life anymore, and besides, she was in no mood to attempt any part of a job search. The idea of watching TV just made her feel more depressed. Even reading held no appeal.

As a last resort, she decided to start looking through the boxes of papers from G-Ma's closet. She carried a couple of them from the computer room into the living room where she turned on some music and prepared herself to sort. Taking a deep breath, she opened a box and dived in.

The first box was filled with Lucky's old drawings and papers from elementary school. She found herself smiling as she remembered how proudly she had presented them to G-Ma as gifts. G-Ma, it seemed, had kept them all. She made slow progress through the contents of the box, lingering over drawings, letting herself dwell in the happy memories they evoked. When she had finally looked at everything in the box, she had amassed a small stack of drawings and finger paintings that she wanted to turn into a collage to hang in her room, something that would remind her of simpler times, when she felt certain of her grandmother's love and was secure in her place in the world—and when the notion that she would ever have to lie to her loved ones for their own protection would never have even crossed her mind.

At first, she thought the contents of the second box were more of the same. But after recognizing nothing familiar in the first few drawings she examined, she knew they were not hers. Then she found one with a name printed in the lower right corner—Marie. Lucky gasped, realizing that these drawings had been made by her mother when she was a child.

Lucky took her time looking through the box. She had never had a chance to know her mother and was grateful for the opportunity to learn something about her through these childhood creations. She wondered why G-Ma had never shown them to her. Surely, her grandmother would have realized that she would have jumped at the chance to find out anything she could about her mother. Then again, maybe it had just been too painful for G-Ma herself to look through things that had been made by her lost daughter.

At the bottom of the box, Lucky found a large envelope. Handwritten in ink across the front were her mother's name, Marie Monroe, and a date a few weeks later than the day Lucky was born eighteen years ago. The return address printed in the envelope's upper left corner was that of a hospital in Ohio. Frowning, Lucky opened the envelope.

Inside she found more drawings and paintings, as well as several pages covered with handwriting. She put the latter aside, as the powerful images in the former beckoned.

Although the strokes with which they had been created were somewhat frenetic, the pieces were well-executed. Clearly, her mother had inherited more of G-Ma's talent in art than Lucky had. But it wasn't the skill of the drawings that captured her attention; it was their subject matter. The drawings depicted figures like those that had become familiar to Lucky in the last few days: figures with wings—some feathered, some bat-like and leathery—and small, gargoyle-ish creatures like the ones she had encountered yesterday at the assisted living facility. The paintings were more abstract, confusions of color, light, and shadow. But Lucky recognized those as well. That was how the world had looked to her as her powers had come flooding in the day before.

Her heart rate increased as she studied the drawings and paintings, and when she turned at last to the handwritten pages, she picked them up with trembling hands. It took her a while to read through them, because the writing was hurried, and she sometimes found it difficult to decipher the scrawl. By the time she reached the final pages, she could hardly see through the tears that filled her eyes, and her hands were shaking so violently she had to lay the papers on the coffee table to finish reading them.

My Dear Little Lucy—

I am so sorry that I will not get the chance to see you grow up. I have only held you in my arms a few times, but you are already so dear to me. It breaks my heart to know I must leave you, but I recognize that I have no choice. I can't be the mother you deserve—or even the mother you need. I can't take care of myself, let alone you.

I want to take care of you. I want to hold you and rock you to sleep, to sing you lullabies. I want to play with you and read you stories and watch you grow up. But they won't let me see you for very long at a time—and never alone. I understand—believe me, I do—but it still hurts. It hurts so much. You're my baby, and I can't be trusted to be alone with you.

I know I'm losing my mind. My thoughts spin around, and my senses are sometimes overwhelming. There's so much noise and color, and my body aches from the feel of things I'm not even touching. I see such things—things that can't be real—and yet they seem to me as real as anything I've ever seen. I've been drawing and painting what I see, and that's given me some peace. But most of the time, I just want to put my arms around my head and scream. And a lot of the time, I do. No wonder they won't leave you alone with me. It's a miracle they let me see you at all.

I've tried to be strong—for you. But I just can't. No matter what I do, the visions come, and the noises come, and it's all too much. I struggle just to write this letter to you. And when I read back over what I've written, I wonder if I should tear it up. It's probably better if you never read it. You really don't need to know what a mess your mother was. I just want so much to have some sense of connection with you. And this is the only way I know to do that. Besides, like the drawings, writing gives me some peace—if only for a few minutes at a time.

Whatever else you may believe about me, please know that I love you. Oh, my little girl, I love you so very much. More than my own life.

Your grandparents are coming tomorrow. You're going to live with them, and they will take very good care of you—as they did of me, for as long as I let them. It's better this way. You'll have a good life—and you'll grow up to be a good girl and not make a mess of things the way I did.

I love you, my Lucy, my baby. You must believe that. Forgive me.

Your Mama, Marie

Scrawled beneath the name was a date the day before the one on the envelope. Lucky wiped the tears from her eyes with trembling hands and scanned back through the pages again. She had been told that her mother had died giving birth to her, but it wasn't true. According to the date on the letter, her mother had been alive for at least a few weeks after her birth. As she wondered why G-Ma hadn't told her the truth, she felt a sickening sense of betrayal. All her life, she had believed a lie. She wondered what else she hadn't been told.

Her mother had obviously been a Sensitive too, and like Lucky, she hadn't known it. But, unlike Lucky, she hadn't had anyone like Aidan or Zeke looking out for her. She had had to face the onset of her powers all on her own, and they had driven her mad. Why hadn't anyone been able to help her mother? And why had she herself been fortunate enough to wander into the Icarus show and encounter Aidan at just the right time? Maybe her nickname was more appropriate than she had thought.

The final item in the box was a manila folder, inside which Lucky found a death certificate, indicating that her mother had died on the same day the letter had been written, and naming the cause of death as blood loss from cuts to the wrists and the manner of death as suicide. Also tucked in the folder were a yellowed newspaper obituary announcement and a program from the memorial service that had been held a few days later.

Once she had read through all three documents, Lucky simply stared at the papers scattered across her lap. When awareness returned some time later, she had no idea how much time had elapsed. She had no memory of thinking or seeing anything she stared at. It was as if she had disappeared, checked out, for an indeterminate period of time. Taking a shaky breath, she placed the papers back in the folder and everything back in the box, this time putting the envelope of drawings and the manila folder on top, instead of burying them beneath the childhood artwork.

Then she curled up in the corner of the couch, her arms wrapped around her knees, her mind struggling to integrate these revelations. Gradually, she realized that Uncle Matthew and Aunt Beth had been as much a part of the conspiracy of silence as had G-Ma. She even wondered if Josh was aware of more than he'd ever let on. He had only been five when her mother had died, but that was old enough to have maybe heard something. He may have even been present at the memorial service. Tears filled her eyes again. She had never felt so alone.

"I can't believe we're still discussing this!" Aidan managed to keep himself from shouting, but he spoke loudly enough to drown out Sambethe, who was again holding forth on the primary importance of convincing "the human girl" to be Made Nephilim. "What part of 'No, it's way too dangerous' do you not understand?"

"Aidan," Zeke said in warning.

Aidan's anger flared higher. He hated it when Zeke used his name like a reprimand, just like he was still a child under his tutelage. Considering the angel's age, though, he supposed everyone was like a child in comparison.

He took a deep breath and managed to reply in a moderate tone. "You know you aren't any fonder of the idea than I am, Zeke."

"No, I am not. But Sambethe is convinced it merits serious consideration."

"More than 'serious consideration,'" the oracle asserted. "It *must* be done! It is the only way. I have seen several outcomes for the coming battle—and the *only* one that shows our victory includes the girl—as Naphil."

This time Aidan couldn't temper his reply. "But you've seen her die in the Making too! If she's already dead, she won't be any help to our cause!"

Sambethe caught and held his eyes with her pale ones. When she spoke, her voice was slow and deliberate. "If she does not undergo the Making, she will die anyway—*as will we all.* But if she survives the Making, then we will all have a chance. I fear there is no other possibility for victory."

"There has to be." Kev joined the conversation. "Isn't it possible that there are other potential outcomes that you haven't seen, Sambethe?"

The oracle kept silent for a moment before acceding, "Yes, it is possible. But I do not believe it likely."

"Understood," Kev said. "Can you determine why the girl is so important in this?"

Again, Aidan interrupted. "Lucky! Her name is Lucky. She's not just 'the girl'!"

Shaking her head, Sambethe replied to Kev's question as if Aidan hadn't spoken. "No, Kevin, I do not know why—only that she is. As is," and here she directed a raised eyebrow at Aidan, "the obstinate, young half-Seraph."

Aidan sighed. He really had to learn to control himself around her. When his half-brother caught his eye, his expression held equal parts amusement, reprimand, and sympathy.

"Yes," Kev responded to the oracle. "And isn't it possible that *he* is enough? We have always known that Aidan's Gift grants him powers greater than those of most Nephilim—should he choose to use them." He looked back at Aidan, and this time there was no amusement in his eyes.

Aidan shifted uncomfortably in his chair, feeling as if he'd been scolded once again.

But when Kev continued speaking, Aidan heard his half-brother's words with pleased surprise. "And I, for one, am sure that he will. He has agreed to step in as second in command of the Forces, and his training is going even better than we expected. I have no doubt that he will use all his powers to combat whatever threat we face."

When he finished speaking, everyone at the table looked at Aidan. Realizing they were waiting for him to confirm or negate Kev's words, he nodded, clearing his throat. "Of course. I will do whatever is necessary."

"While that is a relief to hear," Sambethe replied, "it changes nothing. We need both Aidan and the girl." She turned toward Zeke and spoke in a voice that allowed no further argument. "Ezekiel, you must convince the girl to undergo the Making. There can be no other choice in this matter. Too much hangs in the balance."

The angel closed his eyes for a moment before responding. When he replied, his low, resonating voice held all the weight of his millennia of responsibility. "I will talk to her."

Aidan bolted to his feet and headed for the door, the discordant scraping of his chair legs on the tile floor his final expression of disagreement. If any of them tried to call him back, he didn't hear them; he was too deep in his own anger and fear. He managed to resist the urge to slam the door behind him, but he clenched his fists and his jaw as his long strides ate the distance to the training center's outer exit.

As soon as the exit door closed, he cursed and slammed his fist into the building's stone wall. The resulting pain in his hand gave him some much-needed focus, and he smiled in bitter satisfaction when he saw that the force of his blow had caused tiny cracks to radiate out from the point of impact. Staring at the cracks, he felt his smile take on an ironic curve as he recognized the opportunity he had created for himself. This was about as safe a test case as he could get.

Concentrating his attention on the cracks, the vulnerability at their center, and the essence of the stone itself, he drew on the part of his Gift he kept hidden even from himself and opened his mouth. The note that issued forth sounded no more like music than had his chair legs against the tile floor. It was gritty like stone and pitched at a point of discomfort for even his own ears. As he held the note, he felt it entwine with the stone of the wall, the frequencies that made up the sound reaching into the stone to open its molecular structure, so that it flowed into the open spaces of the cracks and then knit itself back together, healing that which he had broken. He did not make a conscious decision to stop singing. It was as if the note itself knew when its work was complete and dissolved into silence.

Aidan rested his fingertips against the stone, once again smooth and crack-free. It felt warm to his touch, and he flattened his palm against it, holding it there as the heat of creation faded away. He was in awe of the power he was capable of summoning, knew he could take no personal credit for it, knew that it was indeed a Gift—and knew it was a double-edged sword. The power to create was linked to the power to destroy, so much so that the two were flip-sides of the same coin. His Gift was one that required great care in its wielding. He had learned that lesson the hard way—and the result had been the Renunciation of his wings and the suppression of the greater part of his Gift.

Now, he had to stop suppressing his ability and learn to control it. If he could take on the wings again and accept a position as second, he could do this too. He knew with an absolute certainty that came from a place deep inside him—as deep as the source of his power—that he could never master the Gift. Its power derived from the awesome force of creation itself—wild and primal, beautiful and terrifying—and it wasn't meant to be mastered. But it could be directed and focused, channeled, if treated with the proper respect. As he let his fingers fall from the stone, he realized that the fear with which he had so long regarded his Gift was fading away—and that the space created by its retreat was gradually filling with a sense of rightness and responsibility. This was who he was; it was about time he accepted it.

CHAPTER 21

The sound of a ringtone jolted Lucky awake. She had huddled in a knot of misery in the corner of the couch until she had fallen asleep. Now, she felt dazed, disconnected, as she pushed away the throw she had pulled over herself for warmth and fumbled around for her cell phone. She finally located it on the floor by the far end of the couch. Seeing that the call was from Aidan, she accepted it just before he would have been dumped into voicemail.

"Hi," she said, with far less than her usual enthusiasm.

"Hey," came his voice in reply, sounding concerned. "What's wrong?"

"Almost everything." Lucky felt the prick of tears at the backs of her eyes. "I'll fill you in later. I don't think I can talk about it right now."

"Okay."

Lucky could almost feel the force of Aidan's need to question her further, but he only asked if she was still up for the show that evening. When she said she was, he suggested he come over a little earlier than they had planned, so they'd have more time to talk. Lucky welcomed the idea; she was tired of being alone.

After Aidan had signed off with a "See you soon," it occurred to Lucky to wonder what time it was. Checking her phone, she realized she'd have just enough time to shower and get ready before he arrived. She needed a shower, if only to wash away the remains of her tear-fest. Her eyes were hot and sandy, and the skin over her cheekbones felt tight from the salty residue of her tears.

The steamy shower went a long way toward reviving her. As the hot water sluiced over her head and shoulders, it carried away not only the physical marks of her tears but also the deep despair that had filled her. Aidan was coming to pick her up, and she would see both Josh and Mo at the show. Sure, things might be a little rocky between her and Mo, but they could work through it. She'd figure out a better way to integrate her two worlds. And she'd just have to ask Uncle Matthew or Aunt Beth about her mother. Maybe she could even talk to G-Ma—if she caught her on a more lucid day. With the clearing of her head came the understanding that none of them would have lied to hurt her. Misguided or not, they had kept the truth from her in order to protect her—much like she was keeping the truth from Josh and Mo. Lying didn't necessarily stem from a lack of love; sometimes love was the strongest motivator of all.

Shower complete, Lucky pulled on her best skinny black jeans, which she tucked into a pair of tall black boots and paired with a soft gray scoop-neck sweater with elbow-length sleeves. She slipped the Light-Bringer's Medallion under the neckline of her sweater and covered most of the chain with a jade green scarf she wrapped around her neck. Surveying herself in the mirror, she decided the result wasn't bad. At least, the scarf accented the color of her eyes.

She was just about to pull her hair up into its usual ponytail when the sound of the buzzer announced Aidan's arrival. She stuffed the elastic band into the pocket of her jeans and hurried down the hall to buzz him in. Opening the door, she heard the creaks and groans of the old building's stairs as he made his way up to the top floor. By the time he reached the third-floor landing, her heart was pounding as if she were the one climbing multiple flights of stairs.

"Hey, you," Aidan said, catching her eyes with his own.

"Hey, yourself," she replied with a small smile, stepping aside so he could enter the apartment. Turning toward him after closing the door, she caught him scanning her face with concern.

"Are you alright?" he asked.

She nodded, noticing that the apartment somehow seemed much smaller with him in it, as if it were dwarfed by his height and his sheer presence. "I'm better now. The shower helped."

"Tell me about it?"

She nodded again and, taking his hand, led the way to the living room. He sat down at one end of the couch and drew her down beside him. Keeping her hand in his, he turned so that he was facing her, bent knee resting on the couch cushion. He offered no questions, just waited patiently for her to speak, his fingers warm and firm against hers. Lucky turned toward him, her knee and shin touching his.

"I guess I exaggerated a little when we were on the phone," she began. "Everything isn't so bad."

One corner of his mouth lifted. "I'm glad to hear that," he said, his thumb stroking the back of the hand he had clasped in his own. "What happened anyway?"

Lucky told him about her discomfort with Josh and her subsequent realization that she'd have no choice but to lie to her friends and family from now on, her falling out with Mo, and the unexpected discovery of her mother's unacknowledged Sensitive abilities and resulting suicide.

When she finished the story, she showed him the letter her mother had written to her infant self. It wasn't anything she had planned on doing, but as she told him about the letter, she realized that she wanted him to read it. She not only wanted Aidan to see for himself what she had discovered, but also to bear witness to it. The truth had been denied, hidden away, and she needed someone else to see the letter, to read it and give it a reality outside the paper on which it was written and the confines of her own mind and heart.

After Aidan finished reading the letter, he looked at her in silence for several moments. Then, setting the letter aside, he opened his arms to her.

Lucky didn't hesitate. She was in his embrace in an instant, relishing the warm strength of his arms around her. Pulling her close he positioned her on his lap, and she relaxed against him. She could feel the steady beat of his heart under her palm where it rested on his chest.

Snuggling her head against his shoulder, she said, "If I hadn't met you that night—if Josh hadn't invited me to come to your show—the same thing could have happened to me."

"But you did—and it didn't." Aidan slid his hand under her scarf so he could rest it against the side of her neck.

"It's just—I wish she had had someone to help her too."

Aidan did not reply, but his thumb moved back and forth over her cheek and jaw in a light caress.

They sat like that for several moments, the stroking of his fingers and thumb against her neck and cheek conveying both comfort and support. Lucky couldn't tell how the texture of his touch changed, the shift was so subtle. But suddenly the movement of his fingers against her skin was no longer soothing, and her heart quickened its rhythm at the same time that she felt the acceleration of Aidan's heartbeat beneath her hand. Turning more toward him, she slid her hand up to twine her fingers into the curls at the nape of his neck. His mouth brushed her cheek, feather-light, before settling on her parted lips.

It was several moments later when Aidan drew away from her. "We'd better go—or I'm going to be late."

Lucky was gratified to see that his breathing was as ragged as her own. She nodded but made no effort to move off his lap. With a wicked grin, he leaned down and caught her lower lip between his teeth for an instant. Then he lifted her with ease, shifting her so she was once more sitting beside him.

Now that she was no longer touching him, Lucky's thoughts were a little clearer. She ran her fingers through her long curls and retrieved the elastic band from her pocket.

When she pulled her hair back to secure it into a ponytail, Aidan stopped her.

"Leave it down," he said, the rising inflection on the last syllable making the words more a request than an order. "For me."

Looking into his blue eyes, Lucky let her hair fall back around her shoulders. The warmth of his smile conveyed his thanks. Standing, she put the abandoned elastic band back in her pocket and went to grab a light jacket and the small purse that was the evening's stand-in for her usual backpack. When she returned from her room, Aidan was waiting by the door.

Lucky was surprised when he led her not to the motorcycle to which she had become accustomed, but to a silver BMW roadster.

"You do own a car," she teased. "I thought your only choices were motorcycle or wings."

"Actually, I prefer those," he said, opening the passenger door for her. "But they sometimes have their limitations, especially where passengers are concerned."

"Oh, I don't know," she said, sliding into the seat. "They've both worked pretty well for me."

He chuckled as he closed the door and moved around the car to take his place behind the wheel.

The band was playing at Wild Hare in Wicker Park, and the drive didn't last long enough for Lucky. The closer they got to their destination, the more knots she could feel in her stomach. As anxious as she was to see both her cousin and her best friend, she was also dreading the first encounter with each of them. Not that Josh suspected anything; she just wasn't comfortable knowing how much of the truth had been taken from him. Mo, on the other hand.... Lucky really wanted to clear the air with her, and she was hoping her friend would be more amenable to that tonight than she had been in their morning telephone conversation.

As she followed Aidan into the bar, she pressed a hand to her stomach and took a deep breath. Her anxiety was not alleviated when she found that neither Josh nor Mo had yet arrived. As worried as she was about seeing them, she also wanted to get that first encounter over with.

She managed to navigate the small talk that ensued when Aidan re-introduced her to the band members who were present; then she did her best to stay out of the way while they got set up. A couple of times someone called on her to help place or tape cords, but most of the time she just stood to the side and watched, finally taking a seat at the table at the front that had been staked out for the friends of the band. Soon after she was seated, a waitress stopped at the table to ask if she'd like a drink while she waited for her friends. Lucky ordered a Coke, if only to have something to hold on to.

She had just taken her first sip of the beverage when she saw Mo come in with Eric. He hurried to the stage, apologizing for being late, and dived into the setup activities. Mo stopped when she saw Lucky, and the action caused Lucky's heart to plummet. She met her friend's eyes across the room and offered a shaky smile and a small wave. Mo didn't smile back, but she did walk slowly over to take the seat beside Lucky. She was wearing a hot pink sweater and a scarf of turquoise and yellow stripes. The scarf's turquoise stripes matched her suede boots. It was a combination Lucky would never have thought to put together, but on Mo it worked.

"You look great," she said.

"So do you," replied Mo, in a reserved manner so unlike her usual ebullience that Lucky worried she would never be able to patch things up with her. Then, with a small twinkle in her eye, she added, "Nice scarf."

Lucky smiled, the ache in her chest easing. "Yeah," she said. "My best friend gave it to me."

"She has good taste, that friend of yours." Lucky could see the corners of Mo's mouth fighting to turn upward.

"Yeah, she does," she said. "I don't know what I'd do without her."

At her words, Mo threw her arms around Lucky and gave her a huge hug. "I can't stay mad at you. It's like being mad at my own feet because they made me trip and fall."

Tears of relief filled Lucky's eyes as she laughed and returned her friend's hug. "I'm glad you can't stay mad at me. And I really am sorry about yesterday. I've been miserable all day about hurting you."

"Good," Mo said, releasing her. "'Cause I was miserable all day yesterday. Now, we're even." Her smile took most of the sting out of the words.

Lucky wanted to promise Mo that such a thing wouldn't happen again. But given the changes in her life, she didn't know that she could do so in all honesty. Instead, she gave her friend her warmest smile and said, "Thanks, Mo. I don't deserve you."

"No, you don't," Mo said airily, "but then, no one does."

"Not even me?" asked Eric, who had come up to the table just as she was speaking.

Mo grinned at him. "Especially not you."

"Then I'm a very lucky man," he said, leaning down to drop a light kiss on her cheek. "I'm going to get a drink. You want anything?"

Glancing at Lucky's glass, Mo requested a Coke as well.

"One Coca-Cola, coming up," Eric said as he departed.

"Things seem to be going well with him," Lucky commented. That was enough to keep them chatting until Eric returned, juggling two Cokes and baskets of pretzels and popcorn that he had balanced on his arms.

"Give me those before you drop them," Mo said, laughing. She scooped the baskets off his arms and placed them on the table before taking the Coke he held out to her.

"Thanks." He dropped another kiss on her cheek and then hurried back to the stage.

"I wonder where Josh and Ben are," Lucky said, more than a little worried that they hadn't arrived yet.

Then, as if her words had conjured them, the two appeared in the doorway. Ben hurried toward the stage, while Josh made his way over to Lucky and Mo. Lucky frowned as he sat down in a chair across the table from them, holding on to the chair for support as he lowered himself into it.

"Are you okay?" she asked.

"I'm fine, just tired." He brushed off her concern. "Ben and I played racquetball this afternoon, and I guess I'm not in as good a shape as I thought I was."

"Maybe you're coming down with something," Mo offered. "You should take it easy for the next day or so—and drink lots of juice and eat chicken soup."

Or maybe he wasn't recovered from the Dark toxin after all. Juice and chicken soup probably wouldn't help with that. Lucky frowned again. Zeke and Sambethe had assured her he would be fine—and they should know. She corralled her thoughts as the other chairs at the table began to fill and introductions were made.

A few minutes later, Aidan approached the table. *It isn't fair,* Lucky thought, *for anyone to be so impossibly handsome.* The light blue of his shirt enhanced the color of his eyes, making them look even bluer than normal.

"We're about to get started," he said. "Everyone doing alright here?"

They all nodded, and a few made teasing remarks to the effect that it was about time they got the music going.

Aidan stepped closer to Lucky. "Let me know what it's like for you this time," he whispered in her ear, before planting a soft kiss beside her mouth.

The others hooted and whistled, causing Lucky to blush to the roots of her hair. Aidan gave her shoulder a squeeze and headed for the stage.

Lucky glanced at Josh to see how he'd reacted to Aidan kissing her. He seemed distracted, almost as if he hadn't even noticed, and she thought he was looking a little pale. He was definitely not okay.

Mo leaned toward her. "Looks like things are going well with him, too."

Lucky frowned. "With Josh? No, I don't think—"

"Not Josh, silly," Mo laughed. "With Aidan. You and Aidan."

"Oh, yeah, I guess they are," Lucky said, her attention divided between Mo and her concern for her cousin.

"You guess? Honey, given the very public nature of that little display of affection, I think you can move beyond guesswork. Lucky, are you listening to me at all?"

"What?" Lucky tore her gaze away from her cousin and focused on her friend. "I'm sorry, Mo. I'm just worried about Josh. He's… not acting like himself. I really don't think he's well."

"I'm sure he's just tired, like he said, and maybe coming down with a cold or something." Mo reassured her. "He's a big boy, Lucky. He wouldn't be here if he felt all that bad."

"Yeah, you're probably right," Lucky said, but she had her doubts. Josh didn't remember what had happened to him. He didn't know that he might need to worry about something more dangerous than a rhinovirus. And she could do nothing to warn him. So much for her special powers. So far, they'd brought mostly trouble.

As Aidan broke into the haunting *a cappella* opening of the first song, Lucky acknowledged that at least one good thing had come from her powers—or from the fact of her possessing them: her budding relationship with him. She wouldn't have gotten to know him otherwise. Casting a last worried glance at her cousin before turning her full attention to the stage, she squashed the superstitious voice that wondered if the acquisition of a new relationship might have to be balanced by the loss of an old one.

CHAPTER 22

Listening to Aidan's voice grow louder and more powerful, increasing in volume so as to stand up against the addition of the band's instruments, Lucky realized she was more than just curious about how that voice would affect her tonight. She also *wanted* to get caught up in it, *wanted* it to take her away from her uncomfortable thoughts and fears. The opening song was about frustrated love, unrequited longing, unfulfilled desire—not the most positive of emotions. Still, she wondered what it would be like to be swept up in Aidan's voice as he sang about them. Closing her eyes for a moment, she located what she was coming to think of as her inner control room and chose just one aspect of her abilities, the one that would enable her to see what she heard; then, she opened her eyes.

Aidan's voice filled the room like colored smoke. It was muted blues and grays, shot through with rich reds and purples, thin in places like a light silk veil and thick in others, like satin or velvet. She let the textures in too, and suddenly she could feel the silk beneath her fingertips, the satin against her cheek—but only in the briefest of touches, each teasing feather-stroke evoking the desire for more. A velvety ribbon of sound wrapped itself around her throat and then snaked down over her heart before slipping away, and she almost reached out to catch it, so great was her need to hold it close. She caught her breath and looked toward the stage.

Aidan was looking at her, directing all the longing and unrequited passion of the song toward her. As her eyes met his, she felt him add his Gift to her powers, and she gasped. She could almost, but not quite, feel his arms around her, almost, but not quite, feel his breath on her cheek. It was as if he were mere millimeters from her, and yet she could never close the distance, could never complete the touch. She could hear the words of the song, the timbre of his voice, see its colors, and even experience its textures in those brief, tantalizing moments, but she wanted more. She wanted to grab on to all of it, to clasp it close to her, to hold *him* close to her—his voice, his body, his heart, his soul, all of him. But she knew she never ever could, because no matter how near he seemed, he was completely out of reach.

Just as she was beginning to wonder if one could actually die from frustrated longing, the song ended. Aidan's voice faded away, his Gift losing its hold on her, and the intense feelings that had filled her drained away as well. Focusing on her own abilities, she watched the smoky tendrils of sound as they diminished and drifted into the corners of the room. Taking advantage of the break afforded by the crowd's applause, she sought Aidan's eyes once again. In answer to the silent question posed by his raised eyebrow, she mouthed the word "Wow." The corners of his mouth curved upward. Then he turned away from her and directed his attention to the general audience.

Well, that was interesting, Lucky thought. She had wanted to be swept away, but she hadn't been prepared for the intensity of the experience. She felt both emotionally drained and strangely energized. She wanted to try the experiment again, but she decided she was going to give herself a song or two to recover.

For the rest of the set, she experimented with her Sensitive abilities, drawing first on one aspect of her powers and then another. With a little effort, she found she could even manage to control her powers while responding to the occasional comment from Mo or Josh. On the one hand, she supposed her experimentation distracted her from the show somewhat, but on the other, it offered her a deeper—if strange and synesthetic—experience of it. The set was almost over before she realized that she hadn't felt Aidan's Gift after that first song—and she knew he had deliberately used it then. She wondered if the reason she was no longer drawing his power as she had at the last show was because she was now aware of and could control her own abilities.

The set ended and a few of the band members, including Ben, stopped by the table to see if anyone there needed a refill. Commenting that she could use another Coke, Lucky offered to accompany Ben to the bar and help carry the drinks back to the table. She was grateful for the opportunity to talk to him apart from Josh for a few minutes. When she noted that Josh didn't seem like himself, Ben agreed. He said Josh had started feeling weak and tired during their afternoon racquetball game, and his symptoms had worsened as the day progressed. Although he also remarked that it was probably just a cold or the flu, Ben seemed to share Lucky's worry.

She didn't get a chance to talk to Aidan during the break. When she and Ben made it back to the table, he and the guitarist were working with the sound guy to make some adjustments. Ben had only a few minutes to down what he could of his beer and chat with Josh and his friends before he and the rest of the band returned to the stage.

Icarus was halfway through the second song of their second set when Lucky sensed a non-human presence in the room. She couldn't tell which of her heightened senses had tipped her off. And while she couldn't be sure this new presence provided a threat, the jangling of her nerve endings didn't bode well. Shifting more fully into Sensitive mode, she scanned the room, searching for the source of her odd discomfort.

She located them a few yards away, not far from the door: two figures covered in dark cloaks. The space around their bodies was slightly blurred, fuzzy, and she understood that they were cloaked in glamour as well. None of the other patrons seemed to be aware of them at all. Lucky looked toward the stage, wondering if Aidan had also sensed them. From the direction of his gaze, she could tell that he had. Otherwise he gave no indication that anything was amiss. He continued to give his all to the song, working the audience as usual. He glanced her way, and she acknowledged, with the slightest of nods, that she too was aware of the strangers.

Studying them through the corners of her narrowed eyes, Lucky wished she could see what they looked like, but the long, hooded cloaks covered them so completely that she could discern nothing about them. They stood in that same spot for what seemed like several minutes, as Lucky watched them as surreptitiously as she could. Then, as if they had finally located what—or whom—they were looking for, they turned their heads toward her table. With effort, Lucky kept herself from moving, so as not to betray her own observation of them.

The strangers moved through the bar with ease, the crowd parting for them even as the patrons evinced no conscious awareness of their presence. Lucky wondered what she should do if they reached her table. Surely, they wouldn't try to take her from a crowded room? Or, she suddenly thought, what if they were here for Josh? What if they were the ones who had administered the toxin, and they had come back to finish the job?

Anonymity forgotten, she stood up and pushed through the crowd to the other side of the table, so she could be nearer to Josh. She had almost reached his side when her scarf snagged on something and tightened around her throat. Reaching up, she jerked it aside, and the action caused the Light-Bringer's Medallion she wore to slip free of the scoop neckline of her sweater. As if the action were in slow motion, she saw the medallion flash as it caught the light from the stage, and she stared in surprise as the two strangers froze in reaction.

Then the smaller of the two moved its hood back enough to reveal a fall of scarlet hair and a beautiful, pale face with startling emerald eyes. Catching Lucky's eye, the woman gave her a small smile that somehow managed to convey a smug satisfaction. Then she and her companion dematerialized, but not before Lucky had seen the flash of yellow eyes beneath the other hood.

"Lucky? What are you…?"

Her cousin's voice snapped Lucky's attention back to the rest of the room, making her realize that her actions must have seemed more than strange to everyone else at her table. Josh had partially risen to his feet, a slight frown between his brows. Now, he grasped her arm to steady himself, but as soon as he was standing, his breath hitched, his eyes rolled back in his head, and he collapsed against her.

She cried out his name as she staggered under his weight and struggled to lower them both to the floor. Then she knelt beside her cousin, stroking his hair back from his forehead and listening to his shallow breathing. She was vaguely aware of the people nearest them pushing their chairs aside and making noises of concern, remarking that someone should call a doctor.

Suddenly, Josh grasped her wrist with surprising strength, stopping the motion of her hand on his hair, and when he lifted his eyelids, Lucky gasped. The eyes looking up at her from her cousin's face were those she had seen in the dream she had had the night Sambethe had given him the antidote to the toxin. Blood-red and feral, they bore no resemblance to Josh's warm brown ones. Then, just as suddenly as he had grabbed her, his hand fell away from her arm, and his eyelids closed over those red eyes.

By that time, Aidan and Ben had pushed their way through the crowd gathered around them. His face pale, Ben dropped to his knees on Josh's other side and took Josh's hand in one of his, murmuring worried endearments.

Kneeling beside Lucky, Aidan said quietly, "Zeke's on his way."

Even as he finished speaking, Lucky heard the angel's resonant voice. "I'm a doctor," Zeke lied, shouldering his way through the crowd to kneel beside Ben, who shifted back to allow him clearer access to Josh.

Lucky had become accustomed to seeing more than Zeke's human form when she looked at him. Still, it was a bit disorienting to watch his four faces morph in and out in this bar surrounded by other humans. She shifted her perspective bit by bit until she saw him as she had when she had first met him, as a tall, long-haired, gray-eyed man. His wheat-colored hair spilled over his shoulders as he leaned over Josh, checking his pulse and then touching his head, hands, and heart in a pattern she recognized. He was activating a healing stasis once more. She could see the blue triangle of light wrapping around her cousin's upper body, but she could tell by the blurriness of its edges that Zeke had also cast a glamour so that the other people surrounding them could not.

"We need to get him out of here and back to Aidan's, where Sambethe can examine and treat him," Zeke said, his voice just loud enough for Lucky and Aidan to hear.

Aidan nodded, and rising to his feet, he made his way back to the stage. He assured everyone that Josh was going to be alright and promised that while the band wouldn't play a complete set, they would do a few more songs, once Josh had been moved. Everything would go much more smoothly, he added, if everyone would return to their seats and step aside for "the doctor."

Ben had returned to Josh's side as soon as Aidan's departure had cleared a space for him. "I'm coming with you," he said.

Lucky promised to call him as soon as she had any news and was trying to think of an excuse strong enough to make Ben stay, when the young man turned to Zeke with a determined expression. "Zeke," he said, "tell her it's okay if I come with you."

Wordlessly, Zeke nodded his assent. Casting a curious look at Ben, Lucky said quick good-byes to Mo and Eric, and after receiving a supportive squeeze from Mo, she fell in beside Ben so they could follow Zeke as he carried Josh out of the bar.

To her surprise, Malachi was waiting outside. Dressed more casually than she had ever seen him in black jeans and a black ribbed sweater, he was leaning against a black SUV, which was double-parked with flashers activated. She wondered how he'd gotten there so quickly. He opened the back door as Zeke approached and helped the angel slide her cousin into the vehicle.

Lucky and Ben slipped into the back seat as well, and Ben lifted Josh's head to pillow it on his lap. Zeke climbed into the front passenger seat as Malachi slid behind the wheel. He drove fast and skillfully, somehow managing to maneuver in and out of traffic, breaking every possible speed limit, without once making Lucky fear for their safety.

As soon as they'd parked in the visitor's section of the garage for Aidan's building, Zeke dematerialized, flashing himself to Aidan's apartment, so that he could let them in. Ben wouldn't allow Malachi to take Josh from his arms. And Lucky was surprised when the slender young man carried her cousin as easily as if he weighed nothing. Malachi nodded to the security guard while they awaited access to the building. Lucky gauged from the guard's easy response that he was unable to see her cousin's unconscious body in Ben's arms. When she focused her attention, she was able to see a slight blurriness around Josh's figure, an indication that he was hidden by some kind of glamour.

To Lucky, it seemed as if time expanded the closer they came to getting help for Josh. The elevator ride to Aidan's apartment seemed to take as long as the entire trip from the bar, and as she followed Malachi's long strides down the hall to the guest room, she felt as if they were moving in slow motion. It was only after Ben had placed her cousin on the bed, and Sambethe, who had arrived while they were transporting Josh up from the garage, had begun her examination, that Lucky felt time resume its normal speed.

When Sambethe shooed the rest of them from the room because she said they were interfering with her concentration, Lucky led the way down the hall to Aidan's sparsely furnished living room.

Déjà vu all over again, she thought, as she stared out the large windows overlooking the city lights and the lake. Was it really only two days ago that she'd stood in this same place, worrying about Josh, as he lay encased in blue light in Aidan's guest room? It had seemed too good to be true when Zeke and Sambethe had assured her he was healed, but she had wanted to believe it. And with Zeke's assurances, how could she not have? She shivered as she remembered the strength of Josh's hand on her arm and that flash of red eyes. If he didn't survive this, or was somehow permanently harmed because of it, she wasn't sure she could ever forgive herself. If it hadn't been for her, the members of the Dark who had done this to him would have had no reason to single him out as a target.

She was shaken out of her thoughts by a hand on her shoulder, and she turned to find Ben at her side. As soon as he had called Zeke by name, she had suspected the young man was Naphil, and she wondered why neither she nor Aidan had ever realized it. She never voiced the question. Before she could speak, Zeke had come to join them, holding out steaming cups of tea.

Lucky took hers gratefully, feeling its warmth seep into her fingers. She even managed a small chuckle when Malachi remarked, "You must have lived in England at some point, Zeke. Like the British, you seem to find tea to be the appropriate response to almost any situation."

"It's no cure-all, but I find that it offers some small comfort." With a wry smile, the Cherub added, "Besides, making it gives me something to do other than wait."

Lucky wondered how many times in his unimaginably long life Zeke had felt helpless to do anything other than wait—or make tea. It was hard to believe a being so powerful could ever feel helpless, but she knew there were many things outside of his control. She couldn't decide if that knowledge was reassuring or immensely troubling.

"Ezekiel," Sambethe beckoned from the hallway, "I would speak with you, please."

That can't mean anything good, Lucky thought, as Zeke followed the oracle-cum-healer down the hall, and Ben found a seat on the couch. She shot a troubled glance at Malachi, seeking some indication that she was wrong, but she found her own fear reflected in the tightening of his jaw and the small frown that knit his brow. The look he turned her way was sympathetic, but he made no attempt to offer empty reassurances. Like her, he remained silent—and waited.

When Zeke returned, his expression was grimmer than she had ever seen it, as if his responsibilities weighed more than heavily on his winged shoulders. He looked at Lucky, still standing by the windows, and gesturing toward the black leather couch, said quietly, "Sit down. Please."

Heart filling with dread, she sat down between Ben and Malachi. Then she turned to Zeke with wide, anxious eyes.

"Sambethe—," Zeke cleared his throat. "Sambethe says she was mistaken about the nature of the toxin that was given to your cousin. His condition is much more serious than any of us suspected." He studied her for a moment, his gray eyes containing a depth of sorrow that nearly made her heart skip a beat. "He will die, Lucky. And, worse than that, when he dies his human death, he will become a Wraith."

At his words, Malachi bit out a quiet oath.

"What's a Wraith?" Lucky asked, afraid of the answer.

It was Ben who answered. "A Wraith is a kind of demon—one that lives by taking the souls of humans."

"And there's nothing you can do?" Lucky turned to Zeke in desperation. "Nothing Sambethe can do?"

Zeke shook his head. "No, there is nothing *we* can do." Again, he paused and looked at her in sorrow. "Helping your cousin is up to you, Lucky."

"Me? What can I possibly do to help him?"

"The only thing that will save him is the blood of a Naphil, and one who shares his own blood."

"He needs my blood?" Lucky was filled with relief. "And the blood of a Naphil? Ben is Naphil, right? We can mix some of his blood with mine and give it to Josh."

Zeke shook his head again. "No, Lucky, it's not that simple. The *Naphil* has to be of Josh's own blood."

"But I'm not...," Lucky began. Then her heart plummeted as realization struck. "I have to go through the Making."

As if pulled by magnetic force, her eyes swung toward Malachi. "They said it *killed* you, that you only survived because of your Gift."

Malachi nodded. "That is true."

Lucky made a noise somewhere between a sob and a humorless laugh. "So, it's likely to kill me, but it's Josh's only chance? If I die, we both die, but if I survive, we both live."

She held that thought for a moment, then made the only possible choice.

"I'll do it. Of course, I'll do it."

Decision made, she once again turned to Malachi, her face determined. "Can you help me? Can you teach me anything that will help me survive it?"

"I don't know." His deep voice was thoughtful. Leaning forward, he took both her hands in his, his long braids sliding over his shoulders as he did so. "But I will help you in any way I can."

Lucky swallowed the lump that had appeared in her throat. "Thank you," she whispered.

"You are quite certain about this?" Zeke asked. "Once the agreement is made, you cannot change your mind."

Lucky answered without hesitation. "Yes, I'm certain. I have to try. If there's the slightest chance…." Her voice trailed off.

Zeke nodded his understanding. "Yes. Very well. I will contact—"

He stopped speaking as the apartment door opened, announcing Aidan's return. None of the group said anything as they listened to his booted footfalls crossing toward them, with a brief pause for him to retrieve the piano bench.

Once he had joined them, he stood, holding the bench, his eyes shifting from Zeke to Ben. "I should have known."

Then, looking at each of them in turn, he added, "I take it Josh isn't doing well."

Zeke cleared his throat. "No, he is not. Sambethe is with him."

"Take your seat, Aidan," Malachi added quietly. "There's more."

Aidan lowered himself onto the piano bench, his face settling into grim lines.

"The toxin will kill Josh," Lucky explained, her voice hushed, "and worse than that, it will make him become a Wraith when he dies."

"A soul sucker?" Aidan interrupted, shocked.

A muscle working in his clenched jaw, Malachi nodded.

"The only cure is the blood of a Naphil who is also a relative." Lucky watched Aidan as she spoke, and she knew the exact instant that the full import of her words sank in. His mouth tightened, his eyes blazed, and his hands clenched around the edge of the bench, as if to keep him from launching himself off it. She paused, giving him a chance to speak, but he maintained his silence, just staring at her with those blazing eyes.

"I've agreed to go through the Making." The way he was looking at her made her feel like she was confessing to some kind of crime. Still, he said nothing.

Zeke's voice cut through the palpable tension. "I will contact Uriel and arrange for the Striking of the agreement. It should be done as soon as possible. I fear we do not have much time."

"Even if the Striking is tomorrow," said Malachi, "the Making will be four days from now. Do we have that much time?"

Although he spoke in general terms, Lucky knew what he meant: Did *Josh* have that much time?

"Sambethe has given him a tonic that will alleviate his current symptoms, and we have placed him in a stronger stasis that will keep the toxin from completing its work for a few days, perhaps even a week. I will communicate the urgency to Uriel and request that the Striking be set for tomorrow."

"She has agreed to the Making, then?" Sambethe's voice startled Lucky. She hadn't heard the oracle enter the room. The woman moved silently across the floor to stand beside Zeke.

Aidan made a strangled sound, and his hands clenched so tightly around the bench that his knuckles were white knobs. "Of course, she's agreed," he said, each cold word as hard as a bullet. "What else could she do? You must be very happy about that, since it's what you've wanted all along."

"Aidan," Zeke cautioned.

Uncurling his fingers from the bench, Aidan threw his hands up palms out. "I'm not arguing. The decision's made. I'm just saying...."

"He is correct," Sambethe said coolly. "You all know that is true. The circumstances are somewhat less than ideal, but the outcome? Yes, it is what I have wanted." When no one replied, she continued, "The stasis is stable, and the young man is sleeping comfortably, so I will take my leave now. Should the stasis become unstable or his condition change for any reason, I will know, and I will return immediately."

"Thank you," Lucky said, as Ben slipped by Sambethe to get to the guest room and Josh.

The oracle brushed away her thanks. "It is the least I could do," she said.

Zeke looked at her with a strange expression on his face, but when he spoke, he only offered his own words of thanks and farewell. Lucky watched him as Sambethe dematerialized and saw that a small frown had settled on his forehead. She refrained from asking him about its source. She didn't need anything else to worry about at the moment.

"I must depart as well," Zeke said, his tone heavy. "If we are to arrange the Striking for tomorrow, I have a long night's work ahead of me."

Before he could dematerialize, Lucky went to him and, laying a hand on his arm, stood on her tiptoes to place a kiss on his cheek. "Thank you, Zeke, for everything."

Cradling her cheek in his hand, he regarded her with serious eyes. "I do not know that I deserve any thanks in this, my dear. Like you, I do that which must be done." Redirecting his gaze to the tall, dark man who had risen from his seat on the couch, he added, "Do whatever you can to help her, Malachi. She is too valuable to be lost."

Malachi silently inclined his head in assent, a gesture that struck Lucky as oddly formal, even somehow ceremonial. Then Zeke was gone.

"It seems we must all leave at once," Malachi said, looking at Lucky. "I have some studying to do in order to determine how best to help you with the Making. We will begin our work together tomorrow after the Striking ceremony."

Holding his hand out to Aidan, he added, "Until tomorrow, Commander."

Aidan raised a questioning brow as he clasped his friend's outstretched hand, and Malachi added, "I thought you could use a reminder of your status."

Aidan smiled wryly. "Yeah, Sambethe and I—well, I guess she sort of brings out the rebellious teenager in me. I'm attempting to work on that."

Malachi placed a hand on his shoulder. "Your anger and concern is understandable, my friend," he said, casting a quick glance in Lucky's direction.

"I'll take the elevator down," he added by way of farewell, as he headed toward the door.

Lucky took a couple of deep breaths as she waited for Aidan to return from seeing Malachi out. She wasn't sure what to say to him, and her feelings were all jumbled together. She was terrified of what she had to do, but she was equally determined to do it. She was fighting to remain positive and trust in Malachi and her own strength and determination to survive. And she didn't need Aidan making her feel defensive. She was already scared to bits about the Making; defending her decision to do it was more than she should have to deal with.

Aidan walked slowly back into the room and stopped a few feet away from her, his hands in his pockets. "I wish you weren't doing this," he said. "I understand why you are. I know you have to—you don't really have a choice—but I wish you weren't. I just—"

He stopped, as if the words stuck in his throat, and then continued raggedly, "I don't want to lose you."

His fear for her safety and the pain he felt at the anticipation of her loss were reflected in his blue eyes and the muscle that worked in his jaw. Lucky felt strangely as if she were the stronger in this situation. It did make sense, she supposed. Even though the Making might be the death of her, she had made the decision to attempt it. She held the power of that decision, no matter what its outcome, while Aidan could do nothing but support her and fear for her.

Wordlessly, she went to him and slid her arms around his waist. His arms went round her in return, and he hugged her close, pressing his face into her hair. Neither of them said anything as they stood there, holding one another. Words seemed both inadequate and irrelevant, incapable of expressing what they wanted to say and too far removed from the immediacy of their feelings to matter. They needed not abstractions, but the simple reassurance of touch, the tangible evidence of life found in warm, strong arms, steady heartbeats, and the rhythmic movement of breath. They held on as tightly as they could, as if the strength of their embrace could fuse them into one.

After a time, Aidan lifted his head and, releasing her with one arm, he pushed her hair back from her face. "We should get some sleep," he said softly. "Tomorrow is going to be a long, hard day."

"I want to look in on Josh," Lucky said, withdrawing from his arms. "Ben is with him, but…."

Aidan nodded. "Sure. Tell Ben he's welcome to stay if he wants."

Ben was standing near the bed, staring down at Josh. He looked up as she stepped into the room. Lucky glanced from Ben to her cousin. His body was encased head to foot in bands of pulsing blue-green light. He was motionless, and as Sambethe had said, he appeared to be quite comfortable. His face held the relaxed, peaceful expression of deep, dreamless sleep. Looking at him, she issued a silent prayer to whoever might be listening that she be allowed to survive the Making, so that she could save him.

"Aidan says you're welcome to stay as long as you like," she told Ben.

"There's nothing I can do, so I might as well go. But tell him thanks for the offer," Ben said. "It seems it's all up to you. That's a pretty heavy burden to lay on your shoulders. Thank you for accepting it."

"How could I not?" she whispered, tears filling her eyes.

Ben bent forward and dropped a kiss on her cheek. As he pulled away from her, he was already dematerializing. When he was gone, Lucky offered her sleeping cousin a whispered "Good night" before she left the room, closing the door behind her.

The door to Aidan's room was open. Lucky hesitated only an instant before stepping inside.

"Oh," she gasped.

Aidan was standing at the closet, his back to her. He had removed his shirt, and she could see the lean muscles of his back shifting beneath his skin as he moved. But it was not the sight of his bare torso—impressive though it was—that made her gasp; it was the design that spanned the top of his back between his shoulder blades. Vaguely circular in outline, the symbol was an intricate pattern of interlacing swirls and loops. She would have assumed the design had been tattooed in black ink, except that it seemed to be retracing itself in gold as she watched. It was as if an invisible hand were inking the pattern in gold, which then turned to black as it set, to be re-inked in gold once more.

Hearing her gasp, Aidan half-turned toward her.

"Your back…," she faltered.

"Oh, right. That's my sigil," Aidan said. "Every Naphil—and every angel—has one. It's sort of like an angelic fingerprint. Each is unique. It's on both my palms too; it just doesn't show up there unless it's activated."

Walking toward her on bare feet, he held up his hands palms out. His palms looked normal at first; then a smaller version of the symbol she had seen on his back appeared on each of them. The smaller designs were not traced in moving black and gold, but appeared almost fiery, more like molten gold.

"Does it hurt?" she asked, reaching her fingers toward one of the designs.

He jerked his hand back before she could touch it. "I just feel a slight burn. If you touch them, though, they will burn you badly enough to leave a scar." As he spoke, he deactivated the sigils in his palms, closing his fingers over them until they faded away.

"What about the one on your back? Will it burn me too?"

He shook his head.

"Can I touch it?"

He swallowed, then nodded and turned so his back was facing her once more.

Lucky rested her hand on his back, her fingers touching the sigil's outer swirl. It was slightly raised, like a scar, and felt a tiny bit warmer than the rest of his skin. With one fingertip, she traced its outline, following the flash of gold as it moved around the design. Aidan shivered.

"Can you feel it?" she asked. "The gold part that moves?"

"Not usually," he replied, his voice deeper and thicker than normal, "but I can feel you."

"Sorry," she breathed, letting her hand fall to her side as she stepped away from him.

"Not a problem."

He moved back to the closet and pulled out a t-shirt which he tossed to her. As she caught it, she noticed that the button of his jeans was undone, and the denim hung low on his hips.

"I can take the couch this time," she offered, a little breathlessly.

He shook his head, his shoulders stiffening. "You're undergoing the Making in a few days. I want to be with you every possible moment until then. You'll sleep here—with me. If that's alright with you."

"It's alright with me."

"Good." His shoulders relaxed.

"I'll just go—brush my teeth then," she said.

"You know where everything is."

Lucky escaped to the bathroom, where she readied herself for bed, brushing her teeth and pulling on the t-shirt

Aidan had given her. When she returned to the bedroom, he had turned back the covers on the bed. He had also replaced his jeans with navy blue pajama pants, which rested equally low on his hips. She swallowed and tugged nervously on her borrowed t-shirt.

"Go ahead and climb in," he said. "I'll be back in a minute."

Lucky slid onto the bed and under the covers, her heart threatening to pound its way out of her rib cage. She didn't know what to expect; she wasn't even sure what she wanted. But, like Aidan, she wanted to spend every possible minute together.

Aidan's breath caught in his chest as he stepped into his bedroom and saw Lucky in his bed. She had tucked a pillow behind her and was sitting up, her blanketed legs pulled up in front of her, her arms wrapped around her knees. Her long dark curls spilled over her shoulders, and her jade green eyes were huge. She looked so fragile, so simultaneously scared and determined and brave. The thought of her going through the Making made him quake inside—and filled him with frustrated anger. He wanted to protect her from everything that could harm her, but he could do nothing to protect her from this. He respected her choice—knew she would have found it impossible to make any other—and her loyalty and strength and bravery made his heart ache as he walked slowly toward the bed.

Sliding his legs under the covers, he settled himself beside her and put his arm around her shoulders, pulling her tight against his side. She sighed as she leaned into him, resting her head on his shoulder and her hand on his blanket-covered thigh.

"Tell me about the Making," she said in a small voice. "How does it work?"

Before he could respond, she lifted her head and looked at him, asking hopefully, "Will I have a sigil like yours?"

His lips curved even as the pain in his chest increased. The very question took her survival for granted. "Sort of," he answered, his hand slipping under the overlarge sleeve of her—his—t-shirt to caress her upper arm. "Once the Making is over, your own unique sigil will appear on your upper back, yes, and it will burn itself into your palms as well. But you—you will have more than just the one sigil on your back."

He stopped, hesitated, steeling himself for what he had to say next. "During the Making, a number of angels or Nephilim—who they are will be revealed to you during your preparations in the three days between the Striking and the Making—will each grant some of his or her powers to you. It's done through the palm sigils."

He paused again as she pulled away enough to look into his face. He could tell from her expression that she was already beginning to understand what she was about to endure.

"Go on." Her voice was surprisingly steady.

"Turn around," he said.

She shifted so she was sitting with her back to him.

"They will each put a hand here," he said, placing his palms on her back, one on each side of her spine, near the base of her shoulder blades. He slid his palms a hand-length lower on her back and positioned them slightly wider apart. "And here." Again, lower, the base of his palms now at the bottom of her ribs, and his hands even farther apart. "And here."

"Like the wings," she whispered.

"Yes," he replied. "They mark the positioning of the wings."

"And they will—burn their sigils into my back."

Lucky's words were more statement than question. Still, he answered her, "Yes."

He felt her shiver beneath his hands. Then she turned back around to face him.

"It sounds painful."

He nodded. "I've never experienced it first-hand, but watching Malachi's Making.... It looked unbearable."

As soon as the words were spoken, he wished he could take them back. She didn't need to hear that. "I'm sorry," he added quickly. "I shouldn't have...."

"No," she said, laying her hand on his arm, "I need to know—so I have some idea of what to expect."

He lifted her hand from his arm, planted a lingering kiss on her palm, and then closed her fingers around it. "I wish I could make this different for you, take it away from you, go through it for you—anything, rather than see you endure it yourself."

"I know," she said, "but you can't."

Kneeling, she leaned forward and kissed him, wrapping her arms around his neck. He pulled her close, his hands slipping beneath the t-shirt to slide over the smooth skin of her back, skin that would be marked with excruciating burns in a matter of days. Stifling a groan, he met her kiss with increased urgency.

Later, as she lay curled next to Aidan, his body spooned around hers, Lucky wondered if sleep would even be possible. She had expected him to take their embrace somewhere beyond kisses and touches, but he hadn't. He seemed content to simply hold her close while they slept. Although she was a little disappointed, she was also touched by his tender consideration. She knew he was trying to protect her in the only way he could.

She stroked his arm where it rested around her waist and raised his hand so she could brush her lips across his knuckles. In response, he caressed her cheek with the backs of his fingers before repositioning his arm around her. Nudging her hair aside with his nose, he placed a soft kiss on her jaw, just beneath her ear. When he whispered, "Go to sleep," she yawned. Snuggling back against him, she closed her eyes. It was only moments before she slept.

CHAPTER 23

Aidan wasn't sure if it was the ringing of his cell phone or Zeke's mental push that woke him up. He silently cursed the Cherub as he carefully disentangled his limbs from Lucky's, hoping to give her a few more minutes of sleep. Swinging his legs onto the floor, he retrieved the cell phone from his bedside table. By the time he accepted the call, he was halfway to the living room.

"By all that's holy, Zeke, you're worse than a freakin' alarm clock. What time is it anyway?"

Zeke chuckled. "Thank you, Aidan. I had not expected to laugh today. It is approximately two minutes past 6:00 AM."

"Just because *you* never sleep…."

"The Striking has been set for 10:00 this morning. You and Lucky should plan on arriving here no later than 8:00. We have to get her ready for the ceremony."

"Of course. We'll be there." Aidan was fully awake now. "You've outdone yourself, Zeke. How did you manage to get the ceremony scheduled so soon? I was expecting this afternoon at the earliest."

"There are some advantages to never sleeping, my young friend," Zeke answered before ending the call.

Aidan shook his head at his silent cell phone, then sighing, raked a hand through his hair. If he just let Lucky sleep, maybe they wouldn't have to face today's ceremony—or the resulting one three days from now. Yeah, and then Josh would die and become a soul-sucking monster. Not a lot of good options to choose from, were there?

With another sigh, he headed back down the hall to wake Lucky and tell her the news.

The morning sky was a mass of gray clouds, and small rain was starting to fall as Aidan guided the silver BMW into a parking spot a couple of blocks from Zeke's Hyde Park brownstone. Lucky had to struggle against the wind to close the passenger door. That same wind whipped her hair around her face as she and Aidan hurried down the sidewalk toward Zeke's house. She shivered and clutched the too-large jacket she had borrowed from Aidan more closely around her.

She had been surprised to learn that Zeke lived just a few blocks from her own Hyde Park apartment. Strange to think the angel had been so near her all this time. She wondered if she had perhaps passed him on the sidewalk in her previous life, unaware of who—or what—he was and how important he would become to her.

She glanced at Aidan as they climbed the steps to the front door. Like the sky, his usual glow seemed overcast, and his eyes were shadowed. He rang the bell and then stepped back from the door to wait. Her eyes sought and found his, but he looked away. She had sensed his withdrawal the moment they stepped into the elevator and began their descent to the garage. And he had seemed to move further away from her the closer they had come to their destination, responding to her attempts at conversation with such monosyllabic answers, she had finally given up and remained silent for the remainder of the trip.

When Zeke opened the door, Aidan gestured for her to precede him inside, still without saying a word. Zeke hadn't spoken either, and as Lucky followed his tall, silent figure through a chilly, unused-looking formal living room and down a hallway to a set of descending stairs, she began to think silence might be a necessary part of the preparation for the Striking ceremony.

Given what she assumed would be the formality of the occasion, she felt underdressed. She was once again wearing the black jeans and gray sweater she had put on the evening before. When they had exited Lake Shore Drive for Hyde Park, she had asked Aidan if they should swing by her apartment so she could change, but he had answered with a clipped "No need."

Zeke turned right at the bottom of the stairs and ushered them into a large, warm room that seemed to serve as both office and sitting room. At one end sat a huge, old-fashioned desk, surrounded by stuffed bookshelves and topped with an incongruous-looking silver laptop, open and humming softly amid a nest of papers and scrolls; at the other, four worn leather armchairs were grouped into a cozy seating area around a low, round table. Lucky guessed this was where Zeke spent the majority of his time.

"Please, have a seat," the angel said, indicating the leather chairs.

Lucky sat down, feeling even smaller than she was, since the large chair all but swallowed her. As Aidan settled into the chair next to hers, she tugged off her boots and pulled her feet up under her to sit cross-legged, so she took up more space.

Zeke gave her an affectionate smile. "And, by all means, make yourself comfortable," he said.

"I suppose I should have asked before I put my feet up," she responded. "This chair's just so big and cozy."

"It pleases me that you felt at home enough here to do it without asking." Tilting his head toward Aidan with a raised brow, Zeke added, "Some people have even been known to engage in wrestling matches on those chairs without so much as a 'by-your-leave.'"

"Can I help it my brother's a barbarian?" Aidan finally spoke.

"*I'm* a barbarian? As I recall, you instigated more than your share of those wrestling matches."

Lucky looked toward the door to find the source of the amused baritone. A man she had never seen before, but who was apparently Aidan's brother, was lounging in the doorway, one shoulder propped against the frame, a fragile-looking china teacup cradled in one hand.

"Kev," Aidan said, rising to his feet, "I should have known you would be here for the pre-game show." His tone held a disconcerting mix of warmth and reserve.

Kev pushed away from the wall, taking Aidan's extended hand with his free one. Not content with a handshake, he drew his brother into a half-embrace, shifting the cup so as not to slosh tea down his back. When Aidan stepped away from him and turned toward Lucky, his face showed the beginnings of a smile.

Before Aidan could speak, Kev said, "You must be the girl I've heard so much about. It's nice to finally meet you, Lucky." The eyes that raked her from head to foot before coming to rest on her own were a deep green flecked with gold.

Lucky rose to take the hand he held out toward her, while Aidan completed the introduction. "Lucky, this barbarian is my half-brother, Kevin Drake—also known as Satan." Much of the warmth left his voice on the last word.

"Satan?" Lucky squeaked.

Kev cocked an eyebrow at his brother. "Nice," he muttered.

Turning back to Lucky, he said, "You can call me Kev. And it's *Ha-Satan,* actually—not a name, but a title—one I've had the dubious pleasure of holding for about two weeks now. As you might have guessed, my little brother is somewhat less than pleased about that."

"It's just because I'm worried about you, Kev."

Aidan dropped back down into the chair beside Lucky's. Kev shrugged out of his beat-up brown bomber jacket and took the chair on the other side of the table from him.

"Yeah. I'm kind of worried about me too, but, hey, what's one more item added to the list?"

As Lucky curled back up in her chair, she studied the two young men, looking for a resemblance. She could see some similarity in their bone structure, and they were both lounging back in their chairs in similar positions. Other than that, they looked almost nothing alike. Where Aidan, with his golden hair and blue eyes, was like a summer beach, all sunlight and sky, sand and water, Kev was like a shady forest, with light filtering in patches through a canopy of leaves. The dark green shirt he was wearing somehow served to make the gold flecks in his eyes more pronounced, and the wavy brown hair that fell just to his shoulders was streaked with honey blond. He was a little shorter than Aidan, she had seen when they were still standing, and broader, his frame more heavily muscled, where Aidan's was whipcord lean. She guessed he was about the same age as Josh.

"Is either of you going to explain the whole Satan thing to me?" she blurted. Then, realizing she had spoken without thinking and interrupted their conversation, she added, "Sorry. I didn't mean to interrupt."

"No, it's alright. It's even relevant," Kev answered, surprising her. "I'm not here just because I'm Aidan's brother."

He paused as Zeke, who had left the room a little earlier, returned bearing a tray laden with tea and food. After Zeke had supplied them all with tea, and they had each filled a plate from the selection of muffins and breads, hard boiled eggs, bacon, and smoked salmon, Kev continued, "*Ha-Satan* is Lucifer's representative to the Metatron. The term means 'the adversary,' and in some ways, I guess that's what I am. As

Lucifer's representative, you could say my role is to act as a sort of devil's advocate with them."

"What does that have to do with why you're here?" Lucky asked, selecting a mini poppy seed muffin from the items on her plate.

Kev paused with his lox and bagel halfway to his mouth. "Well, over the years the position has evolved. *Ha-Satan* serves as Lucifer's representative in many ceremonies as well as in communication with the Metatron. That includes such things as Strikings and Makings. Lucifer may decide to come to the Making himself, who knows? But at least for the purposes of today's Striking ceremony, I'm it."

As Kev bit into his bagel and lox, Zeke picked up the explanation. "The Striking ceremony is very formal. You will be asked a series of questions and expected to give the standard responses. I asked you to arrive early so we could give you a general idea of what to expect, and so we could coach you on how to act and what to say. Once we have finished breakfast, we get to work."

After her coaching session was over, Lucky was shown to a spare room where she exchanged her re-worn jeans and sweater for a loose-fitting silver-gray silk shift. She left her boots and socks with her discarded jeans and sweater, since Zeke had informed her she must be barefoot for the ceremony. Exiting the room, she felt more like she was dressed for bed than for a ceremonial gathering.

Joining the others in the cold formal living room, Lucky discovered that Zeke had changed clothes as well. He was now wearing a loose, long-sleeved robe of heavy ivory silk. Covering his chest and secured at his shoulders and waist was a gleaming breast plate marked with a complex design of curving loops and straight lines. Lucky assumed it was a sigil of some sort, since its style reminded her of the mark on Aidan's back. Aidan was still dressed in the jeans and dark sweater he had donned that morning, since he would not be participating in the ceremony. Kev had left to prepare himself for his role as *Ha-Satan.*

Lucky's uncomfortable sense that she was wearing a nightgown lessened somewhat when she learned her costume was not complete. She stood with raised arms, while Aidan wrapped her waist with a white belt decorated with black sigils. After the sigil belt had been wrapped and secured, Zeke dropped a long stole over her shoulders. It too was white and marked with sigils, not black like those on the belt but a fiery red-gold. The stole looped around her neck so that the two long ends hung down her back. She guessed its fiery sigils were meant to mimic those that would be burned into her skin during the Making.

Once the stole was in place, Zeke placed his hands on her shoulders. "You are sure about this?" he asked, his gray eyes steady on hers. When she nodded, his hands closed in a brief squeeze.

Aidan stepped in front of Lucky as Zeke released her. Cupping her cheek in his hand, he stared into her eyes, his own reflecting his fear for her, a deep respect, and something more that she couldn't quite name, but which threatened to bring her to tears. He placed a soft, lingering kiss on her mouth. Then, letting his hand fall from her face, he whispered, "See you on the other side." And he was gone.

Gesturing for her to follow, Zeke moved out into the hallway. He led her back down the stairs to the basement level, where his office was located, but instead of turning right at the base of the stairs, he turned left. Following behind him, Lucky stopped and stared.

Directly in front of them was a massive set of double doors. They were not set into one of the ivory painted walls but were free-standing in the middle of an otherwise empty room. Made of what appeared to be heavy, dark wood, they were carved to look like a pair of folded wings, each feather of which was exquisitely detailed. Unable to resist, Lucky reached out to touch the polished material. As her hand moved over the carved feathers, she could feel a slight vibration beneath her fingers, like she was stroking a purring cat.

"They are called the Gates of Heaven," Zeke said. "They were originally created to facilitate passage between the earth and the Heavens for the Fallen. Once we chose to leave the Heavens, we could no longer simply dematerialize here and rematerialize there; we had to use the doors, to knock and seek entry, as it were. Now, only *Ha-Satan*—and I on rare occasion—are allowed entry to the Heavens even through the Gates."

He sighed and was silent for just a moment before continuing, "The Gates have since been modified for other uses. Since human Sensitives are unable to dematerialize, they can, with the help of an angel or *Ha-Satan*, use the Gates to reach places outside the earthly realm—like the Alliance Council Hall, which is our destination."

"Are these Gates the only ones?" Lucky asked.

"Oh, no. This pair is one of many. Every community of Fallen around the globe has a pair of Gates, each placed in a secure location and protected with wards. Not only is this house heavily warded against unauthorized entry, but no human—even a Sensitive as powerful as you—can so much as see the Gates without my permission."

When he finished speaking, Zeke held his hand out to her. "Ready?" he asked.

Lucky took his hand. "I'm ready."

Zeke placed the palm of his free hand into the slight indentation in the center of the pair of doors, where the wings met. Lucky could see a golden glow begin to emanate from beneath his hand. When he removed it, a complex sigil was marked in fiery lines and curves against the dark background. Then the flames subsided, sinking inward as if absorbed, and the wings began to open.

Lucky's eyes widened in astonishment. The doors didn't open outward or inward like any doors she had ever seen. Instead, the wings unfolded, and as they did, they began to glow with a light that was almost too bright to bear. She closed her eyes, shielding them with her free hand. When she opened them again, she was looking at a wing-shaped opening through which she could see distorted images, as if they were on the other side of a field of clear, flickering flames.

Feeling a tug on her arm, she realized that Zeke had taken a step toward the opening. Moving forward, she joined him, and they stepped through together.

CHAPTER 24

That single step seemed to take forever. Lucky felt like her body was being compressed, stretched. It was hard to breathe, as if the air were too thick to take into her lungs. She heard the crackle of flames, the rushing of water, and something like the beating of powerful wings. She tightened her hand on Zeke's. Then they were through to the other side.

They were standing on a grassy boulevard, leading up to a huge building constructed of white and black granite and topped by a golden dome. Perched on the top of the dome was a weathervane in the shape of two angels facing one another, arms raised, with bent elbows and hands clasped. The sky was blue, and although she couldn't find the sun in the sky, she felt the warmth of sunlight on her bare arms, and feet.

Looking around, she saw angels—some Light, some Dark—flying through the sky, and descending to the ground to enter the Alliance Council Hall. Other beings, some winged and some not, were strolling on the boulevard or hurrying toward the great building.

"Are they all here for the Striking?" she asked.

Zeke shook his head. "No. Some of them may be, but most are here for other reasons. Many ceremonies and meetings are held here."

"How was the passage?" Aidan called, as he came strolling across the grass toward them.

"I felt a little squished," Lucky answered. "Otherwise, it was fine."

"Shall we?" Zeke asked, and headed down the boulevard toward the Council Hall.

Lucky and Aidan fell in behind him, Aidan catching Lucky's hand in his. As they walked, Lucky took in her surroundings. Except for the winged and otherwise inhuman figures and the lack of a visible source for the sunlight, they could have been somewhere in or around Chicago on a mild summer day.

"Where are we anyway?" she asked Aidan.

"Elsewhere," he answered, with a smile. "This place was created as a meeting place for everyone who is part of the Alliance—Light, Dark, Fallen. Since no one from any one group wanted the others to have the advantage of having the Council Hall in their world—on their home turf—it was decided that the Council Hall should be, well, elsewhere. So, in Elsewhere we are. The place belongs to everyone in the Alliance, and it's considered neutral territory."

"Does it have weather? Seasons? Day and night? Or is it always like this?"

"It's always like this as best I can tell. At least, it has been any time I've been here."

"Always midday in summer. Not bad."

They had reached the steps leading up to the Council Hall. Lucky gripped Aidan's hand more tightly as they climbed the stone steps, and he laced his fingers through hers. Zeke held the heavy door open for them to precede him inside. A long hall floored with pink marble stretched out before them, and black marble stairs with ornate golden banisters curved up on either side. People—beings—were hurrying down the hall and turning into the corridors that branched off it, just like in any office or governmental building Lucky had ever visited. Zeke directed them to the stairs to their right, and they began to climb. The marble felt cool beneath Lucky's bare feet, in contrast to the warm grass and the heated stone steps outside.

The stairs led them to another pink marble tiled hall, this one narrower than the one on the first floor.

"Here we are," Zeke said, stopping outside a door about halfway down the hall and on the left.

Lucky took a deep breath as Zeke turned toward her.

"Remember to make your responses as we rehearsed," he said.

Lucky nodded.

Aidan squeezed her hand before releasing it. *This is it,* Lucky thought. Once through that door, there was no turning back. No sooner had the thought crossed her mind than Zeke opened the door and ushered them through.

The room was oval-shaped and looked like a cross between a church and a courtroom. The walls were paneled in dark wood with tapestry depictions of angels hung on alternate panels. Gilded trim circled the frescoed ceiling that arched high overhead. A single large chair sat in the center of the room, facing a raised dais upon which sat a podium flanked by two heavy tables. The entire wall opposite the podium was filled with graduated gallery seating, made from dark wood and looking to Lucky much like church pews. Aidan left them to head toward the gallery, while Zeke directed Lucky to the chair that was the room's focal point.

As they drew closer to the chair, Lucky saw that it too was raised. Zeke held her hand as she climbed the three steps leading up to it, releasing her when she reached the top step, so she could turn and face the podium. She remained standing, as she had been instructed, while Zeke moved toward the table to the right of the podium. Positioning himself behind it, he too remained standing, with his arms behind his back. Lucky's breathing quickened as her stomach began to knot. She wished she could turn around and look for Aidan in the gallery, but Zeke had told her she must face toward the podium at all times. Without turning her head, she shifted her eyes toward Zeke. His eyes met hers, and he tilted his head in the tiniest nod of encouragement.

Out of the corner of her eye, she saw someone approach the table on the podium's other side. Moving only her eyes, she looked in that direction. She managed to keep from starting in surprise as she recognized Kev. In his formal role as *Ha-Satan*, he bore little resemblance to the warm, smiling man who had teased his younger brother and helped prepare her for this ceremony. His face looked hard, almost cold. No longer in his green shirt and faded jeans, he was dressed in loose-fitting black silk trousers and a blood-red robe that fell to his knees. The robe was open down the front, revealing an expanse of bare chest, on which rested a large, circular black pendant with red markings. Like Zeke's and her own, Kev's feet were bare. He took a position identical to Zeke's behind the other table. His eyes caught hers before she could look away, and he dropped one eyelid in a quick wink. Somehow, that wink helped to calm her more than had Zeke's nod—perhaps because it made her realize that, whatever happened, she had at least three friends here. She wasn't going through this alone or unsupported.

She could hear the sounds of others entering the room and climbing the gallery steps to find seats, and again she wished she could turn her head. To distract herself, she studied the podium in front of her. Carved into its front in *bas relief* was the image of an angel, robed and barefoot, facing forward, wings arcing up behind. The angel's left hand rested on the hilt of a sword, the tip of which pointed toward the floor; the right was held up, palm out. The palm was marked with a sigil that had been traced in gold. The gold marking stood out against the dark wood, and Lucky swallowed the lump that formed in her throat as the purpose of today's ceremony rose to the front of her mind again. She had gotten so caught up in the preparations and her nervousness about the ceremony itself that she had almost managed to forget why she was here.

Suddenly, she heard the beating of wings, and the space behind the podium was filled with a light so bright she had to close her eyes. When she opened them, the light was fading, as if being drawn into the body of the being now standing behind the podium. Zeke had told her that the Archangel Uriel would be presiding at the ceremony, and she had tried to imagine what he would look like. Her imagination had not come close to the reality. The Archangel was huge, easily four times the size of Zeke, and his massive wings stretched half the length of the room. The wings seemed to be in constant motion, like water or light, and sparked with the iridescence of opals and mother of pearl, shimmering with colors she had never seen before. The hair which flowed down to his shoulders was like spun gold and moved as if lifted on a faint breeze. His eyes were closed.

As the brightness was absorbed into his body, the Archangel shrank until he was perhaps only twice Zeke's height and breadth, and his wings folded inward, arcing up behind his shoulders. His entire being pulsed with the golden-white light as if it were barely restrained and could explode into that unbearable radiance at any moment. Heat radiated out from him as well. Even with the space between them, Lucky felt as if she were standing in front of a roaring fireplace. His glowing face was stern, set in hard, unforgiving lines, and when he opened his eyes, the sockets appeared to be filled with flames. He was beautiful and awful, compelling and terrifying. Lucky couldn't tear her gaze away.

He lifted one hand, and she realized it held a large book, ancient-looking and bound in leather trimmed in gold. She was amazed it didn't burst into flames in his hand. He placed the book, unopened, on the podium and, lifting his head, gazed out over the room. It seemed to Lucky as if he saw everything and nothing all at once, as if his flame-filled eye sockets took in everything and everyone in the room, but that he remained untouched by anything he saw.

He lifted his arms, spreading them wide, and opened his mouth to speak. The voice that issued forth was like the rushing of wind or the roar of a tremendous fire. Lucky sensed more than heard the words he spoke.

We gather in the spirit of Alliance—Light, Dark, and Fallen. Let the representatives speak. I AM URIEL, ARCHANGEL OF THE HEAVENS.

"I am *Ha-Satan*, the Adversary," Kev's voice rang out, strong and clear.

"I am the Cherub Ezekiel, Ambassador to the Fallen." Zeke's voice was more resonant than ever. Like the fluid chime of a deep, clear bell, its tone lingered after the words were spoken.

The Sensitive is present?

Lucky gave her response. "I am Lucinda Lily Monroe, known as Lucky."

Let the Striking begin.

That was the signal for Lucky—and everyone besides the Archangel—to take their seats. The dark wood of the chair was hard, and the ornate carving bit into her thighs through the thin silk of her shift, but the chair was warm to the touch, warmed as was Lucky herself, by the heat radiating outward from Uriel.

Who speaks for the Sensitive?

Zeke rose to his feet. "I do," he replied.

What is your request?

"Lucky would undertake the Making, Archangel."

And the reason for this request?

As she listened to Zeke's response, Lucky felt almost as if his words had nothing to do with her, as if he were talking about people she didn't know. Zeke explained in formal terms what had happened to her cousin. He stressed that Josh was a human, an innocent, who had become an unwitting victim in a conflict he knew nothing about. He described Josh's condition with stark simplicity. "He will die and become a Wraith without the blood of a Naphil of his own blood. Lucky would save him from this fate."

You are aware of the danger of that which you would undertake? The Archangel's words were addressed to Lucky.

She stood and swallowed to ease the sudden dryness in her mouth and throat.

"I am."

You make this request of your own free will?

"I do."

You have not been coerced or compelled in any way?

You mean, other than by the fact that my cousin was given a poison that will turn him into a soul-sucking demon? Lucky thought, but she gave the expected response. "I make this choice freely."

Ha-Satan, have you any objection to the granting of this request?

"I have no objection." Kev's words lacked inflection. Lucky knew from their morning's conversation that, like Aidan and Zeke, he wished she weren't going through the Making, but knew that she had no real choice and would not stand in her way.

Then let the contract be Struck.

So saying, the Archangel opened the book that lay before him. Light sprang forth from its pages as it opened. Uriel raised his right hand palm out, and as he spoke, a complex and intricate sigil glowed on his palm like red-hot embers.

The contract is absolute. Once Struck it cannot be revoked. The Sensitive, Lucky Monroe, will be Made Naphil in three days time.

As soon as he finished speaking, Uriel pressed his burning sigil against the pages of the book. A wind swept through the room, and it seemed to Lucky as if everything went dark except for the Archangel and the book he touched.

She felt as if she were underwater, the pressure on her ears drowning out all sound except the beating of her own heart. She tried to take a breath, but the air wouldn't enter her lungs. Her hands and feet began to tingle, and within seconds the sensation spread throughout her entire body. Directing her attention deep inside herself, she tried to reach her control room only to find that access was denied. It wasn't that the interior space was no longer there; it was like a door had been locked and barred against her. She wanted to scream with frustration, but she couldn't even breathe.

Then something shifted—inside of her and, she somehow sensed, in the very substance of being itself—and the force of that shift was enough to knock her off her feet. She felt a sudden flash of pain as her knees hit the wooden platform, and then there was nothing.

Aidan felt the shockwave wash over and through him as the fabric of reality adjusted to accommodate the terms of the Striking. He saw Lucky fall as if from a distance. Decorum forgotten, he staggered to his feet and raced down out of the gallery in a stumbling run. An aftershock hit before he'd reached the bottom step, and he tripped and fell. When he hit the floor at the base of the gallery stairs, he rolled into a crouch, pushing off into a sprint that brought him to Lucky's side in time to catch her before she tumbled off the raised platform onto the floor. Dropping to his knees, he cradled her against him. As he ran his hand over her hair, he felt something sticky. He pushed her curls back with trembling fingers. The blood had come from a cut on her temple, and a goose egg was rising on the spot even as he watched.

"Is she okay?" Kev asked, as he crouched down beside him.

"She's unconscious, but she's breathing normally." Aidan gestured to the wound on her temple. "She must have hit her head on the chair when she fell."

"The force of the Striking made *me* stagger. I can only imagine how much more intense it must have been for her."

"I've never attended a Striking before. Is it always like this?"

Kev shook his head, his face grim. "The only one I've been to that came close was Malachi's."

Aidan clenched his jaw but said nothing.

"She should come to in a moment or so. We must put her back in the chair." Zeke spoke above them. Directing a sharp glance at Aidan, he added, "And you need to return to your seat. I will take care of her."

"I didn't notice you keeping her from crashing to the floor," Aidan hissed.

"There was no need," Zeke answered. "You were already here. Now, go. I have her."

As he spoke, the Cherub lifted Lucky from Aidan's arms. Aidan reluctantly made his way back to the gallery and found a seat off to the side, where he thought he would have the best view of Lucky. But when he sat down, he could see only Zeke. The Cherub was bent over the side of the chair, blocking Aidan's view. In a moment, Zeke stood up, and Aidan saw Lucky's hand come forward to rest on the angel's arm. She was conscious then. Zeke said something to her, listened to her response, and then patted her hand, before returning to his place at the Ambassador's table.

Even with Zeke out of the way, Aidan couldn't see much of Lucky. The high carved sides of the Petitioner's Seat hid everything except her hand, which in lieu of Zeke's arm now rested on that of the chair. He would only see her well if she stood again.

Directing his gaze back to the front of the room, he saw that the Archangel had not moved. His hand was still pressed against the glowing pages of the book, and the wind that had swept through the room when his palm first touched the book now seemed concentrated around him. His hair and robes whipped about him as if he were in the direct path of a hurricane. As Aidan watched, the wind suddenly ceased, and the light coming from the book abruptly dimmed, as if both were sucked into the volume's pages. Uriel raised his hand from the book and again held it palm out. The sigil that had before burned red-hot was now black with hints of red sparking here and there, like banked embers. The Archangel spoke.

The Striking is complete. What has been done cannot be undone.

At the words, a shiver snaked up Aidan's spine. He knew the Striking was unalterable, but somehow when put like that in the Archangel's unearthly voice, the comment struck him as distinctly ominous.

Are there any final words? Ambassador? Ha-Satan?

Zeke and Kev both declined to speak. Aidan wondered if they felt as impatient as he did to get out of here. They had done what they came for. Now, they had to do everything they could to prepare Lucky for the Making—or, at least, Malachi had to do everything he could.

Out of the corner of his eye, Aidan saw a dark-robed figure slip from the far end of the gallery and glide into the center of the room.

"I would speak, if I may."

The voice was female and rang out clear and unexpected in the silence. Aidan's pulse rate increased as his anxiety ratcheted up several notches.

The Archangel's flame-filled eyes shifted to the hooded figure.

Who speaks?

The woman raised her hands to push back her hood. Crimson hair flamed against the black of her cloak. Aidan heard several members of the gallery gasp in surprise.

"I am Lilith, the Banished."

And what would you tell us, Lilith the Banished?

"Only this," Lilith said. "The girl, Lucky, is not as human as she seems. Her mother, an unfortunate Sensitive named Marie Monroe, coupled with my son Luil, and this girl is the result. Lucky Monroe is my granddaughter."

"*What?*" Lucky had risen from the Petitioner's Seat and was staring at the scarlet-haired woman. Sheer force of will kept Aidan from rushing to her side.

"Did you never wonder how you came by your middle name, child?" Lilith said to Lucky. "In the crease of your left arm there is a mark like a Dark Moon, is there not? All of my children and all of my children's children have such a mark."

"This?" Lucky raised her arm and pointed toward the inside of her elbow. "*This* means I'm your granddaughter?"

"Show me, Lucky." Zeke commanded, stepping up close to the platform of the Petitioner's Seat.

She turned her outstretched arm toward him.

"It is true." Zeke's words were so quiet that Aidan almost didn't hear them. Then raising his voice, he repeated, "It is true. She bears the mark of Lilith."

The gallery erupted in a flood of protests: "No child of the Banished can be Made Naphil." "The girl cannot have been ignorant of this." "It is an outrage!" "Is a Making even possible? Does she have a chance of survival?" "How could the Ambassador not know of this?" "No wonder *Ha-Satan* had no objections." "One can only hope she will not survive the Making. Who knows what kind of power she might have if she does." "The Making must be stopped!"

SILENCE!

Aidan looked back toward the Archangel, who had increased in size until he dwarfed the podium and everything surrounding it. The top of his head reached almost to the ceiling, and his unfurled, iridescent wings nearly encompassed the length of the room. His flaming eyes blazed brighter, and his features looked, if possible, even harder and sterner than when he had arrived, as his hair tossed in that invisible breeze.

Lilith the Banished, your words have been heard. They alter nothing. The Striking is absolute. What has been done cannot be undone. Lucky Monroe, Sensitive, Granddaughter of Lilith the Banished, will be Made Naphil in three days time.

As he finished speaking, light exploded outward from the Archangel's body, and with a sound like the rushing of a great many wings, Uriel was gone.

CHAPTER 25

There was a moment of stunned silence after the burst of light created by Uriel's departure had faded. Taking advantage of the lull, Aidan joined Zeke and Kev, who had moved into postures of defense, one on either side of the platform on which Lucky stood. He hoped the neutrality of the Council Hall would be respected, but he too wanted to be in a position to protect Lucky should it become necessary. Based on the comments he'd heard when Zeke pronounced his confirmation of Lilith's statements, many of those present were not feeling especially neutral about the coming Making. Aidan wasn't sure how he felt about it himself, except that he now had more reservations than ever about Lucky's safety. Otherwise, he was refusing to think much about Lilith's revelations until they were all safely back at Zeke's.

He noticed with some surprise that Lilith too had moved closer to the Petitioner's Chair, while keeping a wary eye on the members of the gallery. It looked like Lucky had a fourth protector. He bit back a bitter chuckle. Lilith owed her at least that much. If she hadn't decided to make her little revelation in this public venue, Lucky wouldn't be in quite as much need of protecting, would she?

Conversations resumed as the observers stood up to leave the gallery. Aidan was relieved to find that, although several cast venomous glances toward Lucky and the little group surrounding her, no one either approached them or made any verbal threats. He wasn't stupid enough to think that Lucky's safety was thereby ensured—he knew better—but at least everyone seemed to be respecting Elsewhere's status as neutral zone.

As the last of the observers left the room, the heavy door closing behind them, the group gathered around the Petitioner's Chair relaxed their defensive postures and drew together. Kev, who was nearest to Lucky, reached up to give her a hand as she descended the platform's steep stairs.

Zeke shifted his eyes from one member of the circle to another, coming to rest on the scarlet-haired woman.

"That could, perhaps, have been better managed, don't you think, Lilith?" he asked.

The wide sleeve of Lilith's cloak fell back as she lifted a pale, elegant hand in an airy gesture, as if brushing the question aside. "You know me, Ezekiel. I've always had something of a penchant for drama."

"And that extends to willfully endangering your own granddaughter?" Even though his words were harsh, the Cherub's voice was quiet and contained. Aidan recognized the signs. When Zeke was upset, he didn't shout, he just got calmer and quieter. Aidan had seldom seen the angel this angry.

"Oh, give me some credit, Zeke!" Lilith said with a laugh. "I chose to make the announcement here, in the presence of her supporters and in neutral territory—and in the presence of the Archangel, I might add. If something were to happen to her between now and the Making, Uriel would exact a strict punishment, and everyone knows that."

"But it's not as if she's under the Archangel's protection in the meantime," Kev remarked. "And there are some who would risk punishment—even death—to keep one of your blood from a Making."

"Yeah, about that," Aidan inserted. "Shouldn't we—or at least Lucky—have known about—her parentage—before the Making was Struck? How much more dangerous will that process be for her now?"

"It wouldn't have made any difference," Lucky said, reaching out to brush his hand with her fingers. "I would still have done it."

Zeke's quiet words were addressed to Lucky, but Lilith was the recipient of his pointed look. "Yes, you would have, because of your cousin, but Uriel, had he known, might never have agreed to consider the Striking at all. Your—grandmother's timing was—impeccable."

Lilith laughed again, the sound somehow both musical and sardonic. "'Impeccable'? Why, I was expecting something more like 'calculated'—or 'strategic,' at the very least. But, yes, I agree. I think my timing was quite 'impeccable.'"

When Zeke just continued to look at her, a muscle shifting in his jaw, she asked, "With whom are you angrier, Ezekiel—me or yourself?"

Zeke did not deign to respond but turned his face toward Lucky. "You have been awfully quiet. Is there anything you wish to say—or to ask?"

Lucky's eyes shifted from Zeke to Lilith and back again. She shook her head, her face expressionless. "I have nothing to say to her. Can we go now?"

Aidan thought he saw something flash in Lilith's emerald eyes, as if Lucky's words might have caused her pain, but whatever it was, it was gone in an instant—if it had been there at all.

"Yes, I must go now too," she said airily, already walking away from them toward the door. "But we'll talk before long, Lucky. We have so much catching up to do."

Raising her hood over her scarlet hair, she slipped through the door, leaving them alone.

At her departure, the expressionless mask slipped from Lucky's face for a moment, revealing all her uncertainty, confusion, and fear. Aidan wanted to pull her into his arms and hold her close. But he didn't. He knew she wouldn't thank him for it. Not now. She took a deep breath and, squaring her shoulders, steeled her expression once again.

"Let's go home," she said.

Lucky changed out of the ceremonial garb and back into her own jeans and sweater with automatic, mechanical movements. As she pulled on her boots, she felt almost as if she were dressing a doll. She had barely registered the trip back from Elsewhere. She vaguely remembered following Zeke to the Council Hall's Gates of Heaven, and she could recall with the visceral precision of physical memory the sensation of compression and the frightening inability to breathe that accompanied the transition through the Gates. Otherwise, the trip was a blur. She didn't remember when Aidan and Kev had left her and Zeke. She couldn't remember climbing Zeke's basement stairs to find the guest room where she'd left her clothes. She had just known that she had to change back into them as soon as possible. She needed the feeling of those familiar things against her skin, something of her own to pull her back into herself, back into her body.

The internal shift that had happened during the Striking had shaken her to her very core, which had been terrifying enough in itself. And then that woman—could she really be her grandmother?—had said what she'd said. Lucky had witnessed what remained of the ceremony as if she were watching a play. Even Uriel's final pronouncement had seemed distant, apart from her, something that had no bearing on her future, but affected someone else.

She wasn't sure how long she had been sitting on the edge of Zeke's guest room bed, staring into space, too numb to move, when someone tapped on the door. She knew she should ask whoever it was to come in, but she couldn't shape the words with her lips, let alone find the energy to breathe sound into them. A moment later the door opened, and Malachi stepped inside, quietly reclosing the door behind him. He was dressed in something that looked a lot like scrubs, except, like everything else she'd ever seen him in, they were black. His long braids were pulled back and tied at the nape of his neck. Her eyes followed him as he moved to the wall in front of her, lowered himself to the floor, and sat cross-legged, like he was going to meditate.

He studied her for a minute or two without speaking and then asked, his deep voice just loud enough to be audible, "Are you alright?"

She shook her head.

"It was a powerful Striking. I felt it myself—and I wasn't even there."

Her gaze sharpened as she looked at him, but still she said nothing.

"What was it like for you?" he asked.

Again, she shook her head. "I—I don't know—how to explain," she said. "I feel like everything is different—and not just with me. Like nothing, anywhere, is ever going to be the same."

As she spoke, she found to her surprise that she did want to talk about it, that it was something of a relief to put the experience into words. "It felt like I was pulled out of my place in the world and then put somewhere else, and that—I don't know—like everything else moved around, something sliding into the place I left, while other things shifted to make room for me in the new place. Sort of like a piece of furniture that's been moved off the showroom floor and into someone's house, I guess." She paused for a moment and then added in a whisper, "But bigger than that, a lot bigger—and more important."

"Scary." The soft-voiced word was a statement, not a question, but Lucky nodded anyway.

"It's alright to be scared. I was terrified."

The words surprised a smile out of Lucky. "You? Terrified?"

It was Malachi's turn to nod. "Oh, yes. I felt like the new place I'd been given had no floor, that the ground had fallen away beneath my feet, and I would never have anything solid on which to stand again."

"I know the feeling. It gets better?"

One side of Malachi's mouth lifted in a half-smile. "Eventually."

"Great. And here I thought you were trying to make me feel better." As Lucky smiled back at him, she realized that she did feel better. She still felt shaken and sort of like she was walking on eggshells, but for the first time since she'd come to in that big wooden chair, with her knees and temple bruised and aching, she felt like she just might make it through this passage and manage to come out on the other side—wherever that was.

"Did Zeke tell you about—Lilith?"

Malachi nodded but said nothing as he waited for her to continue.

"Who is she? Zeke said Uriel might not have allowed the Striking if he had known she was my—grandmother." Lucky found it hard to say the word; it felt more than strange to use it for anyone other than G-Ma. Of course, everyone had two of them, but she had only ever known the one. Besides, the term seemed too intimate to refer to a complete stranger,especially one who was not exactly human.

"Lilith is an ancient being—as ancient as Zeke—and, like him, she was once worshipped as a deity. She and Zeke have known one another a very long time, and while I am not privy to the history of their relationship, I believe they were once quite close. I do know that when the ancients divided into Light and Dark, she aligned herself with the Dark. She has been one of Lucifer's more rebellious subjects. That alone is enough to cause Uriel to refuse the Striking. In addition, there is the question of your mixed blood. The Making ceremony is intended for humans."

"That's why Aidan's afraid the Making will be even more dangerous for me? Because we don't know what will happen when someone with mixed blood like mine is Made Naphil?"

"Yes," Malachi nodded. "It is possible that the combination of powers could kill you."

"But we've known it might kill me anyway. Is it really so different than when I was just plain old human Lucky?"

"The Making is always dangerous, the chances of surviving it roughly fifty percent. Your mixed blood is a wild card. It could be that the two powers are like matter and antimatter—the reaction when they mix so strong as to annihilate you, meaning the chance of surviving drops to zero."

Lucky shivered. "Okay, that doesn't sound good. Still, dead is dead, right? I was always risking that anyway."

"Alternatively," Malachi continued as if she hadn't spoken, "you could become immensely powerful. And the thought of one of Lilith's blood having so much power strikes fear into the hearts of many angels—both Light and Dark. That, I'm afraid, means that someone might try to kill you before the Making."

"My odds of surviving for more than three days don't seem very high, do they?"

"Not when looked at from a certain angle," Malachi conceded. "But you have a number of powerful beings who are willing to risk their lives to protect you between now and the Making, and that raises your odds considerably. In addition, while what happens at the Making is largely out of our control, I believe I can help you increase your chances of surviving it."

Lucky's heart lifted as she latched on to the slightest possibility of surviving the coming ordeal. "I knew you'd think of something," she said. "When do we start work?"

"Soon," he replied, rising to his feet. "But first you need to get something to eat. The Striking depleted your energy, and our work together will be intensive. You need to replenish your reserves before we get started."

"Yeah, I guess I do," Lucky said when she found the simple act of standing surprisingly difficult.

"Don't worry. Your strength will come back once you've eaten."

As he led Lucky to the dining room, Malachi shortened his steps to accommodate her slow ones. If she hadn't felt so generally not herself, Lucky would have been embarrassed by her weakness—she had no more strength than if she had spent several days fighting the flu. But since nothing else about her felt at all normal, she accepted the weakness as part of the package and walked as slowly as she needed to, pausing every few steps to lean against the wall and rest. Malachi made no comment. He just waited with her until she was ready to go on. He could no doubt have picked her up and carried her to the dining room without even noticing the extra weight, but she was grateful that he didn't. She assumed it was because he had been through his own Striking that he understood her need to do this on her own—no matter how difficult it was or how long it took.

When they finally reached the dining room, it was to find a feast awaiting them. Zeke had pulled out all the stops. There were salads and meats and pastas, tiny sandwiches and quiches and vegetables of various sorts—and the desserts! Lucky didn't know if he'd had the food delivered, somehow managed to prepare it himself, or magicked it into existence, and she didn't care. Looking at the laden table, she realized that she had never felt so hungry in her entire life.

"Ah, there you are!" said Zeke, entering the room through a door that appeared to open into the kitchen. He was carrying a large pitcher. "I was just going to fill the water glasses. Sit, please. Anywhere is fine."

Happy to oblige, Lucky dropped into the chair nearest her. Malachi took the seat across the table from her.

"Aidan and Kevin should be joining us soon," Zeke said, as he filled the final glass with water and headed back toward the kitchen.

As he exited through one door, the brothers strolled in through the other. They had been in mid-conversation, but Aidan stopped speaking when he caught sight of Lucky at the table.

Crossing the room in two long strides, he sat down in the chair next to hers and turned toward her, concern filling his blue eyes. "How're you doing?" he asked.

"I'm weak, but Malachi says that'll pass once I eat—which I'm definitely going to do," she said, managing a small smile. "I think I'm hungry enough to eat half of everything on this table."

Kev chuckled, surveying the table's contents. "That's saying something. There's enough food here for a small army."

As Kev settled into the seat next to Malachi and across from Aidan, Lucky noticed that he too had discarded his ceremonial clothes and was back in the jeans and green shirt he had been wearing that morning. She was intrigued by how different he seemed when he was in his *Ha-Satan* role. She had to admit she liked the way he looked in his ceremonial garb, but he seemed more comfortable, and more approachable, when he was just being Kev.

Aidan's touch on her hand drew her attention away from his brother, and she felt a momentary flash of guilt. Turning her hand so she could wrap her fingers around Aidan's, she gave him what she hoped was a reassuring smile, just as Zeke returned from the kitchen and took his place at the head of the table.

As she ate her fill of the delicious food, Lucky learned that she was the reason for the feast. She had until midnight that night to eat as much as she wanted. After that, she had to fast until the Making was over. Maybe her enormous appetite was a blessing in disguise, since it would enable her to eat more than she normally would have. She had the feeling she'd need every bit of energy she had to make it through the next few days. *If I make it through.* She cut that thought off right there. Such thoughts offered no help, and she didn't have the time, the energy, or the inclination to dwell on negative possibilities. If she was going to get through this—and she had every intention of doing so—then she had to focus on what she needed to do to succeed.

"Are we starting work after we eat, or do I have some time to take care of some things?" She directed the question at Malachi as she dropped a large dollop of whipped cream on top of a generous slice of berry tart.

"We will start at midnight, when your fast begins," her mentor replied. "You have until then to make whatever preparations you wish."

Lucky turned to Aidan. "I'd like to see Josh again—and G-Ma. And I want to talk to Mo. I can't just disappear on her. If anything happens…." Her voice trailed off.

"I'll take you to see them," Aidan said, wrapping the fingers of his right hand around those of her left.

"Thanks," she whispered. "Hey, have you talked to Ben by any chance? Is he doing alright?"

"I called him a little earlier while you were with Malachi. I told him what happened at the Striking and that the Making is scheduled. He's worried about the three-day wait—and about you. Same as the rest of us."

Lucky's eyes caught and held Aidan's. The possibility that the Making might fail, that she might not survive, that Josh might never be okay, remained unspoken. He released her hand and raised his own to rest it against her cheek, his thumb brushing over her cheekbone.

Kev cleared his throat. "Not to intrude where I'm not wanted, but I think I should maybe go with you two."

"I won't let anything happen to her," Aidan said, his tone betraying both irritation and defensiveness.

"It's not that I don't trust you, Aidan," Kev responded. "Lucky is a walking target right now. She needs all the protection she can get. Plus, you're going to be around other people—and we don't want them getting caught in any potential crossfire. I know you want to handle this alone, but now isn't the time. Admit it; you need me."

Aidan nodded, sighing. "Right. Point taken. We'll both go with her."

"I'm going to call Mo," Lucky excused herself, as she pushed her chair back and rose to her feet. "See when would be the best time to catch up with her." Reaching across the table, she snagged another roll and a slice of cheese before leaving.

Zeke chuckled. "The food will still be here when you have made your phone call."

"So you say. But what if you all ate everything while I was gone? Then where would I be?" Lucky said with a teasing smile.

Looking around the table at all of them—Zeke, Malachi, Aidan, and Kev—she felt a fullness in her chest, accompanied by a rush of tears to her eyes. She had known them for such a short time, but she felt close to each one of them. If anything did happen to her, and if she was somehow still capable of missing what she'd left behind, she'd miss them all as much as she would miss G-Ma or Josh or Mo.

"I'll be back in a few minutes." She managed to force the words around the lump in her throat. Then she left the room before she started to cry.

CHAPTER 26

It was getting dark by the time Lucky, Aidan, and Kev met Mo at Salonica. The little Greek diner on the corner of 57th and Blackstone was a favorite, and Mo had suggested meeting there for a late dinner, since that would give Lucky plenty of time to check in on Josh and to visit G-Ma.

The stop at Aidan's to see Josh had lasted less than an hour—and had gone pretty much as Lucky had expected it would. Her cousin was still sleeping in his cocoon of pulsing light, which, according to Sambethe, whom Aidan had contacted at Lucky's request, was holding the toxin at bay as planned. While Aidan and Kev talked to Sambethe, Lucky talked to Josh, telling him again how sorry she was and explaining as best she could what they were doing—what *she* was doing—to try to help him. She didn't know if he could hear anything she said, but she felt better for being able to tell him the truth, whether he could hear her or not.

Her visit with her grandmother had been more difficult. When Lucky first entered the room, she could see a Still One crouched by G-Ma's chair, one clawed hand resting on her knee, while two more of the creatures waited in the room's far corner. She acknowledged them with the tiniest tilt of her head. Although they simply stared back at her, their large eyes unblinking, she could sense their acceptance of her, both as G-Ma's visitor and as someone who walked at least in part in their world.

It didn't take Lucky long to figure out the reason so many of the creatures were present. G-Ma was less herself—something that often happened later in the day—seeming more confused than usual and quite anxious. She didn't recognize Lucky and kept talking about how worried she was about her granddaughter and how she wished she'd come to visit her. Lucky's attempts to reassure G-Ma that her granddaughter was, in fact, fine and standing right in front of her, didn't seem to penetrate her consciousness. G-Ma just continued to ask for Lucky, insisting that she was in danger.

Lucky felt weighed down by guilt and fear and sorrow. It was bad enough having to lie to G-Ma and tell her she wasn't in any danger and was perfectly alright, when Lucky herself was terrified about what lay ahead of her. Worse yet was being unable even to comfort her grandmother with the fact of her presence.

Lucky finally gave up on conversation and wandered over to her grandmother's art table. The disturbing painting she had seen on her earlier visit was once again on its surface. G-Ma had done more work on the piece since she had last seen it. The black cloud on the right side of the picture seemed less amorphous, more defined, more anthropomorphic—those yellow spots were definitely eyes—and it seemed even more menacing that it had before. The smaller figures on the left of the sheet were still just sketches, but Lucky could make out what appeared to be faces and limbs.

She frowned as she noticed that some of the indistinct figures looked almost as if they had wings. After examining the figures for a few moments, she shook her head. She couldn't be sure; the sketch was still too incomplete. Maybe she was just seeing wings because she was beginning to expect to see them.

She wondered if she should take the painting and hide it away where G-Ma couldn't look at it or work on it. There was no wonder she was feeling anxious and sensing danger if she was working on such a disturbing piece. Then again, maybe the painting was disturbing precisely because it gave her a way to release those feelings. Better for her to paint them out if she could. Lucky sighed as she turned away from the canvas, deciding it was best to leave it for now.

When Lucky leaned down to kiss G-Ma good-bye, her grandmother surprised her by grasping her hand.

"Lucky!" she said, smiling up at her as if she had only just arrived. "I'm so glad you came to see me. I've been worried about you."

Lucky caught her grandmother in a warm embrace. "G-Ma, there's no need to worry," she said, her voice catching in her throat. "I'm fine. I'm right here."

"Well, then," G-Ma patted her cheek as Lucky drew away from her. "That's good."

Now that G-Ma knew who she was, Lucky sat and talked with her for a long time. She told her about some of the changes in her life and about her new friends, especially Aidan, at least as much as she could without revealing the whole unbelievable truth.

It took her a while to get up the nerve to raise the topic she wanted most to talk about: her mother. She didn't want to upset G-Ma, and she wasn't quite sure how to ask the question. In the end, she blurted it out.

"Why did you tell me my mother died giving birth to me?"

Lucky held her breath as she waited for G-Ma's response.

"Because she did, in a way. She was not—herself after your birth."

"I found the letter she wrote to me."

"I meant to give it to you someday, but somehow I never did. And then…." G-Ma's voice trailed off, and her face grew anxious. "Where's my Lucky?" she asked. "I'm so worried about her. I wish she'd come to see me. Why doesn't she come to see me? She's always been such a good girl."

Lucky's eyes filled with tears. Giving G-Ma a quick hug, she whispered, "I love you so much." Then, leaving her grandmother to the care of the Still Ones, she exited into the hallway where Aidan and Kev awaited her.

As Kev maneuvered his old Jeep Cherokee into a parking place almost in front of the restaurant, Lucky pushed her memories of her visit with G-Ma to the back of her mind. She'd think about it later, when she wasn't trying to concentrate on spending quality time with her best friend—*for perhaps the last time.* Pushing that thought away too, she began a wrestling match with the car door, from which she eventually emerged victorious, and slid out of the backseat into the drizzle that seemed to have continued unabated all day. After Kev ended her struggle to reclose the stubborn door with an effective push-and-kick combo that he'd clearly used before, she jogged toward the restaurant, ready to be out of the chilly dampness.

"You really need to get a new car, Kev," she heard Aidan say as he and his brother fell in behind her.

"Why?" Kev responded. "That one still works."

"Barely," said Aidan, disgust evident in his voice.

"Gets me where I need to go," Kev said. They had caught up to Lucky, and he gave her a wink as he added, "We can't all drive designer sports cars."

"You could do better than this," Aidan answered.

"Maybe. But the Jeep suits me."

"Because, like you, it's battered and hard to handle?" Aidan asked with a grin.

Smiling, Kev pushed open the diner's door and held it for Lucky to precede them. "There are days when that description seems generous."

Mo was already sitting in a booth against the right wall, and she grinned and waved as they came through the door. She scooted over, and Lucky slid into the seat next to her, leaving the other for the brothers to share.

"Hi, I'm Mo." Mo smiled across the table at Kev as he slid into the spot opposite her. "You must be Aidan's brother. Kev, right?"

"That would be me," Kev responded, smiling back at her. "It's nice to meet you, Mo."

Introductions over, the four chatted about nothing in particular while they studied the menus. Only after the waitress had taken their orders—a Greek salad and fries for Mo, spanikopita and egg lemon soup for Lucky, and gyros for both Aidan and Kev—did Mo turn to her friend. "You said we needed to talk?"

On the drive to the restaurant, Lucky had informed Aidan and Kev that she intended to tell Mo everything—unbelievable as it all might sound to her. She had had enough of lying to her best friend, and she wasn't going to spend what could be her last visit with Mo making up things to tell her about why they might never see each other again. The brothers had made a few token protests about how telling Mo might put her in some danger as well, but both had been sympathetic enough with Lucky's wishes that neither had argued with much force.

Still, now that Mo was right in front of her, Lucky wasn't quite sure how to begin. "You first," she said. "What have you been up to since I saw you last?"

"Just last night, you mean?" Mo asked, her expression indicating that she recognized the question for the stalling tactic it was.

When Lucky nodded, trying to look innocent, her friend answered the question, telling her about her day—and the rare treat of lunch with her father—until their food arrived. As soon as the waitress had placed the last plate on the table, Mo commanded, "Okay, your turn. Spill!"

Lucky hesitated for the space of a breath or two before complying. "Remember when we were at the Med, and that man made my head hurt?"

Mo nodded and took a bite of her salad.

"Well, I have a better idea of what that was all about now." And, while still managing to enjoy every bite of her delicious egg lemon soup and spanikopita, Lucky told Mo everything that had happened in the last couple of weeks, excluding the private moments with Aidan, which were just that—private. Mo took in the whole story, occasionally looking to Aidan or Kev for confirmation. At Aidan's nod or Kev's "It's true," she would indicate that Lucky could continue.

When Lucky got to the part about the Striking, she found she was unable to relate that experience to her friend, or to talk about the danger she would face in the coming Making. Both Kev and Aidan noticed the difficulty she was having. Kev took up the tale where she had left off, while Aidan reached across the table to place his hand over hers. Lucky was grateful for Kev's gesture but, for some reason, vaguely irritated by Aidan's. Slipping her hand from beneath his, she stole one of the few remaining fries off his plate and shot him a mischievous grin before popping it into her mouth.

She noticed Kev glancing her way as he related the story of the Striking to Mo, his intelligent green eyes scanning her face, as if gauging her reaction to the tale. She could tell he was attempting to convey the information to her friend as accurately as possible while limiting the emotional impact that hearing her own story recounted would have on her. The care with which he chose his words revealed a subtle and understated attentiveness that she found somehow moving.

"The Making will be two and a half days from now," Kev said, bringing the story to a close, "and as of midnight, Lucky will be fasting and working with Malachi to prepare for it. She wanted to make sure you knew everything before midnight tonight." His eyes caught and held Lucky's for a second or two after he finished speaking.

Lucky mouthed a silent "Thank you" to him before she turned to look at Mo.

"Wow, girlfriend," Mo said. "I'd say your *life* is most definitely nuts, but at least you don't have to worry that *you're* going crazy anymore."

When Lucky responded with a strangled half-laugh half-sob, Mo threw her arms around her and pulled her close. She offered no further comment as she held on to Lucky, her embrace conveying all her love and support.

Lucky felt a chill creep up her spine and was already withdrawing from her friend's arms when Kev's muttered curse reached her ears. Something that looked like fog was filling the restaurant. Standing at the door and staring through a gap in the fog-like substance were two large, winged beings, garbed in some kind of chain mail and armed with gleaming swords. Their eyes, notably silver even from this distance, held the coldest expression she had ever seen.

"Powers," Aidan and Kev said simultaneously.

Leaping to their feet, they positioned themselves between the two girls and the cold, silver beings, each raising a hand, into which appeared a flaming weapon. Aidan held what looked to be the same fiery sword he had wielded the night he fought the shadow creatures and the gray-haired man. Kev held a broadsword.

"What are they doing?" Mo asked in alarm, her fingers clenching on Lucky's arm. "Lucky, what's going on? Why do Aidan and Kev look like there's about to be a fight?"

"Because there is," Lucky said, pulling her friend out of the booth and drawing her into a crouch behind the two Nephilim. She understood that Mo couldn't see the fog or the two beings—"Powers," Kev and Aidan had called them. She remembered enough of her Catholic school theology classes to know that Powers, like Cherubim and Seraphim, were angels, but that was all she knew. From the looks of things, though, these angels weren't on their side. Odds were good that they were among those who thought allowing one of Lilith's blood to go through the Making was a really bad idea. Even while she berated herself for bringing Mo into this, she was edging them toward the back of the restaurant.

"Get them out the back way," Kev said to Aidan, jerking his head toward the girls. "I'll handle Tweedledum and Tweedledee. At least long enough to take this outside."

Then he lunged toward the two Powers, the broadsword and a shield that had suddenly appeared in his empty hand, flashing. That was all Lucky saw before Aidan rushed her and Mo toward the back of the restaurant, through the kitchen, and out into the alley behind the building.

Once outside, they raced to the end of the alley, skirting around foul-smelling dumpsters and miscellaneous pieces of scattered refuse. They stopped at the alley's end and peered around the corner back toward the front of the restaurant. Lucky could see that the street was filling up with white fog. She could hear the sharp clang of metal striking metal and the dull thuds of flesh impacting flesh. She hoped Kev was holding his own against the Powers. She didn't doubt that he was strong and skilled, but there were two of them to his one.

Aidan's voice cut through her worries. "Across the street," he said. "See that abandoned church? That's a safe house. If we can get you inside, they can't reach you there."

"*Angels* can't get inside a *church*?" she asked.

"Not this one. Zeke's warded it against everything but specific members of the Fallen. I used to be one of them. Let's hope Zeke didn't revoke my access when I renounced my wings."

"When you *what*?" Lucky asked.

"Another time," Aidan said. "Now, you and Mo need to run as fast as you can across the street and to the church. I'll be right behind you. Go!"

Her hand clenched around Mo's, Lucky ran. She resisted the urge to look back, even when she heard the sound of steel on steel close behind her and realized Aidan was fending off an attacker. They had reached the sidewalk in front of the church when she heard Aidan's cry. "NO!"

Pain sliced through her middle, and she looked down in blank surprise to see a blood-covered sword protruding from her abdomen. She heard Mo screaming her name as if from a distance and opened her mouth to say—something—but then she fell forward. The last thing she felt was the sword retracing its path through her body as she slid off of it onto the wet concrete of the sidewalk.

As Kev launched himself at the two huge angels flanking the doorway of the diner, he pushed all worries about his brother and the two girls to the back of his mind. The key to being an excellent warrior was the ability to focus on the matter at hand, eliminating all distractions while taking in everything with direct bearing on the immediate situation. And right now, concern for Lucky and her friend was a distraction he couldn't afford. He'd left Aidan to protect the girls, and he had to trust his brother to do his job. His own task was either to kill the two angelic thugs or to wound them badly enough that they'd dematerialize back to the coldest reaches of the Heavens from whence they'd come—where they could await the wrath of the Archangel Uriel.

Warding off their blows with the shield he'd called as he leapt toward them, he swung the heavy broadsword with a lethal grace that belied its weight. He felt the impact in his shoulder as the weapon struck against the nearly impenetrable chain mail of one of the Powers. Focused as he was on the fight, it was as if time slowed for him. He knew each move they would make before they made it and so was able to maneuver them out the door and onto the street in a matter of moments. Still, he had to take some body blows to make it happen. He chose those with care, ensuring that he was struck only by a fist or the broad side of a sword. He let the shield absorb the bites of the swords' keen edges. He'd definitely be bruised, but if he could help it, he wasn't going to be blooded by one of the deadly blades.

Once outside he was free to move more aggressively as were his opponents. The white fog filling the street would hide them from human senses just as it had in the restaurant. People passing by would avoid the site of the battle without even being aware they had done so. Even so, taking the combat off street level seemed the best plan. The farther he could get the Powers away from Aidan and the girls, the better chance they'd have to get to safety. Shield up to defend his left side, Kev ducked a blow aimed at his right and felt the heavy weight of his wings as they settled into place. Shifting the huge appendages out of the range of the Powers' weapons, he shot upward, his own sword flashing out to slice against the neck of one of his opponents.

Growling his rage, the Power surged after him. Just as Kev had hoped, anger made the angel careless. Kev dodged a blow leveled with more strength than skill, and the angel was knocked off balance when his strike failed to impact a target. Flexing one wing to circle around behind the Power, Kev swung his broadsword with enough force to cut through the angel's neck. Golden ichor flowed from the wound for the second or so it took the head to fall free. Then both head and body disappeared, leaving nothing behind but a slight golden shimmer that was already fading as Kev turned his attention toward the second angel—who hadn't followed him into the air.

No, he was still at street level, exchanging blows with Aidan, while Lucky and Mo ran toward the safe house on the other side of Blackstone. As Kev dived toward the street, he saw a third angel materialize right behind Lucky. Before he could begin to reach her, the angel's sword had already run her through. Aidan's cry was still echoing in his ears as Lucky fell forward off the sword, and her assailant dematerialized.

CHAPTER 27

Cursing himself as twenty times an idiot, Kev dropped to the ground at Lucky's side, disappearing his wings as his feet touched down. He should have realized the first two Powers were themselves the distraction, meant to capture his and Aidan's attention while someone else got to Lucky.

Behind him, he could still hear Aidan's sword as he battled the remaining Power. Scooping Lucky into his arms, he ran to the door of the abandoned Christian Scientist church, Mo hard on his heels. He had to hand it to the blonde girl. He could see the terror on her face, but she wasn't screaming, and she seemed to be as focused as he was on getting her wounded friend to safety. Repositioning Lucky so he could cradle her against him with just one arm, he held up his right palm, hardly noticing the slight burn as his sigil activated. He pressed his palm against the locked door, which opened almost as soon as it felt his touch. Bless Zeke for realizing the need for safe houses.

Lucky moaned as he shifted her weight onto both arms once more. He took it as a positive sign: she still lived at least. Mo swung the door shut behind them, and Kev cursed aloud. Dim light filtered through the grime-covered windows high in the walls of the church. Shifting Lucky into one arm again, he summoned his flaming broadsword once more. Not exactly a torch, but almost as effective. At least it would provide enough illumination for them to find a light switch. Zeke would have made sure the safe house had electricity.

"There," Mo said, moving toward the switch even as she spoke. As she flipped the switch, illuminating the bulbs high overhead, Kev released the sword, allowing it to return to the great ethereal weapons room it called home until he needed it again.

"What happened to her anyway?" Mo asked in a shaky voice. "We were running and then—there was all this blood—and she fell."

It took Kev a moment to realize that the girl wouldn't have been able to see the Power or his sword. To her it must have seemed as if the wound just suddenly appeared on her friend's body.

"She was stabbed," he said. "By a Power—a kind of angel—who apparently didn't want her to go through the Making."

"That's who you and Aidan were fighting?"

Kev nodded, his eyes scanning the room.

Since the dusty wooden pews looked narrow and uncomfortable, he decided the floor would suit their purposes just as well—even though it was cold stone and none too clean. He knelt, laying Lucky on the floor as gently as he could. He had slipped out of his jacket and was folding it into a pillow for her, when he heard the door open and Aidan's running footsteps on the stone floor.

"The Power?" he asked, glancing at his brother.

"Beheaded." Aidan knelt beside him. "How is she?"

"She's breathing," Kev said. With gentle hands, he lifted her blood-soaked clothing away from her skin.

"The sword went straight through her." Aidan's voice was choked.

"I know," Kev said, stripping off his shirt. "Get Zeke."

As Aidan made the call, Kev ripped his shirt into pieces. Folding two of the fragments into thick pads, he instructed Mo to press one against the wound in Lucky's back while he lifted her. Together he and Mo slid a longer strip of fabric beneath Lucky's body before he lay her back down. After placing the other pad over the wound in her abdomen, Kev tied the ends of the long strip together to hold the bandages in place.

"Zeke's on his way," Aidan said, returning to his brother's side, "and he's summoning Uriel."

"Good." The grimness in Kev's voice belied the word.

If Lucky had been stabbed with a normal weapon, her wounds would be bad enough. As it was, he wasn't sure there was anything they could do to save her. It wasn't just the blood loss or the damage the edge of the blade could do. The angelic metal itself could be deadly—especially so to a human, even a hybrid like Lucky. If she had been part angel instead of part demon—or whatever she was—she might have been able to withstand it better. Since she wasn't, the poisons from the metal would already be moving through her bloodstream, making their way through her system and killing her organs as they went.

Lucky moaned again, and he and Aidan each took one of her hands in theirs, while Mo stroked her friend's hair back from her damp forehead and murmured soothing words.

Only a few moments had passed since Aidan had called the Cherub, but it felt like forever to Kev before Zeke appeared in the dusty sanctuary. Presumably due to his worry and haste, the angel wasn't enveloped in his usual human glamour, and Kev found it hard to look on his shifting form, as bull, man, lion, and eagle intermingled amid multiple pairs of great blue wings.

"Zeke, please," he said, averting his eyes.

"My apologies," Zeke resonated, as he knelt beside him, a long-haired man in khakis once more, his efficient hands already moving over Lucky as he examined her wounds.

Mo gasped, and Kev realized that she must have been able to see Zeke only after he took his human form. Just as well, really. The poor girl had been through enough this evening.

A blinding light suddenly filled the sanctuary, so bright it blocked out not only the pews, walls, and grimy windows but also Lucky and the other people kneeling around her. Kev could see nothing but the brilliance of the light itself, and he had to close his eyes against that. When he sensed the light dimming and opened them once more, he saw that Mo had collapsed to the floor. He moved to check her pulse, but Zeke's voice stopped him. "I thought it best that she not be conscious while the Archangels are present."

Kev nodded and contented himself with repositioning the girl's limbs, so she wouldn't be too stiff and uncomfortable when she awakened. Then the full impact of the Cherub's words struck him. *"Archangels?"*

"I requested that Uriel bring Raphael with him," Zeke said.

Kev looked up at the two huge, glowing beings before them. As he watched, they shrank until they were each only a foot or so taller than Zeke when he was standing, their glow diminishing as they did so. Uriel he recognized. Even in this smaller form, the Archangel was intimidating, with his emotionless, flame-filled eyes. That unearthly breeze seemed to accompany him wherever he went; his hair and the iridescent feathers on his wings moved in it even now.

The Archangel Raphael Kev had never seen before. Though still awe-inspiring, he looked altogether much more approachable than Uriel. Like the other Archangel, Raphael's eyes were absent of pupils and completely inhuman, but where Uriel's sockets were filled with flames, Raphael's somehow conveyed the impression of water, holding all the blues and grays and greens of every ocean or lake or sea imaginable. His hair, its strands ranging in color from the palest white to the deepest green, curled around his shoulders in a manner reminiscent of vines. His wings, like Uriel's, were iridescent and sparked with colors seen nowhere on earth, but even those colors were more subdued than those found in his cohort's wings, not dimmed in any way, but somehow soothing rather than terrifying.

Ha-Satan. As Uriel spoke, he directed his fiery gaze at Kev, who felt as if the Archangel were looking through him rather than at him. *You were a witness to the attack?*

That's one way of putting it, Kev thought. "Yes, Archangel. I was in combat with the two Powers who threatened us, while my brother sought to direct the Sensitive, Lucky Monroe, and her friend to safety. As I was dispatching one of the Powers, the other engaged my brother, distracting his attention from the girls, while a third Power materialized and ran Lucky through with his sword."

Aidan, son of Lucifer, does your brother speak the truth?

"Yes, Archangel." Aidan moved a few steps closer to Kev. "My brother had taken on the two Powers, so that I could get Lucky and Mo safely away. We were running toward the safe house when one of the Powers attacked me. While I fought him, another appeared out of nowhere, stabbed Lucky, and then dematerialized. Kev—my brother—brought the girls into the safe house while I—finished off the Power."

Since the girl's wounds were inflicted by angelic means, in a direct attempt to thwart the decree of today's Striking, I have some leeway to intervene.

Although Kev sensed more than heard the words of both Archangels, Raphael's voice was as distinct from Uriel's as was a tumbling waterfall from a raging inferno. Both were powerful, but while the intensity of the one burned its way into his mind, the other flowed like liquid between and through his senses.

"I confess I was hoping that would be the case," Zeke said. He spoke softly, but the powerful resonance of his voice filled the sanctuary like distant echoes. "Which was why I requested that Uriel ask you to accompany him. Is there anything you can do to help the girl, Raphael?"

I have healed her wounds and stopped the progression of the sword's poison through her body. I cannot undo any damage the poison has already caused, but there will be none additional. She will not die this night, tomorrow, or the next day, but she may or may not awaken. Only one of angelic blood can withstand a wound from a sword of Heaven.

Aidan laughed harshly. "Then the Making may actually *save* her?"

Zeke nodded. "It could, if we can do it in time. Uriel, do you, like Raphael, have any leeway in this matter?"

I can give you some time, Ambassador. The third day from the Striking begins at midnight—a little more than 48 of your earthly hours from now. We can hold the ceremony then, and we can do so in a location other than the Council Hall, if your Sensitive is unable to make it there.

"Thank you, Uriel. That should suffice. And, Raphael, many thanks for your healing."

Would that I could have done more, Ambassador. Actions such as those taken by the Powers who attacked the Sensitive cannot be condoned. I would have preferred to have alleviated all the damage they caused.

"You have done a great deal," Zeke replied. "And to both of you we are most grateful."

Zeke had barely finished speaking when Uriel's words burned through Kev's brain.

The Making will commence at midnight on the second day from this. Send us word of the place of your choosing.

Kev gathered the Archangel had grown impatient with the niceties. As if to corroborate that thought, no sooner had Uriel spoken than both Archangels supernovaed, bursting into that blinding light once more. Kev slammed his eyelids shut and clapped a hand over his eyes for good measure. When he lowered his hand and lifted his lids, the dusty room, lit only by the electric light of the overhead bulbs, seemed dim by comparison.

His eyes flashed to the floor where Lucky lay—to find that she was nowhere to be seen.

"Where's…?" he began.

"Hmm," Zeke mused. "Raphael must have determined he could do something more after all. I believe we will find her resting in my guest room. I will return there as well and bring Malachi to her, if you two will see that her friend gets safely home."

Mo was sitting up, groaning and rubbing her head as she did so.

"She did not observe any part of the Archangels' visit, so she will have no memories of that," Zeke continued. "I assume she is to be allowed to keep the memories she does have of this evening's events?"

"Yes," Aidan said. "Lucky told her everything before the Powers attacked. She would want her to know."

"Then so be it. I will see you both shortly." With that, the Cherub vanished.

"I can take Mo home, Aidan," Kev said, shrugging into the jacket he'd retrieved from the floor. He could feel a slight residual warmth left by Lucky's body as the jacket settled against his bare skin. "If you want to go to Zeke's and help tend to Lucky."

Aidan hesitated, and Kev could see how much his brother wanted to take him up on his offer. Instead, his training as a soldier won out. "She's safe now—as safe as she can be anyway. And you might need my help—in case there's another attack."

Kev nodded, feeling both proud of his brother's decision and sad that such a decision had to be made. "I don't think it's likely, but you're right. It is possible someone might try to hurt Lucky through her friend."

Aidan sighed. "Like they did with Josh."

Kev turned toward Mo, who looked as if she was about to crumple to the floor again. Stepping up beside her, he slid a supporting arm around her shoulders. "Right," he said briskly. "Let's get you home."

They ran into no difficulties on the trip back to Mo's apartment. No one attacked; no one appeared to be following them. Nevertheless, Kev and Aidan took the precaution of setting up protection wards on both the building and the apartment itself. Unlike the complex, personalized wards that protected Aidan's condo and Zeke's brownstone, these were simple and generic, designed to protect the inhabitants from anyone who intended them harm.

By the time they were finished with the apartment and were ready to move outside to work on the building itself, Mo had fallen asleep on the couch. Noticing her shiver in her sleep, Kev pulled the throw from the back of the sofa and tucked it around her before they left.

CHAPTER 28

Aidan paced back and forth outside the closed door to Zeke's guest room. In his mind, he could still see Lucky lying on the bed, with Malachi hovering over her. She'd looked so small and fragile, the lashes of her closed eyes dark against her pallid cheeks, her sweater and jeans stained with her blood. He clenched his hands and jaw at the memory.

He and Kev and Zeke had all been standing around the bed waiting for some movement, some sign to indicate that Lucky was okay. Although they had spoken very little, their presence, or perhaps their fear for the girl on the bed, must have gotten to Malachi, because he'd shooed them all from the room, saying he needed absolute peace and quiet in order to concentrate deeply enough to reach Lucky. Zeke and Kev had wandered downstairs, but Aidan hadn't been able to bring himself to go any further than the hallway just outside the door. He wanted to be as near her as possible, even if there was nothing he could do for her. So he paced. And worried. And paced some more.

He started when a hand fell on his shoulder.

"Sorry," Kev said. "Why don't you come downstairs? Since there's nothing else he can do at the moment, Zeke is making tea. We might as well do our part and help him drink it."

Wordlessly, Aidan glanced from his brother to the closed bedroom door.

"I know," Kev said. "I'm worried about her too. We all are. But Malachi is the only one who can help her right now. And he will. He knows what he's doing. He'll bring her back to us."

Aidan heaved a sigh and then managed a weak half-smile. "Wouldn't want Zeke to think his tea-making was wasted, I guess."

Kev grinned. "Plus, if you wear a hole in his antique rug you'll really piss him off."

His hand tightened on Aidan's shoulder for a moment. Then he turned and headed for the stairs, adding in a deliberately cheerful voice, "Fighting off those Powers made me kind of hungry anyway. I could use a snack."

Aidan cast a last worried look at the closed door before he followed his brother down the stairs.

She was floating in the dark. Waves of sensation washed over her. Pain, numbness, nausea, fatigue, more pain. She caught flickers of light against the blackness, like distant lightning in a night sky. She thought she could hear the murmur of voices, but they too were distant—too far away for her to make out any words. Fatigue flooded over her, and she offered no resistance as it swept her away.

The darkness parted, the swirling in her head subsiding. She was with G-Ma. In the Oriental Institute, like when she was small. But she wasn't small anymore. She stood at G-Ma's side, while her grandmother pointed at something she wanted her to see. Lucky followed G-Ma's pointing finger to a huge stone sculpture. It looked like a bull, but it had wings and the head of a man. As she watched, the statue's wings seemed to move, multiply, and she caught flashes of blue. Then, for a moment, the bull-man's hair seemed to lighten to gold-brown, a mix of wheat and honey, and his eyes were warm and gray. Something in the back of her mind whispered a name, but she couldn't quite grasp it. She reached toward the bull-man, but he disappeared as darkness closed around her.

Aidan threw back the covers and sat up on the side of bed, shoving a hand through his hair. This was pointless. He wasn't going to be able to sleep, never mind how tired he was, until he knew Lucky was okay. Zeke and Kev had urged him to go to bed—and he'd finally complied, against his own better judgment—but all he'd done was toss and turn and worry. He couldn't seem to clear his thoughts, no matter how hard he tried. Maybe he'd wander downstairs to Zeke's study and help himself to several fingers, perhaps even a whole hand, of the fine scotch the Cherub always kept on supply. Either that or make his way to the large personal gym hidden in the brownstone's extensive basement. Drink or sweat, how to decide?

Sighing, he pushed himself off the bed and rummaged through the bag of clothes he'd retrieved from his place before trying to call it a night. Sambethe had been in the guest room checking on Josh when he'd arrived, and she had assured him Lucky's cousin was still as stable as possible. At least they had that going for them. His hands closed around the pair of *gi* pants he'd stuffed into the bag almost as an afterthought. Pulling them on, he quietly opened the door and stepped out into the hallway.

He paused for a few moments outside the door behind which Malachi labored to find Lucky and restore her to consciousness. He reached toward the doorknob, but let his hand fall back to his side. He knew better than to interrupt Malachi. If he broke the Naphil's concentration at a critical moment, Lucky could be lost to them forever. Squaring his shoulders, he turned away from the door and made his way down the stairs, his bare feet making little noise on the hardwood.

No one was moving on the main floor, and all the lights were turned off. No matter. The perpetual city glow provided enough light for him to follow the familiar path to the basement stairs. As he descended the stairs, he was unsurprised to see light emanating from the door to Zeke's study—the angel never slept. Not in the mood for conversation, Aidan passed the study door without even glancing inside and headed toward a tapestry hanging on the far wall.

It was a medieval piece, depicting the traditional version of the battle in Heaven that led to Lucifer's eviction. Michael's sword was raised, ready to strike the victorious blow. Aidan noticed, not for the first time, that for whatever its flaws in accuracy of story, the tapestry's portrait of Lucifer was pretty much dead-on. Lifting the tapestry, he pressed his palm against the door hidden behind it. No sooner had he felt the burn of his sigil than he heard the click as the door opened beneath his hand. Slipping inside, he let the tapestry fall back in place behind him.

Apparently, his brother had had the same idea. At the far end of the room, Kev was moving through the familiar postures of *tai chi*. Like Aidan, he was wearing only a pair of *gi* pants. Squelching a momentary flare of resentment at finding the gym occupied, Aidan reluctantly acknowledged that some company might be welcome. Padding down the length of the gym, he positioned himself beside his brother, and taking a few deep breaths to center himself, he picked up the routine at the point Kev had reached, letting his breath and physical movements fall into the rhythm Kev set.

His body remembered the postures, knew them well. Although he had left much of his training behind when he renounced his wings, he had kept up with his *tai chi* practice. For the first six months or more, it had been the only thing that had prevented him from drinking himself into a stupor more often than he had. Now, the concentration required to move through the slow, deliberate postures was exactly what he needed. As his body flowed from posture to posture, the movements and controlled breathing gradually stilled his mind.

Pain ripped through her entire body. Nausea so intense she craved the release of vomiting—which didn't come. Then numbness—starting at her abdomen and radiating outward, downward to the soles of her feet and upward through her chest and shoulders to her head, a welcome relief from the nausea. When the wave of exhaustion slammed into her, she was grateful to let go.

She was standing in a vast expanse of darkness. Far away on the horizon, she could see a gleam of light, faint, more moonlight than sunlight. Darkness stretched away from her in every direction. And this darkness wasn't a mere absence of light; somehow it was palpable, as if pulsing with presence. She could feel it sliding along the bare skin of her upper arms, like smooth, cool hands. She shivered and took a step toward the distant light. Her feet and legs were heavy, and moving through the darkness felt like swimming in molasses or honey. The phantom hands tugged at her arms, as if trying to prevent her movements. She took another slow step. And another. And another. She could feel herself perspiring from the effort required to put one foot in front of the other, and she was breathing as hard as if she were running, but with each step, the movement became the tiniest bit easier. And gradually, the hands on her arms fell away, no longer trying to pull her back. She didn't know if she could ever reach the light. She only knew that for some reason she had to try. Then she stumbled and fell, her knees and hands striking something that felt as cold and sharp as ice. She cried out as the icy substance morphed into something the consistency of sludge and rose up around her, engulfing her and pulling her under.

When he stepped under the shower spray, Aidan wasn't sure how much time had passed since he'd climbed out of bed and made his way down to the gym. After a lengthy *tai chi* routine, he and Kev had practiced hand-to-hand sparring. Then they had made the circuit of weight machines that lined one end of the room. Then they had sparred again, until both of them were drenched with sweat, and Aidan at least was aching all the way down to his bones. Finally, by silent mutual agreement, they had settled into another round of *tai chi* to make the circle complete. Aidan's muscles had trembled through the last slow, careful movements.

As the warm water ran over his body, rinsing away some of the aches along with the sweat, he noted gratefully that the intense physical exercise had had the desired effect. He was still worried about Lucky, but he no longer felt like he was going to jump out of his skin. And he was tired—both physically and mentally. Maybe he'd be able to get a little sleep after all. Finishing his shower, he dried himself off, pulled on a pair of boxer shorts, and walked down the hall to the room he was using. It took only a few minutes after he'd climbed into bed for him to fall asleep.

Josh's childhood room. Toys and sports equipment scattered on the floor. Clothes tossed over chairs and desk. She and Josh were sitting cross-legged on the bed, a game board between them. She remembered spending afternoons like that, playing with Josh. But they weren't children anymore. The Josh sitting across the game board from her was the Josh she knew now, the adult Josh. There was something about him, something she couldn't remember, but which filled her with a sense of misgiving, of dread. He moved a piece forward on the board and looked at her. One of his eyes was its normal warm brown; the other was red, feral, inhuman. She glanced down at the board to determine her next move, but she couldn't see the board. It was covered with some kind of dark cloud. She put her hand into the cloud, feeling for the game pieces. The pain was immediate. Crying out, she jerked her hand back out of the cloud. It was covered with blood.

"Any news?" Aidan asked, pulling off his wet leather jacket and hanging it over the back of one of Zeke's dining room chairs.

The Cherub, who had been staring out the rain-slicked window, turned toward him and shook his head. Eyes alighting on the girl behind Aidan, Zeke added in greeting, "Good morning, Mo. May I offer you anything—coffee, tea?"

"I'd kill for a cup of coffee," Mo responded with a shiver, removing her own rain-soaked jacket and shaking her head from side to side, flinging water droplets from her hair into Aidan's face.

To his surprise, Aidan found himself laughing, despite his worry. "Watch it, Mo. Who raised you, anyway? Dogs?"

"That would be the local Chicago wolf pack, thank you very much," she responded, with another toss of her head. "Didn't Lucky tell you I was raised by wolves?"

"She must have forgotten to mention that," Aidan chuckled.

He was glad Mo had called him that morning. She had been hoping for better news about Lucky, and when none had been forthcoming, she had asked if she could come over and wait with them. Zeke had had no objection, so Aidan had gone to pick her up. Even though he, Zeke, and Kev all agreed that the chances of her being in danger were minimal, they'd decided it was best that she not walk to the brownstone alone.

"Really?" Kev asked with mock surprise, as he strolled into the room. "She told *me* about her friend the wolf-girl. As

I recall, she especially warned me about her 'nasty, sharp, pointy teeth.'" As he uttered the last words, he held his curled fingers up by his mouth to mime fangs.

Mo bared her teeth at him and growled, then laughed and settled into the chair before which Zeke had just placed a steaming mug of coffee. "Thank you, Zeke," she said, inhaling the fragrant steam. "This smells wonderful. You may have just saved my life."

At her words, the laughter faded from all their faces.

"Isn't there something else we can do, Zeke?" Aidan asked. "It's been over twenty-four hours. Can you pick up anything from Malachi?"

"I can implant commands in the minds of others, Aidan—"

"Yeah, don't I know that?" Aidan interrupted.

"—but I cannot read minds," Zeke continued as if Aidan hadn't spoken. "I would know though if Malachi were in danger of losing consciousness or getting lost in the darkness himself, and I have sensed nothing of the kind. We just have to wait."

"We don't have much time," Kev inserted, "if the Making is to be at midnight. And the ceremony can't be performed if she doesn't regain consciousness."

"She will," Zeke said softly. "She has to."

The darkness in which she floated was so thick she could feel the weight of it pressing on her. And it was cold. Far, far on the edges of her consciousness, she heard a faint murmur. No, it was gone. At least the nausea had abated, and the pain had lessened to a dull throb. She was tired, so tired. She let the cold weight of the dark take her under once again.

Light. Just a pinprick at first. But growing larger, pushing back the dark, to surround her with the soft red-gold glow of an autumn sunset. She was sitting on a hill, an island in a sea of red-gold light. She could feel the cold mass of the darkness behind her, pulling like a magnet, trying to keep her from the encroaching light. A few yards away was a huge tree, its silhouette black against the fiery sky. She tried to move toward it, but the darkness tugged her back. A soft breeze ruffled the leaves and blew her hair away from her face. The air smelled like fall, dusty and crisp, but with some other scent mixed in, something strong and smoky, almost like incense.

The wind blew harder, and the leaves began to tumble from the tree. As they fell to the ground, she saw that they weren't leaves at all. They were birds. Crows. Hundreds, thousands, of crows, fluttering out of the tree to the ground. She watched, curious, but detached, feeling the deepening chill as the darkness drew closer at her back. One of the birds separated from the crowd and marched toward her. The red-gold light glinted off the rich, iridescent black of its wings. It stopped just in front of her, cocking its head first one way then the other as it looked at her with amber eyes.

"Lucky?" it cawed.

"Yes," she said, leaning toward it, holding out her hand. The darkness at her back wrapped strong arms around her, and she leaned further forward as it tried to pull her away from the amber-eyed bird.

Suddenly, the crow grew, morphed, shifted, and a tall, dark man with dusky black wings flaring up behind him knelt before her. His mass of long braids fell loose around his black-clad shoulders, and his amber eyes searched hers as he bent toward her, thrusting out his arm and grasping her outstretched hand in his. At his touch, the cold weight of the darkness receded, and as it departed, a wave of recognition and relief washed over her.

"Malachi?"

He nodded.

"You found me. Your birds were able to find me."

Again he nodded, as his grip on her hand tightened. "Even here," he said.

She had to work to open her eyes. Her eyelids felt so heavy, like tiny weights had been implanted in her lashes. When she was finally able to lift them, she found herself looking into a familiar pair of amber eyes.

"You found me," she whispered.

"Yes," he responded, his own deep voice quiet. "If you get trapped in the darkness again, find the tree. We will come for you there."

"Find it? How will I find it?"

"You will figure that out should the need arise."

"Okay," Lucky sighed. She still wasn't sure she understood, but she had a feeling she wasn't going to get any additional information out of Malachi without some very precise questions, and she was too tired and weak to think of anything else to ask.

When her stomach growled, she thought of a different question. "What time is it?"

"A little after noon."

"It's tomorrow, already? That means I can't eat anything, right?"

Malachi gave her a quick, closed glance, before offering, "You may have water."

He turned to reach for something on the bedside table, and she heard liquid being poured into a glass. Then he was lifting her head and shoulders with one arm and holding the filled glass to her lips. With his help, she drank all of it.

Malachi rested her back against the pillows and studied her for a moment, his face grave. When he spoke, his words were slow and deliberate. "Lucky, it is the day before the day of the Making. You have been lost to us for over thirty-six hours. Had Raphael not healed many of your injuries, I doubt that even I could have found you."

Lucky felt her heart rate increase, and she could hear the fear in her own voice as she responded, "Th-the Making is tomorrow? I—I'm not strong enough…."

"Shh." Malachi's hands came to her shoulders as she tried to sit up. "The Making is just past midnight. But do not worry. You are more prepared than you think."

Lucky subsided against the pillows, heart rate decreasing. She was more than willing to comply with Malachi's demand not to worry—though she wasn't sure it would be possible—and she wanted to believe his reassurances. But she was so tired and sore and weak. She couldn't muster either the mental or physical energy necessary for any kind of preparatory exercises now. Of course, that meant she might not be strong enough to survive the Making itself. At that thought, she felt her stomach tighten and her heart begin to pound again.

Malachi must have sensed her renewed fear, for both his hands closed over hers. "Do you trust me?" he asked, holding her eyes with his own.

She nodded.

"Then know that you will be ready for the Making when it comes," he said. He tightened his grip on her hands before releasing them. "Now, you need to get some real sleep." Glancing at her blood-stained clothing, he added, "You will probably want to get cleaned up first." He looked at her with a raised eyebrow, "Shall I send Aidan to assist you? He's very worried about you, you know."

Lucky frowned. She wasn't sure she wanted Aidan to help her get cleaned up, but when she tried to sit up on her own, she knew she'd never manage to get undressed and showered without help. And she guessed she'd rather have Aidan's help than anyone else's. Unbidden came the image of Kev carefully undressing and bathing her, and she felt herself blushing. Why was she thinking about him? Pushing the unwanted thoughts aside, she answered Malachi's question with a small nod, "Yes, please."

"He will be here shortly," Malachi said, rising from where he knelt beside the bed. From her prone position, he seemed even taller than usual. "Do not try to move until he gets here. You are very weak, and you do not want to fall and injure yourself further."

He didn't close the door behind him when he left the room, so she could hear his footfalls, light as they were, as he descended the stairs. Just as she could hear Aidan's rapid ones as he ascended them. It sounded as if he were running up them, taking two stairs at a time.

He halted as he reached her door, then walked slowly into the room and over to the bed. The control he exerted to slow his movements was almost tangible. When his anxious blue eyes met hers, Lucky smiled into them. She really was glad to see him. He rested his hand against her cheek, and she could feel a slight tremble in his fingers. His touch felt familiar and right, and the relief that filled her made her turn her head to press her lips to his palm.

"Let's get you cleaned up then, shall we?" he said, gathering her gently in his arms. She groaned as he lifted her, her aches and pains springing back to sudden life.

"I'm sorry," he apologized.

She rested her head against his shoulder. "It's okay," she said into his shirt. "I think some pain is unavoidable. It's worth it to get rid of all this blood."

She relaxed against him as he carried her into the bathroom. Settling her into a seated position on the closed toilet, he began to remove her clothing. She tried to help, but she felt so weak that she made no protest when he brushed her hands aside. She let him move her body about as he needed to, concentrating on staying upright, as he slipped her jeans and panties down her legs and unhooked her bra to slide it off her arms. When she was undressed, he stripped down to just his jeans, then picked her up again and stepped into the shower with her.

The warm water streaming over her revived her somewhat, and as Aidan stood her on her feet and leaned her back against the shower wall, bracing her with one knee on each side of her, she realized that she would probably be embarrassed when she remembered this. Right now though, she didn't feel much of anything except relief and pleasure as the water and Aidan's soapy hands washed the blood and dirt out of her hair and off her skin. She gasped with surprise as his hand ran over her abdomen. Pushing weakly at his hand, she looked down at her unmarked skin.

"But the sword…," she began, looking back up at him with a puzzled frown.

"Raphael healed your wounds," Aidan said, sliding his hand back to the spot where the wound had been.

"Oh, right. Malachi said something about that. Who is Raphael?"

"He's another Archangel, like Uriel—though not as scary. He's a healer. Zeke called him after you were—hurt."

"If he healed me, why do I still feel so weak?"

"Part of it is blood loss," he replied. He paused a moment before continuing, "And part of it is poisoning from the sword itself."

"Poisoning?" she asked.

Aidan didn't answer her question, but repositioned her so he could soap her back and legs.

After he had let the shower rinse all the soap away, he bundled her up in a huge towel, carried her back into the bedroom, and set her down on the bed. Someone had changed the sheets while they were in the shower. She was sure the ones that were on the bed before must have been stained with her blood. Excusing himself, Aidan left the room, to return a few moments later having traded his wet jeans for a pair of gray sweat pants.

He was carrying a navy silk pajama top, which he helped her into, after disengaging her from the towel.

"Zeke's," he offered, by way of explanation.

It was only as he sat behind her, carefully drying and brushing her hair, that he returned to their earlier conversation. "The sword was made of an angelic material that is poisonous to humans, to anyone who is not at least part angel."

"Will I get better?" she asked, feeling strangely unconcerned about the answer.

"Once you are Made Naphil, you will be immune and will heal completely."

"Yet another reason for the Making."

"So it seems," Aidan sighed.

Moving from behind her, he repositioned her so that she was reclining on the bed again, her head resting on a pillow.

"Thank you," she said, forcing her eyes open as they drifted closed.

"You're welcome," he responded. "Is it okay if I stay with you?"

"Yes," she said, rolling onto her side. "S'okay."

She was almost asleep when she felt him slide into the bed and spoon himself around her. She drifted away to the soft touch of his lips against her neck.

CHAPTER 29

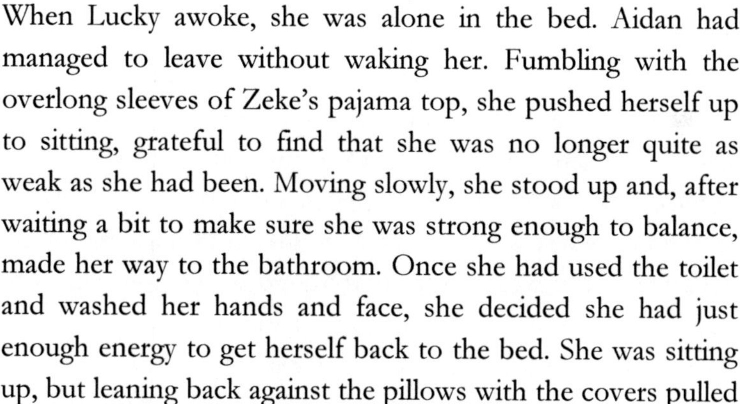

When Lucky awoke, she was alone in the bed. Aidan had managed to leave without waking her. Fumbling with the overlong sleeves of Zeke's pajama top, she pushed herself up to sitting, grateful to find that she was no longer quite as weak as she had been. Moving slowly, she stood up and, after waiting a bit to make sure she was strong enough to balance, made her way to the bathroom. Once she had used the toilet and washed her hands and face, she decided she had just enough energy to get herself back to the bed. She was sitting up, but leaning back against the pillows with the covers pulled over her legs, when the door opened.

"Good evening," Malachi said, as he stepped inside. He was carrying a tray holding a steaming tea pot, two cups, and several other closed containers.

"You remember that I can't eat, right?" she said with a smile.

He smiled back at her and set the tray on the bedside table. "You seem to be feeling a bit better."

She nodded. "I'm not up to fighting off any attacking Powers, but I don't feel quite as weak as I did."

"Good. We have some work to do, and we do not have much time."

He moved a chair nearer the bed, positioning it so he was within easy reach of both Lucky and the items on the tray.

The closed containers seemed to contain dried herbs of some sort. As Lucky watched, Malachi placed a pinch of the contents of each container in each of the cups, before filling the cups with hot water from the teapot. Then he sat back in his chair.

"Now, I want you to relax," he said. "Close your eyes. Take deep, slow breaths."

She did as he asked, relaxing into the rhythm of her breath. After a few breaths, she realized he was speaking again, in a language she didn't know, but which sounded familiar somehow. It took her a few more breaths to remember where she'd heard it before. Although she didn't understand the words, the rhythm and intonation were like those of the language Aidan had spoken the night he changed the wards on his apartment to allow Sambethe access.

Malachi paused his chanting to speak to her again in English. "Open your senses, Lucky. Allow your powers to work."

She obeyed, activating her powers bit by bit, while he resumed the chant. Senses open, she could see the words he spoke spiraling around her, letters of fire in an unknown alphabet but somehow familiar. She felt as if she were on the verge of being able to read the circling words, but their meanings kept eluding her, their secrets stored away just beyond her reach. She frowned in concentration, pushing her senses farther in an attempt to grasp that which was hidden.

"Do not struggle so."

The English words were oddly muffled, as though she had cotton in her ears, but she recognized Malachi's deep voice. Then she realized with some surprise that she could still hear him speaking the other words, the ones that were circling her, the ones she could almost, but not quite, understand. She focused on one word in particular. If only she could read at least one of them. Perhaps that would be the key to unlocking the mystery of the rest.

"Lucky." Again that muffled voice, and with it the realization that Malachi was speaking the English words inside her head. "You do not need to understand the words. Just let them in."

She did her best to comply, softening her gaze so she couldn't even see the fiery words as distinctly. But the desire to understand, to know, kept goading her, and she found herself, almost against her will, concentrating on a single word, her mind pushing against the locked door of its meaning, mental fingers feeling for a way in.

Then Malachi spoke in her head once more. "Hear me, Lucky. You do not need to understand. Relax, breathe, and let them in."

Taking a deep breath, Lucky closed her eyes, so she could no longer see the spiraling words. Slowly, she released the desire to understand, the need to know. Opening her eyes again, she allowed herself to see the fiery letters simply as shapes, lovely calligraphy writ by fire on air. The letters spun around her, and she opened herself to their beauty and power. The sound of Malachi's voice speaking the foreign words licked at her mind like tongues of flame.

The scent of dark herbs, spicy and pungent, filled her nose, and she felt the touch of a cup against her lips. "Drink," commanded Malachi's voice in her head, and she drank.

The words spun so quickly now, she felt as if she were in the center of a fiery tornado, one that was closing in on her. When the spiral was so near she could almost feel the touch of the letters as they circled her, the spinning ceased. Then the words settled onto her body, wrapping her in warmth, like a blanket, before they sank into her skin, each letter burning like a tiny cinder as it did so. Lucky felt detached from her mind and her thoughts, and her eyes closed as her awareness centered in the stinging of the letters on her skin.

"Now," said Malachi, the English words falling on her ears instead of into her head, "we wait. Let your spirit call your Makers. Do not try to force anything. They will come to you as they are called."

The stinging of her skin intensified until Lucky longed for a pool of cool water to quench the myriad tiny sparks. Then the burning sank through her skin, through her muscles, and into her bones—and a stillness deeper than any she had ever known settled around her like drifting snow. She opened her eyes, and it was as if that stillness had blanketed the world: she was alone in a field of undifferentiated white, blankness stretching out in all directions. She drifted in the white void, waiting for whoever—or whatever—would come to her.

After what seemed like hours, but could have been a matter of minutes, something began to take form in front of her, like a film coming into focus on a screen. As the image took shape, she saw that it was G-Ma as she had been during

Lucky's last visit to the assisted living facility, in those moments of clarity when she had recognized Lucky and they had been able to talk.

"G-Ma," Lucky said, reaching toward the image, but it shifted and changed, flashing to a scene of her grandmother and herself on that fateful evening when they had realized G-Ma could no longer live in the apartment but had to be moved to assisted living. Lucky had held her grandmother, comforting her as best she could. Tears rose to her eyes as she witnessed the scene from the outside, seeing her own arms around her grandmother, the older woman's head pillowed on her shoulder.

Then the scene shifted again, showing a much younger Lucky cradled in G-Ma's arms. The child she had been was laughing as she looked up into the smiling face of her grandmother, who had eyes only for the granddaughter on whom she had lavished a world of love.

"Oh, G-Ma," Lucky choked, tears streaming down her face, "I miss you so much."

The image faded away, and Lucky stared at the place where it had been, wondering if she would ever stop grieving her grandmother's loss.

Then, into the midst of her grief, came memories of G-Ma holding her, laughing with her, teaching her to cook or throw a pot, and telling her she loved her. G-Ma's voice filled her head in a rushing chorus of "I love you, Lucky," and "Lucky, I love you." Fresh tears followed the tracks down Lucky's cheeks as she was enveloped in her grandmother's loving presence. She closed her eyes and let the sense of

G-Ma's love sink through her skin and into her bones like Malachi's fiery words.

Lucky had no idea how long she rested in that tender place before she became aware of another presence near her. She opened her eyes and nearly screamed aloud. Standing only a few feet away, lashing its thick tail, was a massive dragon. Its scales were mingled green and gold, and huge dark green wings flared from its back. Lucky gasped as the creature reared up on its hind legs and roared, flame spouting from its open jaws. When it settled down to the ground, its great head resting on its curled front feet, much like a cat, its wings trailing away on either side, Lucky had an absurd desire to pat its head. Before she had time to think better of the action, she had covered the distance between herself and the beast and rested her right hand between its eyes.

The creature's large gold irises with their cat-like pupils were on a level with Lucky's head. As her hand stroked back over the smooth, dry scales, those eyes closed, and the dragon began to shrink until it fit into the palm of Lucky's now upturned hand. It continued to shrink as it climbed up her arm, onto her shoulder, and down her chest to disappear with a flash of golden light into the Light-Bringer's Medallion resting on her breastbone. The amulet heated until Lucky feared it might burn her, before cooling to a temperature that no longer caused her discomfort, but was warm enough to make it impossible for her to forget the medallion's presence against her skin.

No sooner had the dragon disappeared into the amulet, than another large shape appeared before her. Lucky recognized the statue of the *lamassu* and, without surprise, watched it morph into her friend and mentor as she saw him when her senses were wide open—multiple pairs of lapis blue wings surrounding a form perpetually shifting from man to bull to lion to eagle and back to man again. Then the Cherub settled into his more familiar human form, clad in khakis and a white button-down shirt, his long wheat-blond hair pulled back from his temples. Only now, three pairs of blue wings extended from his back and curved inward at their ends. He reached out his hand toward her, and she saw that he was holding a china tea cup. She took it from him and raised it to her lips. The contents slid down her throat like warm honey, filling her with a sense of safety. As Zeke's form began to fade, she had the sense of being enveloped in the protective embrace of his great blue wings.

When Zeke had disappeared, Lucky was once again alone in a field of white. After a time, she noticed that the blank whiteness was taking on a ruddy hue. Soon she was enveloped in golden-red light, and she found herself on a familiar hilltop facing a familiar tree. A crow cawed three times, and then a man-sized bird rose up from the ground in front of her. He regarded her with Malachi's amber eyes, cocking his head from side to side as he studied her. Without warning, he lunged forward, pecking at her chest with such force that his beak sank into her heart. She dropped to her knees, gasping in shock, a trembling hand rising to press against the bloody wound. The crow took a few backward steps away from her, before studying her once again with cocked head. She could see the wetness of her blood on his shiny black beak. Then, lifting his wings, he cawed three more times and flew away. When the bird's black wings had disappeared in the sunset sky, Lucky looked down at her chest. There was no blood, no wound, but she could hear the crow's caw with every heartbeat.

Sensing a change in her surroundings, she looked up to see the redness fading from the sky, leaving the blank, white field behind, as all the color was drawn to a spot a few feet from her, where it condensed and dropped like blood into a vial that appeared to catch the droplets as they fell. A hand appeared to clasp the vial, and then a body attached to the hand, and Lucky heard an eerie sing-song voice proclaiming over and over, "Both Naphil and not Naphil, she will unwind the threads. Light and Dark, she will unwind the threads."

Sambethe marched toward her, the vial clasped in her outstretched hand, her pale eyes unfocused, seeing not Lucky, but something beyond. When Sambethe reached her, she thrust her free hand into Lucky's hair and jerked her head back. Tipping the vial, she let a drop of liquid fall from its lip onto the center of Lucky's forehead. Lucky drew in her breath with a hiss, feeling as if acid were eating through her skull. The pain intensified and she cried out, falling back onto the ground. She could still hear Sambethe's sing-song chant as she faded from consciousness.

Lucky awakened to find that the pain in her forehead had lessened to a slight tingle, of an intensity to match the temperature of the amulet on her breast. Or the bruised tenderness of her heart. Or the warmth in her bones. Or the sense of being embraced by protective wings. In addition, she felt a sharp, burning pain in her abdomen and back. Her hand had located the source of the pain by the time she focused her eyes on it: a sword was run through her body, the hilt and an inch or so of the blade protruding from her abdomen. Clenching her teeth, she grasped the hilt with both hands and pulled. A scream ripped from her lips, and she collapsed panting, her hands falling away from the sword that still pierced her. As she lay there, a glowing hand closed around the sword's hilt and the weapon was withdrawn. Immediately, she felt as if she were floating in sea water. Warm and silken, it surrounded her, buoyed her, cleansed her, soothed her. The sensation faded, and she was left lying there, with a small ache in her abdomen to add to her list of new awarenesses.

"Lucky!" She heard Malachi's muffled voice in her head. And then his hands were on her shoulders, shaking her, and she heard him with her ears. "Lucky, come back now. It is time."

"Did I call them all?" she mumbled.

"I believe so. I did not see what you saw. I only know that I am among those you called to you, and that the veil around you had cleared by the time I called you back. How many others were there?"

She thought for a moment. "Five, besides you." She frowned. "But one of them was G-Ma. How many are there supposed to be?"

"Generally, there are seven altogether."

"But I only saw six. And G-Ma can't possibly be one of them. Even if she somehow managed to get to the Making, it's not like she has a palm sigil."

"It is done. You called whom you called. The Making will be as it will be."

"Thanks, Malachi. Cryptic is just what I need right now." Lucky swung her legs out of bed and stood, grabbing onto the nightstand when her balance threatened to desert her.

"Still weak I see," Malachi remarked. Opening the door, he added, "Your attire is on the end of the bed. Call for me once you have changed. I will be just outside."

The attire he'd referred to turned out to be a simple, backless, red linen sheath. When she slipped it over her head, its hem fell to her ankles, but there were slits to just above her knees on either side. She preferred not to think about the reason her back was left bare. Once she had put on the dress, she sat down on the side of the bed, winded. Her weakness, she feared, did not bode well for the coming ceremony. Her hands shook as she removed the Light-Bringer's Medallion from around her neck and placed it on the bedside table, and her heart accelerated its rhythm as butterflies clustered in her stomach.

Then she heard the echo of the crow's caw in her heartbeats and felt the other tiny pains and awarenesses that witnessed to the Makers who had revealed themselves to her. Somehow, she found the subtle reminders reassuring, as now were the cryptic words Malachi had uttered earlier, which repeated themselves in her head. The Making would be what it would be. They had done all they could to get her ready for it; the outcome was out of her hands.

She called Malachi's name, and he was through the door in an instant. "I realize that you would prefer to do this on your own, but we do not have time for that. I hope you do not mind being carried."

Before she could respond, he was already scooping her up in his arms as if she weighed no more than a feather. Lucky replied anyway, "I don't mind. Much as I hate to admit it, I'm not sure I could make it down the stairs on my own right now."

They were halfway down the stairs when she spoke again. "Malachi?"

"What is it, Lucky?"

"Thank you. For everything you've done for me. I really am grateful."

"I am sorry for the necessity of some of it, but I am glad I could help."

Lucky tightened her grasp on Malachi's shoulder and rested her head against his chest. She sensed that was as close as she could get to hugging the Naphil; an outright embrace would probably make him uncomfortable. She brushed her cheek against the fabric of his shirt and settled more closely against him. She might have imagined it, but she thought he tightened his hold on her in response.

When they reached the basement and turned left into the large room that housed the Gates of Heaven, they were greeted by a torrent of words as a familiar blonde almost pulled Lucky out of Malachi's arms to sweep her into a bear hug. "I've been so worried about you. I'm so glad you're okay. Well, not that this Making thing sounds like a piece of cake or anything, but you survived getting skewered, so I'm sure you'll get through this just fine." Mo paused to take a breath and then continued more slowly. "You have to, you know. You have to get through this—I'm not giving you a choice. You're my best friend. If you don't make it, I'll find you, wherever you are, and kick your butt myself."

Lucky chuckled as she returned the embrace. She wasn't strong enough to squeeze Mo back with the vice-like grip her friend had on her, but she did her best. "Thanks, Mo," she said. "If things get bad, I'll picture you waiting in hob-nailed boots, and that'll scare me into surviving."

Mo laughed, but there were tears in her eyes when she pulled away from Lucky. "Seriously, Lucky. You come back to me, okay? I can't stand to lose you."

Lucky's eyes filled as she pulled her friend close again. "I'll do my very best, Mo. I promise."

"We must go," Zeke said, and Lucky looked in his direction in time to see him give a small nod to Malachi. The tall, dark man ushered Mo back up the stairs as Zeke moved to Lucky's side, sliding a supportive arm around her and helping her take the few steps to reach the Gates. He pressed his palm against the slight indentation between the huge wings, and they unfolded, flooding the room in brilliant light. He swept her up into his arms and stepped through.

CHAPTER 30

Lucky took a deep breath, relishing the feeling of relieved expansion as her body adjusted to normal after the squish of the passage through the Gates.

"Are you alright?"

Even though Zeke spoke quietly, the resonance of his voice vibrated through his chest into Lucky's body, causing her to wonder if this was how a tuning fork felt. The sensation wasn't unpleasant; in fact, it carried the same essence of protection that had accompanied Zeke's visitation in her vision of her Makers.

She nodded, wishing he'd say something else—especially as the touch of Elsewhere's unnatural sunlight reminded her of how long it had been since she'd been outside. Not that it had been sunny; it had been rainy and dark when that Power had skewered her like a kabob.

"I'm scared, Zeke." The words tumbled out, surprising her. She had been determined to remain stoic about this whole business, to be strong and think positive.

"I would be very surprised if you were not," he replied—and Lucky soaked up the vibrations of his voice like a sponge. "There is no shame in feeling fear, Lucky. It is a natural response—one necessary for survival. Bravery is not the absence of fear, but the willingness to do what one must even in the face of it." He paused for a moment, then continued, "What you are doing is very brave. And I am more than proud of you."

The tears that seemed far too close to the surface lately filled Lucky's eyes once more. Swallowing the obstruction that had appeared in her throat, she wound her arms around Zeke's neck and hugged him as tightly as she could. He wrapped her close, the protectiveness that was a part of his nature settling around her like a cloak.

When she lifted her head from where she had buried it against Zeke's neck, she saw Aidan standing nearby. Dressed in black denim jeans and his favorite black leather jacket, he had one hip cocked, and his arms were crossed over his chest.

"Hey," he said softly, as his blue eyes met hers. "Zeke, could we have a minute or two alone?"

Zeke set her gently on her feet, his arms tightening around her in a last quick embrace before he released her. "I will wait for you at the door to the Council Hall."

Aidan took a few steps toward her, stopping when there was less than a foot between them. His arms now hung at his sides, his hands clenching and releasing, as he studied her in silence. Lucky understood at least something of what he must be feeling—she had no idea what to say to him either. Everything that came to mind seemed to offer too much or too little. Silently, she placed her hand against his cheek, stroking her thumb across his cheekbone. Aidan let out a shaky breath, clenched his jaw, and closed his arms around her. She wrapped her arms around his waist and pressed herself against him. She wanted to keep holding on to him, to put off what was about to happen, to ask him to pick her up, spread his wings, and fly them both out of here. But she knew she couldn't do any of those things. So, after far too short a time, she pushed away from him and raised her face to look up into his. His hands coming to rest on either side of her face, gentle as butterflies, he bent his head and kissed her. Her own hands lifting to cover his, she kissed him back.

Neither spoke as Aidan picked her up and carried her to where Zeke awaited them. After transferring her to the Cherub's arms, he held her gaze for a moment, before he turned to open the door to the Council Hall. He held the door long enough for Zeke and Lucky to pass through, and then, still without saying a word, he left them to head toward the stairs to their right. Zeke, carrying Lucky, moved at a slower pace, and Lucky's eyes lingered on Aidan's long legs as he preceded them up the stairs.

She had assumed that the Making would be held in the same room as the Striking, but she was wrong. When Aidan stopped outside the double doors to the great room, Zeke gestured for him to move farther down the hall. Bypassing the next set of double doors, which, Lucky remembered, also provided access to the great hall, Aidan stopped when he reached the only remaining door in the corridor. Lucky guessed the room it opened into must be considerably smaller than the great hall, since only this single door seemed to provide entry, and when Aidan turned the knob and swung the door inward, she saw that her assumption was correct. The room was quite small—and surprisingly empty. She had assumed there would be spectators as there had been for the Striking, but the few pew-like benches that ran down the center of the room were vacant. Perhaps, she, Zeke, and Aidan had arrived early?

Aidan stepped through the doorway—and disappeared. One minute he was there, and the next he wasn't. The room stretched before them as empty as before.

"A small magic that offers us a bit more protection for the ceremony," Zeke remarked. "This might feel strange," he added, before he too stepped through the door.

At least she wasn't squished this time, Lucky thought gratefully, as the magic that screened the doorway washed over her, leaving her feeling as if they had passed through a waterfall. The sensation of being deluged with cool water was so real, she was surprised to find herself undrenched when they emerged on the other side.

The actual room was roughly the same dimensions as it had appeared through the veil of magic at the doorway, high-ceilinged and probably one-third the size of the great room, but it was differently arranged. A few curved benches were placed in a semicircle around a central circular dais upon which stood something that looked like a cross between a chair and a piece of sculpture. Its surfaces appeared to be padded, but the angles looked all wrong for sitting. Floor-to-ceiling banners in alternating red-gold and white softened the corners of the room, rounding them into curves which echoed the semicircular arrangement of the benches. The banners were covered with angelic sigils, black on red-gold, and fiery red-gold on white.

The room was not unoccupied, as the magic had made it appear. Not only Aidan, but Malachi, Kev, and Sambethe peopled the far ends of the benches in the innermost row, those closest to the dais. Lilith, flanked by two dark-cloaked figures, sat in the outermost row. Zeke lowered Lucky onto the central bench in the innermost semicircle, positioning himself beside her. Scanning the grave faces of her friends, Lucky's mouth went suddenly dry. What had she been thinking? She couldn't possibly go through with this. Her hands twisted together in her lap, her fingers squeezing so tightly her knuckles whitened, as she willed herself to stay on the bench, instead of crawling, whimpering, beneath it.

Zeke's big hand covered her joined ones just as she heard the now familiar rushing of wings. The Archangel Uriel and a companion whom Lucky assumed to be another Archangel appeared in a brilliant flash of light, at first seeming to stretch from ceiling to floor, dwarfing the room and its other occupants, then shrinking to a size still larger than human, but more in keeping with the room's dimensions. Everyone stood as the Archangels made their appearance, Zeke sliding an arm around Lucky's waist to help her to her feet.

Lucky had a vague sense that Uriel was speaking, but she heard nothing over the sound of her own accelerating heartbeat. Gradually, she became aware that Zeke was urging her toward the dais. As he helped her onto the oddly shaped structure, she realized it was designed to support a kneeling figure, with pads for the front of the shoulders and bars around which to wrap the hands. Clenching her fingers around the bars, she felt Zeke lift her long hair so it fell forward on either side of her neck, leaving her back bare. Her heart pounded so hard, she felt as if it would beat a hole through her chest. Then Zeke placed a hand between her shoulder blades, and a kind of calmness settled over her, not displacing her fear, but lowering its intensity, so that it no longer eclipsed her awareness.

The Sensitive has called her Makers, said Uriel, *and I call them now. With your Powers, your Gifts, your Marks, she will be Made Naphil. Grandmother-Crone, come forward.*

Lucky held her breath. It wasn't possible that G-Ma could be here.

A wind swept through the room, whipping Lucky's hair across her face, and with a blinding flash of light, another huge figure appeared to Uriel's left. Shrinking, he stepped forward to the edge of the dais. His hair was the brilliant white of heat lightning and floated on the breeze that Archangels seemed to generate; his pupil-less eyes were like screens upon which shown a film of clouds scudding across the luminous blue of a summer sky. He turned those eyes on Lucky, and she shivered as they looked at, and through, and beyond her.

I will stand for the Grandmother. Even his voice was like lightning, flashing into the mind, leaving behind a strange frisson of excitement tinged with fear.

Gabriel, Grandmother, Crone, you are the first to make your Mark. Let the Making commence.

The Archangel held Lucky's eyes briefly with his uncanny ones, and for a moment she could see G-Ma's smiling face reflected in their depths. Then Gabriel stepped around the dais, so Lucky could no longer see him. She sucked in a breath as she sensed him approaching her back. Fire seared the skin and muscle below her left ribs, and she sank her teeth into her lip to keep from crying out. Her mouth filled with the slightly metallic, salty taste of her own blood. Dear God, it hurt! She felt like she might pass out from the pain, wished she would. How could she possibly endure six times this? And that was before the Power rushed through her, rolling her over and under, like an ocean wave. A few years before, the entire family had spent a week at Cape Cod, and she and Josh had passed much of that time body-surfing in the ocean. Once, a wave had swept her off the body board, turning her around so that she no longer had any idea which way was up toward air and which was down deeper into the water. She had discovered which way was down when her face had slammed into the sand. This felt surprisingly similar: a rush of adrenaline and fear as she was tumbled in the wave of power, and then pain as that power smacked against the limitations of her still human self.

Reeling from the onslaught, she sensed Gabriel remove his hand. Unfortunately, the burning sensation did not abate in the slightest. It felt as if his sigil were tunneling a fiery path through each layer of skin and muscle.

Will the Dragon please come forward?

Lucky forced her eyes to focus, wondering who the Dragon would be. Aidan? He had given her the pendant. But the medallion had belonged to his father. Would the Dragon be Lucifer himself? With a start of surprise, she saw Kev step to the front of the dais. Apparently, he was here as himself and not as *Ha-Satan.* Instead of the open blood-red robe, he wore his standard faded blue jeans and a soft green buttoned shirt open at the neck, sleeves rolled to the elbows. His sun-dappled brown hair looked as if he'd recently shoved a hand back through it. When his eyes met hers, she saw they were not the gold-tinged dark green she remembered but a strange yellow-gold with vertical, cat-like pupils.

Dragon, make your Mark.

Lucky closed her eyes, steeling herself against the pain, as Kev stepped behind her. His hand touched her back over her left ribs, above and to the right of the fierce burning of Gabriel's sigil. This time, the pain was not immediate. Kev's touch was warm, gentle, on her skin. His fingers flexed against her in a tiny caress. And then she felt as if a red-hot coal had been placed on her back, just where his palm rested. Sucking her bleeding lower lip into her mouth and squeezing her eyes shut to block the tears, she understood that Kev had not yet activated his palm sigil when he'd first touched her. He had instead placed his hand on her back, skin to skin, in a gift of simple human touch. She offered him silent thanks for that momentary, soothing contact, even as his sigil seared another path through her, adjacent to the one Gabriel had left behind.

Kev's Power didn't slam into her, tumbling her over as Gabriel's had. Instead, it ran through her limbs like fire. Every inch of muscle and sinew in her body burned, and she couldn't hold back the whimper that escaped her lips. She knew when Kev removed his hand from her back, though how she could sense that absence in the midst of the various fiery pains that filled her she had no idea. She thought she felt his fingers brush over her hair before he stepped away from the dais.

Protector, Cherub, come forward.

Lucky raised her head to watch Zeke move to stand before her. Her hold on her heightened senses was shaky, and she could no longer limit her view of him. As a consequence his form flickered before her, morphing and changing, only his kind gray eyes remaining the same. Feeling dizzy, Lucky closed her eyes to block the sight.

Protector, make your Marks.

Uriel's use of the plural penetrated Lucky's awareness when she felt not one but two sigils searing their fiery tunnels through her skin and muscles and bones, one on each side of her spine, just beneath her shoulder blades. Like molten worms, they seemed to be crawling through her lungs and out the front of her chest. Sweat ran down her forehead to drip off the end of her nose, and she wondered that it didn't evaporate in the heat. Then she no longer had the presence of mind to wonder anything. Zeke's Power took her like a whirlwind, a sandstorm of dizzying force. The physical pain she had endured was as nothing compared to the mental agony that ripped through her. Thoughts disappeared and senses swirled as the fabric of her being seemed to unknit itself. She might have heard herself screaming, but there was no way to be sure. There was no way to be sure of anything. Everything was chaos.

She was vaguely aware of the burn of Malachi's sigil over her right ribs, and the rush of his Power into her added a swirl of darkness and the echoing caws of crows to the already overpowering jumble of her senses and her self. By the time Sambethe's sigil seared her right side, completing the upside down V Gabriel had begun, she was barely conscious. Surprisingly, the onrush of the oracle's Power brought with it something of a clearing, a momentary cessation of thoughts, senses, pains—a blessed moment of empty, velvet darkness. Then everything crashed back upon her, leaving Lucky reeling once more.

Raphael, Healer, step forward.

Lucky heard the words as if she were underwater, yet somehow she understood them all the same. She couldn't lift her head to see Raphael, couldn't open her eyes, couldn't have focused them even if she had been able to open them. She sensed the Archangel's presence beside her and felt his hand on her back, spanning the distance between her shoulder blades. There was no burn of a sigil. Where he touched felt cool, as if bathed in a healing balm. That space on her back was the only part of her whole being that didn't feel completely ripped apart.

Then he lifted his hand. And a cry tore from her lungs as she arched backward in agony. She would have flung herself off the structure on which she knelt if not for the death-grip her hands had taken on the support bars as soon as Gabriel's palm had touched her. She felt as if every sigil burned into her was crawling up her back to writhe and swirl in the space between her shoulder blades where Raphael's hand had been. Simultaneously, all the Powers that had been gifted to her with the Marks swirled and writhed inside her, coalescing into a ball of intensity that wrung another scream from her as it exploded outward. Then, blessedly, there was nothing.

It was with a strange sense of relief that Aidan watched Lucky collapse against the supporting pads of the kneeling chair. As she slumped in unconsciousness, his muscles relaxed as well. He had tensed a little more every time another Maker had touched her, had wanted to rush forward and push each one away from her as the pain seared her. And when his brother had run his fingers over her hair after he'd Marked her, Aidan had wanted to slam his fist into Kev's jaw. Not just because he'd hurt her, but because he'd been in a position to offer her a gesture of comfort that Aidan could not.

At least the bestowing of the Marks was over. Now, they had to wait, for the requisite three hours, for the Making to complete itself. Aidan feared they were going to be three of the longest hours he'd ever endured. Then again, they might not be any worse than all those hours he'd spent outside her closed bedroom door, waiting for Malachi to come out and tell them if he'd been able to save her or not. He clenched his jaw again as Zeke and Kev lifted the unconscious Lucky from the kneeling chair and laid her facedown on a mat that someone had placed beside the dais for that purpose. He wanted to help, wanted to care for her, but as he was not one of her Makers, he couldn't touch her until the whole thing was over.

She was still breathing. He could hear each ragged breath she took. And, yes, there it was—faint, but growing louder:

the accelerating beat of her heart. Lucky's heartbeat filled the room as her body labored to assimilate the changes worked by the Making.

Aidan remembered how Malachi's heart had thudded, echoing in the great room, which had been filled almost to capacity for the ceremony. He also remembered the deafening silence when that heartbeat had ceased, a full two hours before the required three-hour waiting period was complete. Waiting in that room, knowing Malachi had died, well, those two hours ranked right up there with the worst. Not once in the history of Makings had anyone's heart ever started back up when it had stopped for more than a few beats.

Not until Malachi. Just as the final few minutes of the third hour were ticking down, they had heard a loud gasp, like that of a man near to drowning breaking the water's surface to fill his lungs with life-giving air. And then Malachi's heartbeat had resumed, strong and steady. Aidan guessed he should take some comfort in the fact that Malachi himself had been one of Lucky's Makers. Maybe he'd passed on something of his gift of survival to her.

With that thought Aidan shifted his eyes from Lucky's still form to the big, dark man across from him. Malachi was sitting still, spine straight, eyes cast down. Aidan wondered if he were meditating, or if he'd gone inside himself or wherever it was he went when he did his battles with death and darkness. Maybe he'd figured out a way to help Lucky through this ordeal. Aidan hoped he had.

Unable to look away from Lucky for long, Aidan turned his gaze back towards her, wincing as he scanned the wounds on her back. The burns from the palm sigils looked raw and painful. Once the Making was complete, and she was Naphil, the burns would heal, leaving behind scars that would look much like slightly raised tattoos. Between her shoulder blades, in the spot where her personal sigil would take form, was a swirling, writhing mass of intermingled black and gold. The way it moved reminded him of worms. Just watching it made him shift uncomfortably, shrugging his shoulders beneath his jacket. His own sigil had simply manifested at puberty. His back had burned when it first appeared, but he didn't recall ever feeling like worms were crawling beneath his skin. And he was pretty sure that was a sensation he would have remembered.

As time passed, and he and the others continued to wait without speaking, Aidan started counting the beats of Lucky's heart. One beat, two beats, three beats, four beats. He counted to ten, then started over, then counted to a hundred, before starting again at one. He didn't know how many times he had counted to a hundred, when suddenly the heartbeat stopped. In the silence, he found himself counting the beats that should have been there. One beat, two beats, three beats, four beats, five beats, six beats. *Seven hells! Lucky, don't you dare die on me.* Seven beats, eight beats, nine beats. And it was back, slower and quieter than before, but strong and steady in its rhythm. Aidan released the breath he hadn't been aware he was holding in an audible sigh of relief. Glancing at Kev and Zeke, he saw that same relief reflected in both their faces. The Cherub looked up and, catching Aidan's eye, gave him a tiny, reassuring nod. So far, so good.

Lucky's heart stopped beating twice more before the three hours were up. Each time, Aidan found himself holding his breath and counting the absent beats. And, each time, thank all that was holy, only a few beats were missed before the heartbeat resumed, slower, steadier, and stronger than before. Then, as Aidan watched, the livid burns on Lucky's back began to heal, changing, in the space of a few minutes, to beautifully intricate black patterns. As the wounds healed, the swirling blackness between her shoulder blades gradually settled into an even more intricate pattern, which somehow combined all the Marks as well as something of Lucky herself into a new sigil that was uniquely her own.

The gradual fading of the sound of her strong, even heartbeat filled him with a sense of relief and satisfaction rather than alarm. It had worked! He wanted to whoop with joy. As a huge grin crawled across his face, he could feel the tension in the room, which had ratcheted to nearly unbearable levels, dissipate in a rush, as if it couldn't wait to vacate the premises.

Zeke and Kev were also grinning; even Malachi's lips turned upward in a smile. Sambethe just looked satisfied and smug, which sort of made him want to slap her, but he was so relieved that Lucky had survived the Making—that she was now Naphil and could fight off the blasted poison in her system—that even Sambethe's smug expression couldn't annoy him for long.

Soon after her wounds had healed and her sigil had settled, Lucky began to return to consciousness, making small movements and quiet waking sounds. It took every ounce of control Aidan could muster to stop himself from shooting off the bench, on which he'd sat far too long, and rushing to her side. Instead, as was appropriate, it was Zeke who moved to kneel beside her, whispering instructions and words of encouragement as he helped her rise to her knees.

Precisely as the last second of the three-hour waiting period ended, Uriel appeared in all his distant and terrifying brilliance in front of the dais upon which Lucky and Zeke knelt. With no small amount of surprise, Aidan realized he'd forgotten all about the Archangel. He hadn't been aware of Uriel's presence during the waiting, but he hadn't sensed his absence either. How was it possible for one so sublimely noticeable to fade into the background so completely? He'd have to ask the Archangel about that someday. He and his fellows among the Forces of the Fallen could put such a skill to good use.

You have great strength, Lucky Monroe.

As was usual when the Archangel spoke, Aidan couldn't tell if he heard the words or if they were somehow communicated to him through his other senses.

I offer congratulations on your successful completion of this Making. Sensitive no more, you are now Naphil. Exactly what this means remains to be seen. As a child of the Banished, with two Archangels serving as Makers, your circumstances are rather more than unique.

Uriel paused, his unblinking, flame-filled eyes seeming simultaneously to study Lucky, scan the room, and look beyond this time and place toward something only he—and perhaps Raphael and Gabriel, who now stood on either side of him—could see.

Your wings and your particular Gift will reveal themselves in time. We await the revelation with interest. In the meantime, newly Made Naphil, you are now counted among the Fallen. May your Making be of benefit to us all.

Even with his eyes closed, Aidan felt like the radiance and heat of the Archangels' sudden departure was burning his retinas. As soon as the brilliance faded, he was on his feet and headed toward the dais and Lucky.

His progress was halted by the unexpected touch of a hand on his arm. Aidan's impatience turned to surprise when he saw that it was Lilith who had detained him. Curious as to what she might want with him, he took in her bright scarlet hair before locking his eyes on her impossibly emerald ones. It was hard to believe this woman was anyone's grandmother, let alone Lucky's, even though he knew that, like Zeke, she was much, much older than she looked.

He said nothing, just raised an eyebrow as he continued to hold her gaze.

Letting her hand fall from his arm, Lilith answered his silent query in light, husky tones. "I know she will not want to see me or talk to me now. But I also know that at some point, she will." Withdrawing something from the pocket of her dark cloak, she held her hand out to him. "Please give this to her. Tell her I offer my congratulations and a grandmother's love."

At the sound of disbelief Aidan was unable to hold back, her lips twisted in a mocking smile. "You're right, of course. Scratch the 'grandmother's love' bit. I can hardly expect her to believe it. Take it, boy—it won't bite!" This last was uttered as she thrust her outstretched hand toward him. He held out a palm to accept her offering, and she dropped a delicate gold locket into it. "Give her this, and tell her to call for me when she is ready. I can provide some of the answers she seeks should she see fit to ask."

A frown settled on Aidan's forehead as he regarded the locket in his palm. "Where did you get this?" he asked.

Lilith either didn't hear his question or chose to ignore it. She hurried toward the exit, lifting the hood of her cloak to cover her brilliant hair.

"Wait!" he called, but she had already stepped through the door and disappeared.

His frown deepening, Aidan slipped the locket with its broken chain into the pocket of his jeans and went to join the others who were gathered around Lucky.

CHAPTER 31

Exactly what this means remains to be seen. May your Making be of benefit to us all. Uriel's words echoed in Lucky's ears as she scanned the faces of the friends surrounding her. Behind their relieved smiles and quiet congratulatory words, she could sense the same gravity that now filled her. She had survived the Making, but she didn't feel at all like celebrating. Emotionally, she felt as drained and empty as she had after the Striking. *Exactly what this means remains to be seen.* She felt as if her life, her personality, her self had been burned away. She was no more than an empty vessel waiting to be filled. And what might fill that emptiness was a mystery. *Your circumstances are rather more than unique.* They weren't even sure her Making would have positive results. *May your Making be of benefit to us all.* What if she'd gone through this for nothing? Or worse, what if, somehow, something bad would come from what had been done here?

"Josh," she whispered. At least she knew of one good thing she could do now. Helping him was why she'd agreed to the Making in the first place. Not knowing or caring if she was interrupting or speaking over anyone else, she said in a louder voice, "I have to get to Josh. I can help him now. We have to go now, so I can help Josh."

"Of course," Zeke said, his big hand coming to rest on her upper arm. "I will escort you through the Gates one more time. You may be Naphil now, but you need training before you will be able to dematerialize and reform at will in the place you desire."

Aidan's warm hand closed around her cold fingers in a quick squeeze. "See you on the other side," he said, and dematerialized.

As Kev, Malachi, and Sambethe followed suit, Lucky was already moving toward the door, tugging Zeke behind her. When she passed through the entryway, the magic that veiled the room struck her like a cold shower, causing her to release Zeke's hand. Once through the veil, she was, as before, surprised to find herself dry.

Now that she thought about it, she was surprised by a lot of things. Like how the weakness had left her limbs. And how she was no longer in pain. Yes, she was emotionally exhausted, but her body felt strong and healed, which was pretty amazing considering. The Making had hurt like nothing she'd ever experienced before, and she had been convinced she'd feel the burns on her back for weeks. But she felt no pain, only a tingle of awareness at the location of each Maker's sigil on her back and the slightest sense of movement in the space between her shoulder blades, where she had learned from Aidan her own sigil would be. She wondered what her back looked like with all those Marks, wondered what her personal sigil looked like. She'd have to find a mirror, so she could take a look.

Zeke came through the door behind her, and she grabbed his hand, already starting to run.

"There's no need to rush, Lucky," he said, drawing her to a slower pace. "Your cousin's condition will not alter in the time it takes to reach him. Sambethe checked in on him before the Making. She said he would remain stable for another day, if necessary."

"But it's not necessary. I'm not going to wait another day, Zeke."

"I did not mean to imply that you should, but you might slow down a bit. The Gates are here, just down this hall."

Lucky felt a slight frisson as they passed through the wards protecting the room that housed the Council Hall's Gates of Heaven. She had been too preoccupied on her last trip through these Gates to pay them any attention, but this time she realized they were quite different from the pair hidden in Zeke's basement. Whereas those appeared to be carved from dark wood, these seemed to have been chiseled from some kind of glistening stone. As soon as Zeke pressed his palm against the central panel and activated his sigil, the wings began to unfold. Light flared around them, glinting off the glittering stone feathers, giving them the appearance of flame. Lucky caught her breath at their beauty, even as the brilliance of the light forced her to close her eyes. Preparing herself for the uncomfortable compression of the passage, she gripped Zeke's hand and stepped through the Gates—and into the familiar brownstone's lower level.

She made a move toward the stairs, but Zeke detained her, refusing to release her hand. Catching hold of her chin so he could look into her eyes, he said, "You are wondering if this Making was a mistake, are you not—except for what you can do for Josh?"

At her hesitant nod, he continued. "It was not. That we don't know the exact outcome does not mean it was a mistake, or that anything bad will come from it. You are strong and kind and brave. Whatever Gift manifests itself in you will be shaped by that."

Lucky's eyes filled with tears, and she reached up to clasp his wrist where he gripped her chin. "Thank you, Zeke," she whispered.

The Cherub leaned forward and pressed his lips to her forehead before releasing her. She gave him a quick, teary smile, then lifting the fabric of her long skirt so she wouldn't trip on it, she hurried up the stairs.

When she ran into the guest room she had already come to think of as hers, she found Aidan standing by the bed. He turned as she entered, a bundle of clothes in his hands.

"I was just leaving these for you," he said. "The jeans are yours—the bloodstains washed out of those. Your sweater was a goner though, so I brought you one of mine."

"Thanks," she said. "I'm more than happy to trade in this dress."

"No doubt," he said, as he took a couple steps toward the door. "I'll wait for you in the living room. Then I'll take you back to my place, to Josh. Zeke and Sambethe will meet us there."

"Okay. I'll be quick."

She was pulling the dress over her head even as the door closed behind him. Hurrying into the adjoining bathroom, she splashed water on her face and dragged a brush through her bedraggled hair. She needed a shower, but there'd be time for that later.

Turning her back to the mirror, she took a quick peek over her shoulder. Intricate black patterns, like tattoos, formed an upside down V on her back. The sigil between her shoulder blades, like Aidan's, was black perpetually traced in gold. For a moment, she allowed her eyes to follow the movement. Then she looked away. There'd be time for that later too. Right now, she needed to get dressed.

Not only were her jeans among the clothes Aidan had brought, but so were her socks, bra, and panties. She offered a silent thanks to whoever had washed them and to Aidan for his thoughtfulness in bringing them to her. After she'd pulled on her jeans, tucking the legs into her boots, which she found on the floor beside the bed, she slipped Aidan's sweater over her head. It was a black turtleneck, meant to fit snugly, and she was sure it did on Aidan, the ribbed knit outlining his lean muscles. On her, like everything she'd borrowed from him, it was loose and long. It was also clean and warm, and after cuffing the sleeves, she decided it probably looked no worse than a slightly baggy tunic.

When a quick check of her jeans pockets failed to yield an elastic band, she took a step toward the door, resigning herself to loose, messy hair. She stopped when a glint of light from the bedside table caught her eye—the Light-Bringer's Medallion. She slipped the chain around her neck and tucked it under her borrowed sweater before exiting the room and jogging down the stairs to meet Aidan.

He was sitting on the couch in Zeke's seldom used formal living room, deep in conversation with Mo, who surged to her feet and tackled Lucky before she could make it through the doorway.

"Those were some of the longest hours of my life, girl! Not that I doubted you or anything, but if it's all the same to you, I'd really prefer never to have to go through that again." Mo released Lucky and stepped away from her, a curious reserve passing over her expression. "So, you're not just human now, right? You're, like, half-angel or something—what do you call it?"

"Naphil," Aidan answered, from his seat on the couch.

Lucky shrugged. "I guess so," she said. "I don't feel like I have any extra-special powers or anything yet, but since I don't seem to be poisoned by whatever that sword left in me anymore, something must have worked." Smiling, she added as an afterthought, "Oh, and I now have some serious tats on my back."

When Aidan lifted a quizzical eyebrow, she raised her hands in defense. "Not that I recommend going through a Making to get them. I'm just saying, from the quick glimpse I got, they look pretty cool. Are you ready to go?" Turning to Mo, she added, "Sorry to rush, but, well, …."

"I know," Mo said quietly. "Josh."

Lucky swallowed. "Yeah. We can give you a ride home, though, if you want."

"Already taken care of," Kev said, striding into the room. "I'll drop Mo off and make sure the wards on her apartment are still strong—just in case. Then I'll catch up to you at Aidan's."

Lucky gave Mo a quick squeeze. "Thank you for being here. It means a lot to me. We'll talk soon, I promise. Right now, I just need to help Josh—and then crash. I think worrying about him is all that's keeping me moving at the moment."

"I understand," Mo said, returning the hug. "Go do what you gotta do. Kev will get me home—and Dad will be there. Even asleep, he'll be more company than I've had for the last several hours." She made a face. "Sorry, I don't mean to complain. It was just hard being here alone, you know, when you were all, well, wherever you all were."

"Trust me, Mo," Aidan said. "You wouldn't have wanted to see it. I'm sort of expecting to have nightmares myself."

"Aaannnd on that cheery note," Kev interposed, saving Lucky from a response she couldn't even begin to formulate. "Mo, you got all your things? You live close enough even my Jeep should be able to get you there safely."

On her way out the door, Lucky followed Kev's lead. "Just make sure you sit in the front, Mo. The back seat has aspirations of becoming the Hotel California."

Throughout the drive to Aidan's building—even with him exceeding the speed limit whenever possible—and the tiresome follow-up activities of parking the car, waiting for the elevator, and then riding the elevator all the way up to his floor, Lucky wished they could move more quickly.

Once through the door though, she found her steps unaccountably slowing as she made her way toward the guest room where her cousin lay. She wanted to help him, but she had to admit she was feeling pretty squeamish about what she was supposed to do. Plus, she had her doubts about its efficacy. Except for her sudden healing, she didn't feel all that different. Could her blood truly now have special properties that would somehow save Josh from becoming—what had Aidan called it?—a "soul sucker"? And what if it didn't? She shuddered at the thought.

As if sensing her unease, Aidan rested a hand on her shoulder and gave it a brief squeeze. She took a deep breath and, steeling herself for what lay ahead, stepped into the guest room. Josh looked as he had before, encased in ribbons of blue-green light. The armchair in which Lucky had curled when she waited with Josh when he'd first been attacked was pulled close to the bed, and Ben was seated in it, angled toward the bed, one hand resting on the covers just outside the blue-green light rings, as close to Josh's hand as he could get. Sambethe and Zeke stood on the far side of the bed, looking down at Josh, as they exchanged whispered words. Malachi, as usual, was propped against the windowsill.

At Lucky's entrance, Sambethe looked up. "Ah, Lucky, our newly Made Naphil. How quickly you must move from one ordeal to another. Come here, please, and I will prepare you for this one."

Zeke stepped away from Sambethe to make room for Lucky beside the oracle, but he remained close.

"Push up your sleeve," directed Sambethe.

Lucky did as requested, pushing the sleeve of Aidan's over-large sweater up to her elbow, and then held her bare arm toward Sambethe. The oracle swabbed Lucky's skin, just as if she were getting blood drawn in a hospital, except that the area swabbed was around her wrist instead of her inner elbow. And it wasn't a needle Sambethe withdrew from her bag of supplies but rather a gleaming silver blade. Lucky couldn't hold back a gasp.

"The cut will be shallow," said Sambethe. "A few drops should suffice. As soon as Ezekiel releases your cousin from the stasis, I will make the cut. Are you ready?"

Lucky swallowed and nodded. "Yes."

"Good." Sambethe held Lucky's arm steady with her left hand, while she clasped the gleaming blade in her right. "Ezekiel."

Lucky didn't see what Zeke did to remove the stasis. She kept her eyes locked on Josh's face. She needed to stay focused on him, to think about not what she was doing, but why she was doing it. As the last of the blue bands faded away and Josh began to open his eyes, she felt a coolness against her inner wrist, followed by a flash of pain. Sambethe had cut her with the blade.

When Josh's eyes opened, Lucky gasped and jerked back. She couldn't help herself. They were red and feral, just as they had appeared in the dream—or vision or whatever it was—

she'd had when she was lost in the darkness. And what gazed out of them bore little resemblance to her gentle best fam.

"The process is accelerating." Zeke's voice whipped through the room with the force of a shockwave. "A few drops will not be enough."

Lucky cried out as the blade sliced her wrist again, deeper this time, and she half-fell onto the bed when Sambethe jerked her arm toward her cousin's mouth. After shifting into a more stable position, Lucky glanced at her arm and almost passed out. Blood ran from the cut in her wrist down over her hand, glazing it with red. Again she was reminded of her dream-vision. As Josh's mouth fastened on the wound, she curled her bloody hand up over his cheek and forced herself to look into those frighteningly foreign red eyes. She held her position, eyes locked on Josh's, hearing only the pounding of her own heartbeat and feeling the pulse of the blood at her wrist and the sucking pull as he drew the fluid into his mouth. She didn't move or pull away, just held still until the feral red disappeared, and the eyes she looked into were the familiar warm brown ones she'd known all her life.

It was Josh who drew back, his face filled with shock and confusion. Scrambling up to a seated position, he grabbed Lucky's bleeding arm and gasped raggedly, "God, Lucky, what have I done?"

"It's okay," she said, resting her other hand against his cheek before Sambethe pulled her away to clean and bandage her arm.

While the oracle took care of her wound, Lucky looked around the room. Ben was climbing onto the bed with Josh and pulling her cousin into his arms. Malachi was slipping out the door. Kev, who had joined them at some point, was standing behind Aidan and disengaging restraining hands from his brother's upper arms. As soon as he was free, Aidan rushed toward her. He stopped short of throwing his arms around her, but his desire to do so was obvious.

"Are you okay?" he breathed.

Unable to speak, Lucky just nodded and squeezed his fingers with her free hand.

When Sambethe finished bandaging her wrist, Lucky moved back to the bed, where Josh and Ben now sat side by side. Ben had one arm around her cousin, and his other hand was linked in one of Josh's.

"Thank you," Ben said to Lucky, then after a brief pause, "Oh, and—congratulations—on the Making."

"Which made this possible," Lucky finished. "Thanks—I guess."

Josh reached out a shaky hand and caught Lucky's bandaged arm. After studying the bandages for a moment or two in silence, he looked up at her with haunted eyes. "I'm so sorry. I didn't mean to…. You're my little cousin. I'm supposed to take care of you, not hurt you."

Lucky sat on the edge of the bed, facing toward him. "It wasn't your fault. None of it was your fault. I put you in danger in the first place. I'm the one who's sorry."

Slipping out of Ben's embrace, Josh pulled her into a tight hug. When he released her to settle back against the headboard, he once again took hold of her hand. "Ben gave me a seriously abridged version of what happened."

"Yeah," Ben inserted. "It went something like, 'You got poisoned and were going to die and turn into a soul-sucking monster, but Lucky let herself be made half-angel so she could give you her blood and heal you.'"

"Yep, that was pretty much it," Josh agreed. "Sad lack of detail. I have lots of questions for you—later. Now, well, 'thanks' somehow seems inadequate, but—thanks—for doing what you did, going through what you did, letting me…." He stopped, growing pale. "God, just the thought…. I am *so* sorry that you had to…. Anyway, *thank you.*"

"Hey," Lucky said, giving his fingers a squeeze. "What are best fams for?"

Hoping that Malachi hadn't yet left, Lucky slipped out of the overfilled guest room and hurried down the hall, her boots clicking on the marble tile. She breathed a sigh of relief when she saw the object of her thoughts silhouetted in front of the wall of windows, staring out at the city far below. Slowing her steps, she moved to join him. For several moments, they both gazed out at the city lights in silence.

"So, it worked, I guess," Lucky said, her voice subdued.

Malachi neither spoke nor moved, but Lucky did not take his non-response to mean a lack of interest or a refusal to engage. She recognized it for what it was: an opening, a kind of space into which she could speak until she found what it was she wanted to say.

"Remember, after the Striking, when I told you I felt like I'd been pulled out of my place in the world and put somewhere else? Well, I still feel like that. Only now, I feel like I've been emptied out too. It's like I not only don't know *where* I am, I don't even know *who* I am anymore. Does that make any sense?"

Malachi remained a tall, silent presence at her side.

"I don't know what to do. I mean, I knew I had to help Josh, but now that I've done that—I don't know. I'm not *me* anymore, Malachi. I don't know who *I* am. What do I do now?"

As the silence stretched, Lucky thought maybe Malachi wasn't going to talk to her after all, but he finally spoke, his deep voice as quiet as hers. "Now, you rest. You don't have to *do* anything. Tomorrow, you will do—whatever you do. Do not try to force yourself into doing or being anything in particular. Just wait and rest and let the work of the Making reveal itself as it will. Do not fear emptiness. It is the dwelling place of possibility. Nothing can be added to a vessel that is already full."

It was Lucky's turn to stare silently out the window, contemplating the city lights below and the dark depths of Lake Michigan beyond.

After a time, she sighed. "I must be getting used to your cryptic ways, because I think that might actually make sense—especially the part about resting." She stood beside Malachi for another minute or so, watching the lights of the tiny cars going up and down Lake Shore Drive, like blood flowing through the city's veins. Then, turning away from the window, she wandered over to the couch and, after pulling off her boots, curled up on one end, tucking a throw pillow under her head. She was asleep within seconds.

Ben and Josh were the last to leave. Aidan had invited them both to stay, fearing that Josh might still be feeling weak. But Josh had insisted that he wanted to go home, and Ben had been more than ready to take him. Aidan thought about carrying Lucky to the bedroom, but he didn't want to risk waking her. Instead, he just covered her with a blanket, before he too got ready for bed. The sky was still dark, but it wouldn't be long before it began to lighten. It had been a long night, and he could use some sleep himself.

Before removing his jeans, he checked his pockets, and his fingers closed around the locket Lilith had given him. He'd forgotten all about it—not that he'd had an opportunity to give it to Lucky anyway. He frowned as the chain slipped from his fingers and onto the dresser, wondering once again how the object had come into Lilith's possession.

CHAPTER 32

Lucky cried out, jolting herself awake. She pushed herself up to sitting, hoping she hadn't been loud enough to awaken Aidan. Running a shaky hand through her hair as her heartbeat slowed to normal, she recalled the dream. She had been standing on the roof of Aidan's building looking down on the moving lights that brightened the night. The wind had buffeted her the way it had that night Aidan had flown her back to Hyde Park, and she had been exhilarated by it. Giddy with the wind, with the lifeblood of the city flowing and circulating around her, and with her own newly born Naphil powers, she had leapt out into the air, spreading her wings.... But she had no wings, and she wasn't flying but falling, faster and faster, plummeting toward certain death. Her heart began to race again just remembering.

She pushed the blanket that was covering her aside, and the bandage on her wrist caught her eye. She unwound it to find that the wound made by Sambethe's silver knife was healed; her wrist bore not even the faintest of scars. Without the evidence of the blood-stained bandage, she might have believed she had never been wounded. Apparently, her new status as Naphil had given her some extra abilities after all.

She stood up and wandered into the kitchen. Making as little noise as possible, she filled the teakettle and started it heating, while she located a mug and teabags. She began to understand why Zeke was always making tea. There was something soothing about the familiar everyday motions, and the heat of the steaming mug in her hands brought her attention back to her body and out of her anxious head.

She wrapped her fingers around her mug as she padded back to the window. The day was well underway; the sun had advanced high enough in the sky that she couldn't see it through the glass. She couldn't believe she had slept through the early morning hours when the sun would have shone directly into the room.

In the light of day, the events of the night before—of the past few days—seemed unbelievable. She knew they had happened though. Her memories were too intense to be anything but real—and, besides, she was still wearing Aidan's black sweater.

"Hey." His voice, husky from sleep, intruded on her thoughts.

"Sorry if I woke you," she replied, turning toward him. No wonder she hadn't heard him approach. His feet were bare, as was his chest. He was wearing nothing but a pair of low-riding, faded blue jeans. He stretched and ran a hand through his sleep-tousled hair, and she was struck anew by his masculine beauty.

Without thinking, she reached a hand toward his chest, but then let it fall before she touched him. Since the Striking, she'd been less sure about her feelings for him—and that uncertainty had only increased since the Making. It wasn't that she was no longer attracted to him—she couldn't imagine a world in which that would even be possible. It was just that she felt so confused about everything—about herself, her world, her place in it—that his apparent certainty about their relationship, whatever it was, made her uncomfortable. Plus, if she was completely honest with herself, she had to admit that his brother had been creeping into her thoughts more and more. She had a vague sense that she had dreamed about Kev the night before as well, although the threads of the dream remained stubbornly beyond her grasp.

"It's alright," Aidan said, his lips curving into a sleepy smile as he stepped closer to her. "You can touch me. In fact, please do."

Reluctantly, Lucky gave in to the smile that tugged on her mouth. It was hard to resist the blue-eyed Naphil. When he leaned in to kiss her, she allowed her hand to slide up over his bicep and shoulder and curve around his neck. But when he tried to draw her closer, she pulled away.

He frowned at her sudden withdrawal. "Lucky?"

"I'm sorry, Aidan," she said, wrapping both hands around her mug of tea. "I just—I feel kind of confused right now. The last several days have been—well, 'intense' doesn't even begin to cover it. My whole world is different, upside down. I just need some time to think, to be alone."

"But I thought...." Aidan's voice trailed off.

He looked so hurt Lucky couldn't bear it. Resting one hand on his waist, she leaned her forehead against his sternum. His hands slid up and down over her upper arms.

"Between Lilith and the Making," she said, "I don't even know who I am anymore." She could feel the warmth of her breath as it collected in the small space between her mouth and Aidan's chest. "I need some time to figure things out."

She raised her head to look up at him. "Okay?"

Aidan sighed and nodded. "Just keep this in mind, will you?" he said, pressing a deliberate, lingering kiss on her mouth. Lucky let her lips part beneath his, allowed herself the pleasure of his touch. He'd done so much for her, and she did care about him. How could she not respond?

"That's definitely something to consider," she breathed, when he lifted his head and moved away from her.

He chuckled. Her response to his kiss had erased the wounded look from his face. "So, does that mean you want me to take you home now?"

Lucky shook her head. "I'd rather take the bus, if you don't mind."

"Alright," he sighed, "if that's what you want. But be careful, okay?"

Lucky nodded. She had taken only a few steps toward the door when she stopped. "My keys. Is my purse here? I had it that night at the bar, when Josh collapsed. I don't remember taking it to Zeke's."

"It's probably in my room. I'll check."

Aidan was back in a matter of moments, with her purse and her scarf.

After she'd thanked him and taken the items from him, he said, "I have something else for you."

"What is it?" she asked, noting his slight frown.

He held out his closed hand, and she placed her open palm beneath it.

"Where did you get this?" she gasped, when the locket on its broken chain dropped into her hand.

"Lilith gave it to me—at your Making. She told me to tell you to call for her whenever you're ready for some answers."

"Where did *she* get it?" Lucky asked, suspicion darkening her voice.

Aidan shrugged. "She left before I could find out."

Lucky opened the locket, relieved to find the picture of her mother still inside.

"Your mom?"

Lucky nodded. "Hold this," she said, snapping the locket closed and handing it back to him.

She pulled the Light-Bringer's Medallion out from under her sweater and removed the chain from around her neck. Then she slid her locket off its broken chain and dropped it onto the one on which the medallion hung. As she went to clasp it around her neck once more, she stopped and dropped her hands.

"I should give this back to you," she said.

Aidan shook his head. "No, you shouldn't."

"But you just loaned it to me."

"I know, but I don't want it back. It's more yours than mine now, somehow."

Lucky hesitated. "Are you sure?"

"Lucky, I want you to keep it."

"Thanks," she said, clasping the chain around her neck and tucking the dual pendants beneath her sweater. "I've gotten used to wearing it. Your sweater I'll give back though. I promise."

Aidan chuckled. "No worries. I have more just like it."

"Find something you like," she began.

"Buy several," he finished.

Lucky had made it to the door and turned the knob when his voice stopped her. "Is it okay if I call you?"

"As if it would make a difference if I said 'no,'" she teased.

Aidan didn't laugh; he just looked at her, his face serious and unsmiling, as he awaited her answer.

"Yes," she said softly. "You can call me." Then she stepped out into the hallway, closing the door behind her.

As she walked toward State Street where she could catch the #6 bus back to Hyde Park, Lucky did her best to let her thoughts wander as she took in the sights and sounds and smells of the city. It was one of those perfect fall days, with a few puffy, white clouds adorning the clear blue of the sky and the light soft and mellow, like nature itself was taking a break after the intensity of summer. The faint breeze blew a few strands of hair about her face, and though the air was cool, the heat of the sun collected in the dark fabric of her borrowed sweater, warming her skin. She took a deep breath and then sighed in relaxation. It was good to be outside, in real sunlight, to walk through the city and feel almost normal.

A sign for a coffee shop caught her eye, and on impulse, she popped inside. Latté and scone in hand, she returned to the sidewalk, walking slowly, alternating sips of coffee and bites of scone.

She relaxed enough to begin to play with her Sensitive powers. She had wondered if the Making would have any effect on them, make them stronger, or maybe alter them in some way. The only difference she found was that it was even easier for her to access her control room now. And she could turn her extra senses on and off in a flash. After a few moments of experimentation—during which she moved out of relaxed mode long enough to determine as best she could with her senses wide open that no danger presented itself—she turned all the extra switches off and settled into being normal, human Lucky, or at least what passed as that these days. For now, for as long as she allowed herself, she refused to worry about what had happened or what might happen. She was just a girl enjoying a coffee and pastry—and the freedom to walk through the city on her own.

By the time she'd finished her latté, Lucky had decided she didn't want to go straight back to Hyde Park after all. She wanted to see G-Ma. She knew she'd have to contact Lilith soon; she was unable to resist the lure of whatever "answers" the red-haired woman who called herself her grandmother might be able to offer. And Lucky wanted to go into that conversation with the sense of grounding that seeing her real grandmother could provide. Even if G-Ma was no longer quite the same woman as the one who had raised her, she was still enough herself to provide the sort of lodestone Lucky feared she might need. She didn't trust Lilith, but she had no doubt that the woman had strong powers of persuasion—and if she wanted something from Lucky, she'd use everything in her arsenal to get it.

As if affirming the rightness of her decision, a 151 pulled up just seconds after Lucky had reached the bus stop. She stepped on board, swiped her card, and found a seat.

G-Ma was in the activities room, participating in an exercise session that appeared to be winding down, when Lucky arrived. Lucky watched through the door as a staff member led the residents through a series of simple stretches. She was pleased to see that G-Ma not only followed the leader's instructions and was able to perform the movements, but that she also seemed to be enjoying herself. She was exchanging laughing comments with the instructor and some of the other residents.

The class ended, and the participants began to trickle out of the room. When G-Ma saw Lucky standing by the door, her face lit up with a brilliant smile, and she held her arms out to her granddaughter for a hug. Looking into her bright, alert eyes, Lucky could almost believe her grandmother didn't have Alzheimer's after all. She stepped into G-Ma's embrace, and the sense of homecoming caused her eyes to fill with tears. She held on to her grandmother as if to a lifeline.

"It's so good to see you, G-Ma," she said.

"It's always good to see you, my dear," G-Ma said, releasing her and reaching up to pat her cheek. "I didn't know you were coming to see me today."

Lucky laughed. "I didn't know I was coming to see you either until just a little while ago. I'm glad I did though. It's such a pretty day. Why don't we find you a jacket and go for a walk in the garden?"

G-Ma agreed that a walk sounded pleasant, so after retrieving a light fleece for her, they went outside into the enclosed courtyard that the facility had landscaped for the use of the residents and their visitors. They seemed to have the space to themselves. G-Ma held on to Lucky's hand as they strolled over the walking paths, noting the changing colors of the leaves and admiring the last of the summer blooms. Several times, she commented on how much she liked the large sprays of ornamental grasses that dotted the area.

When G-Ma started to tire, Lucky directed her to a secluded bench, where they could sit and rest while still enjoying the outdoors.

They had been sitting there for several moments when G-Ma placed her hand beside Lucky's. "How different they look," G-Ma said, studying their hands. "Yours is so young and pretty. Mine used to be like that, but now it's old and ugly."

Lucky took her grandmother's hand in hers, caressing the back of it with her own smooth fingers, noting the prominence of the veins beneath the thinning skin. "Just think of everything these hands have done though, G-Ma: all the people you took care of—including me—all the meals you cooked, all the paintings and pottery you made. Your hand isn't ugly; it's full of all that life."

Lucky turned to smile at her grandmother, and G-Ma's eyes locked on hers. "My life is in you now, dear," she said. Then the intensity faded from her eyes, and she glanced back down at their joined hands. "So young and pretty. Yes, mine used to look like that."

"Lucinda?"

Lucky looked up to see a young woman with straight dark blonde hair escaping from its ponytail walking toward them. She was dressed in the regulation khaki pants and maroon polo shirt that marked her as a staff member.

"Sorry to interrupt," she said as she came closer. "But it's snack time, and I wanted to see if Miss Lucinda wanted something to eat."

Turning to G-Ma, she added, "Would you like a snack, Lucinda? We have cookies or cheese crackers—and either milk or juice."

"Cookies and milk would be nice," G-Ma said.

"Alright, then. Let's go back inside, and we'll get you some," replied the young woman—Jenny, according to her name tag.

She smiled and extended her hand to G-Ma, and the older woman accepted the offered support as she rose to her feet. Then she released Jenny's hand to take Lucky's again.

As they strolled back across the garden, Jenny smiled at Lucky. "You're her granddaughter? Lucky, right?"

Lucky nodded. "That's me."

"I'm glad you came to see her. She's been so worried about you the past few days. And last night, the overnight staff said she was really agitated. I guess it was early this morning—around three or four sometime, I think—when they were finally able to get her settled enough to sleep. But when she got up—a little later than usual, no surprise—she was all smiles. When I told her she seemed bright and cheery today, she said, 'I know my Lucky is okay now.' Strange, huh? Anyway, I'm glad you came, so she can see for sure that you're okay."

Lucky said good-bye to G-Ma, so Jenny could get her settled in the lounge with the other residents who were having snacks, and after thanking Jenny for taking care of her grandmother, she made her way out of the facility, her thoughts filled with what the young woman had told her as well as the echo of G-Ma's voice saying she lived in Lucky now. The Making would have been completed between 3:00 and 4:00 AM; she would have regained consciousness somewhere in that time period. Lucky blinked to clear the sudden moisture from her eyes. Somehow, G-Ma had known. She really had been part of the Making.

It was good to be home. As Lucky ascended the stairs of the three-story walk-up, the creaks and groans of the treads welcomed her with comfortable familiarity, and when she turned her key in the lock and swung the door open, she sighed with relief.

"Hi, honeys, I'm home," she called, as Shu and Tef came running to curl around her ankles. Lucky knelt to stroke and snuggle the neglected beasts.

"You're just in time," came Josh's voice from the kitchen. "We're getting ready to order pizza. Any requests?"

"Pepperoni and mushrooms?"

"You got it!"

After giving the cats a few final pats, Lucky headed to the kitchen, pausing only long enough to toss her purse and scarf onto her bed. Shu and Tef trotted along beside her, as if afraid to let her out of their sight. "I know," she crooned to them, "I missed you too."

As she entered the kitchen, Ben turned from the open refrigerator door to hand Josh a beer. "Hey, Lucky, what's your poison?"

Both Lucky and Josh shot him a look.

"Sorry, my bad. Beverage?" he amended.

Lucky chuckled. "A Coke would be great, thanks."

"Did you just come from Aidan's?" Josh asked, as she popped the top on her soda.

Lucky shook her head. "I left his place early afternoon—not long after I woke up. Then I wandered around downtown for a while and went to see G-Ma."

"How was she?"

"Today was a good day. She was more like herself."

"Good. I need to go see her soon."

"She'd like that." Lucky paused before continuing, "And how are you?"

Josh shrugged. "Great. Never better. I feel completely back to normal—except for still being a little weirded out about the whole thing."

"Yeah, I got that too."

Josh studied her for a moment, then after taking a long drink of his beer, he asked, "So, can you maybe give me less of a Reader's Digest Condensed Version of what happened?"

"Let's move to the living room, people," Ben inserted, making shooing motions, before Lucky could reply. "We need comfy chairs for this."

While they waited for the pizza, Lucky filled in the missing details for her cousin, starting with the night at the Icarus show when she'd seen Aidan's wings. As she described her first meeting with Zeke and the subsequent revelations at and after his lecture at the OI, she looked at Ben with a frown.

Interrupting her own narrative, she asked, "You're Naphil too, right? Why haven't I ever seen your wings? Or gotten any visible hint that you're anything other than human?"

"I was wondering when you'd get around to asking about that," Ben replied, grinning like the Cheshire cat.

Lucky raised her eyebrows. "And are you going to give me an answer, now that I've *finally* figured out the question?"

Ben remained silent for a few moments, his mischievous eyes laughing into hers. Lucky kicked him. He was enjoying keeping her in suspense way too much.

"Ow!" Ben said, laughing.

"Out with it," Josh said, giving his boyfriend's clubbed hair a tug, "or I might start kicking you too."

"Alright, alright. I have the Gift of Glamour. Appropriate, right?" Here he directed a raised eyebrow at Josh, who rolled his eyes. "My ability to glamour is so strong that Sensitives, other Naphil, even full-fledged angels can't see through it. That's why Zeke chose me to keep something of an eye on Aidan when he renounced his wings. The fact that I happen to play a *fine* bass was an added bonus."

Lucky frowned. "What is this about Aidan renouncing his wings? What does that even mean? He mentioned it in passing, when those rogue Powers were after us, but then I got skewered, and given everything else, I completely forgot about it."

Ben held up his hands and shook his head. "You'll have to ask Aidan about that, sweetie. I don't think he'd appreciate my spilling that story."

"Fine," Lucky sighed. "So, can I see you without your glamour?"

"Yeah," Josh seconded. "Can we see you without your glamour? I mean, I *can* see you if you drop the glamour completely, right? Now that I know what you are?"

Ben nodded. "Yes, dear one, you'll be able to see me too. In all my glory."

Josh rolled his eyes again. "Oh, saints preserve us! Just get on with it, will you?"

Lucky and Josh both giggled as Ben stood up and struck a pose. Then Lucky's breath caught in her throat as the young man transformed into a beautiful, shining thing. He still had Ben's shape and features, but his skin glowed translucent, and great bronze-colored wings dusted with gold arched upward behind him.

"Be still, my heart," Josh muttered, as the vision before them was replaced by Ben's familiar form.

"I know, right?" Ben said. "I wasn't kidding when I said 'glory.'"

"Oh, please," Lucky said, dissolving into giggles. "Shut up, or I'll have to kick you again."

Just then, the buzzer sounded, heralding the arrival of the pizza. Lucky glanced from her cousin to Ben, neither of whom seemed to have heard the noise. "I'll get it," she said, "since you two seem to be having 'a moment.'"

"How does it feel to be part angel?" Josh asked later, after Lucky finished telling them about the Making. He'd grown pale when she had mentioned the burns from the palm sigils, so she had kept the more painful details of the experience to herself.

Lucky shrugged. "I'm not really sure. I don't have wings or a Gift yet. And since I'm apparently also part demon or something—whatever being a descendent of Lilith's makes me—I have no idea what to expect. Even Uriel seemed to find it all a mystery."

When Lucky started yawning, they said their goodnights, Josh and Ben offering to handle cleanup so she could get some rest. Lucky gratefully took them up on the offer, feeling the residual exhaustion of the last several days seep into her bones. A warm shower and an early bedtime beckoned. As she pulled Aidan's sweater over her head, she felt a momentary pang and thought about calling him. She'd do that after she showered and got in bed, she decided. But by the time she'd finished her shower and slipped under the covers, her eyelids were beginning to droop. She'd call him tomorrow—after she'd gotten some much-needed sleep.

CHAPTER 33

But she didn't call him the next day, or the next, or the next. Nor did he call her. And as the days passed, it became more and more difficult to think about calling or texting him. She began to worry that she'd irrevocably damaged whatever relationship they were beginning to have with her need for time alone. She played their last conversation over and over in her mind, and it always ended the same way: she told him he could call her. And yet he hadn't. Maybe after some time without her, he'd decided he didn't want to wait while she figured out who she was and what she wanted. And it wasn't as if she'd figured anything out, after all. She just missed him.

And she was tired, so tired. The bone-deep exhaustion that had sent her to bed early on her first night back in her own apartment stayed with her for several days, leaving her with little energy for anything besides sleeping and brooding. When she wasn't brooding about Aidan, she brooded about Lilith and when she might feel ready to contact her. When she wasn't brooding about Lilith, she brooded about the changes in herself. She kept staring into mirrors, searching her face for the girl she had been and puzzling over the marks on her back for some clue about who she was now. She knew she could never go back: since she had undergone the

Making, the past was a locked door—or a brick wall. And the future? Well, that was a gigantic neon question mark, flashing on and off: *What do you do now, Lucky? Who are you now?* What *are you now?*

When she finally did pick up her phone, it was Mo she called. She had promised to catch her friend up when she had a chance, and after days spent thinking thoughts that chased their own tails, she was in need of some of Mo's contagious effervescence. And besides, Mo was the one person other than Josh who could maybe help her stay connected to the Lucky she had been as she moved into the black maw of uncertainty before her.

Mo only razzed her a little about how long it had taken her to call. And before they hung up, she had invited Lucky over for French Toast à la Mo on Saturday—which, Lucky was surprised to learn, was the following day. She couldn't believe she'd spent an entire week doing little more than sleeping and worrying.

She awoke the next morning with a feeling of anticipation. And she looked over her shoulder into the bathroom mirror for just a minute or two before she climbed into the shower. Naphil or demon or whatever she was, she had brunch plans.

It was almost two o'clock before Lucky left her friend's apartment. Mo's special French toast was fabulous, as usual, and the two lingered over brunch, laughing and catching up.

Mo told Lucky about her first week of college classes. She told her how much she liked Eric, and how surprised and pleased she was that her dad liked him too. And she told her how scared she had been waiting at Zeke's house while Lucky hovered between life and death.

Lucky told Mo about the strange dream-state in which she'd lingered after the Power had stabbed her, and how Malachi had come to her rescue in a vision of crows. She told her about how Aidan had taken care of her and held her while she slept. She told her how much the Making had hurt, and how afraid she'd been that she wouldn't be able to survive the pain. She did not tell her how Kev had rested his hand on her back for the briefest of moments before he activated the sigil that burned his Mark into her skin, or how he had touched her hair after. Those memories were hers to keep and ponder in secret.

Once the meal was finished, they made quick work of cleanup, laughing and joking so much that by the time Lucky was ready to leave, she felt almost normal. Even as she acknowledged the undoubtedly fleeting nature of *that* feeling, she took comfort in knowing that no matter how much her life had changed, she still had her best friend.

She was on her way out the door when Mo stopped her. "Oh, I almost forgot. Are you going to the show at I-House tonight?"

"What show?"

Mo looked at her in surprise. "Icarus is playing. You didn't know? Aidan didn't tell you?"

Lucky shook her head. "He probably forgot. I'm sure I'll hear from him soon."

"Well, the music starts at 9:00. See you there?"

Lucky murmured something noncommittal. She didn't want to tell Mo about her last conversation with Aidan—about how hurt he'd seemed. And since he hadn't called—after she'd *told* him he could—she wasn't sure if she should go to the show or not. Maybe he didn't want her there. She told herself she had no right to feel hurt, when she was the one who had said she needed time—and, whispered her conscience, when she was the one who kept thinking about Kev—but the sense of loss pierced her heart. She'd said he could call her. Why hadn't he called?

Thinking and worrying, Lucky drifted south, toward the University of Chicago campus. She wandered past the main quad and down to the Midway, where she turned west. She hadn't been conscious of having a particular destination in mind, but when she reached the Midway's end and looked up, her lips twisted into an ironic smile. Rising before her was the Fountain of Time.

She'd always found the Lorado Taft sculpture haunting, with its mass of people swept inexorably along in its sandy waves, that lone, imposing figure watching over them. She had never been able to decide if this mysterious being controlled the tide that swept the others forward, or if he just watched. Was he unable to intervene—or unwilling to do so? Now, she wondered if maybe he wasn't biding his time, waiting for the right moment. She could imagine him thrusting out the staff he held, halting the forward motion, while he made some adjustments, moved this one here, that one there, until, satisfied, he again planted the staff beside him, and the waves rolled forward once more.

Crossing the street, she moved to one end of the reflecting pool and perched on its lip, positioned so she could see both the lone figure and the roiling masses. She studied them in silence for a long time. Then, feeling as if she too were being swept forward by that relentless wave, she tugged the chain with its dual pendants out from under her shirt. Slipping the chain from around her neck, she studied the medallion and the locket with the same intensity that she had directed toward the sculpture. Locket and medallion. Past and future. G-Ma and Lilith. Aidan and Kev. Her thoughts were waves, crashing and receding, only to rush forward once again.

After a while, she wrapped the chain around her left hand, and clasping the locket in her right, she called to mind the image of the flame-haired woman who said she was her grandmother. She imagined Lilith in as much detail as she could remember—scarlet hair, emerald eyes, pale skin, dark cloak, voice bright and mocking, laugh tinkling and airy. When the image was as sharp as she could make it, she squeezed her hand around the locket, closed her eyes, and concentrated, calling to the one the image represented.

"I'm not sure whether to be surprised that you called me this soon or to ask what took you so long."

Lucky turned her head toward the source of the light, teasing voice to see Lilith strolling around the corner of the sculpture. She had exchanged her dark robes for an equally dark tailored pantsuit that, coupled with her sleekly styled red hair, made her look like a successful and somewhat glamorous business woman.

Lucky made no reply as Lilith came closer, graceful in her high-heeled pumps, and took a seat beside her, crossing one elegant leg over the other and clasping her hands around her knee.

"Just look at you. My, what big eyes you have, grand-daughter! And so beautiful too—they're quite an unusual shade of green, aren't they?—but so filled with suspicion. I suppose it's too much to ask that you might trust your grandmother just a little?"

Lucky's gaze did not waver. "I don't know you. I have no reason to trust you."

"I suppose not," Lilith sighed. "If it's any consolation, I only recently learned of your existence. Not that my knowing about you sooner would have made much difference. It's not as if I could have shown up on your doorstep and introduced myself. Before you came into your powers, you would never have believed me—or even believed *in* me for that matter."

Lilith looked at Lucky as if she expected an answer, even though she hadn't asked a question. Lucky responded with a question of her own. "And how did you find out about me?"

"My son—your father—told me of you. He said he'd unexpectedly encountered a girl who could almost penetrate his glamour, despite his ability to scramble Sensitive powers. At first, he was just shocked and angered by your talent. Then he realized you reminded him of a woman he'd once known—almost even loved—and he started to wonder. So, he sought you out—and found you had already been drawn into Ezekiel's little circle. Being, shall we say, somewhat reluctant to show his hand to them, he availed himself of the opportunity to take a personal item of yours."

Lilith tapped the locket in Lucky's hand with one manicured fingertip. Lucky resisted the urge to snatch the pendant out of the woman's reach. "Finding this locket in your backpack was an extraordinary piece of luck. Not only was it so personal that it could be used to track you, which was all Luil had originally been hoping for, but it also held the answer to his question. He recognized the woman in the picture, and he became convinced that she had borne him a daughter."

"And in an effort to show his love for his long-lost child, he tried to kidnap me?" Lucky's question was equal parts angry and incredulous.

"I'm not saying I condone his methods. I had no part in that. He'd told me none of this yet. If he'd asked, trust me, I would have assured him that abduction was not the appropriate course of action. But he believed he had to get you away from Ezekiel and his Fallen by any means necessary. As a consequence, he acted somewhat rashly—Luil has never been very good at impulse control—and succeeded only in taking a bit of a beating and terrifying you. It was after that little fiasco that he came to me."

"And you showed up at Wild Hare." Lucky's suspicion hadn't abated in the slightest.

Lilith's lips, tinted a deeper scarlet than her hair, curved in a smile. "Yes, I wanted to see you for myself. I hadn't been aware of how easily you would penetrate our cloaking glamour. As soon as I looked in your eyes, I knew my son was correct. I could feel the pull of my blood in you. Curiosity satisfied, I departed, but before I could determine how best to approach you, I learned that a Striking had been called. The rest you know."

When she finished speaking, Lilith sat back and looked at Lucky expectantly.

"Oh, there's still a lot I don't know," Lucky said, studying the flame-haired woman with narrowed eyes. "For one thing, why did you attack Josh? What could you possibly gain by hurting someone I love?"

Lilith's eyes widened. "My dear, I didn't attack anyone; nor did my son, outside of his misguided attempt to abduct you. I assume Josh is the person—your cousin, was it?—for whom you underwent the Making?"

Lucky nodded as a frown settled between her brows. "If you didn't attack him, who did? And why?"

"I'm afraid I don't know the answer to that," Lilith replied. "But if you like, I can make some inquiries. I'm quite good at finding out secrets."

Although she still didn't trust Lilith, Lucky was tempted by the offer. The woman had seemed surprised when Lucky had accused her of attacking Josh. And while Lucky did not doubt Lilith's acting abilities, something told her that the emotion was genuine. If Lilith was willing to help her figure out who had targeted her cousin, she was willing to accept—provided the price wasn't too high. "And what would I have to do for you in return?" she asked.

Again, Lilith looked surprised, although this time her expression struck Lucky as somewhat disingenuous. "Why, nothing, of course. My son did you more than one disservice. Putting a few feelers out for information is the least I can do for you. Shall I then?"

Lucky hesitated before nodding. "Please."

"Very well, then," Lilith said, rising to her feet. "I shall see what I can find out. Now, I must be going." She glanced down at the slim, expensive-looking watch that circled her left wrist. "I have an appointment."

"Wait," Lucky said. "I wanted to ask you—"

"Your questions will have to wait for another time, I'm afraid," Lilith interrupted. "But I'll be in touch to let you know what I discover. We'll have a nice, long chat then. I promise."

Lilith's form was already fading away as the last words left her lips. Lucky sighed. She had no idea what Lilith's promise was worth, but it looked like she'd have to accept it at face value for now.

She wondered once again who had attacked Josh. Once she had discovered that Lilith or her son—Lucky couldn't bring herself to think of him as *her* father—had taken her locket, she had assumed that one or both of them had perpetrated, or at least orchestrated, the attack. Of course, Lilith had just denied performing the act. Could she or Luil have hired someone to attack Josh? Lucky was certain Lilith would be capable of the hair-splitting logic that would make her denial truthful even if she had. But the question of what she—or they—could have hoped to gain remained unanswered. Unless, for some reason, they wanted to force Lucky to go through the Making in order to save her cousin. If so, then they would want something from her at some point. Maybe Lilith was just waiting until Lucky's wings and Gift revealed themselves. Still, while all that was possible, Lucky was somehow inclined to believe Lilith—which left the identity of Josh's attacker undetermined.

Sighing once more, Lucky unwrapped the chain from her left hand and slipped it over her head, hiding the medallion and locket beneath her shirt. And, though the unanswered questions continued to beat against her thoughts like the wings of birds against the bars of a cage, she felt a subtle settling as the pendants nestled against her skin.

She had taken only a few steps back toward the Midway when she felt something else, a not-so-subtle need to stop by the OI and visit her old friend the *lamassu.* Before she could formulate a question regarding the source of the sudden compulsion, her lips twisted into a wry smile. Zeke. Of course. She stepped up her pace even as she wondered why he wanted to see her so urgently. At least that question was one for which she'd soon have an answer.

Lucky entered the OI with cheeks flushed from her brisk walk in the fall air. Slipping through the glass door into the museum area, she slowed her steps as she walked straight through the gallery toward its presiding spirit. As usual, she was both awed and comforted by the great beast. It might have been minutes, but it seemed like only seconds had passed before she heard a familiar resonating voice.

"Your quick response is commendable."

She turned toward the sound, her smile softening her words. "You have heard of cell phones, haven't you?"

Zeke chuckled. "Ah, but my way is much more interesting, don't you think? Besides, unlike a call or a text, my messages cannot be ignored."

"As if I would have ignored you," Lucky responded.

Zeke shrugged, a mischievous glint in his gray eyes. "Old habits."

Lucky studied her mentor for a moment, noticing the faint shadows of multiple blue wings behind him. "Just how old are you anyway?" she asked.

Zeke sighed. "Let's just say 'ancient' and leave it at that. Now, come up to my office where we can talk freely."

With that, he ushered her out of the museum and up the stairs. As she entered the cluttered room with its piles of books and papers, Lucky's thoughts turned to the last time she'd been here. And when Zeke pushed aside some papers to clear a space for her on the leather couch, she remembered awakening to find herself lying there with Aidan's jacket draped over her and Aidan himself sitting nearby. Why hadn't he called? Should she call him? It was the sound of his name that drew her attention back to Zeke.

"Aidan tells me Lilith wants you to contact her."

Lucky nodded. "I already did. I just saw her."

"I figured as much. I did not think you would waste too much time before getting in touch with her." Zeke studied her for a moment or two in silence. "And was your meeting—satisfactory?"

"In some ways, I guess. In others, not so much."

Zeke's only reply was a lift of the eyebrows that encouraged her to continue.

"Well, she explained that it was her son—my…," Lucky's voice trailed off as she shook her head. "It was Luil who stole my locket from my backpack in the auditorium"—she gestured in the general direction of the room—"and who tried to kidnap me at the country club. She said he didn't want to hurt me; he just thought he needed to get me away from you and the Fallen."

"Lilith and her sons have never had the highest opinion of the Fallen," Zeke said, answering her unasked question. "I am in part to blame—ancient history between Lilith and me. Aside from that, they think we are too loyal to the Light."

Although Lucky wanted to know what had happened between Zeke and Lilith, she could tell he had no intention of elaborating. Stifling her curiosity, she continued with her story. "She said that neither she nor Luil attacked Josh, though. And she offered to see if she could find out who did."

"Did she?" Zeke asked. "And did you accept her offer?"

"Yes, but not until I'd asked what she wanted from me in exchange."

Zeke's surprised laughter kept Lucky from continuing. "Smart girl. How did Lilith respond to that?"

"She acted shocked and said she didn't want anything, that she felt like she owed me because of what Luil had done. And then she left. She said she had an appointment."

The hint of bitterness that flavored her last statement took Lucky by surprise. She had meant to speak objectively, just stating the fact, but the disappointment she had felt at

Lilith's hasty departure—and which had been unacknowledged until now—refused to remain hidden.

"Lilith may be your grandmother, Lucky, but do not make the mistake of expecting her to act like one. Like me, she is ancient. And her powers are elemental. Her thoughts, values, and emotions are not human."

"Neither are yours." Lucky again surprised herself. Why did she feel a need to defend the red-haired woman?

"No," Zeke acknowledged, "I am not human. But I have spent much of my extremely long life living among them and protecting them. I have not been unchanged by that contact. Lilith has not—lived the same sort of life. Human well-being has never been her prime motivator. I believe she is genuinely intrigued at the thought of having a part-human granddaughter, but the fact is unlikely to change who she is."

Lucky winced when Zeke called her "part-human," but she knew the description was accurate, maybe even as accurate as it was possible to get. What was she anyway? Part human and part angel since the Making, which made her Naphil. But never really human, which made her—what? She made no attempt to disguise the uncertainty in her reply. "It's not as if I'm very human myself."

"You were fully human, Lucky, before the Making, just with a little something more is all," Zeke said. "Your father is a Shedim demon. His true state is less physical than, well, elemental, like the wind. He can take on almost any form, and when he does so, he completely becomes that form, simply adding himself to the mix like extra pieces of genetic code. He fathered you in human form, so your genetic makeup is—

or was—human, except that you have some of those extra bits as well."

"And the Making? Did that give me additional 'extras'?"

"Yes and no. Some extra genetic coding is added during the Making, but the existing DNA is also rewritten." Zeke paused before continuing, "You were human, but you are not any longer. Now you are Naphil."

"With some mysterious little extras," Lucky added.

"Yes."

Lucky sighed. "This isn't what I thought it would be like—being part angel," she confessed. "I don't know exactly what I thought it would be, but not this. I thought I'd feel—confident, maybe even powerful, that all of this would make sense—once I was on the other side of the Making. But I just feel—kind of lost, like I don't know who I am or what I want."

"You know something of who you are. For example, you still love your grandmother and your cousin, do you not?"

"G-Ma? And Josh? Of course, I love them. But they're not—we're not—*I'm* not the same anymore."

"Do you think anyone ever is?" said Zeke. "We all change, and we all feel rudderless at times. There is nothing wrong in allowing yourself to drift. Perhaps you could try letting yourself be whoever or whatever you turn out to be in any given moment. In that way, maybe you will learn what you want."

Lucky looked at him through narrowed eyes. "You and Malachi, you're like Yoda and Obi-Wan. Do you two decide ahead of time just which bits of cryptic wisdom each of you is going to spring on me?"

Zeke chuckled. "Drift you will, and strong in the ways of the Force you will become," he said, his voice a match for that of the small, green Jedi master.

Lucky burst out laughing. She wasn't sure what surprised her most: Zeke's pitch-perfect impersonation, his ready grasp of the pop-culture reference, or the blatant display of humor.

"See," Zeke said with a grin, "you are not so lost."

Lucky smiled back at him. "Not hopelessly, I guess. Just rudderless and adrift."

"Would you feel less rudderless, do you think, if you had a job?" Zeke asked, leaning back in his chair and steepling his fingers.

"A job?" Lucky asked. "Are you offering me one?"

"Would you be interested in being my assistant?" He waved his hand around the room. "Obviously, I could use some organizational help. And, as you learn, you could maybe assist with research."

"I can't believe *you* would need a research assistant," Lucky scoffed. "Besides, I'm not even in college."

"If nothing else, you can cart books back and forth from the library for me." Zeke leaned further back in his chair, crossing his arms over his chest. "And, enrolled in a program or not, you will be my student."

Lucky's mouth twisted. "Yeah, I'm majoring in Fallen Studies, with an emphasis on Survival. Not exactly your standard college curriculum, is it?"

"No," Zeke agreed. "So, what do you say? Interested? I would pay you, of course." He named what sounded to Lucky like a fair wage, perhaps more generous than she would have expected for such work.

"Sure, I'm interested," she said. Then, frowning, she added, "You're not just doing this because you feel sorry for me or anything, are you? I mean, did Aidan or Kev do assistant duty?"

"They did not; their circumstances were somewhat different from yours," Zeke admitted. "But I am not doing this because I feel sorry for you. I am offering you the job because I could use the help. I remembered you saying you were interested in ancient religions and archeology, so it seemed a good fit. You might pick up a few things by osmosis."

"Okay, thanks," Lucky said, satisfied with his answer. "Then I'd like to be your assistant."

"Excellent. Can you start on Monday?" Zeke asked, rising to his not inconsiderable height.

Lucky stood up as well. "Absolutely. Was that everything you wanted to see me about?"

"Yes, you are free to go. Perhaps I shall see you later tonight?"

"Tonight?"

"At I-House," he clarified. "I've never heard Aidan's band play, so I thought I might go tonight."

Lucky tried to ignore the ache that had started in her chest. Apparently, Aidan had invited everyone but her.

"Yeah, maybe I'll see you there," she said, and hurried down the hall, away from the Cherub's perceptive gaze.

Once she was outside the OI, Lucky took her cell phone out of her pocket and double-checked to see if Aidan had tried to call or text, and she had somehow missed it. Nothing. She hesitated for a moment, her fingers hovering over the keypad. Then, with a sigh, she tucked the phone back in her pocket and headed toward home. Although she tried to think of other things—like the fact that she now had an actual paying job—she spent most of the walk worrying and wondering if she should go to see Icarus at I-House or not. She had come to no solid decision by the time she made it home.

Only the cats responded to her greeting when she entered the apartment, leaving Lucky with mixed feelings. She didn't really want to talk to anyone—except maybe Aidan, she admitted, giving herself a mental dope slap—but she didn't like the thought of her own company at the moment either. Tossing her jacket over the back of her chair, she flung herself onto her bed and wrapped her arms around a pillow. She wanted to cry. And she had no one to blame but herself.

When Shu jumped up on the bed and head-butted her, she supplied the requested petting and snuggling, grateful for the comfort of his soft fur against her hands. After several minutes, he wound himself into a purring ball and settled against her. She curled her body around the cat's warmth and closed her eyes, allowing the tears that had filled them to slide down her cheek to her pillow.

CHAPTER 34

"Wake up, sleepyhead." Josh's voice penetrated her sleep-fogged brain. "Get a move on, or we're going to be late."

"Mmmm?" Lucky mumbled. Then she came fully awake as her cousin poked her in the ribs. "Good grief, Josh, what are you, six? What are we going to be late for?"

"Icarus. At I-House. If you don't get up soon, you won't have enough time to make yourself presentable."

"Oh, right. I don't know if I'm going," she said, her voice subdued.

"Why wouldn't you go? Everyone's going to be there. C'mon, get dressed. You know you'll regret it if you don't."

"Alright, fine," she muttered, sitting up and swinging her legs over the side of the bed. "What time is it anyway?"

"We need to leave in half an hour."

In the bathroom, Lucky splashed water on her face in an effort to wash away the dregs of grogginess her extended nap had left behind. She was glad Josh had forced her hand; she really did want to go. But now she had to decide what she was going to wear.

Back in her room, she searched through her closet for something appropriate and responded to Josh's fourth reminder to hurry by yelling "You're not helping!"

Finally, she settled on a short gray-green slip dress, topped with a little black bead-embellished cardigan she and Mo had found at a vintage resale shop. Black flats completed the outfit. With some minimal make-up and a pair of sparkly earrings, she was ready to go. She slipped the strap of her small purse over her shoulder and, grabbing her jacket from the chair she'd flung it on earlier, headed down the hall to the living room.

"Five minutes to spare," she said.

"And me without a single gold star," Josh responded, checking his watch. When he looked back up, his eyes settled on her necklace. "Is that your locket? You got it back?"

Lucky glanced down at the pendants. She had told Josh and Ben about the theft of the locket, but she hadn't mentioned its return. She hadn't been ready to do so until she had talked to Lilith. "Yeah. I'll tell you about it on the way," she said.

"You up for walking?"

She nodded, shrugging into her jacket as she followed Josh out the door and down the stairs.

The temperature had dropped a few degrees since she was last out, but the chill in the air was exhilarating rather than unpleasant. As they made their way south toward campus, Lucky filled Josh in on Lilith's return of the locket and her subsequent conversation with the red-haired woman. Recounting Lilith's denial of playing any part in the attack on him made Lucky realize just how much she had feared that her newfound grandmother had been responsible for hurting one of the people she loved most in the world. Even though she didn't fully trust the scarlet-haired woman, she wanted to get to know her, to spend more time with her. Lilith was her grandmother after all; she would be able to help Lucky solve the mystery of her new self. But if Lilith had been involved in Josh's attack, accepting any kind of advice or help from her would have been out of the question; Lucky would never have been able to forgive her.

Lucky shivered as she remembered her fear for her cousin. "I'm so glad you're okay," she said, sliding her arm around his waist.

He put his arm around her shoulders and drew her to his side in a quick hug. "Me too. And I have you to thank for it. I know you blame yourself," he added when she would have protested, "but what you went through…. I'm glad you're okay too."

They joined the crowd streaming into I-House and made their way to the ballroom where the band was playing. Lucky saw Aidan as soon as they walked into the room. He was impossible to miss, with his golden blond hair glinting in the light where he stood adjusting a microphone. As if aware of her regard, he looked up and stilled, his eyes locking on hers. For several seconds, Lucky was conscious of nothing but the intense blue of his eyes. Then another band member called for his assistance, and he looked away. At the same time, Josh tugged on her arm, urging her toward the raised platform that served as a stage.

Tables were arranged on each side of the front of the room with the rest of the room left open to serve as a dance floor. As they neared the stage, Lucky recognized Mo's messy blonde waves at a table nearby. She was standing, her back to Lucky, talking to someone seated next to her. Mo turned as Lucky and Josh approached, and Lucky smiled at both Mo and her companion, a tall, wheat-haired Cherub, who looked a little out of his element.

"Oh, good, you're here!" Mo said, giving Lucky and Josh quick hugs. She looked radiant in a slim-fitting fuchsia pink dress and black boots, a skinny silver scarf serving as necklace.

Zeke was wearing his usual khakis, but he had exchanged the button-down shirt and corduroy jacket he'd had on earlier for a heather gray sweater. It fit more snugly than anything Lucky had ever seen him wear before, and she was somewhat surprised at how muscular he seemed. She supposed she shouldn't be. The fact that he was a teacher did not discount his status as one of the Fallen. As such, and a Protector at that, he'd have to be ready and able to fight if necessary. It was just that she thought of him as a scholar and a caretaker.

When the shadows of his blue wings crossed her vision, she silently laughed at herself. As if she knew everything there was to know about him. He was an ancient angel, had once been viewed as a kind of deity; he had lived through more than she could even begin to imagine. She would probably always be surprised by him. With that thought came a rush of anticipation. How amazing was it that she would be working and studying with him? There must be no end to the things she could learn.

"I'm glad you came," he said, interrupting her thoughts. "I got the impression earlier that you might not. Is something amiss between you and Aidan?"

Lucky shrugged. Before she could formulate an answer, Mo had grabbed her arm. "Come and help me get some drinks."

Lucky cast an apologetic smile at Zeke and let her best friend drag her away.

She and Mo separated to work their way through the crowd gathered around the refreshments. Lucky had picked up four cans of soda and was heading back to their table, when a hand settled on her arm.

"Here's someone I recognize."

She turned toward the deep voice and looked up into Kev's smiling face. A thrill shot through her—accompanied by a pang of guilt.

"Kev! Hi," she said, hoping she wasn't blushing. "I didn't know you were coming."

"I think everyone's coming—even Malachi, though he's not usually into this sort of thing. We—Zeke and Malachi and I—have never seen the band perform. Aidan started Icarus after he renounced his wings, and things weren't exactly—comfortable—between us."

Something in Lucky's expression must have given her away, because his voice trailed off as his dark green eyes scanned her face. "He hasn't told you about that, has he?"

She shook her head, noting the tiny bits of gold that flecked his irises.

"Well, you should hear about it from him. Let's just say I'm glad to have my brother back and happy to be able to come to a live performance." Kev scanned her face again. "I'm also glad to see you looking none the worse for wear after the ordeal of the Making."

His gaze dropped lower, and he touched the dragon medallion with his forefinger. "I recognize that. Aidan gave it to you?"

Lucky just nodded, remembering how the dragon had come to her in her vision of her Makers, how it had disappeared into her medallion, and how the dragon had turned out to be Kev.

"That's how you called me," he said.

"Did you—did you have the vision too?"

"Probably not the same as yours." Kev's voice was quiet, as if conveying a secret meant for her alone. "I dreamed of the medallion and a girl I knew with jade green eyes, and when I woke up Uriel's voice was like a brand in my brain. I've never been a Maker before. Did you know that?"

Lucky shook her head. She was powerless to speak, mesmerized by his gold-flecked eyes and the voice that touched her like a caress.

"I didn't want to hurt you. I'm sorry about that."

"What you did, it meant a lot to me," Lucky whispered. "When you touched me… with just your hand…." She couldn't say anything more. The sense of intimacy was almost more than she could bear.

Fortunately, Malachi chose that moment to make his appearance. "I am not late, am I?" he said, coming to stand beside them.

Kev blinked and shook his head. "I—don't think so," he said.

"We should get to our seats though," Lucky added, dragging herself free from the waking dream. "I think they're almost ready to start. Zeke and Mo snagged us a table near the stage."

The first chords were beginning to fill the room by the time they reached the table. As they settled into the three remaining chairs, Lucky found herself sitting between Mo and Kev. She tried to focus all her attention on the stage, but she was uncomfortably aware of Kev's big body beside her, the chairs so close that his denim-clad knee brushed hers every time he moved. She did her best to ignore the shiver that passed through her at the contact.

She was relieved when Aidan stepped up to the microphone and began to sing. Listening to his beautiful voice, she opened her senses the tiniest bit, just enough to allow his husky baritone to wrap itself around her mind, eclipsing her awareness of his brother's closeness.

After the number had ended and the applause had died down, Aidan introduced the band and promised that the remainder of the set had been chosen with dancing in mind. When the music started, Mo jumped to her feet, grabbed Lucky with one hand and Kev with the other, and pulled them toward the dance floor.

"Come on, you guys," she called to the remainder of the group. "You heard the man. Let's dance."

Josh readily complied, but Lucky was not surprised when Malachi and Zeke just shook their heads and remained seated. She was surprised that Kev had offered no resistance, but maybe, like her, he realized that Mo wouldn't take no for an answer. Before the night was over, Lucky was sure, her ebullient friend would get even Zeke and Malachi to dance.

The four danced together as a group, moving to the beat of the music as they saw fit, mingling standard dance moves with whatever happened to catch their fancy. Lucky had been to many dances with Josh and Mo, and she knew they were comfortable with this light-hearted, impromptu style. She didn't know Kev well enough to guess how he would feel about it.

She hardly had time to wonder, let alone worry. He joined in easily, following another's lead or making up moves of his own, and laughing along with the rest of them. He was a good dancer, and he didn't take himself too seriously. He also seemed to be enjoying himself. She wondered how often he got a chance to just have fun. She guessed the opportunities were probably few and far between, which made her doubly glad he could do so tonight.

By the time the first set ended, Lucky was laughing and breathless and hot and thirsty. After a stop at the refreshment table for a glass of punch, she headed out the front door for some fresh air. Once outside, she stopped for a couple deep breaths before descending the stairs to the sidewalk. The cool night air felt good against her heated skin.

She had just stepped onto the sidewalk and was contemplating crossing the street to stroll along the Midway, when she heard footsteps coming down the stairs behind her.

"Mind if I join you?" Aidan asked.

"Not at all," she said.

He fell into step beside her as she started across the street. Neither of them spoke until they reached the grass of the Midway, and then Aidan broke the silence.

"I wanted to apologize for the other day," he said, shoving his hands in his pockets and looking down toward the toes of his boots. "I pressured you, and I shouldn't have. You've been through so much lately. It's all been pretty intense and sudden. I can see why you'd want to have some time, to get used to—everything. I couldn't see it then, but I can now. So, anyway, I'm sorry."

"Thanks," Lucky said. Then, before she could stop herself, she added, "I missed you. I kept hoping you'd call."

Aidan looked up, his blue eyes shining in the glow of the street lights. "Really? I wanted to, but I didn't want you to feel like I hadn't heard you. I'd pressured you enough." One corner of his mouth turned up in a smile. "You could have called me, you know."

"I know. I just felt like I didn't have a right to, when I was the one who asked for time. Besides, I told you you could call. Do you know how upset I was when I heard about tonight from everyone but you?"

"I didn't even think about that. I just knew you'd find out from Mo or Josh or someone and was hoping you'd show up."

Lucky chuckled. "I guess we've both been kind of stupid, huh?"

"I guess we have." Aidan held out his hand. "Walk?" he asked.

"Sure," Lucky whispered, taking his hand. He threaded his fingers through hers as they began to stroll down the Midway.

"I've been wondering about something you mentioned the night the Powers attacked us," Lucky said, after they'd taken several steps in silence. "You said something about renouncing your wings…?"

Aidan didn't speak or look at her, but she felt his fingers tighten around hers.

"It had to do with your mother, didn't it?" she asked.

He drew them to a halt, and then waited so long to speak that Lucky began to wonder if he was going to answer her question.

"Yes," he finally said, releasing her hand. "You know she was human, right?"

Lucky nodded. "You said she was a concert pianist."

"Yeah," Aidan sighed. "You also know my world—our world—is dangerous for humans. Well, that danger is compounded when you are intimately involved with someone like Lucifer. My father tried to keep my mother safe by keeping his relationship with her—and with me—a secret. Only a chosen few—Zeke among them—knew Lucifer was my father—even after I'd completed enough of my training to join the Forces."

He paused, and Lucky could see from his tightened lips and distant eyes that he was reliving something that was almost unbearable to him.

"It was my fault the secret got out. Not that I *told* anyone. I just.... Everyone acted like I was the Fallen's Golden Child. I was great in battle. And there was my Gift." His voice trailed off, and he paused another moment before continuing, "The Gift of Song carries with it some of the power of Creation. I haven't tried to use it much, but I can create things, fix things, heal things, with my voice."

Lucky didn't speak into the silence that stretched between them. She waited for Aidan to face his memories and continue his story.

"You've heard Sambethe's prophecy about you. Well, there was one about me too. I was supposed to be the one to lead the Forces of the Fallen and bridge the gap between Light and Dark." He turned to look at her, one side of his mouth lifted in an ironic twist. "I didn't exactly greet the news with the calm maturity you've shown."

Lucky raised her eyebrows. "I was too shocked and scared to do anything else."

His eyes were still haunted, but Aidan's features relaxed into a warm smile, and he reached out to brush her cheek with his fingers before letting his hand fall back to his side. When he resumed his tale, he had turned away from her again to look down the Midway.

"It was all such a rush, and I encouraged it. I drew too much attention. Somebody put two and two together and figured out who my father was. Then some rogue angels of

Light kidnapped my mother. They threatened to kill her unless my father ceded control of the Dark to the Metatron."

A small sound of sympathy escaped Lucky before she could stop it, but Aidan continued as if he hadn't heard.

"Kev was the newly minted Captain of the Forces of the Fallen then, and he and Zeke and my father were still plotting strategy, when I decided to take matters into my own hands. I should have known better, but I was cocky, arrogant. I convinced a few of my closest friends in the Forces to join me in an unauthorized rescue mission. We discovered that they were holding my mother in an abandoned warehouse. When we got there, there were no guards outside. It all seemed so easy. I should have realized something was up, but I didn't stop to think. The ambush took us by surprise.

"We fought hard. And I was actually thinking we might make it out alive, when Zeke got into my head, compelling me to return to the training center. He didn't know we were already in the thick of it; he just wanted to protect us. But with him in my head, it was almost impossible to concentrate on fighting. It was worse for the others. By the time Kev and a band of the Forces had arrived, along with Zeke and Lucifer, I was the only one still standing—well, I was on my knees by then, but I was still fighting.

"Once Zeke realized I was fighting him as well as the kidnappers, he got out of my head, and together we were able to defeat the rogues. But it was too late for my mother."

Aidan paused, and Lucky laid a hand on his arm.

"No," he said, stepping away from her, refusing the offered comfort.

He took a deep breath and let it out before speaking again. "They had strung her up with cords, had her hanging from the ceiling. She was beaten and cut and bloody. The others cut the cords and lowered her to the floor, and I ran to her. She was still alive, but just barely, and I knew she wouldn't last long. Sambethe had been training me, and I thought I could heal her, save her. But I ended up… killing her. It looked like she was healing, like her flesh was reknitting itself, but then it kept growing and growing, like cancer…."

Aidan's voice broke, and he took a few shuddering breaths. Lucky could see his hands clenching and unclenching at his sides.

"After that, I didn't want to be part of the world of the Fallen anymore, didn't think I had a right to be. I certainly didn't want to be responsible for doing to anyone else what I'd done to my friends—or my mother. So I renounced my wings—formally stated my intention in front of the necessary witnesses. Zeke wouldn't accept total Renunciation; he argued that my wings should be returned to me after a time. I know now that he just wanted to give me the opportunity to reconsider, but at the time his interference pissed me off."

He paused again, his lips curving in an ironic smile as the haunted look left his eyes. "Anyway, my wings were returned to me about the time we met. I've gotta say, it freaked me out more than a little when you saw them that night."

"No more than it did me," Lucky said. She wanted to comfort him, to ease his sense of loss, but she knew his feelings were still too raw. "How long were you without your wings?"

"Two years. You dragged me back into this, you know. After I met you, realized what you were, I had to tell Zeke about you."

"Are you sorry?" Lucky asked.

Aidan shook his head. "I convinced myself that I wanted to live a normal, human life, but I was just punishing myself. I'm not normal and human. I'm Naphil, one of the Fallen. Even though I ran away from the life, I missed it. So, no, I'm not sorry. I—"

Lucky cried out as her back suddenly began to burn. Doubled over in pain, she sank to her knees, feeling as if someone were using a blowtorch to trace an upside down V on her skin. Then, in place of the burn, she felt a heavy weight. At the same time, she felt Aidan rest his hand on her head. A slight ripple washed over her at his touch.

"Speaking of wings," he said softly, "yours are quite beautiful."

Lucky gasped and turned her head to look at the great wings that were weighing her down. They glowed in the light from the streetlights, feathers ranging in color from celadon to a green so dark it was almost black, all dusted with pale gold.

"They're heavy!" she said.

Aidan laughed. "You'll get used to them."

She concentrated, opening her extra senses, letting them tell her how to flex the new muscles that would operate the appendages. Once she had drawn them closed, tucked them in against her back, so their weight was not stretched out to either side of her, they did not feel quite so heavy. When Aidan offered her his free hand, keeping the other on her head, she accepted his aid without hesitation.

"Can you hide them yourself?" he asked, once she was on her feet. "I'm going to have to let you go."

"I don't know. How do I—?" But even as she asked, Lucky could feel the glamour beginning to shape itself in her head. She just had to imagine the wings hidden, invisible, and in some part of her mind, she had to maintain that thought. She felt another ripple as the glamour took hold.

"Good," Aidan said, removing his glamour from her as he lifted his hand from her head. "Now, you should be able to summon them and dismiss them at will. That might take a bit of practice."

Closing her eyes, Lucky thought the wings gone. It took her a few moments to frame the thought precisely, but the instant she did so, the weight lifted from her shoulders. Then, shifting the thought 180 degrees, she thought the wings there. As the thought settled into her mind, the weight of the wings settled against her back.

She was still practicing when they heard Kev calling Aidan's name from across the street. "Ben sent me to find you. It's past time for the second set. They're playing an instrumental until you get back."

"Are you okay to go back in there?" Aidan asked her.

"I think so," she said, thinking the wings away once again. "They're gone now."

"They might show up without you summoning them for a while—until you get the hang of it all," Aidan said, taking her hand and running back across the street. "Just be aware of that, and be ready to dismiss them if necessary."

Kev held the door for them. They could hear the chords of the instrumental number spilling out of the ballroom. Aidan headed for the stage, and Lucky and Kev went to rejoin their friends.

Lucky's head was spinning, and her heart felt full to bursting. She wanted to cry for Aidan's past; she wanted to celebrate the healing of their relationship, her future work with Zeke, and her new wings; and at the same time she couldn't completely stop worrying about who—and what—she was and what that might mean. She was able to release some of those spinning thoughts when Aidan grabbed the microphone and started to sing, because he caught her eye and closed one of his own in a wink.

Then the dancing started up again. And just as Lucky had predicted, only a couple of numbers had passed before Mo managed to drag Zeke out onto the dance floor. Malachi took a little more persuading, but eventually he followed as well. Dancing and laughing, surrounded by her friends, Lucky finally let go of her worries and allowed herself to be caught up in the rush of the moment. The necessity of keeping a part of her mind focused on making sure her new wings stayed away only added to her excitement.

When the music stilled, everyone waited while Aidan conferred with the rest of the band before stepping back to the microphone.

"We'd like to end with a brand-new song called 'Falling into Flight,'" he said. "This one is just a few days old, and we can count the number of times we've practiced it on one hand, but it'll be on the next album. We hope you like it."

He had been scanning the crowd, and his eyes came to rest on Lucky. As the notes of the guitar began filling the room, he smiled right at her. "I'd like to dedicate this one to Lucky, who helped me find my wings—and who recently found her own."

Looking from Aidan's warm blue eyes to the surprised faces of her friends, Lucky threw back her head and laughed with joy.

ACKNOWLEDGEMENTS

Two years ago, when I told my brother I was writing a novel, the first thing he said was, "Congratulations—for finally doing what you've wanted to do your whole life." I'm so glad I finally did it. Writing and publishing this book—even with the worries that such a huge project can bring—has been a joyful experience. And while much of the work has involved me sitting at my computer, writing or researching or formatting, this has not been a solo journey.

I offer thanks to my family and friends, who provided encouragement and support—and believed in me even when I didn't. Their willing participation in many, many conversations about the story and my obsession with the process of writing, publishing, and self-publishing helped make this book possible.

I am more than grateful to all the friends who so kindly served as beta readers for the book or sections of it, especially those who patiently re-read through various versions: Carolyn Allen, Michaelangelo Allocca (who gets bonus points both for hours spent accompanying me to various Chicago sites in the interest of "research" and for giving me an explanation for the significance of the number 18), Dan and Katie Brogan, Sue Caulfield, Peter Jabin, Laurie Phelps, Traci

Selvidge, Ami Snow, and the Wildcats, the best book group ever (Barb Erickson, Pat Relf Hanavan, Shirley Hebert, Kathy Huffman, Jil Larson, Carol Leigh, and Lauren Longwell). Your feedback helped make this the best book it could be. Any remaining faults are entirely mine.

Thanks to Roxanne Manders for her great copy editing and for a refresher course on comma usage.

Much praise and gratitude to Cindy Koshar for her beautiful cover design and the sweet little feathers in the chapter heads—as well as for the patience she showed in putting up with me during the design process.

Thanks to Jeremy Brown for advice about publishing and self-publishing. And thanks to all the indie writers who have made their stories and information about the process so accessible.

Finally, I want to thank Mark Nepo and the wonderful people who have been part of the workshops in which I've participated. Your wisdom and the support of the circles we create together have helped me find the courage to listen to the voice of my heart and to shake my own wings free.

AUTHOR'S NOTE

This is a work of fiction. While many of the locations mentioned are real, they are used fictitiously, and I have taken liberties where necessary for the story. For example, I have never been in the abandoned Christian Scientist church near the corner of Blackstone and 57th Steet, so I have no idea what it looks like inside. Nor do I know if there is really a lecture hall or a lounge or office space on the second floor of the Oriental Institute. The statue of the *lamassu,* however, is real. You can see a picture of him on my website at www.stephanieastamm.com.

ABOUT THE AUTHOR

Stephanie Stamm grew up in Kentucky and then moved to Chicago, where she lived for 10 years, before settling in Southwest Michigan. She holds an advanced degree in Religion & Literature and has been a press operator, a teaching assistant, a research assistant, a part-time English and Humanities instructor, a potter, and, for the last 12+ years, a technical writer. An avid reader of fantasy, she finally decided to combine her fascination with angels, ancient religions, and world-building and write the novels she wanted to read. *A Gift of Wings,* the first volume of the Light-Bringer Series, is her first novel. You can visit her and read more about the Light-Bringer Series at www.stephanieastamm.com.